Foiled Again

Also by J. S. Borthwick

Foiled
Again

J. S. Borthwick

ST. MARTIN'S MINOTAUR ❧ NEW YORK

This is a work of fiction. All of the characters, organizations, and events portrayed in this novel are either products of the author's imagination or are used fictitiously.

www.minotaurbooks.com

ISBN-13: 978-0-312-36655-1
ISBN-10: 0-312-36655-8

First Edition: February 2007

10   9   8   7   6   5   4   3   2   1

This is again for James Alexander, who has long put up with a wife who was writing about murder when she should have been doing something useful.

Acknowledgments

Thanks again to my faithful medical advisors, Mac and Rob. And a grateful nod to Malcolm Creighton-Smith for details on the finer points of foil, épée, and saber.

Acknowledgments

Cast of Principal Characters

FACULTY AND STAFF OF BOWMOUTH COLLEGE
ALENA FOSDICK—Dean of the College of Arts and Sciences
DANTON DAVIS McGRAW—Chairman of English Department
VERA PRUCZAK—Director of the School of Drama
AMOS LARKIN—Professor of English, husband of Mary Donelli
MARY DONELLI—Associate professor of English, wife of Professor Amos Larkin
SARAH DOUGLAS DEANE—Assistant professor of English, wife of Alex McKenzie
ARLENE BURR—Chief clerk in English Department
LINDA LaCROIX—Senior secretary of English Department

STUDENTS
KAY BIDDLE (JULIO)—Drama major
TERRI COLMAN (ROMIETTE)—Drama major
TODD MANCUSO (MERCUTIO, FRIAR LAURENCE)—Drama major
MALCOLM WHEELOCK (TYBALT)—Drama major, captain of fencing team
WEEZA SCOTINI (PARIS)—Drama major, dance minor, nurse's aide
GRIFFIN STARR (BENVOLIO)—Drama major, fencing team member
SETH NUSSBAUM (extra in crowd scenes)—Drama major
DEREK MOSELY (UNDERSTUDY FRIAR LAURENCE)—English major, son of Alena Fosdick
GROVER BLAINE (UNDERSTUDY MERCUTIO)—English major

POLICE, OFFICIALS
GEORGE FITTS—Sergeant, Maine State Police CID
MIKE LAAKA—Sheriff's deputy investigator
KATIE WATERS—Sheriff's deputy investigator
JOHNNY CUZAK—Forensic pathologist

HOSPITAL STAFF
DR. ALEX MCKENZIE—Physician, husband of Sarah Deane
DR. JONAS JEFFERSON—Psychiatrist
HANNAH FINCH—RN

Also cameo appearances by: THE REVEREND NICHOLAS COPELAND of the Church of the Troubled Waters; JULIA CLANCY, Sarah Deane's aunt; PATRICK O'REILLY, farm manager for Julia's High Hope Farm; PROFESSOR EMERITUS SILAS ULYSSES MORGAN; PATSY, Irish wolfhound; PIGGY, orange kitten.

Foiled
Again

Prologue

A hit, a very palpable hit.
Hamlet, act 5, scene 2

ALTHOUGH Terri Colman about had it up to here with that so-called comedian Todd Mancuso, it had not been her intention to kill the guy. Or maim him. Of course, when her best friend, Kay Biddle, got into the act, well what could you expect? And Kay was really pissed off, because she'd been kind of close to him last year and figured he was due to shape up, turn into someone she might be interested in. Anyway, things got really out of hand. Right there on center stage. A smash to the head and a clip to the ear.

Of course, the Todd business had been ready to explode anytime. There he was at every rehearsal bugging Terri and Kay every chance he got. Tripping them up just before entrances, chasing them around backstage with a can of aerosol Kool Whip. Talk about juvenile behavior, and from a college senior no less. Then trying to put on a sex fiend act, asking if he could run his hands down their beautiful bodies, all the time pretending he was shocked he'd said such a thing. Well, Kay really came through when the chips were down. Kay with her black belt in judo was always ready for some overreaching male. Or a nutcase like Todd.

All summer. How had they stood it? Todd thinking he was so damn special and God's gift to the part of Ariel when poor Terri was doing *The Tempest* and God's gift to the part of Puck in the August production of *Midsummer-Night's* with Kay playing Tita-

1

nia. And at last night's rehearsal of the Drama School's crazy production of *Romeo and Juliet* just before Terri's entrance Todd pulled down the zipper on the back of her costume. Well, she couldn't make a commotion onstage—it was the last rehearsal before the full-dress one—so she had to play the whole bloody scene trying to keep her back to the front-row watchers and half the drama faculty. And then, would you believe it, Todd, standing upstage, muffled the delivery of her last lines by a little extra swordplay—make that horseplay.

Okay, so they both lost it. Right after her exit Terri grabbed a lantern backstage, left from the previous street scene, and Kay, quick as lightning, seized a foil propped against the wall, and they made a wild re-entrance. They chased Todd around the set, Terri swinging the lantern. Then as Todd ran by, Kay made a lunge at his head. Nicking his left ear. He kept going, but Terri closed in on him, raised the lantern, and crashed it down on his head. And splat! Todd hit the stage, slid all the way to the edge of the apron, his feet sticking straight out at the front-row seats. But even as Todd lay there, not moving, blood dribbling down from his ear, making little dark pools on the boards, Terri felt no immediate sympathy. Or sense of blame. Nor did Kay. They had stood silently by, Terri arms folded, chin up, Kay holding the foil, its tip down on her shoe, while someone called 911. And later, even after Todd had been toted off to the hospital, both women declared only a strong sense of vindication.

Later that evening, the rehearsal being necessarily canceled, word came that Todd was doing well, the concussion was not serious, the facial injuries and the cut to the ear would not cause lifetime disfigurements. This news came to Terri and Kay, who had met in a booth in a dark corner of the student cafeteria for restorative fluids and a serious talk. They each needed to explore a rising sense of guilt.

"You know," said Kay, "the show goes on in two days. If you had to attack someone, you should have a made a better choice."

"Back up," said Terri. "Make that *we*. We attacked. This was a joint effort."

"Maybe. But you lost it. Temper, temper. I had to come in as a helper. But you know me; I usually keep my cool unless things are dire."

Here Kay took a long sip of her coffee, made a face, and then dumped in the contents of two sugar packets and stirred it irritably. "As for you losing it onstage, for Christ's sake let the curtain come down and then nail him backstage. Not in public. Talk about asking for trouble. Besides, Todd isn't that evil. Actually, I really like the guy. But emotionally he's about nine years old. But there are a couple of other assholes I wouldn't mind taking care of."

"We'll probably get a big F for performance this semester along with ending up in jail," Terri said. She sighed heavily. Even two cups of herbal tea were doing nothing to soothe her. "You know," she added, "maybe it serves our dear director right. Vera Pruczak shouldn't be putting on this upside-down *Romeo and Juliet*. Calling it *Romiette and Julio*. Half the time I don't know whether I'm playing a man or a woman."

"Forget the play," said Kay. "What's important is action. Why not go after someone we can't really stand? Like the man said, I've got a little list. Anyway, face it. Todd is so full of himself he's ready to burst, and he's an out-of-control tease. But he's a damn good actor and he's a drama student. One of us. Not one of those mongrels, those half-baked English majors, Drama School minors, always looking down their snoots at us because we're not academic." Kay shook her head angrily and took a gulp of her coffee.

Terri nodded, frowning. There certainly were better victim choices for hitting over the head with a stage prop lamp. Or playing touché with a foil. Even if the tip had a button on it.

"Like Grover Blaine," suggested Kay. "I wouldn't mind seeing that guy sliced in two."

"Or smashed with a lamp," said Terri. Certainly, she thought, Grover Blaine, called by the female drama students "Groper," would qualify. If she had to slam someone, why hadn't she chosen a more deserving object? Grover was one arrogant character, a would-be predator with a huge ego and a reaching hand. Not just a damn fool playing games like Todd Mancuso, who, for all his stupid childish tricks, hadn't actually ever laid a hand on anyone she'd heard of. As Kay had said, Grover was another of those "mongrels." A guy who came from the English Department along with a few other like-minded sorts who hung around together making obscene jokes when they met up with Drama School students.

"Of course," said Kay, "like you said, we're probably going to be charged with assault. And since we're already in hot water, why not hunt down Grover and give him a good knee to the groin if he makes one false move? Which he will."

"And," said Terri, "while we're at it, nail his pal, Derek."

"The gruesome twosome," said Kay. "But Derek is really just a second-rate yes-man. He follows Grover around like a puppy dog. Can't really make it up onstage. He can move but can't project. As for Grover, yetch. A loud voice is all he's got going for him."

"But don't forget who Derek belongs to," said Terri. "Number one son of our esteemed lady Dean of Arts and Sciences. Probably admitted to Bowmouth because of her. But I don't think we should do anything to Derek until after we graduate. We've still got the whole year to get through."

It was a somber thought and both students subsided. Terri bent over a third cup of tea and Kay returned to her now tepid coffee.

Terri Colman, Kay Biddle, and Todd Mancuso, aspiring students in the Bowmouth College Drama School, after a summer of plays ranging from Shakespeare, to Ionesco, to Tom Stoppard, had been cast in the annual Halloween night presentation set up by Bowmouth Drama Chair Professor Vera Pruczak.

Terri was really a wonder. She could handle comedy, farce, tragedy, do the Elizabethan heroines, Major Barbara and Eliza Doolittle types, and those smart alcoholic flappers from the Roaring Twenties repertoire. She was fair-haired, with one of those wide, lopsided mouths that can go in any direction, dark hazel eyes that could narrow with menace or open wide with horror. As for her body, she was a choreographer's joy: she could slink, stride, hunch, and dance lightly around the stage. Plus she could handle accents from Catskill Jewish to Charleston belle, from London to Glasgow, across to Paris, south to Italy, to Frankfort, and even at a stretch make authentic throat sounds from the Middle East and catch the intonations of the Far East language groups.

Kay Biddle was another valuable asset. She could play the

heavy-duty parts with an edge: those deadly women in Ibsen, sex-starved drudges, the wronged wife (Gertrude in *Hamlet*) or the loving mother, the caring mate with a homicidal side. Her alto voice could sink to a grumble or rise to a soprano shriek. Unlike slender Terri, Kay was a dark-haired, dark-eyed, strong-chinned, healthy-looking woman built on the lines of a soccer player, but like Terri, she had been born with a flexible body that could hunch down or rise in a queenly way as was necessary for a given role.

Todd Mancuso, to complete the trio of gifted seniors, was also a sort of genius. He could fly like Puck and Ariel or stump about like wizened ninety-year-old. Tan wispy hair, black arched eyebrows, and despite a wide mouth and a strong straight nose, he had been born with a face of putty, a face that could go ardent with passion, soft with pity, playful as Peter Pan, and menacing as Iago. Like Kay, he had a voice that could go anywhere. A perfect match for Terri. Or Kay. At least onstage. Offstage he was a constant annoyance, mostly to Kay. Maybe it was love. Terri had suggested to Kay that Todd might be engaged in juvenile foreplay, working up to a big offstage scene. Or, suggested another friend, Todd could be gay and trying to push the ladies into some sort of response and then laugh like hell at them. Who knew for sure? Certainly not Kay. Nor Terri.

The trouble was that when two of these—or the three—came together onstage they created enough sparks during their scenes that it was a wonder the stage set didn't start smoking. Drama professor Vera Pruczak, however, tended to ignore her star students' antics because she wanted to showcase her wares by the middle of the fall term.

Drama schools almost do invite offstage dramatic scenes. Many of the aspiring student actors, quite a number of the drama instructors—often actors themselves—the choreographers, even a student stage manager here and there, were often a volatile, peppery lot, and a display of temperament from time to time was not surprising. But although an occasional punch or kick or shove had occurred in the past, this was the first time that actual blood—not manufactured by the prop department—had appeared on the stage, the curtain rung down, the actor taken to the hospital.

All in all, the whole affair overshadowed the positive publicity the Drama School had intended to harvest from the performances. Instead the presentation of a lively scene from Vera's particular version of *Romeo and Juliet* now lingered in the minds of the rehearsal audience as a production that featured two raging female students who, for some unknowable reason, had gone completely berserk.

And getting the last nitty-gritty details of the affair the next morning, a certain Professor Danton Davis McGraw, English Department chair, also lost it.

"Goddamn it to hell," shouted Professor McGraw at the long-suffering senior secretary of the English Department, one Linda LaCroix.

Linda, a cool and highly focused woman, long used to such outbursts from McGraw, waited for enlightenment.

"That Drama School is a total zoo. No, it's worse than a zoo. It's a pit. A pit with wild animals. *Romiette and Julio*. Christ! Vera Pruczak doing her own damn thing as if there's no connection with the Arts and Sciences. Well, I've had it. She's really done it this time."

"The last straw?" suggested Linda, who was used to last straws. At least from the chairman of the department.

"Goddamn right," bellowed McGraw, turning on his heel and striding toward his office. Then he stopped abruptly on the threshold and said, "Call the hospital. See how the Mancuso kid is doing. He's taking English classes, so send flowers to the family. Condolences from the English Department."

"Has the family filed suit?" asked Linda, who had a healthy interest in the law. She herself had been thinking of hitting up the English Department for long-owed overtime.

"Not that I've heard, but with our luck it's already been filed. I've heard his father's a selectman in Appleton."

"Vera Pruczak called in to your office," said Linda. "She said to tell you Todd's being discharged and everything's under control. An emotional flare-up. Talented kids. Regrettable."

6

"Vera Pruczak is what's regrettable," muttered Danton McGraw, and he slammed into his office.

Back at his desk, taking drinks from a thermos of hot coffee while at the same time trying for calm by studying his nicely framed collection of citations, commendations, and diplomas that hung on the walls of his office, Professor McGraw found his temper cooling. And better than that. Something positive was emerging from the Drama School fracas.

He smiled. A grim, self-satisfied smile. Danton McGraw believed he had in the palm of his hand the exact cause célèbre that would allow for both the enlargement of the English Department and a most desirable shrinkage of the Bowmouth School of Drama.

1

LINDA LaCroix thought that twelve years in the service of Bow-mouth College's English Department should count for something. She had done her stint as a general clerk and had risen to be the department's number one secretary. So why was she being treated by the department's new chair, Professor Danton McGraw, as if she were fresh out of some second-rate two-year business school? All those little lectures on office management and academic proto-col. Didn't the guy know she was a grad from Bowmouth's own School of Business—with honors yet? Didn't he see her bachelor's degree diploma framed right there on the secretaries' wall, where he couldn't miss it when he headed into his office? And this se-mester she and Arlene Burr, the department's chief clerk and as-sistant secretary, had to sign In-and-Out slips whenever they took off on a two-minute trip for coffee or to run something off the copy machine. Hit the cafeteria for lunch. Stop in the halls for two min-utes to say hello to some other human.

Now as the late October chills were turning the remaining leaves brown, Linda and Arlene each looked back on her past workstation as something like lost Eden. It had happened with the speed of a falling ax. Last spring and all the years before, the secretary and the clerk had had two adjoining but separate offices, both of which were placed at a safe distance across the corridor from the chairman's office. But then along came Dr. Danton McGraw, who had caused walls to be moved and partitions eliminated. The end result was that now Linda and Arlene found themselves yoked together like conjoined twins fixed in side-by-side desks in the newly created secretaries' space outside Dr. McGraw's office. Here neither could get two paces away from her chair without arousing suspicion from the sharp-eared department chairman. Worse still, neither woman could get away from the other and hunker down in the privacy of her own office space. Take shoes off, sneak a candy bar without sharing it, send a private e-mail to a friend, make a personal phone call. The result was that two good friends and coworkers were beginning to feel an unpleasant tension in their everyday work life.

"Trapped," said Arlene to Linda on the Monday of Halloween week. "That's what we are. Say I want to step out of this cage to maybe get a breath of air or go pee. I've practically got to leave fingerprints and bring back a urine sample."

But Linda was otherwise focused. She looked around, sniffed the air, and wrinkled her nose. "I don't know about you," she said, "but this place is really starting to stink, and it's not just grungy students coming in and hanging around. Something smells real funny, like there's a fungus growing somewhere. In a file drawer maybe."

Linda was a striking woman with a strong opinion on all things. Tall, thin as a wire coat hanger, with a mane of white-blond hair caught into a crown on her head, she had a sharp little chin and narrow blue eyes. And with her whole face bravely covered in a heavy duty makeup and eye enhancements, Linda could have passed for anywhere from thirty-seven to forty-seven. Actually, she was closing in on fifty, a fact she kept quiet about. Her choice for clothing ran to clinging shirts and sweaters—all about a size 3—that still allowed her breasts full presentation rights together with constricted breathing. Then there was the snug skirt, the high-fashion boots and long purple fingernails. Altogether, Linda, known to some of the faculty clowns as "Linda Lovely," was a female who resembled one of those handsome slender but lethal insects that stand on two legs and eat family members. Most of the English Department regulars, faculty and adjuncts, did well to stay on the right side of Linda.

The yin to Linda's yang, Arlene was a perfect contrast. She was a comfortably built woman with a cheerful round face, an almost comically turned-up nose, and dark brown hair pulled back with two clips. While Linda dealt with the public with the verbal equivalent of a scalpel, Arlene soothed, comforted, and counseled patience. However, until the beginning of the new semester, Arlene had pretty much taken the faculty ego clashes, the complaints of unhappy English majors, the pleas of adjuncts and teaching fellows as they came. But with the arrival of Dr. McGraw and the new secretary-clerk double-desk setup, her nervous system seemed to have developed a greater sensitivity and her natural buoyancy showed signs of leakage.

Now Arlene herself took a long sniff. Well, Linda was certainly right about the smell.

"I mean," went on Linda, "maybe it's the new carpet they laid before we moved over here, but I wouldn't put it past someone to poison us. A little bit. And even if no one is doing that, some new carpet dyes have fumes that make you really sick. But this smell seems to be coming right from under your desk."

Arlene grimaced. "I don't think it's the carpet. But you know, I'll bet it's that mouse. I'd forgotten the mouse."

"Mouse?" said Linda, lifting her feet up and peering at the floor.

"Found him two days ago with that batch of blue exam books left over from the spring semester," said Arlene. "On top of those shelves." She waved at a line of shelves packed with catalogues, directories, student handbooks, and reams of printer paper. "I felt kinda bad. You know, like he reminded me of Stuart Little. But all dried up and skinny. He must have starved to death."

"*What,*" demanded Linda, "did you do with this mouse?"

Arlene grinned. "I wanted to slip him into McGraw's desk drawer but lost my nerve. I need this job. Besides, the mouse might have carried that virus, what's its name?"

"Hanta virus. Spread by rodents," said Linda. "So *where* is the mouse now?"

Arlene shrugged. "I think someone distracted me just after I'd found him, so he may be right there in one of the wastebaskets. Like my wastebasket."

"Oh, ugh," said Linda.

"Ugh," agreed Arlene.

"Okay, okay," said Linda. "I'll call Maintenance and they can set some traps or whatever they do about mice. And, for once," she added firmly, "I agree with McGraw. With everything else going on, we don't need mice." She nodded in the direction of a door with a window and the legend Chairman (gold on a black plaque) fixed below the glass.

"Please, no traps," said Arlene, apparently still affected by the idea of Stuart Little. "I mean not real ones. I have a little Havahart trap thing for mice. I can bring it in. And it's no wonder this one starved. Before McGraw turned up there used to be plenty of snacks for mice. I used to keep pretzels in my drawer, and the students were always leaving foodstuff around, and of course we were allowed to have our lunch in here. I even had that one mouse, you remember, the one I called Rosie. Last winter."

"I don't remember Rosie," said Linda. "We each had our own office space then, remember. But, whatever you do, don't encourage mice. McGraw is absolutely right about bringing in food. If mice really start moving in, he'll probably start having a major housekeeping inspection. He'll be going around with white gloves and a microscope. Like the army."

"He was in the navy," Arlene reminded her.

"Whichever," said Linda. "But listen to this. Yesterday he just found out that old Professor Morgan keeps a hot plate in his office closet—you know how far away that guy's office is, way down by the back stairs, so he must have missed it. Well, there was Morgan with a teakettle going and he'd had Chinese brought in. All those little white cardboard boxes. Talk about a fire hazard. And mouse heaven. That office is ripe, really ripe."

"The poor old guy," said Arlene. "He's been here since World War Two. Or Korea. You can't change him; you can't *inspect* his office. You can't even get in the place without a shovel. And he's emeritus. Me, I think he's kind of a cute old geezer. And he's pretty smart. But he'll probably be given the boot by the end of this semester."

"Wrong. Professor Morgan was asked back again because we lost that new nineteenth-century guy last spring to NYU. Anyway, he's been given those grad seminars on Wordsworth and Keats and Byron, and he's scheduled to go through the spring semester. I've had to print up a whole new guide and syllabus for his students."

"Forget about mice. McGraw has Vera Pruczak on his mind," Arlene pointed out.

"And who's to blame him there?" said Linda. "I mean, talk about a disaster. That Todd Mancuso assaulted right on the stage. In the middle of a scene. His ear practically cut off, plus almost having a fractured skull."

"Yeah," said Arlene. "It was that Terri Colman and Kay Biddle who did the job. I heard from a friend who saw the rehearsal that there was blood spattered everywhere. But you know theatre people. They do things like that."

"For the record," said Linda, "A lot of these gals change their names. Some have lousy ones and want something jazzy that looks good up in lights. That Louisa Scotini made me cross out her first name and use 'Weeza.' I end up making corrections whenever I send in the grades to the dean's office. As for that Todd Mancuso, honestly."

"What I've heard," said Arlene, "is that Todd Mancuso is too much of a smart-ass for his own good. Thinks females are just drooling for his attentions."

"So good for Terri and Kay, beating him up like that," said Arlene. "And you know they're both pets of Vera's. Anyway, the Drama School is in hot water. I heard McGraw going on about uncontrolled violence and no discipline. And the students are joining sides. The Drama School majors think our students doing a minor in drama are sort of half-baked. Not serious."

"Drama School kids call them mongrels."

"An insult to dogs," said Arlene, the animal lover. "Mongrels are the best kind. Better than some of our students any day."

"What I'm trying to say," said Linda, "is that if McGraw's on a housekeeping binge, Vera might just get the shaft."

"Or at least be ousted from her number two office in the English Department."

"That office," said Linda. "Another god-awful mess. It needs McGraw. Plays and scripts up to her boobs, a recliner, and all those masks and skulls and voodoo dolls."

"Plus that little refrigerator," said Arlene.

"And alcohol stashed in her desk. Brandy and vodka. The maintenance people told me all about it. Little parties after evening rehearsals. But she can't get away with it forever. McGraw will grind her into chopped liver before she knows what hit her. Of course, she's got that other office over in the Drama School building and people ask why one faculty member needs two offices."

"Shhh. Can it," said Arlene, bending over her computer screen. "I think that's him in the hall."

Professor Danton McGraw—Dan to those faculty associates still speaking to him—had arrived in late summer to take over the English Department at Bowmouth College. He was a tall, angular man with brown hair cut to military shortness, had large hands and pointed ears, and brought to his office a sharp eye, a sharper tongue. Further, he showed a poorly concealed contempt for the previous recent chair, an unfortunate vacillator and fusspot called Ellis Humber. Professor Humber had been ousted by a series of flanking maneuvers and moved into the woodwork: a seat on a number of unpopular committees and several drab evening teaching assignments all designed to keep him out of Danton McGraw's hair.

Now in the normal course of things, the chair of many academic departments at Bowmouth College was taken in turn: a year or two, at the most three, and then turned over to the next victim. Victim because despite a certain prestige attached to the job and the glint it gave to a résumé, the position was generally regarded as a pain in the neck. Too much paperwork. Too many committee meetings. Too much time spent soothing tempers, dealing with ruffled feelings, complaints about teaching assignments, soothing prima donna visiting writers, poets, and dramatists. In short, most chairs gave up the job with a huge sigh of relief.

Not Professor Danton McGraw. Being the chair of the English Department was for him a goal reached. And not about to be surrendered because of some foolish tradition of letting some other faculty member rotate into that office.

Danton McGraw, an Annapolis graduate, had done a fifteen-year stint in the navy, mostly under the water in an atomic submarine—a fact that department wags claimed had compressed his judgment—and spoke and acted as if he had a deck under his feet or, more accurately, a periscope over his head. Even after leaving the navy and going the academic route: Ph.D. in English, full rank as professor with tenure, he was given to naval terminology and spoke of making the English Department "shipshape" (an impossible task by any definition). However, submarine veteran that he was, by the beginning of the fall term he had cleaned the department with the academic equivalent of a new broom. A broom made with long sharp metal spokes and designed to not only achieve a "clean sweep" but also plow under anything that threatened to hinder the cleaning operation.

Outspoken junior faculty members disappeared into distant offices. Authors (unless of the Pulitzer variety) running loose writers' workshops were eyed with suspicion and required to submit outlines of their courses—this anathema to any self-respecting writer. Prima donna professors on esoteric subjects, such as the lesser novels of lesser novelists, translations from the Sanskrit, the diaries of early American Baptists, were rescheduled to teach popular mainstream courses—"popular" meaning mandatory high-enrollment, ergo profitable, classes.

The natural result of the "shipshape" approach to academic management was that secretaries, clerks, and those of such lesser ranks as teaching fellows, lecturers, and other adjuncts became adept at keeping their shoulders hunched, their voices low, and in an effort to become invisible took to gliding along the walls corridors of the English Department's Malcolm Adam Hall. But these "lowlifes" were relatively fortunate. Unlike the senior faculty and those professors on tenure track, they were housed in a distant sector of the building. As for the "Poets in Residence"—always a temperamental bunch—they had been safely stashed in the West Quad. Thus possibly troublesome members of the English faculty only had to appear in the central Malcolm Adam Hall for committee and faculty powwow, or to have copies of assignments and exams run off. Then back to their lairs out of sight, out of touch.

But Danton McGraw had developed another and more questionable aspect to his persona. He had theatrical aspirations. Loved to take part in stage productions of all kinds. Had shone in small parts in small-town theatres in and around the state and had had walk-on roles in the seasonal Portland Stage productions. Lately, however, his dramatic efforts had been showcased closer to home in midcoast Maine's little-theatre efforts and library readings. And he wasn't that bad, as even his enemies would admit. Naval training stood him in good stead; his gestures were sharp and definite, his bearing upright. No, he couldn't, nor did he want to, play the beggar, the cripple, the sot, but as the straight player he could pull a scene together. He had that great dramatic virtue: a loud, clear voice, so that audience members well beyond the first few rows could hear every spoken line. Added to these talents was the fact that Danton McGraw was a fencer of note. Foil, épée, and saber. Particularly the épée. Ten years ago he had won a state championship in the épée. And only last year in a Camden theatre production he had starred as Laertes in a particularly dazzling duel with a local Hamlet.

The result of this aspect of Dr. McGraw's résumé was that he had added an undergraduate course in dramatic literature and a graduate Shakespeare seminar to his workload. Further, he had mentioned teaching a beginning course on aspects of directing come the winter semester. Plus, in his desk he had an agreement, already in motion, that allowed him to supervise the swordplay choreography for the Drama School's new production of *Romiette and Julio*. After all, Dr. McGraw would point out, although she was undoubtedly a multitalented drama instructor, Vera Pruczak had certainly never shown any aptitude for fencing.

16

In short, from many points of view, colleagues, clerks, students, and would-be thespians, Professor McGraw was trouble. An ill wind that blew no good. A wind that was set to blow down the fine unwieldy system whereby Associate Professor Vera Pruczak held sway as chief in the Drama School but at the same time had long occupied a second office in the Malcolm Adam building. This latter office sat some five doors away from the department chair's office and gave her a base for teaching and meeting students taking her academic drama courses. So not only did the woman take up space in two offices, as Dr. McGraw had pointed out with ill-concealed irritation at a restricted committee meeting, but she also seemed to run a one-woman dictatorship at the Drama School. She hovered over rehearsals, contradicted guest directors, and rode herd on student stage designers. Worse yet, Vera's choice of last season's productions had resulted in that school losing hunks of money on a two-week Ionesco festival that had really turned off a number of the community of playgoing regulars.

"The college is supposed to be making *some* money on those. Or not losing it, anyway. Think about goodwill. We're part of the Maine midcoast area. We don't need to alienate the entire countryside," McGraw had told Vera.

Here Vera had smiled her Delphic smile. "We are bringing contemporary drama to areas that might not have an opportunity of seeing it. Not everyone can drive to Boston or New York. Or even to Portland and Augusta."

"But Vera," said McGraw, trying for patience. "People began leaving halfway through that Ionesco one, *The Bald Soprano*. One parent of a senior—he's a trustee—stopped me on campus complaining that the thing was written for babies. Or for the insane. And three church members wrote about the language used in that Stoppard play last spring. And then there's that anti-American bullshit. Please keep politics out. It'll be frontal nudity next, I suppose. Listen, for God's sake give the audience something pleasing. Or serious. Something classic. Old favorites. *Julius Caesar, Pygmalion, Our Town, Arsenic and Old Lace. A Raisin in the Sun* is okay. So is *The Glass Menagerie. Death of a Salesman.* And a musical or two, and I don't mean *Chicago*. We're talking farmers and merchants and fishermen and veterans. Parents of active-duty servicemen. Mothers, first-grade teachers, and checkout ladies. They all want to feel comfortable going to a play. Not to put up with academic artsy types and student oddballs spouting a lot of what the audience thinks is a lot of shit."

Vera had quietly informed Dr. McGraw that he was not yet head of the Drama School, thank you very much, and departed.

Which remark fertilized a very sharp seed already planted in the fertile brain of Professor McGraw.

It was not surprising then that this same Monday, October the twenty-ninth, found several persons by mid-morning who had reached boiling points. It started when Arlene, thinking that Dr. McGraw was safely stashed in his office, began tiptoeing out of the office, the dead mouse wrapped in a crumpled piece of paper. Arlene, seeing no need to sign out for such an unusual excursion—burial of mouse under a campus lilac—had almost made it to the outer office door when she tripped over the backpack of a female student waiting to see the chairman, went splat, and the mouse—now hardly more than a rigid bit of gray fur—shot out and landed on the bare instep of the student. Who screeched. Jumped up.

And brought forth Professor McGraw, who had just about had it with this unshipshape part of his domain.

Arlene was told to get back to her desk. Linda was told to call Maintenance and find some Lysol; the student was told that he did not have open office hours and to make an appointment. Then seeing another figure approaching the door, Professor McGraw pointed out in a voice rising to an upper baritone register that it wasn't open season on his office. Didn't anyone make appointments? Was there no consideration for people who wanted to get some work done? Was there no sense of order anywhere?

The figure, someone he should have certainly known at least by sight, was one Assistant Professor Sarah Douglas Deane arriving to check with Arlene on the midterm exam schedules.

Sarah halted. She knew that she was on the bottom rung of the tenure ladder and so hardly a worthwhile object of Professor McGraw's wrath.

But the chairman was beyond reason. "Out," he said. "This isn't a freeway." Then seeing Vera Pruczak looming up behind Sarah, he said, "Not now, Vera. Not until this afternoon. Make it after four. Your office. We need to talk." And to Sarah. "You there, Deane, isn't it? Dr. Deane. Or Ms. Deane? Not now. Appointment. Always make an appointment."

Then Professor McGraw wheeled on Arlene and pointed to what was left of Stuart Little. "See that this rodent is out of the office and if I ever see another one, alive or dead, I'll . . ."

Here he paused, hesitated, took a deep breath—good office people like Arlene and Linda were hard to come by—clamped his mouth shut, turned again, headed for his office, and disappeared.

Sarah found herself backing out of the office. She turned around and found herself facing Vera Pruczak, who hadn't moved an inch and was now scowling in the direction of Dr. McGraw's office door.

"Damn him," said Sarah in a low voice. "If I had any guts, I'd . . ." She hesitated. What would she do?

Vera reached over an arm and spun Sarah around. "No, you wouldn't. You have guts but no clout. Fighting with the chair of the department isn't your thing. As I've told you before, thin, wispy females without tenure are raw meat for guys like Danton. Come back to my office—which if I read the tea leaves correctly may be an endangered object. I'll give you strong drink and dangerous advice."

Sarah, recovering her temper, grinned at Vera, a friend of at least two years and easily one of the more interesting figures in the college. But it was no time to visit Vera and get caught up in her Halloween play as a gofer girl or part of the set crew. Vera was omnivorous when it came to her dramatic productions, and Sarah, with three classes to teach, was up to her ears in work and not ready to be thrown into the Drama School's vortex.

But as Sarah shook her head, Vera tugged more sharply on her sleeve. "I need your advice," she said. "I think it's time to circle the wagons. Follow me."

"Remember," called Sarah, scuttling down the hall after the drama professor, "what you said about clout. I'm a new assistant prof. No one in his right mind would listen to me."

"You're a body, a warm body," said Vera, opening the door to her office, a door covered with a carved death mask from one of the more obscure Pacific islands.

Sarah, agreeing that she was, still, a warm body, followed into the office and then, as usual, found her mouth gaping at the interior. She had not been inside this term, and changes had been made. Linda LaCroix had hardly done justice to the mélange in the office. Not just masks and Vera's favorite winter headdress, a hand-knitted balaclava, not the pile of scripts and paperback plays, but now a large wire cage holding what appeared to be a parrot in a high state of irritation.

"Have you seen Tom Fool?" asked Vera, sweeping a tartan cape from a chair. "I thought he was lonely at home, so I've started bringing him to work. He only speaks French, which is a bother, but I think he adds color."

"Yes," said Sarah, thinking resentfully about the preparation for her next class. Why hadn't she ever learned to say no to this woman?

"I won't keep you," said Vera, who often seemed to have second sight. She settled down into her office chair, a rocker with a tapestry pillow. "But now listen. I'm going to take you into confidence. Never mind that you're not number one or even number eleven in the department. We've done things together and I need a listening ear."

Sarah withheld a sigh and prepared to provide the ear.

A contrast, the two women. Vera Pruczak had the sharp face of one of the more dubious Italian aristocracy, one of the Medicis perhaps. But on top of these features, sharp nose, glittering hazel eyes, mobile mouth—thin one minute; pursed and rounded the next—she had a head of gray hair, hair that always appeared to have just suffered a severe jolt from a strong electrical device. Her hands were covered in rings with bulging stones (the kind, Sarah thought, that flip open and deliver cyanide); scarves, jackets, vests, flowing skirts, knitted stockings, completed the look. This was her "drama persona."

But Sarah knew another Vera who, as Olivia Macbeth, wrote gothic romances and when doing a book signing wore flowing velvet, feather neck pieces, and jingling bracelets. This aspect of Vera, however, was usually hidden from college eyes.

As for Sarah Douglas Deane, assistant professor of English, Vera was right. Sarah wasn't built for conflict. At least not physically. Her narrow figure, thin limbs, large dark eyes, high cheekbones, and short, clipped brown hair created the sort of look that made strangers think of offering chicken broth, wheaten biscuits, and nutritious milk drinks. All this to Sarah's annoyance and made her consider wearing black leather jackets with hanging chains, motorcycle boots, and having a serious tattoo—a coiled rattlesnake or dragon perhaps—engraved on a conspicuous part of her body.

"You see," said Vera, with an imperious gesture pointing to a wicker chair for Sarah, "I've been hearing remarks. Literally. Danton McGraw has a loud voice. I'm sure he's planning a coup and God help the Drama School. And me. All I've worked for. So I need your help. Naturally."

"Naturally?" said Sarah, startled, sinking into the indicated chair. Her one escapade with Vera had been a few years back when was Sarah was still in graduate school.

"Of course. You weren't really part of the department then but so helpful in that business of the body in the ice sculpture."

"Which I had nothing to do with finding," Sarah pointed out.

"Don't quibble. McGraw wants me out. My second office in this building anyway. And he'd like to have the Drama School under his big thumb so he can squash the life out of our productions. I'll be allowed to put on *Peter Pan* and *Little Women*."

"Not that bad, I hope," said Sarah soothingly.

"The hell it isn't," said Vera fiercely. "And now the Drama School has got this big black eye because that idiot Todd Mancuso had to play the joker with Terri Colman and Kay Biddle. A whole rehearsal scene ruined and the opening coming up in two days. All right, so he deserved some of what he got. But I need him because he's good, a natural. And yes, I suppose I've taken the thing too lightly. Now I'll have to try and straighten the boy out, cut the other ear off, something like that."

"Oh, great," said Sarah. "That ought to make the front pages."

"Don't take me literally. With me it's the velvet glove."

"Over the iron claw?"

"Don't be funny. This is serious. McGraw isn't to be trusted. He won't go the faculty meeting route. He'll go right to the nearest power center. The provost? No, more likely the dean. I think she's vulnerable. In the meantime, you, Sarah, keep your ears open. And your eyes. You'll hear things in the English Department that I won't be able to catch. Try Arlene and Linda. They absorb gossip like sponges."

"I should glide hither and thither in a black cloak?"

"No, that's my act," said Vera with a short smile. "Now get out of here. I'm busy."

2

SARAH had barely reached the end of the hall before Vera scooted up behind her and grabbed an elbow. "Wait up. One more thing."

"You've already had one more thing," said Sarah. "I'm supposed to be your undercover agent, which means I'll probably be tossed out of my own department."

"The play," said Vera, forcing Sarah to back up against the wall. "The one we've been rehearsing."

"I thought we'd covered that."

"I want you in the afternoon after your classes. We need help with the costume changes. That's something I don't want to worry about. I've got enough on my plate with these last rehearsals. A complete run-through tonight. Troubleshooting Tuesday afternoon, dress rehearsal Tuesday night. Some of your own students are extras in crowd scenes, playing small walk-on parts. Being understudies."

"Okay, I'll help you this afternoon. But why have the play on Halloween night?"

"Tradition. A Halloween Masque."

"Great," said Sarah, taking a quick look at her watch. She'd give Vera five minutes and then split.

"Now please listen," said Vera, now speaking as if to a junior student with a small brain. "Here it is in a nutshell. Every October the Drama School has put on a play. I call it a Masque. Actually, the first one we did was the *Masque of the Red Death.*"

"Nice choice," said Sarah, beginning to feel like the wedding guest being pinned down by the Ancient Mariner. Was she about to hear the history of theatricals since the founding of Bowmouth College?

"It was over-the-top," said Vera. "A star production. Every fall after that we took a well-known play and exploded it. Turned it upside down. A big effort, costumes, set, lights, orchestra in the pit. The works. Ask any of your students to volunteer; we need ticket takers and ushers."

"But why Halloween night? How does that work with all the kids in town in costumes asking for tricks or treats? Hitting up the college probably."

"Curtain goes up at nine o'clock Halloween night—Wednesday—to allow the grad students and faculty who want to trick-or-treat with their kids or their sisters and brothers. Actually, the undergraduates really get into it, cause more trouble than sixty little kids."

"In the true spirit of All Hallows' Eve," said Sarah. "Okay, Vera, good for you. I'll be at your play and make Alex come, too." Alex was Sarah's physician husband, long-suffering in the matter of being dragged to student productions, recitals, faculty parties, and such. This worked as a payback for Sarah being pushed into a number of stupefyingly dull medical receptions and staff affairs of the Mary Starbox Memorial Hospital.

"Alex can come on his own," said Vera, gripping Sarah's arm even more tightly. "I need you at *all* the rehearsals, not just this afternoon. We've got actors taking several parts, so there will be many costume changes. You know we're doing a turnabout *Romeo and Juliet.* The balcony, street fights, music, people dancing. But with an upbeat ending. Of course there's usually some last-minute improvising."

"Like hitting Romeo over the head with a lantern?"

"Please listen. We're calling it *Romiette and Julio.* Gender

24

mix. The character Mercutio is in love with both Julio and Romiette, which adds to the confusion. Friar Laurence is an enabler for an illicit wedding—which it really was. Nurse is a tough fraulein from Dusseldorf. Paris, the suitor of Julio-Romiette, after he's killed comes back to life as a woman to lead the finale. Professor McGraw will be around since he's been working on the sword scenes. And that means both of us will be able to keep an eye on the man."

"Perhaps he could understudy Romeo, or Romiette," suggested Sarah, sliding out of Vera's grasp and beating it down the hall, her brain crackling with the thought of a reverse-gender balcony scene.

Professor McGraw was having an early lunch that same Monday with the dean of the College of Arts and Sciences, one Dr. Alena Fosdick. He thought that a quiet lunch in one of the smaller conference rooms away from student commotion and faculty bustle might serve his purpose. This because Danton McGraw usually had a purpose, sometimes unspoken, sometimes a direct in-your-face purpose.

But he would begin with gentle pleasant conversation. Intelligent inquiries into the problems of being dean of a college division that included the Drama School, an entity Danton considered the most unruly in the entire college. Professor McGraw needed Dr. Fosdick's attention, her interest—this last ensured by Danton's knowledge of some awkward parts of her domestic life. Not that he intended knocking her over the head with such. No, sympathy quietly expressed was in order, so by the time they reached the second cup of coffee—or perhaps the second or third glass of a pleasant white wine—he should be almost sure of her unqualified support.

Alena Fosdick had style. A presence. Was a strikingly good-looking woman who gave the impression of being someone in charge of herself, who walked about with her head up, dressed usually in a dark pin-striped executive suit. Alena had been gifted with the ability, particularly useful for one in her position, to focus her deep blue eyes on someone's face so that her gaze seemed to be one of sympathetic understanding. She was somewhere in her mid-fifties, had taffy-colored-by-bottle hair that, being thick and lustrous, could be augmented by braids and falls and so should see her well through her sixties. And due to careful attention to clothes shown in the more expensive fashion magazines, her appearance when she walked down the hall was impressive: designer costumes, contrasting scarves tossed around the neck, and never too much jewelry, two rings at the most and a single statement pin set with a modest emerald or diamond. And to complete the whole look, the sort of costly footwear that complimented her shapely leg when Alena, in a short skirt, swung it forth from a sitting position.

But Alena, although she hardly acknowledged this to herself, already had several strikes against her. In fact, she was a setup for whatever scheme Dan McGraw had hatched.

First there were those two very messy divorces. Husband number one, George Mosely, a professor of chemistry who had apparently used Alena as a punching bag and then had defected to the University of Maine at Orono. The next marriage and almost immediate divorce happened with a teaching adjunct named George Printer from the Sociology Department, a heavy drinker given to public denunciations of her failure in bed.

Of course, everyone on campus knew that Alena was the victim, one who had bravely broken free from two unsatisfactory men named George and had returned to her maiden name, Fosdick. But it was only human for her academic associates to wonder what there was about the woman to (a) have attracted these losers in the beginning or (b) have encouraged these questionable partners to morph after marriage into genuinely abusive beasts.

Then there was her son, Derek, by first husband George Mosely. Age twenty-one, Derek Mosely, now a senior, had been accepted at Bowmouth College despite reservations expressed by the admissions people. But Alena was one of their own and the boy had periodically shown spasms of good work and had been something of a star on his high-school soccer team. Make that one of his high schools or preparatory schools, since he had tried several. But Derek last spring semester had gotten involved in some drug-making scheme in his dorm and been suspended. Now, with Alena working behind the scenes, he was back for the fall term and, although feeling sorry for himself, was taking a reasonable course load. Furthermore, at the prodding of his best friend, Grover Blaine, Derek had signed on as an English major doing a minor in drama. Because of this last he had been given the part of an understudy to Friar Laurence in Vera Pruczak's Halloween play.

The third and possibly the most fatal chink in Alena's armor was her choice of a doctoral subject. Alena had been a Bowmouth graduate but had done her graduate work at small Windamere College in southern New Hampshire. Windamere was the sort of institution that first brought puzzled looks to faculty faces as if they were trying to remember such a name, and then, with their brows clearing, they changed expressions into those that clearly said, "Oh, that place." The subject of her scholarly work had centered on a particular set of children's books and was titled *Gender Stereotypes and Recurrent Themes in Johnny Gruelle's Raggedy Ann and Andy Series*. This work Alena had tried to conceal from her associates with ill success, because even the title of her dissertation was always good for a chuckle in faculty circles.

But through perseverance and organizational ability Alena had won out in the end. Her appointment as dean of the College of Arts and Sciences had come about when two other candidates had squared off in an unseemly manner, so that Alena was chosen because of the need seen for a compromise, but she was, all things considered, something of a success in the job. She looked the part, acted the part, and by flattering the egos of difficult associates had won through to a fair popularity.

The small conference dining room chosen by Professor McGraw for the meeting was an intimate space, five or six small round tables, a few pale nineteenth-century watercolors on off-white walls, long windows overlooking a distant view of the Camden Hills. Accepting a pulled-out chair from Danton McGraw, she settled herself with as much authority as she could muster, Danton being more than a head taller than she was. Whatever qualms she might have about this surprise lunch—Danton had not until lately

27

seemed to know she was on planet Earth—she must not lose her cool. No drinks. No unmanageable menu choice such as many-boned fish or a slippery fettuccini. No dessert. A simple coffee during and after.

But Professor McGraw, master of the preemptive move, like a magician produced from under the table a bottle of Italian white Verdiccio. "I hope you'll forgive me," he said, with a smile and modest showing of white teeth, "but this is so special. A gift from my old mentor, Dr. Fiero—wonderful man, you remember him, I'm sure. I've been wanting to share it with someone. And today seemed like the right day. Perfect weather looking at us." Here Dan McGraw waved across to the window view of rolling hills dyed with late autumn's russets and yellows.

Alena arrested her hand that had started to flatten itself over her empty wineglass. What the hell, she thought, a single drink of white wine wasn't going to destroy her. He wasn't going to get her drunk and try to drag her off to some dark, distant bedroom. She smiled up at Danton, murmured something that suggested agreement, all the while hoping that she would not be asked to identify Dr. Fiero—a man she was sure she'd never heard of in her life.

Danton deftly inserted the corkscrew, extracted the cork from the bottle, decanted an inch into his own wineglass, took the de rigueur taste, and then poured a full glass for Alena, another for himself, and raised his glass.

"Cheers," said Danton, smiling broadly.

"Cheers," repeated Alena with less enthusiasm.

"So what do you think of his new book?" asked Danton, reaching for the menu card.

"Book?" said Alena, startled. "What book?"

"Dr. Fiero's. Martin Fiero. Quite a departure, I think. A real turnaround."

"You think?" said Alena, playing for time. Picking up her menu and pretending to be absorbed.

Danton lifted eyebrows. Showed surprise. "You disagree?"

"You know," said Alena brightly, "I'm so hungry I really can't put my mind to giving you a real opinion of the book. Any sensible criticism. Of such an important work. I think I'll go for the chicken with the mushrooms." There, she told herself. I won't play that game. I'll bet there's no Dr. Fiero at all. Alena was not entirely ignorant of Dr. McGraw's reputation as a "strongman." Nor had she yet worked out why she had been singled out to be dined *and* wined by him. Be careful, she prompted herself.

He dropped the subject of his old mentor, Dr. Fiero, chose the seafood casserole with salad, ignored a student in a white jacket who offered him ground pepper, and Danton and Alena sipped and munched their way silently through a third of the meal. Then Danton McGraw put down his salad fork, looked up at Alena, and said in a voice of warm entreaty, "Dr. Fosdick . . . Alena. I need your help."

Alena put down her fork, which had been chasing a slippery slice of chicken breast around on her plate. "My help? Something to do with the English Department? Or the whole Arts and Sciences College?"

"Both," said Danton. "We have . . . and I mean we, you as dean, me as chair of the English Department. Both of us. We've got a mess on my hands, and I'm afraid it will start reflecting on all of Arts and Sciences. It's the Drama School. Which, as you know, thinks of itself as a separate department. But the fact is that it actually started as an offshoot of the English Department. Back when."

"Mess?" demanded Alena, galvanized by the word. "You mean that incident?"

"Of course, there may have been many incidents," said Danton smoothly. "Ones we don't know about. Given the climate over there." Here he leaned forward and frowned at Alena. "But I mean those two drama students, Terri Colman and Kay Biddle, attacking another student. Todd Mancuso. On the stage, halfway through one of the last rehearsals. Right in front of many watchers, including faculty members from other departments. My God, is that the sort of publicity Bowmouth needs? The ambulance called, the local papers running with it. All this in the middle of a capital fund drive that includes, as you know, support for some important Arts and Sciences projects."

Alena bent her head over her plate, successfully speared the piece of chicken, poked the fork in her mouth, chewed, and swallowed. And then, her ideas in place, seeing Danton McGraw sitting like a rock, waiting, spoke up. "You're trying to remind me that the whole Drama School is out of control. And that its management is my responsibility."

"Well, remember the brouhaha in September when Vera Pruczak had to call security during tryouts. Hanging the Music School department chair in effigy after some music students went after a group of drama students."

"That," said Alena firmly, "began with the music students. They started it."

Danton waved away the music students and returned to Topic A. "No one has greater respect or admiration for Vera Pruczak than I do," he said. "She is a wonder. Her productions, so . . . well, so . . ."

"Imaginative?"

"Stimulating, perhaps. Sometimes downright outrageous. I think Professor Pruczak is more than pushing the envelope. She's ripped it open. Her Halloween play. Have you heard what it's going to be this year?"

"No," said Alena, sighing. "I've barely recovered from last year's *Oedipus*. That business of snuggling in bed with his mother. Right onstage."

"Quite a scene," said Danton, pleased at the horror in Alena's voice.

"And doing it while the chorus sang that Civil War thing, 'Just Before the Battle, Mother.'"

Danton put down his fork. And again leaned slightly toward Alena. "What I'm saying is that the Drama School, with or without Vera, is coming unstuck. Giving the whole of Arts and Sciences a very bad name. The English Department, too, because Vera also teaches there. Those courses like The Role of Drama in Literature. She has an office in our department *and* over in the Drama School. Two offices!" Here Danton paused and then leaned forward again. "If I can express a candid opinion."

Alena hesitated and took a long sip of wine. It felt wonderful sliding down her throat and giving her the slightest sense of buzz.

She opened her hands wide and gave a slight shrug of her shoulders. "Go ahead," she said. "I encourage the department chairs to speak perfectly frankly."

"I know you do." Danton reached over, extended three fingers, and pressed for the merest second her upturned palm. "My dear Alena, if you knew how talking to you has helped me put my ideas in focus. I didn't really know where I was going when I suggested lunch. I was simply worried to death about the whole unsavory business. But I can see you're also concerned about a runaway section of the college. What to do about it."

And Alena melted. The warmth. The charm of the man. She'd heard he could be a bit of a brute. But he had sought her out without taking any wild unilateral action. Without going to some higher-up, to the chancellor. Or, God help them, the Bowmouth Trustees. And he did seem interested in her opinion and felt, as she did, strongly about discipline and order. Alena was no rebel and her social experiences—those two miserable marriages—had left her wary of anything that suggested unchecked disorder.

They got down to it. By three o'clock, three drinks of wine and two cups of coffee later, a takeover plan had been touched on and Alena, soothed, her hand twice touched with a meaningful pressure, was Professor Danton McGraw's pussycat. Or meat.

Danton's last move was to ask solicitously about the welfare of Alena's son, Derek Mosely. Was he settling in? Unfortunate about last spring term, but this was a new semester. Everyone deserved a second chance. And he, Danton, had heard that the boy played soccer. Quite a bit of talent there. And he'd been working out in the fencing class.

And Alena purred. She felt that here was someone who understood what it might be like to have such a wayward youth in the family. She smiled, nodded, said yes, Derek was trying, seemed to be serious. Derek was really liking his fencing, hoped to make the team. Then, turning businesslike, she asked Danton if he actually had a plan in mind.

Yes, Danton did indeed have a plan. A simple one. Turn back the clock and reabsorb the volatile Drama School into the sturdy, solid framework of the Bowmouth English Department. Vera

Pruczak to be left in place as "director" of this reformed entity, which would be known in the future as the "drama division of the English Department." It was a plan whose foundation must be laid as soon as possible.

A second luncheon meeting was proposed. Perhaps tomorrow, Tuesday. Both would work on the details, meet and share their ideas. Let Vera have her Halloween Masque, keep their fingers crossed that nothing more would happen.

"Let the idea float around so everyone starts getting used to it," urged Danton. "Not say 'takeover,' anything like that. The word 'merger' would be a good choice."

"I would hate to bother the Chancellor with the little details of this," said Alena. "We can handle the whole thing at a lower level. Then get his approval when the plan is all in place. He ought to be glad we've spared him the trouble. Fortunately, Todd Mancuso's parents aren't suing the college. At least not yet. And so far Terri Colman and Kay Biddle haven't been locked up. I gather they're both awaiting a hearing."

Danton smiled approvingly. They had now become "we," and even if Alena Fosdick was generally considered to have dubious academic credentials—that dissertation about Raggedy Ann, for Christ's sake—her title as dean carried enough weight to help the scheme through its formative weeks.

Assistant Professor Sarah Douglas Deane knew that her doctorate was too new, her college teaching experience too limited, for her to be allowed a say in what English literature courses she would be given to teach. Like all those on the bottom rung of the ladder, she had been handed a mixed bag. At dawn she had an eight thirty class (Business Writing) when no student was properly awake. Then at nine thirty, with hardly time for a trip to the ladies' room, Introduction to English Poetry, this demanding a hip-hop from Chaucer, a glance at Shakespeare and Donne, a swallow of Keats, Wordsworth, and Blake, and then a swift descent into the abyss as rendered by certain dark-minded contemporary poets. But last of all came, at two thirty in the afternoon, a handoff from Vera

Pruczak, an introduction to Greek drama. Vera was not overly fond of this part of drama history and disliked plays featuring messengers, gods, priests of Apollo, and prophecies, with all the real action taking place offstage. However, for this class Sarah was duly grateful. Even though the chosen plays had their stretches (for the students anyway) of tedium, there were moments of refreshment. The students were allowed to read aloud from various scenes, drowse through video offerings, and at the term's end be bused to a theatre showing an honest-to-goodness in-the-flesh play. Also, as Vera had requested, Sarah, at the beginning of Tuesday's class, had asked for volunteers for the new production of *Romiette and Julio*. This idea planted among her students had caused a good deal of restlessness not only from those already acting in the play but also among others who felt that a little theatre was just what they needed at this time of year.

It was some ten minutes after three o'clock on the same October Monday that had seen Professor McGraw and Dean Alena Fosdick reach their understanding. The fine day had vanished, and now a dreary cold rain had begun, which so depressed the view from the classroom windows that Sarah had to prod and push her class through the final moments of *Antigone*. She had hoped that the women in the class at least would be fired up by the heroine's defiance of authority.

But no. This afternoon the class was not with her. Greek tragedy, Greek myth, the whole stupid business of the chorus, left them cold. They twisted in their seats, studied the rain drizzling down the windows, and could not even rouse themselves to take parts. And a video clip of the play—in black-and-white—had done nothing for the torpor that had overwhelmed the class.

Sarah, wondering if teaching was her profession after all, thought about dismissing the class. Then, as she looked over at a somnolent male body sprawled in his chair near the back of the classroom, she had an idea that would allow her to get rid of a substantial number. Send the ones involved in the Halloween play down to the Drama School early.

Lifting a copy of *Antigone*, she raised it, waited, and then slammed it hard on the desk. "Wake up!" she shouted.

The effect was satisfactory. Heads rose; eyes opened; backs straightened. I should do this every ten minutes, Sarah told herself. Then in a loud, clear voice she announced that anyone actually involved in the play could go on down, *now*, to the Drama School. And anyone else who would like to help with set changes, take tickets, hand out programs, act as ushers, might also be welcome.

"Huh?" said Derek Mosely, one of her more inattentive students. "Whaddaya mean, we can go?"

"All of us?" asked the boy sitting next to Derek. This was one Grover Blaine, a student Sarah recognized as being a particular friend of Derek's. The two sat together, hung out in the student lounge, the cafeteria, together. They differed only slightly in physical characteristics. Grover was darker eyed, slightly heavier, more muscular, with wavy yellow hair. Derek had straight blond hair that flopped over his forehead, and was altogether a paler version of his friend, looking rather as if he had been taken out of the oven too soon. But both were tall, bony, and lean, and strangely enough, as if like actually attracted like, they shared the same devious expression on their sharp, almost foxlike faces. Both had an attitude. A hidden sneer and a hint of contempt hovering under their comments and questions.

"I heard it's *Romeo and Juliet*," said a premed student in the rear of the class.

"Yuck," said a student in the second row.

"Why not something like *The Return of the King*?" said another, a music major. "On the stage instead of a movie?"

"That Tolkien stuff is history," yawned a girl by the exit door. "I mean it's very bad retro."

"At Bowmouth College," said Sarah, "the Halloween Masque is famous. Legitimate live theatre. But of course," she added sweetly, "you might not know about it if you only watch TV and the movies."

"Hey," said Derek. "Some of us are doing a minor in theatre. So we like plays. Decent ones with an edge. Like they say something we relate to."

"And," said another student, "you need a play that makes the audience feel weird. Make those boring business types wake up." This voice, coming from the side of the classroom, Sarah discovered belonged to Grover Blaine, whose father, she thought, might well be a "boring business type."

"Where they can see themselves. Like a mirror," added another voice. "You know, like tragedy."

This idea was answered by the only student showing a degree of animation. It came from the now-notorious Todd Mancuso, recently released from the hospital with a bandaged skull, a swollen ear, and a bruised face, all of which reminded the class of his recent meeting with a stage lantern and a foil.

"Tragedy," said Todd in his penetrating voice, "shows what losers we humans are. How we flounder and muck around up to our hips in garbage, how we try to put crowns on our heads, how we want to eat our family members for lunch, how we try to climb some stupid mountain and end up in a ravine. If we didn't have tragedy we'd end up thinking we were pretty neat characters. Which we aren't. Tragedy maybe keeps us paying attention. Or maybe stops us from paying attention."

A rather confused and black view of life, thought Sarah, but she was grateful for anything resembling an interest in the subject.

"Thanks, Todd," she said. "Some of that makes good sense, and we'll be writing a paper in a week or so on tragedy. Are there any comments on what was just said?"

Here she was rewarded with yawns and shuffling feet. And silence.

A hand went up. "You just said we can leave early," a student reminded Sarah.

"You can't waltz out of here unless you're already involved in the play or want to volunteer help. I'll pass around the permission slip. If you're not interested, hang in and we'll go back to *Antigone*."

This thought was apparently so repugnant that two-thirds of the class came forward to sign the sheet and then, grabbing their book bags, took off. The remaining eight students looked at Sarah reproachfully.

"I'm not into theatre," said one. "I'm an engineering major. I just took this class because it fitted my schedule."

"Me, too," added another. "I'm economics and I think *Antigone* sucks and besides, I feel lousy. I've got some kind of virus coming on."

"We can read *Antigone* in our dorm," pointed out a third. "Less noise. We can concentrate."

Sarah took a deep breath, reached for her briefcase, carefully slipped *Antigone* into place. And looked over the remaining students. And decided. "Okay, go. Get out. All of you. But next class we dig into this play even if it kills all of us. Got that? Now beat it."

They did, with the swiftness of persons fleeing floodwaters, apparently afraid that their instructor might change her mind. Sarah sat for a moment, savoring the blessed quiet. Then she hoisted her briefcase and stepped thankfully into the hall. And directly into Professor Danton McGraw.

There was no chance to change direction or pretend she hadn't seen him coming. He was fifteen feet away, moving down the corridor toward her with fire in his eye.

Like meeting a pit bull, thought Sarah. She lifted her head and called out a hello, remembering to call him "Dr. McGraw," since he had stressed in an early department meeting that formality should be maintained in public. "If we start yelling 'hey there, Joe,' or 'Mike' or 'Emma,' it gives the sense of a slipshod outfit," Commander McGraw, USNR, had declared.

"Wait up. Whoa there," said McGraw, coming to a full halt. "Your class. Some of your students just went by me on the stairs. What's up? The period has another twenty minutes."

Sarah paused, turned slightly in McGraw's direction, feeling like a freshman caught stealing library books. But it was no time to waffle. "I dismissed them early. Professor Pruczak needs the students who are working in the play. And she wanted any other warm bodies to do grunge work."

And before Danton McGraw could exhale, she had slipped by, calling over her shoulder that she had an appointment.

The bastard, she said to herself as she accelerated down the hall. The slightest deviation from routine and the guy thinks the sky is falling. The English Department isn't the navy. He should try the Engineering School. They might listen to him.

Turning the corner, she hesitated. If she went to her own office, he'd nail her. Instead she rapped on the door of an old friend and confederate in past untoward events, Mary Donelli, assistant professor, specialty eighteenth-century lit.

Mary was slumped in a basket chair in an office only a few cubic feet larger than Sarah's, this because Mary had about two years' seniority.

Mary jerked her head up. "Good God, Sarah, you scared the daylights out of me. What are you doing banging in like this?"

Sarah, pushing away a litter of folders and student papers, sank down on the corner of Mary's desk. "McGraw caught me letting students out before the end of class. Some to the Drama School and the others because I was sick of the sight of them and they were sick of the sight of me. Sometimes you have to just wing it."

Mary nodded sympathetically. "And McGraw doesn't believe in winging. I know, I've bumped my shins on the guy."

Mary Donelli was a short dark-haired woman, dark eyed, with a lopsided grin. Since she maintained a total disregard for fashion, she usually dressed in some sort of sack, cotton for summer, denim for fall, wool for winter. As a teacher of eighteenth-century literature, she was humorous, demanding, and at the same time understanding. As she was married to Professor Amos Larkin, a reformed drunk with a tongue like a razor and an ironic sense of humor that often bit as much as it amused, Mary's toughness and accommodating disposition were often tried. But as far as Sarah could tell, Amos had been Mary's true love since the time he had accidentally knocked her off her bicycle in the faculty parking lot. As Mary had said of the event, "It must have been chemistry. There's no other explanation. Except we both love Jonathan Swift."

"Actually," said Mary now, considering Sarah's situation, "the only thing McGraw believes in is McGraw. He's managed to stir up most of the English faculty except the ones who are so well-known that he doesn't dare jerk them around. Did I tell you what he did with Amos—and you know Amos is no one to fool with."

"No," said Sarah, diverted. The idea of Professor McGraw tangling with Professor Larkin conjured up pictures of two wolverines facing off. And if bets were to be made, she would bet on Amos. He was more than a match for any naval officer recently turned English professor. Particularly one who had specialized in the nineteenth-century fiction and biography that covered the naval aspects of the War of 1812. "A monstrous waste of effort," Amos had called it.

"Like this," said Mary. "Amos had a visitation. In his office here. I know because I stopped in to pick up a book. Anyway, there was thoughtful Danton McGraw, who was telling Amos that some students in his class were a little wild. Noisy. Well, you know Amos. If he's disgusted with kids lounging around, not participating in a discussion, he's apt to push them into a dialogue, only sometimes it gets a little loud. On both sides. So McGraw thought a few teaching tips might be in order. The classroom-under-control theme. I thought Amos would shove his pencil sharpener down McGraw's throat. Or up his ass. Fortunately a bell rang and that was that. But then the very next day—"

But Mary wasn't allowed to continue. A rap sounded on her office door and was followed by the opening of the door. The head of Professor McGraw thrust itself into the gap. Followed by the body.

"May I come in," said Professor McGraw, who was already in.

Mary pushed her office chair in a circle to face the intruder. "Making an office call?" she asked pleasantly.

3

SARAH slid off the corner of Mary's desk and turned to the open door. Better to face the enemy standing.

But the enemy for the moment seemed out of place. This because Mary's office was a close fit even for two or possibly three persons of a reasonable size but a real squeeze when a commanding naval presence of six foot two inserted itself. Also, the enemy seemed somewhat confused, because although Danton McGraw had obviously come to Mary's office with some purpose in mind, he had also been hunting down Sarah Deane, and here was his prey four feet away from him, partly shielding Mary.

"Oh," said Professor McGraw. "It's both of you." He paused, frowned, obviously trying to reorder priorities and not lose the advantage of a sudden visit to someone who didn't expect him. Make that two someones.

Mary nodded, really an almost indiscernible downward head movement.

Sarah moved her mouth into a slightly more affirmative shape. McGraw's looking raggedy, she thought. Shirttail visible under the tweed jacket, tie slightly askew. Not the spit-and-polish model we like to see.

Dr. McGraw, unaware of these judgments, managed a smile. "May I sit down, Professor Donelli?" He looked around and, only finding one slender cane chair against the window, shook his head and murmured something about preferring to stand.

"Sorry," said Mary. "I don't keep big, comfortable chairs because there isn't room, and besides, it would let students settle down for too long. And yes, I know you have this thing about all of us using academic titles to keep up the proper academic atmosphere, but for God's sake, we're here in this cupboard of an office and no students are hiding under my desk taking notes on slipshod faculty members."

"Yes, of course—Mary." Danton McGraw, Professor Affable, had apparently decided to let Mary enjoy her small victory and then get onto the real subject of his visit. But first put Sarah in her place. Her place being back in her own classroom.

"Sar-ah," he said, making her name sound as if it were part of some Asian dialect. "Some of your class. On the stairs. Before the period was over. What happened? You said something about Professor Pruczak."

"Yes," said Sarah. "Vera wanted extra rehearsal time and needed volunteers for the usual work jobs. Only a few others were left in the class, so I let them out early. They were restless and it's that time of year, you know."

Professor McGraw stared down at her. "*What* time of year? I've never heard that there's a special time to let a class out before the period is finished."

Sarah, to move the subject firmly away to another area, added, "Vera's productions are always special. I gather that this year's Halloween Masque will be a real hoot."

She paused, waiting while Danton McGraw dealt with the precise meaning of "hoot."

But for the moment he seemed stymied, his face became flushed, and Sarah could see that she had stuck a knife in a very sore spot.

"I think we need to talk," he said finally. "My office in about fifteen minutes. Right?"

Sarah, who had made up the time-of-year excuse, was not going to be badgered about a simple teaching decision. "Can't make it. I'm sorry," she said. "Another appointment. Which I'm afraid I can't cancel." From one lie to the next, she told herself. By the time I'm out of here I'll be up for manslaughter.

But Mary moved in. "What is it, Danton? You look worried." A modest description of a man whose complexion was turning darker by the second.

But naval training now exerted itself. Danton McGraw took a deep breath, exhaled, rotated his shoulders, and, to the great hazard of life and limb, pulled the little cane chair away from the window and gingerly lowered himself onto it.

Then the smile again. The chair of the department had regrouped. "Actually," he said, "I can talk to both of you at once. For now, Sarah, we'll forget the class-dismissal business. This is a matter of two students. I've been looking into their class assignments and find that you both have them in at least one of your classes."

"I'll just bet you're not here about two of the magna cum laude Phi Beta possibilities," said Mary.

"Trouble?" put in Sarah. "Low grades, failing average, calls from parents?"

Now Professor McGraw's smile had a warm, understanding quality, and Sarah remembered that this man, apart from his naval training, actually enjoyed theatre work and had been acting around the area in a number of plays.

"Grover Blaine," said McGraw, carefully crossing one leg over the other so as not to tilt the chair. "Senior. An English major with a minor in theatre. And, of course, an interest in the theatre goes hand in glove with works of literature."

"Well, well, think of that," said Mary, and then, before she could be pounced on for sarcasm, went on to the more immediate issue. "Grover Blaine," she said, "is one pain in the butt. Interrupts discussions. Won't listen to other students. Or me, for that matter."

"Ditto," said Sarah. "Not stupid. But usually late with assignments."

"Sounds familiar," said McGraw. "Some of his other instructors think the same. And he hangs around, or pushes around, my other more serious concern, Derek Mosely."

"Double trouble," said Mary. "Whither one goeth, the other also goeth."

Danton McGraw raised an eyebrow. "Anything else you can think about either of the two?"

"I've heard Grover is called 'Groper' by the female theatre students," said Mary. "As the saying goes, he's 'into women.' But there have been no outright complaints from the students. As for Derek, who knows what he's like? More a follower—at least of Grover—than a leader. A mixed-up guy. Got himself kicked out last spring term."

"I'm trying to be sympathetic," said Danton. "The advisors of these two men have been in touch. Grover is quite able—academically. But I'm not sure about Derek. Both claim to have an interest in theatre. Grover, I hear, is an understudy for the part of Mercutio. Derek for Friar Laurence. And I believe in cutting both students a little slack."

No, you don't, thought Sarah, and out of the corner of her eye she could see Mary Donelli's eyes widen in surprise. Danton was not known for cutting any slack but for moving students off, out, and away. Mandatory college community service, suspension, not so veiled threats of expulsion, were more in his line.

And here was this same guy seeming to take not one but two undesirables under his wing. Okay, she'd play along. If she was really lucky, maybe McGraw would take all of them out of her class and set up special tutoring.

He must have read her mind.

"Special tutoring," said McGraw. "I'm arranging for them to meet with a graduate assistant twice a week until they can bring their studies up to speed. But what I'm trying to say is that I'm asking all of their instructors to be particularly understanding. I'll make an appointment with you both later in the week after you've had time to think about the problem. So try to keep an eye on those two. Check their performances on recent assignments."

Here Professor McGraw allowed a small pause to let these remarks sink in. Then he changed his role again, this time from concerned academic master to a variant of beloved Mr. Chips. "You know, I'm not just the English Department chair. I really care about all the students. Especially the ones having trouble finding their feet."

This statement rang so palpably false that Mary and Sarah accorded it the favor of silence.

Which Danton McGraw took to mean sympathy and assent. He rose and moved the chair back to the window. Smiled once again, the smile fixed on a spot between Mary's head and Sarah's shoulder. Turned to go and then paused.

"You know," he said to Sarah, "I realize that Vera Pruczak may have put some pressure on you to release students from your class, those in her Halloween play. And since she might ask you to assist her in the production I want to say something. May I be frank?" Here Danton favored both women with a serious lowered brow. "I have the greatest respect for Vera Pruczak; she's a"—here he paused, struggling for an appropriate adjective—"a very remarkable person. Creative. But sometimes she gets too close to the edge, and I'm very afraid that she may take a real fall, a real header." Here the chairman paused, pleased with his extended metaphor.

"She forgets," said Danton, "that the College of Arts and Sciences has many priorities and one of them is good community relations. And all of Bowmouth College cares about social conventions beyond its own walls. Accepted values, for God's sake. We should be in sync with the outside world. Half our students come from that world. The surrounding counties, the state of Maine. It's important to show a certain face. Not just by our football games and soccer matches and concerts. But by our theatre productions. I mean"—here Danton's temper reasserted itself—"last year Vera actually allowed an actor to masturbate during a scene in that play about the Marquis de Sade. The Chancellor, the department chairs, certainly heard about that one. I had calls from parents, a bishop, two Catholic priests, a Methodist minister, a rabbi, and even a Unitarian minister. And you know Unitarians tolerate just about anything."

"But," said Sarah, "you're the English Department. Vera is the Drama School."

"Yes," said McGraw, his voice straining with emotion. "She is the director of the Drama School. Which is not like the School of Medicine. Or the School of Law. The Drama School is small potatoes despite the name. Actually, it's associated with the English Department. Or used to be. So along with Vera, I and the whole English Department were also on the hot seat. And you should both know, as faculty members of the English Department, that there is a plan being formed to return the Drama Department to its original status. This plan has the interest of the dean of Arts and Sciences. I will be holding a meeting on the subject of this merger with senior faculty members later today. So I trust that you both will be part of our support team. For the good of Bowmouth College."

With which Professor McGraw reached for the door and departed, the door slamming shut behind him.

"My, my," said Mary. "I think I felt the hot breath of a threat on my brow."

Sarah sat down again. "McGraw wants to have the Drama School for lunch. And dinner."

"That," said Mary, "goes without saying. Vera is focused on drama, not what the Methodist church thinks."

"And for some reason McGraw has singled out two students for love and attention, and never mind the other ninety percent of students who also need a little special TLC."

Mary banged her fist on her desk, an action causing a cascade of exam papers to slide to the floor. "Of course. I've got it. By George I've got it."

"Got what?"

"The dean. Weren't you listening?"

"The dean? Which dean? There are a lot of them around."

"Arts and Sciences, stupid. Alena Fosdick. She's behind McGraw's takeover plan. He just said so. And all that stuff about Derek Mosely. That's Alena's kid."

"Huh?"

"I forget you haven't been around Bowmouth for that long. Missed all the gossip. Dean Alena Fosdick. First marriage to a George Mosely—with whom Alena produced baby Derek. George Mosely was a chem prof here before he skedaddled to U. Maine. Alena divorced George, then married another George—disaster number two. Got out of that marriage, so she's free. But now, with Derek hanging on by his toes, I'll bet she's leaning on Danton. Squeezing him."

"Hard to picture."

"Agreed. But she is the dean. And efficient, I guess. Though everyone gets a charge about her doctoral subject."

"Watch it," said Sarah. "My dissertation was on English fairy tales."

"Yeah, but you attached them to something solid. Biggies like Chaucer and Shakespeare. Poor Alena probably wrote a wonderful thesis, but all in all it seemed featherweight what with references to Nancy Drew and the Bobbsey Twins."

Sarah got slowly to her feet. "I'm still trying to handle Alena Fosdick leaning on Danton McGraw for family favors. I'd bet it's the other way round."

"To repeat, she's the dean. As in boss. As in superior. Sort of."

"Okay. But Grover Blaine. Why him? Just because he's a friend of Derek's? Before I turn myself into a helpful mommy type, I think I'll do a little research."

"You go to it. Why not hit up on Arlene or Linda? They know things nobody else has a clue of."

Mary began shuffling the exam papers into an orderly stack. Looked at her watch. Shook her head. "Time to go. Amos and I are taking in that new movie in Rockland. *Death Comes to the Vice President.* Supposed to be a hot one. You and Alex want to come?"

Sarah shook her head. "We're taking it easy. Alex's been on call for the last three nights. Time to watch the grass growing or the moon coming up. Something peaceful anyway. Danton McGraw's given me enough excitement for one night."

"And you'd rather see a movie called *Death Comes to the Department Chairman.*"

"Don't tempt me," said Sarah, and she headed for the door.

Mary picked up a canvas briefcase from a jumble of objects under her desk and began stuffing the exam papers into its mouth. Then she paused, looked up at Sarah, and grinned. "I don't picture this semester gliding along on smooth ripples toward a tranquil sea of achievement and understanding."

Sarah nodded. "More like forty-knot winds, crosscurrents, riptide, with an occasional waterspout."

"You got it," said Mary.

Sarah walked slowly toward her office with no immediate objective in mind. Then, step-by-step, she was overtaken by the urge to visit Vera Pruczak's embattled kingdom and judge for herself how it was faring after recent events.

But first check her mail and, if Professor McGraw was not lurking, see what Linda and Arlene had to say.

The answer was plenty. McGraw, happily, was at a committee meeting in another building, so Arlene and Linda brought Sarah up to speed. The three women had been together during a particularly unsettled period several years back when Sarah was still in graduate school. Over the strangulation of an inquisitive student and the poisoning of a tyrannical secretary the women had developed a bond. "Nothing like those college murders," Arlene once said. "And which turned the English Department on its ear," retorted Linda with disapproval. However, since that stimulating period they had until lately kept their friendship alive with occasional lunch breaks and at departmental social affairs. But in this current fall semester Sarah had noticed that fractures had begun to appear in Linda and Arlene's friendship.

"But," Arlene objected, "this affair is different. At least it's not murder. Just temperament. You know Drama School kids. They think they should be emoting all over the place or they're not really actors. That guy Stanislavsky has a lot to answer for."

"It could have been murder," said Linda. "That lantern was plenty heavy. And that fencing sword. Talk about dangerous weapons. They need a security guard over at the Drama School."

"Todd Mancuso," said Arlene, "is damn lucky to have his skull still in one piece. And his ear."

"Terri Colman and Kay Biddle should be behind bars," said Linda, moving into her law-and-order mode. "Let people get away with assault and who knows what will happen next? Professor McGraw is right about the mess over in the Drama School. And look what he's done around here. Yes, it's too much of a good thing sometimes, but now you can actually find a file. And we're not always running out of cartridges and copy paper because the whole faculty thinks it's open house in the English office. Under the last two department chairs the place was like a dirty laundry room. And mice were being fed. Made into pets."

Here Linda frowned at Arlene. "The only bad thing now is losing my own space and being fastened next to Arlene."

"Thanks a lot," said Arlene. "You're beginning to sound like McGraw. I don't like it any better than you do. Anyway, Terri and Kay will probably be charged with assault. Satisfied? Vera came with their family attorneys to pick up copies of their academic records. They're trying for some sort of suspended sentence and letting them do community service. Terri's a first-time offender, but Kay got in trouble last year throwing a bottle at someone. An environmental protest group."

"Anyway," said Linda in a tone meant to put an end to the subject. "The dean has been busy in the office looking over student files."

"My spies from the cafeteria kitchen," said Arlene, for whom gossip was her favorite dish, "tell me that Dean Fosdick had lunch with McGraw. And, get this, the lunch lasted practically the whole afternoon. I'd say that the dean's foot is on McGraw's throat for him to do something about Vera. Get a choke hold on her productions."

"Unlikely," said Sarah. "Vera does her own thing. With no help. Anyway, I've sent some of my students to help out with the Halloween play. So I think I'll go on down to the Drama School and get a real feel for the place."

"Sarah," said Arlene with emphasis. "Remember how upset the English Department was that winter when people were putting cyanide in thermos bottles? And at the end of the business you said, 'Thank God it's over.' All you wanted was to get your dissertation done, get a job, and take care of your dog. And spend quality time with Alex."

Sarah shrugged. "Vera's an old friend. She needs help with the production, and it has nothing to do with cyanide. And I don't think Terri and Kay are going to try any more attacks; they're in enough trouble."

"Good-bye," said Linda. "You're distracting me."

Uninterrupted, Sarah made it down the hall, down the stairs, out the side door, and became aware of the fact that the late-afternoon rain had stopped and given way to a stiff October breeze. She bent her head and walked briskly down the sloping path to the Drama School.

And was stopped twenty feet from the entrance.

By husband Alex. He took her shoulder and turned her about. His dark hair was blown across his forehead, his somewhat rumpled white coat was open, his stethoscope was stuffed into a pocket, his tie was loose, and all together he looked like someone who had been working too hard in an overloaded clinic—which he had—and not as a respectable visitor to the campus. But even at his neatest, his dark eyes of the penetrating variety, the rather grim long slice of a mouth, might give someone pause if he met Alex on a dark night in a lonely part of the countryside. But it was an aspect of him that had always fascinated Sarah, who from long experience knew the softer side of the man.

"So," said Alex. "Out for the fresh air?"

"I sent a bunch of my students off to Vera's Halloween production and turned the rest of the class out to pasture. They all needed a break. Including me. And then I thought I'd go over and see what's actually going on. Besides, Vera—"

"Don't tell me. Vera wants you to sneak about in costume and find out if two of her students really intended to murder another of her students with a lantern and some sort of weapon. Probably a battle-ax. Right?"

"Wrong. A foil. And Vera is in a dither because Danton McGraw's acting as if he's going to take over the Drama School. He's acting like some sort of czar about to invade a small country. But Arlene and Linda say he's getting the idea from Alena Fosdick, who doesn't want a big stink starting up in her part of the college. Anyway, why are you visiting the theatre world?"

"On business. Vera wants to be sure that victim Todd Mancuso is up to full rehearsal, which apparently involves a bunch of fencing scenes with a lot of jumping around. I gather Todd's playing Romiette or Julio—if there's a difference."

"I doubt if Vera knows. It seems to be a gender-bending version. And Todd is playing Mercutio, Romiette or Romeo's friend. Possibly as a male. But did the hospital give him an okay to take up normal life?"

" 'Normal life' doesn't mean leaping from balconies or lunging around the stage with a foil in his hand. I said I'd come and have a look at him. What I think she'd like me to do is sit through the next rehearsals with a first-aid kit in my lap waiting for the blood to flow. But I'm not giving in, although Vera's hard to refuse."

"You've noticed. But my job is harmless. I'm just supposed to help with costume changes. And be generally supportive."

"No, your real job will be to sneak around and try and rescue Vera from the jaws of Danton McGraw. Vera will triumph and you'll end up trapped in the middle."

This was an opinion Sarah wished to ignore, and since they had reached the lower step of a flight of stairs that made a grand sweep up the new entrance of the renovated Drama School, Sarah chose a diversion. She pointed and exclaimed, "Oh my God! Look at the place. They've got all the scaffolding down. I haven't been up this close in ages. It's huge."

Alex frowned. "It used to be a big white flying saucer, which wasn't too bad. At least it matched the Music School. But it's metastasized and grown all these appendages."

"Like a turtle with mumps," said Sarah. "Or with tumors."

The description was apt. When first conceived some fifteen years ago by a generous donor with an architect in the family, the flying-saucer design had caused a mighty stir. Traditionalists thought that an eighteenth-century Georgian look of ivy-covered redbrick with white pillars or simple white wooden clapboard boxes with dark green shutters was what a college of the age and dignity of Bowmouth should display. However, time and custom had brought acceptance—until this past year. What had been a simple circular building incorporating several small practice stages, a space for choreographing dance and martial arts, a proscenium stage, two dressing rooms, and costume and set storage areas had been turned into a major theatre complex.

But the additions had roused the community again. The college conservatives, rural neighbors, and local residents of Bowmouth Township who, having swallowed the flying-saucer look, now complained bitterly about being asked to accept additives that in Sarah's words did indeed make the place look like a turtle with mumps. The smooth, round concrete building now boasted a series of extended bulges around its circumference, not all showing the same degree of protrusion. A pile of construction dirt and debris that still remained piled close to the building added to an unfinished and unsightly look.

Vera Pruczak, for whom the outward appearance of her kingdom meant little, had embraced these changes and pointed proudly to increased practice space, a library, an orchestra pit, a fencing practice room apart from the dance studio, an added dressing room. All these plus new storage for props and a shop for building and painting sets. And best of all, the addition of a stage set in a small theatre-in-the-round, a modern variation of one of the many Globe Theatre imitations that peppered the earth.

For a few moments Sarah and Alex inspected the building, Sarah trying hard to think positive thoughts, Alex allowing negative ones. However, he was also a very focused person hitched to someone who, though charming and intelligent, was, in his opinion, also a highly unfocused one. So he returned to his question.

"To repeat," he said. "You and Vera scare me."

"Not me. I can't do a thing about departmental warfare. I'm so far away from any power base that I might as well be in Alaska."

"You're probably being given the role of a low-level spy. And," Alex reminded her, "after all, you have important friends. Mary Donelli, with a backup from husband Amos Larkin, and nobody fools with Amos. And you've got an in with Linda and Arlene, who both know a hell of lot more than they should. Listen, for once in your life, my dearest love, stay away from this stew. Think how you'd feel after someone brained you with a lantern."

Fortunately, they had now reached the topmost step into the main lobby entrance of the Drama School, so Sarah reached for the door, waved to Alex, and slipped inside. Once inside, she headed directly for the main stage. And Alex, shaking his head and remembering his medical mission, turned into the office.

The center stage door facing Sarah bore the name of one Elvira Hoskins, remembered by older area residents as a bad-tempered town clerk with theatrical aspirations who on death had turned out to have no family and a large fortune.

Sarah pushed open the door, went down the aisle, slipped into a seat in the middle of the fourth row center, and settled back, ready to see what was going on. There was Vera Pruczak down by the orchestra pit holding a clipboard and facing a circle of students. Onstage was featured a balcony (stage right), an antique street complete with steps made of painted stones (center stage), and the double door that no doubt led into the Capulet residence (stage left).

Then, like a general addressing troops, Vera raised an imperious hand and called in her penetrating stage voice, "Onstage, onstage. All of you. Act one, scene four."

At which call a number of students, half in, half out of costume, moved onto the stage, from the wings and from seats in the audience. They all looked, Sarah thought, like Elizabethan hybrids cross-matched with American blue-jeaned youth. A doublet here, a feathered hat there, a trailing velvet robe on one, pleated bloomers and striped stockings, or "hose," on another.

"Quiet, quiet," called Vera. She waited a moment while shuffling and whispering settled down. And then spoke, her voice deadly serious, clear, and without inflection. "For the umpteenth time," she said, "I'm going to remind you what's going on. This is just as important for the principal parts as for the crowd extras. Some of you don't seem to have a clue about the plot or what's going on generally. We are following the main script of the original play and simply twisting some of the gender identities. For now I'll just refer to the original names of the characters. Remember that we have two warring families, the Capulets and the Montagues. Romeo is a Montague and Juliet is a Capulet. This is a scene just before Romeo and his friend Benvolio and the others wearing masks sneak into a party being given by the Montague enemies, the Capulets, where Romeo will meet Juliet and fall in love. Remember, you people in the crowd scene, you're not just walking bodies. You are actors. You are to indicate by your facial expressions and slight movements that you are aware of what's happening. Mercutio, Romeo's particular friend, has a big scene here. Mercutio mixes irony and poetry. Somehow you maskers and torchbearers show that you are aware of the importance and humor of what he says by paying attention to his speeches. But without disturbing the scene."

Here Vera suddenly clapped her hands, then cupped her hands around her mouth and shouted, "Benvolio, downstage. Maskers, torchbearers, take your places. Romeo or Romiette, you're on. Stage left. Mercutio, where in hell are you? Blaine, move up."

At which Sarah sat up. Hadn't she just heard from Danton McGraw that one of those two obnoxious boys, Grover Blaine, was understudying Mercutio? Yes, there he was moving forward. He pulled down his sweatshirt, straightened his back, and looked belligerent. As the scene progressed, Sarah observed that although his voice was loud and clear and his gestures wide, the whole impression was not of an Elizabethan wit but of a twenty-first-century thug. And there, among the torchbearers and maskers, she thought she saw another of her students, the girl who thought *The Lord of the Rings* was "retro." And Romiette! Wearing a sort of long velvet jacket, a sword belt, flowers in the hair, raising his—make that her?—hands in the air as he/she came tripping forward saying something about dancing shoes. But then Sarah's concentration was broken abruptly. Vera Pruczak had collapsed in the seat beside her.

"I'm done in. Knackered, as the Brits say. We're going to use all your volunteers, although some of them seemed to expect being handed speaking parts. A day before the real dress rehearsal. Really. I am putting a couple in the later crowd scenes and let the rest be ushers, hand out programs. And as you can see, I've thrown Alena Fosdick a bone and am letting son Derek Mosely understudy Friar Laurence and his friend Grover understudy Mercutio, which is a lot more than either deserves."

Sarah nodded, adding that Grover looked ready to spear someone.

"Well, his star moment is over. Here comes Mercutio. Todd

Mancuso. I'd excused him from this rehearsal because of his injuries. But he insisted on going on. Todd's our Friar Lawrence, too, since Mercutio doesn't live past the third act. Todd's one of those actors who can do any age and use any voice. Even within with all those bandages and bruises, you get a sense of those dark, ironic features—the sexy villain look. And a voice to die for. I'll work on this scene with him and then run through the whole thing tonight."

"Grover will be disappointed. Ten minutes onstage."

"Lucky to have that. Everybody starts at the bottom and the big parts go to the upper classes of the Drama School. The theatre minors can take the small ones. If the English students are really serious they can switch over to us. Meanwhile they can learn to carry spears, open doors, and carry messages." Here Vera heaved a mighty sigh, right from the bottom of her high-top sneakers. "I've given everyone a scare talk. No more incidents. No temperament. No clowning. And the good news is that your Alex just okayed Todd for all the action. Fortunately, Mercutio doesn't have to leap off a balcony. And as Friar Lawrence he just shuffles."

"And the leads?"

"Terri Colman is our Romiette. Kay Biddle is Julio. Latter-day hermaphrodites. Or if you want a better description, they're like the amoebas we studied in biology. Changing shape all the time. However, as I said, we are sticking to the framework of the play."

"You mean," said Sarah, "you're having Romiette and Julio, those two amoebas, falling in love? Doing the balcony business and all that?"

"Exactly, and Romiette's friends, like Mercutio and Benvolio, and enemies, like Tybalt, Julio's cousin, and Julio's suitor Paris, get into fights and are killed with a foil. With Benvolio and Mercutio and Paris I just followed the plot."

"Then the lovers are married in secret and accidentally commit suicide at the end. That's what you mean by framework?"

"Of course. Some things are absolutely sacred."

But Sarah was saved from asking what Vera meant by "sacred" by the arrival of two familiar figures heading up the aisle toward the sixth row. She nudged Vera. "Here comes the deadly duo."

"Wouldn't you know it," said Vera crossly. "They won't take no for an answer. I've done my best. But I'm not about to hand any of them a real speaking part at this point. They should be grateful for the understudy jobs. More I will not do."

Sarah nodded absently; none of this was a surprise. The two boys now shambled—the only word for it—slowly toward Vera. Oddly enough, seen away from the classroom, out of context, so to speak, they almost took on other identities. As a type they gave a sense of a character Sarah had seen on television—or in a movie, perhaps—doing bad things. Or was this because she could picture both students on the wrong side of the law? And now here they were, front and center, confronting Vera. Sarah rose to go.

"Sarah, stay put," ordered Vera. "These students are yours as well as mine. Well, Grover, you first. What's on your mind?"

But Sarah had had enough for one day. Certainly enough of Grover and Derek. She faced Vera. "Look, I promise I'll be back for the evening's rehearsal. But costume changes only." Right now, she told herself, she needed to pick up some food for dinner and take her Irish wolfhound, Patsy, for a long run in the fields outside their old house on Saw Mill Road.

Again, Vera seemed to read her mind. Sarah, darling, you must try and loosen up. You really need more flex."

And Sarah, little knowing how much flex she would need in the next forty-eight hours, took her leave.

4

WALKING down the long flight of stone steps from the Drama School, Sarah became aware that action was not confined to the stage indoors. Students were in motion. Signs had sprung up. Handmade, paint-dribbled signs, and all obviously put together in a hurry. They varied in size, color, and shape, some planted on wobbling sticks, others tacked to a tree trunk. Other signs were held aloft by students, waved at passersby, or handheld and marched about the Drama School entrance. They read in part:

SAVE THE DRAMA SCHOOL. FIGHT FOR OUR SCHOOL. *NO LAST ACT FOR THE DRAMA SCHOOL.* JOIN THE PROTEST. *SECESSION FOR OUR SCHOOL.* DOWN WITH THE UNION!

All these plus a large placard with a nod to New Hampshire with a crudely drawn rattlesnake with the legend: **DON'T TREAD ON US!** And bringing up the rear, more daringly. *F*CK THE EN-GLISH DEPARTMENT.*

Well, Sarah thought, that didn't take long. What with Danton and Dean Alena Fosdick's "merger" plan being aired, not just to

Mary and herself but probably to every soul in the English Department, well, no surprise. Danton McGraw with the vocal cords of a snorting bull had probably been sounding off all afternoon to anyone he ran into. And certainly Vera Pruczak had undoubtedly been busy stamping around to faculty offices, accosting faculty members on the subject. This is what happens, Sarah decided, when two students lose their tempers and attack another one in public, onstage, with a foil and a lantern. Blood is shed, an ambulance is called, and from these sparks is kindled a major campus brush fire. Students, after all, are always ready for some crisis, an opportunity for action. Student cafeteria workers, library aides, alert office chiefs, graduate student teaching aides, all like a number of Paul Reveres, must have "spread the alarm."

For a moment Sarah stood fixed on the bottom step of the Drama School taking in the scene, considering the possible future of such a demonstration. She doubted that the protestors would confine their marching to that school's immediate vicinity. Once under way, like machinery set on "Go," the group would gather rolling power. Students, Sarah remembered from her past experience as an undergraduate, like action. Movement. A cause—even if the cause was something with which they had not previously identified themselves. Many of the most favored were popular causes that involved "stopping" and/or "saving" something. Stop Corporate Globalization, Stop Capital Punishment, Stop AIDS, Stop Global Warming, Stop the War, Save the Forbush Lousewort, Save the Spotted Owl, Save Social Security, Save the Arctic Ice Cap.

Now with the rain just clearing off on this late October day, with Halloween hovering, the students were probably asking themselves, Why not grab this chance to get psyched to stop something, save something? Things intimately connected to their college life. And, no doubt, the demonstrations had the excitement of an in-your-face confrontation with the English Department. And then on to Halloween. Or mix the protests in with Halloween while wearing a costume and mask. Then there were college parties, club parties, and Bowmouth Town costume events coming up. And all to be followed with the climax of Vera's production of

Romiette and Julio, during which signs and fists might be hoisted and a lively time could be had by all.

All right, Sarah told herself. It was time for domestic concerns, not protests. She began to work her way through the marchers. But was halted. A sheet filled with names, obviously a petition of some sort, was shoved under her nose. A woman student wearing a Drama School logo on her sweatshirt stood in front of Sarah and flapped the sheet. "Hey, it's Dr. Deane, isn't it? We need signatures. We're going to the Chancellor."

"But," began Sarah, trying to spot an avenue of escape.

"No buts," said the student. "I know you're the English Department, but I've seen you with Professor Pruczak and so you must know her pretty well. We're getting graduate students to sign, but we need faculty. Because the Drama School is under attack."

"Not quite under 'attack,'" said Sarah, hoping what she said was true but at the same time thinking that things might eventually involve spray-painting college buildings or taking over the Chancellor's office.

"Listen," said the student. "Call it what you want. Dr. McGraw wants the Drama School to fold. So he can grab it. And squeeze it dead."

"Where did you hear that?" demanded Sarah, anxious to find out exactly which gossip mill the student had listened to.

"It's all over. Everyone knows. All the English Department people, well, most of them, probably know. And some of us drama majors are going over to the Music School and get them to sign on."

Sarah indicated the paper. "I'll read your paper, okay? Now I've got to get going." And then, searching for some friendly remark, "Are you in the Halloween play?"

"You bet I am," said the student, looking pleased. "I'm doing some fencing in the street fight scenes, and I'm understudying Lady Capulet and Tybalt."

"Good for you," said Sarah, and snatching the paper, she made her escape. But it was an escape that brought her no farther than the edge of the faculty parking lot, where she was pounced on by one of the students from her poetry class. This one in a Halloween vampire costume but also holding a paper. A petition to the effect that the Drama School was giving the English Department a bad name and "we the concerned signers from the English Department wish to draw this matter to the attention of the dean of Arts and Sciences."

After a short argument on the subject of faculty neutrality (from Sarah) and faculty indifference (from the student), Sarah was released. She hurried to her car, her much-traveled Subaru Outback, noting to herself that not only was the Drama School on the march, but that factions of the English Department had also rallied the troops. All that was needed for a campus rumble was for two marching parties, after a few preliminary skirmishes, to meet in a major engagement in the last hours before Halloween evening.

And to confirm this last thought, Sarah, as she pushed her car into gear and began rolling out of the parking lot, saw out of the corner of her eye a large yellow sign held aloft bearing the message TO HELL WITH DRAMA SCHOOL!!! RALLY ROUND THE FLAG!!!

With the uneasy sense that some messages were beginning to take on the flavor of an academic civil war, Sarah drove down the road, turned into the main route to the town of Bowmouth's small mall that held the local supermarket, Fine Food Mart. On entering through the magic of the automatic doors and rolling forward with her food cart, she could see that Halloween already had a stranglehold on the place. The town of Bowmouth had a tradition of playing the occasion for all it was worth and in the past few years had stretched it into something like a three-day festival. Now on Monday, two days before the day itself, the whole scene vibrated. Black and orange crepe paper surfed along the outer walls, meeting here and there cut-out paper pumpkins, black cats, and witches on broomsticks. The baked-good shelves displayed cookies and cakes frosted in particularly intense shades of orange with black sprinkles. And to complete the almost nightmare effect, the checkout people were done up in hats and masks and capes, paper mustaches, several wearing orange face makeup that suggested a particularly fatal skin disease.

Added to all this, a number of costumed figures roamed the

58

aisles, some pushing carts laden with cider, cookies, and bags of trick-or-treat candy, often with the extra baggage of overexcited small children done up variously as Batman, vampires to knights, fairies, angels, Frodo, Harry Potter, clowns, soldiers, and witches. Others, obviously older high-school students and Bowmouth College types, were wearing wilder, more provocative costumes, some indeed wearing homemade paper badges proclaiming the fall of the Drama School or the demise of the English Department.

Oh God, Sarah thought. All we need. A supermarket fight. Flying apples, hurled oranges, onions, potatoes. Eggs! But as she wheeled from baked goods to fresh produce and on to beer, tea, coffee, yogurt, chicken pieces (cooked), squash (frozen), and finally toilet paper, detergent, and dog food, she felt that the place might be simmering but was not quite ready to blow. Several groups of the college students—two or three she could actually identify despite makeup and costume—had at first glance seemed to be gathering as if in sinister conference. But no action. So, Sarah told herself, stop thinking trouble. Perhaps these were merely meetings of friends ready for upcoming parties. Or in some cases, students heading back to the rehearsal of *Romiette and Julio* with supplies of junk food to see them through the evening.

Sarah, assisting with the bagging of her purchases, was suddenly stopped in her tracks. The store's lights dimmed, and from the loudspeaker system, after a few crackling noises, came that familiar Halloween classic *A Night on Bald Mountain*. The Fine Food Mart was certainly going all out for the eerie atmosphere. Even the checkout woman (done up as a black cat with whiskers) who was dealing with Sarah's groceries seemed startled. But then grinned.

"I heard we were going to do something special. Tonight, tomorrow night, and then maybe something real big on Halloween."

"Don't you need more light to see what you're doing?" asked Sarah, because really the whole business was so completely over-the-top. How could Thanksgiving, Hanukkah, Christmas, or Kwanzaa possibly compete?

"No prob," said the woman. "I've gotten used to it. They started dimming the lights last night just for a trial."

Sarah nodded, wrote a check for what seemed like enough money to feed a family of ten with five Irish wolfhounds, and pushed her cart toward the exit. And stopped.

A strange mewing sound. High-pitched, once, then again. Clear even with the background of shopping noise. It came from somewhere in front of her in an alcove marked by doors indicating the restrooms and between them a door marked Utility.

Was it a whine? Or soft cry. Something unnatural anyway.

A cat? A trapped cat. Or a kitten. But trapped where? In one of the restrooms? Strange. No, more likely perhaps behind the door marked Utility, the space that stood between men's and women's. Sarah stood still, trying to listen. But the clamor from the check-out lines had risen and now was being topped off by an infant strapped into a shopping cart who let out a high-pitched and sustained bellow.

Was that what she'd heard? A preliminary whine before the child sounded off? But there it was again. Now the merest whimper sounding faintly under all that racket. Coming most surely from behind one of those three doors. Sarah pushed her cart over to one side and then pushed open the ladies' room. Packed with a waiting line. But no visible cats as far as she could see, although she could hardly peek under the stall doors.

Retreating, she considered the men's room. Or the middle-section utility room that bore below the title No Admittance.

Get a grip, she told herself. Probably the strange mewing noise was part of the Halloween act, some sound system competing with Moussorgsky's *Bald Mountain*. Okay, time to go home. Shaking her head at her own folly, her own propensity to stick her nose where it was neither wanted nor needed, she pushed her cart through the automatic doors and headed toward the parking lot. Only to be stopped dead by the sudden arrival of a man wearing a blue cotton jacket with Fine Food Mart written on its chest. The man had hold of a partially grown orange kitten by the scruff of the neck.

"Okay," said the man. "You git." He put the cat down, none too gently, and gave it a push with his foot. Then looked up and saw Sarah staring at him.

"I'm not hurting the thing," said the man defensively. "But we got no use for cats inside the store. He'll find his way home. He got in here. Now he can go out."

And before Sarah had time to argue, the man turned and strode back through the entrance doors.

The kitten stood for a moment, one paw lifted pathetically, and then turned and rubbed his head against Sarah's pant leg.

At which point Sarah abandoned all common sense. Or any idea of caution. She reached down and picked up the animal, which first made itself limp and then tensed and let out a squawk, nailing Sarah's hand with a quick claw.

"Goddamn you," Sarah said aloud. But she hung on, moved the orange body under an arm, clamped it against her side, and, abandoning her shopping cart, marched the struggling cat to her car, opened the door, and slipped it into the backseat and quickly closed the door behind it. Then returned with her shopping cart, pushed it to the rear, opened the back gate, shoved in the bagged groceries, watching that the cat didn't escape. Then, climbing into the driver's seat, she tried to think. Okay, the Humane Society. She would offer to pay for its food and depart, letting the shelter take calls from owners of missing or wandering cats. And that would be that. Because surely this cat had an owner. And even if it proved an orphan, the shelter would take it in and try to find a new home. She and Alex didn't need a cat, although she as a child had grown up with a succession of tigers and oranges, blacks and tortoise-shells. Besides, wasn't a giant Irish wolfhound enough for one household? And Patsy had never shown any fondness for cats, had in fact chased every one that had wandered into his territory.

She turned the key in the ignition. And immediately was joined by a loud feline basso profundo from an enraged orange marmalade number now standing on the rear seat, its back arched. What a voice. A sort of miniature lion. This would not be an animal that would take kindly to a Humane Society cage. Or to an Irish wolfhound.

And then it hit Sarah. The cat's voice was nothing like the mewing, whining noise she'd heard by the restrooms of the Fine Food Mart. Of course one cat probably had many voices: the mad cat, the frightened cat, the hungry cat, the cat in heat.

Even so, there might well be a second cat back there by the restrooms. Even worse, a child perhaps? Caught in the utility room. Damn, damn. Sarah looked at her watch. If she didn't hurry, the shelter would close for the day. But.

No. She had to go back to the market and finish the job. Rescue a child, a fallen human. Some tottering senior citizen with memory loss. But, of course, a cat or cats were the more likely captives. Perhaps even a litter of kittens some creep had dumped thinking they were sure to be adopted. Better, Sarah supposed, than leaving the kittens on the highway, which was too often done. Anyway, she had to act. Fast. She jumped out of the car, watching to see that Cat Number One did not escape, and ran back to the market, back to the restroom alcove.

And listened. Nothing. Just the cacophony of distant costumed shoppers, checkout people ringing up purchases, and tired children fussing. Okay, the manager. Or an assistant. Someone. Paranoia was no doubt causing this reaction, but Sarah had too often been close to some commonplace location that involved what might be called "an unfortunate event."

After a certain amount of searching, pushing her way through the crowds, Sarah found a loose man wearing the Fine Food Mart jacket with *Joe* stitched on it. By three clear repetitions of her mission she finally persuaded Joe that something, a child, an adult, an animal, maybe a cat, was hiding out in the restroom area.

Joe, an old-timer with a blotched red face that looked as if it had come in contact with a cheese shredder, shook his head. "Come on; no one's reported a missing kid. Or anybody's lost husband or grandma. And no cats. Fact is, we just got rid of one. But that's all. And no squirrels. No varmints. We keep those restrooms checked. On the hour."

"What about that utility closet?" Sarah persisted.

"Well, no. We don't have to waste time to see if the cleaning stuff is behaving itself," said Joe, trying for humor. "Besides, that's a very heavy door. No little kid or even some older person could pull it open."

"How about a big kid? A half-grown kid? A mixed-up adult, not an older one? Or how about some joker stuffing his little brother or sister in?"

"Okay, okay, okay. I'll check."

"Shall I come with you? I mean if there are kittens or a stray cat we'd have to get in touch with the shelter."

"Thanks, but I know my way. And if any cats or any other animals turn up, believe me, I'll take care of them."

Sarah hesitated. The expression "take care of" had sinister connotations.

"Listen, I'm not an animal killer," said Joe. "You go along and I'll take care of it. And before you ask me, listen, if there's a cat hiding out I'll call the Humane Society."

For some reason, a reason she couldn't account for, Sarah did not admit to having just locked up an angry orange kitten in her car. Instead she pulled out a pencil and scrap of paper—a dry cleaner bill—from her pant pocket and scratched down her telephone number. "Will you have the shelter call me if it is a cat? Or another animal?"

"Take it easy; take it easy. Sure, I'll call," said Joe in the sort of voice used for deranged customers. "Listen, first I've got to check back at the bakery. Where I was heading when you came around. Some kids fooling around. Then, I swear, pronto, I'll come right back and rescue your kitty cats."

With which Sarah had to be content. Telling herself again that there was nothing more she could do, she walked to the door, looking back once at the utility door. Silence. But now the music moved into the Pink Panther theme and the dimmed lights came on full force, brightening up the restroom alcove so that whole area seemed simply a harmless extension of the now-illuminated store.

Sarah, shaking her head at her own qualms, headed for the exit. But no sooner had she passed behind three other shoppers pushing their carts through the automatic Out Door than she wheeled around, entered the automatic In Door, and headed for the alcove. Which was now thick with people waiting to get into the restrooms. Then a lull. The crowd dissolved and Sarah sidled

63

toward the utility room. The place should be checked. Now. No wait for Joe to settle whatever rumble was going on by the bakery section.

The door, as stated, was a heavy affair. Joe was right; it was unlikely that a small child or aged citizen could push it open. Even Sarah had to put her shoulder against it and heave.

A small square room painted a dull beige. Holding the door ajar, Sarah fumbled for the wall switch, found it. The light was barely adequate. Enough, she supposed, for someone coming to pick up cleaning equipment and to turn on the water at the sink that stood by one side of the wall.

For a moment she stood listening. Not a sound. The heavy door must have dulled the racket from the store. Maybe she'd been mistaken about the crying noise. Okay, but take an inventory. The place was pretty clean, a garbage bin facing the sink. A phalanx of pails, mops, and brooms hung from a rack beside an inside narrow closed door. Some sort of closet, which seemed to have been left unlocked and very slightly ajar. Sarah turned its doorknob cautiously, thinking that a bundle of kittens might tumble out at her feet. Along, perhaps, with an enraged mother cat.

In the inadequate light, the first thing that struck Sarah inside the closet, right at eye level, was a long shelf holding a number of cleaning powders, boxes, canisters, and plastic bottles marked Do Not Drink. Then she became aware that something was preventing her stepping inside. Something right by her shoes was sticking out. She looked down.

Feet. At least two things with shoes on. No, not shoes, black boots. Sarah stared, almost hypnotized, at the feet. Feet without apparent legs. She bent over the protruding feet and saw that whatever might be the legs and a body was covered by a heap of cleaning rags, a fallen dustpan, and the handle of a large waxing machine. She took a harder look. Not cleaning rags. Someone's messed-up clothes. A limp, uninhabited sweatshirt stuck out behind the dustpan. And now, Sarah's eyes well adjusted, she made out parts of what was a person. Or a body. Or parts of one. And there was a hand reaching out. And the legs had stockings. One leg in a red stocking, one in a green stocking. But the rest of the body belonging to the legs disappeared under what looked like a drop sheet, which had been thrown haphazardly over it.

And then she heard it. Not a whine or a screech. Nothing more than a low moan. Or groan. Low pitched, anyway. Nothing that would be audible beyond the heavy door.

It, the person, was alive! Or something was. At the sound, Sarah shed any doubts about moving anything. The person had to be reached. Uncovered. Scene of the crime be damned. She seized the end of the drop cloth, a green plastic sheet, and gently slid it away from a twisted figure with two arms. Bent at odd angles. And a head. Rolled back so only a bloody chin and mouth showed. The mouth open and groaning, blood bubbling from some sort of cut or injury below the lip.

As soon as the damaged figure came into view, Sarah went into action. She ran to the utility room door, pulled it open, and screamed, "Help! Help!" And then, "Someone call nine-one-one."

At which the door was dragged away from her hands. Joe, her friendly helper who had sent her home, stood there breathing like an angry furnace. "What the hell, what the hell," he yelled.

Sarah grabbed at his shirt and pointed inside.

And Joe saw the feet, the figure. "Jesus H. Christ," he breathed.

And then it was Emergency Time. Cell phone time. A loud-speaker called for a doctor, any doctor in the store. And like a genie, a Dr. Madison Grasso, who had been standing in the checkout line with her cart, shouldered her way past the cashier, sprinted to the utility room, took the scene in, knelt down, and began, ever so gently, to exam the damaged person, reached for a wrist, the angle of a jaw, put her head down on what might be a chest, and was miraculously joined by another doctor, this a Dr. Santaro, a friend of Alex's, and together the two doctors took charge of what was now their patient.

Joe, seeing a trio of curious heads sticking into the open door, turned, swore, and blocked the entrance. Then beckoned to Sarah, who stood against the wall just outside the utility room and told her to leave. "They'll take care of everything, okay? You go along now. The ambulance is here." And then under his breath Sarah thought she heard him say something like, "You've caused enough trouble as it is."

Biting her lip, resisting the impulse to argue, Sarah stood aside as two EMTs charged into the utility room. Then she elbowed her way past the gathering crowd and left the store. On the curb stood an ambulance blinking and flashing.

And Sarah turned and walked slowly to the parking lot. He, she—the victim, whoever it was—now rested in medical hands. Time to get to her car and deal with her new feline passenger. Concentrate on the present.

Fortunately, the kitten had subsided and was crouched in a corner of the backseat, a dim bundle of orange fur. It was getting dark now; the few street lamps that went along the narrow shortcut road from the town of Bowmouth did little to light the way to the top of Saw Mill Road. The turn, identified only by the mailbox and an ancient oak tree, was a sharp one onto an uneven dirt road. Some hundred yards up the road stood Alex and Sarah's old farmhouse, a structure in a continual state of renovation and repair.

Sarah stopped at the mailbox and grabbed a handful of mail. Then, looking as she often did down the long hill toward Bowmouth College, she saw that the lights had begun to come on in the dormitories, and the line of home-going cars on the highway had thickened into a solid stream. And, weaving in and out of the traffic below, Sarah spotted not one but two ambulances, their flashing lights making their way toward the Mary Starbox Memorial Hospital. Well, this was normal; ambulances came and went with great regularity day and night, since the hospital was a major medical facility drawing from many surrounding towns and the ER was a very busy place. Her battered victim would only be one of many that evening.

So now back to the work at hand. Groceries in. Settle cat in a small, safe place to begin with. The bathroom maybe. But, oh Lord, she'd forgotten cat food, kitty litter. And what if Mr. Orange needed shots—a rabies shot? Or was Mr. Orange a Mrs. Orange and pregnant? Or about to come in heat? Were any vets open at what was now well past six o'clock? But shouldn't she call the shelter first and let them do all that? But that would mean giving up the cat to sit out a waiting period in a cage. Best to call and say a young orange cat had been found, was anyone looking, and leave her number? Meantime confine, feed, and post a bathroom alert sign. Later, much later maybe, a call to Dr. Santaro or Dr. Grasso about the utility room victim. No, that wouldn't work. Doctors were unlikely to share patient information with even the one who had discovered that victim. She'd have to find out on her own.

Back to the cat. But she had no sooner settled her new friend, wiggling and hissing in the bathroom, opened a can of tuna fish—that seemed a safe bet—put some gravel and sand taken from her garden supply in the barn in a dishpan as a default kitty litter box, than the telephone jangled.

Alex. Had she picked up anything for dinner?

She hesitated. And then answered, yes, she'd been shopping, but would he mind stopping off somewhere and picking up a bag of kitty litter and a good brand of kitten food.

"What!" Alex almost shouted.

Sarah let the explosion simmer down. And then told Alex that all would be explained, that it was just one of those things that "happen . . ."

"Only to you," growled Alex.

"Trust me," said Sarah, who had rarely given Alex reason to trust her in such matters. "It's okay. I'm going to look for the owner. See you soon." And she hung up. Ran to the car, hauled in the four grocery bags of food. And the telephone rang again. And again. And again.

Alex, no doubt. She wasn't going to pick it up except to do her duty right now and call the Humane Society. She lifted the receiver, but the caller hadn't given up.

"Wrong number," she said firmly, and was about to slam the receiver down, but a heavy-duty male voice hit her ear. "Sarah Deane," it said.

"Are you selling something?" Sarah demanded. "Because I'm busy. I'm in a meeting. An emergency."

"This is Sergeant Peters of the Bowmouth Police. Am I speaking to Sarah Deane?"

"Is this some sort of Halloween joke?" said Sarah impatiently.

She could imagine a bunch of her overheated students deciding to annoy faculty members.

The return voice was firm: "If this is Ms. Sarah Deane, you are wanted to return to the Fine Food Mart immediately. There's been an incident, or possibly two incidents, in which you may have been involved. We have two notes about you. One from one of Food Mart's assistant managers, Joe Lynch. Something about a cat. Then one from a Dr. Santaro."

"You mean," said Sarah, incredulous, "a cat or a litter of kittens is mixed with the person Dr. Santaro saw? He and Dr. Grasso? What did they tell you about the . . ." Here she faltered. "Person" wasn't really descriptive. Should she say "dead body" or "mangled person" or "victim"?

"If you can't drive down here immediately," said the voice, "we can have someone from the sheriff's department pick you up."

Sarah, breathing very fast, picturing again that tangled bloody body sprawled amid a cluster of mops and brooms, told Sergeant Peters that she would leave now.

"Come to the service entrance by the loading dock," said the sergeant, and the phone went dead.

And Sarah headed, again, for her car. Fifteen minutes later, taking the same back road she had recently traveled, she pulled into the Fine Food Mart service entrance, parking the Subaru between a Knox County Sheriff's Department cruiser and a white and black Maine State Police car.

And on opening her car door was met by an entirely familiar—and right now unwelcome—presence. Sheriff's Deputy Investigator Mike Laaka.

Any other time Sarah would have been happy to see Mike, an old friend of hers and a boyhood pal of Alex's. But Mike had met Sarah on too many odd occasions when events had turned nasty, so that he had begun to blame her for having a sort of noxious aura that attracted everything from civil unrest to murder. He was a tall Nordic type with almost white hair, intense blue eyes, the sort of person Sarah could imagine standing on an ice flow or casting a herring net.

Mike now stepped forward, took charge of Sarah's elbow, and

guided her firmly toward the loading door, this now guarded by a Bowmouth Town uniform type.

"So," said Mike, in not too friendly a voice, "what has Professor Deane been doing? Hearing funny noises in the restrooms? Finding people in closets? Homes for strange animals? Stealing pussycats?"

5

SARAH jerked her arm away from Mike's grasp. "Cut it out. I'm not going anywhere. In fact, I've already spent half the afternoon in this damned place."

Mike sighed. "Why in God's good name, Sarah, can't you ever stay quietly in your office seeing harmless students or at home correcting papers? If I believed in witches you might qualify. You probably have bats hanging in your kitchen. And your brain is wired with a GPS looking for something that's none of your business."

Sarah was spared a reply by their arrival in the rear section of the Fine Food Mart where stood a cluster of employees, still in their logo shirts or butcher's aprons.

What struck her first was the lack of noise. There were some whispers and low-voiced mutters, but that was all. But she had no time to speculate. Mike pushed her on toward a double door that led out from the meat and seafood sections onto the main floor of the store itself.

Again the lack of noise. Only here and there a wailing child, an older child's exclamation, these hastily quashed. Shoppers, or former shoppers, had, like the employees, moved themselves into informal groups. Several older people leaned on the handles of their shopping carts; several even more ancient had taken possession of a line of benches in front of the checkout counters.

"What," said Sarah in her firmest voice, "happened? Did the person I found die? Or was dead? Or just banged up? The ambulance was still there when I left."

But Mike, a man with excellent distant vision, was now peering into the distance, moving his head until he found the head and shoulders he was looking for. A Maine State Policeman. Mike waved, the policeman waved back with a beckoning gesture, and Mike signaled okay with an outstretched hand.

"An accident," said Mike tersely. "Might be a Bowmouth student. Not sure yet. Waiting for a positive ID. No wallet turned up."

"An accident to a Bowmouth student? In the utility room?"

"We don't know. You're the person who heard something. The accident victim trying to call out. Or a cat calling. Together or separately. Anyway, we'll need to have you run through what you saw of the store scene from the time you got here until you left."

"Impossible. I couldn't even guess at what was going on before I heard the noise. There must have been more than a hundred people milling around. The Bowmouth College crowd, and parents—with children—buying trick-or-treat candy, and half the middle- and high-school population. A lot of them in costume. There's a batch of parties tonight. This town always overdoes Halloween. Anyway, I'm sure someone else besides me must have heard the noises."

"Apparently not. Or they're not telling. You apparently suggested to one of the guys here—the assistant manager named Joe Lynch—that someone should check the restrooms and the utility closet. Because of this weird noise you claim to have heard."

"I didn't *claim*. I did hear. But after I got hold of Joe—I didn't know his last name—he said he had to check something going on in the bakery section and I thought . . ."

"You thought you wouldn't wait for Joe?"

"It might have been a child. Someone's grandmother. Someone having a grand mal seizure. Oh hell, Mike, I don't know what I thought except someone had to go look. And there was only me because God only knew when Joe would get loose to do it."

"And what you found was this beaten-up person, half-alive, half-dead. Or maybe more dead than alive. We don't know yet how it's going to go."

"He—is it a he?—was mashed inside of the place mixed in cleaning stuff, a tarp pulled over part of him with his, or her, legs sticking out. And I yelled for help, and someone called the ambulance and for any doctors. And two turned up. That's the whole story."

"It's a man. And so far we haven't heard about what sort of shape he's in. But you're wanted back at the restroom area. To go over the whole business. Time, place. Well, you know the drill. Or should by now. You should have a degree as some sort of veteran witness."

"I did *not* witness. I just heard something. And went to look."

"Good, tell it to the judge. Or better to George Fitts, who's waiting. I'll bet he turned purple when he heard who had been loitering around the crime scene."

"You go straight to hell, Mike Laaka. I wasn't looking for a crime scene. And I didn't set this up because life was boring. I heard some goddamn catlike noise and rescued an orange cat and went back and found this guy and I will goddamn well tell George that."

She turned and strode down the frozen-food aisle with Mike on her heels.

George Fitts, or rather Sergeant George Fitts of the Maine State Police CID, was the human equivalent of a Cuisinart. He could mix and churn and agitate an unhappy witness (and most witnesses were unhappy after a session with George) until evidence or incriminating statements ran out like juice from his victim. He always spoke in a low voice, never shouted, and was only known to have used profanity after a moment of extreme personal jeopardy involving a pointed weapon. And he was relentless in questioning, never seemed either to be tired or need food. Although he was wearing plainclothes, his clothing suggested the military, so that he gave the impression of being ready for inspection. But when all was said and done, there was a deep well, mostly hidden, of an ironic sense of humor. And, once or twice, a few drips of sympathy had been detected. And, as far as Sarah was concerned, the chief thing in his favor was his ownership of two West Highland terriers. This fact Sarah had only learned last summer and for which she forgave him much.

Now she arrived within George's orbit, a small table set up outside the restroom area, took the offered folding chair, and nodded a bleak, unsmiling greeting.

"Professor Deane," said George, pulling a notebook toward himself. He called her Sarah privately, but protocol in public must be observed.

"George," said Sarah, for whom police protocol meant nothing, and she had known George for far too many years, "George, I'm not glad to see you. But I'm sorry if something happened to someone. About which I really know zilch. I yelled for help. And left."

"I think," said George, checking his watch and noting the exact time in the notebook, "that you will be able to elaborate on zilch. Help the police as you have done in the past. By now we would call you an experienced witness. A mistaken one sometimes, but certainly an experienced one."

"Is he someone I know?" Sarah demanded, deciding to get to the heart of things.

"As a matter of fact, we believe it is. The ID just came in. It's a student from one of your classes."

Sarah stared at him. "How do you know that? And is he hurt? Badly hurt?"

George reached for a notepad. "The college identified him as being in a class of yours. And we've just talked to the emergency room people. He isn't as badly injured as it seemed at first. The two doctors and the EMTs, when they first saw him, said he looked like he'd been through a cement mixer. Now we've heard he's only got contusions, superficial cuts, a few needing sutures, a loosened tooth. A couple of cracked ribs. But lucky. No bones, no punctures of important parts."

"I love what people call lucky," said Sarah. "But I'm glad it's not too bad. And George, who, just who, are we talking about? What student of mine?"

George again consulted his notebook. "Name is Mancuso. Todd Mancuso. He's taking your Greek drama class."

"Mercutio!"

"What?"

"Todd is playing Mercutio. The Halloween play at the college. For the Drama School. I just saw Todd going up onstage this afternoon."

George raised his eyebrows a fraction—the only hair on his otherwise clean-shaven face and bald top side. "This afternoon? When this afternoon?"

Sarah considered. The whole afternoon seemed to stretch like a rubber band endlessly to this moment. From letting her class out early, meeting Alex, watching of the rehearsal, the protest marches, the strange noises, the orange kitten, to the utility room and finding what seemed like a body. On and on the afternoon, now the evening, went.

"When," George repeated, "did you actually see Todd Mancuso at the Drama School?"

Sarah tried to focus. She'd let the class out early, been caught by Danton McGraw, gone to Mary Donelli's office, seen Dr. McGraw again. "Maybe around four o'clock," she said. "Something like that. Vera was going over the first act. Mercutio was late coming onstage and I left after that."

"So you got to the store when?"

"I didn't look at a clock. I just pushed my cart around, got my groceries, and after I'd been checked out I heard the noise. A cat or other animal of some sort. Or a child. Someone sick. I told one of the store people to investigate—Mike says his name is Joe Lynch. Anyway, Joe said he'd look into it, and that there'd been a stray cat around, but it had been put out of the store. Maybe the cat got back in. Joe told me to go home."

"And you didn't go home?"

"No. I began thinking that with all the Halloween business going on, the music, the lights going off and on, my hearing a funny noise wasn't going to get top priority."

"So you came back, opened the utility room, and found what looked like a dead body. Or a badly injured person. And called for help. So now we've got to back up and see why and how young Todd Mancuso got himself beaten up and stuffed into the cleaning closet."

"The poor guy," said Sarah, shaking her head. "He's just out of the hospital. He'd been hurt during an earlier rehearsal."

George looked as if he had just swallowed a large chunk of spoiled food. "I heard from one of my sources about that incident, although the Drama School seemed to be trying to cover it up. I was hoping it wasn't the same student. I was told that one of the English Department secretaries passed around the information that two female students went crazy and attacked this Todd Mancuso onstage. Is that correct?"

"Well, not quite," said Sarah. "I think it's more complicated."

George snapped his notebook closed. "I want to see you tonight down at the Drama School. Make it eight o'clock. I'll be talking to Vera Pruczak at the same time. She can fill me in on this early attack so we can get some background." George's voice when the subject was the goings-on at the college always expressed such disapproval of the whole academic machine that it was as if he were speaking of a crowd of psychotic orangutans.

"What about all these people in the Fine Food Mart?"

"We're taking statements, addresses, phone numbers, all the usual. Mike Laaka has three deputies, and I'm leaving two troopers here. Someone may have seen something, heard the same noise you did. And we're stationing a few men on campus for the next few days. According to my sources—"

"The English Department secretaries?"

George ignored this. "I'm told that the Drama School and English Department students, probably some of the faculty, too, are getting themselves in a lather. Students starting protest marches. Well, no one wants the thing to blow up into a real fight. Frankly, I'd rather deal with a Maine State Prison riot than a bunch of empty-headed students looking for trouble. Because they usually find it. And they're quite surprised to find out how much being in trouble actually hurts."

"Do you think that Todd's being beaten up has anything to do with the protests?"

George shook his head. "Nothing would surprise me. But perhaps it had to do with what he was wearing. Red and green stockings. Or tights. The female variety. And some sort of pleated shorts, almost like bloomers. And makeup. A Halloween costume or does he cross-dress? There are still plenty of people around who react to men in women's clothes."

"Mercutio," Sarah said. "Todd is playing a part requiring tights. It's an Elizabethan costume. Doublet and hose. Vera's been having partial dress rehearsals."

"Knowing Vera Pruczak," said George, "I'm surprised she's sticking to the Elizabethan look. I might have expected the actors to be in space suits or dressed like Tarzan."

Sarah nodded, remembering that George had stubbed his toe on Vera during a previous investigation and had apparently no happy memories of the meeting.

"So," said George, making a gesture of dismissal. "I'm off to check on Todd Mancuso at the hospital. I'll see you at the Drama School at eight. Now go home and take care of that orange kitten you picked up outside the store."

Sarah stared. "What! How do you . . .?"

George allowed himself a tight smile. "As I said, I have my sources."

Mike Laaka and his fellow sheriff's deputy investigator, Katie Waters, a square-faced, square-chinned person with square-cut brown hair and a determined manner, had labored long and hard within the confines of the Fine Food Mart. The natives were restless, many moving from reluctantly agreeing to a holding-tank system to vehemently demanding that they be let out and allowed to go their way. The fact that at least a third of the customers as well as the checkout people wore some sort of costume, that the lights had been dimmed, that the usual shopping noise had been augmented by Moussorgsky and "The Pink Panther" plus sound effects that suggested the howling of wolves—all these made the chances that anyone had seen or heard anything of significance to the beating and stowing away of Todd Mancuso most unlikely.

"It's like this," said Mike to Katie as they began boxing their tapes and notes. "Half these people probably know each other. But they can't remember if they saw them in the store. Some students only remember seeing a person dressed like Batman or Spider-Man, or a someone who might have come right from the play rehearsal in their costume. But no one seems to have a grip on the names."

"And," added Katie, "you've got those parents who think all students look alike or were so busy trying to shop and get out of the place that they wouldn't have noticed if Abraham Lincoln turned up."

"Actually," said Mike, "he did. Along with George Washington. Two Bowmouth history majors. Mightily pleased with themselves. There's some sort of history party coming up and they think they've nailed down the prize."

"Not a chance," said Katie. "I took the names of two women who think the same thing. Mother Teresa in her habit and Jeanne d'Arc wearing half-burnt clothes and carrying a Bible. You can't beat that sort of thing."

"Enough jabber," said Mike impatiently.

"You started the jabber," Katie pointed out. "Now let's hit the trail. I think we've drawn a big zero. No one heard a sound. Except for the music and kids crying and students yodeling at each other."

"So first we'll drop these statements off at the state police office and then meet George over at the Drama School. A little before eight."

"Like George said, keep an eye on this protest scene," said Katie. "He thinks the whole business might spill over into other college departments. Maybe into the town."

"The town mostly doesn't give a shit whether the English Department beats up on the Drama School," said Mike. "Though some people in the town might enjoy the idea."

"I know. They think some of the Drama School stuff is, what's the expression, 'offensive to the sensibilities of decent people.' I think they might like to protest."

"Oh, great," said Mike. "What we need just before Halloween, a real Town-and-Gown rumble. With high moral touches. Though you must admit some of those items the Drama School served up last spring were pretty raw. Sex and violence and revolution like they're all going out of style."

"But you need the kind of theatre that makes people think."

"Think?" said Mike. "More like toss their lunch."

Katie, ignoring remarks of an unenlightened colleague, picked up one of the boxes stacked with recorded interviews. "Move it. I'll tell the Fine Food guys that they can open the doors, flush out the place, and go back in business."

And the two deputies stood up. Tall, blond Mike and short, dark-haired Katie, like a mismatched couple in a comedy routine, worked their way through the grumbling crowd, delivered the re-lease message to the store manager—a very unhappy personage—headed for the employees' parking lot, and took off in Mike's old Chevy Bronco.

"Where's your car got to?" asked Mike.

"George had me picked me up at the sheriff's office," said Katie. "Two squad cars are in the shop. Don't worry; I'll get some-one to give me a ride back after George's finished with people he's going to be working on."

"Others beside Sarah and Vera?" Mike turned the Bronco to-ward Route 17 and pointed its nose toward Route 1.

"They'll be two of the stars anyway. But then . . ." Katie hesi-tated.

"Are you thinking what I'm thinking?" Mike said.

"You mean about who else he's going to haul in?"

"Yeah. Because maybe I'm ahead of you on the next two."

"Don't bet on it. George will want to spend quality time with Todd Mancuso. And with that Terri What's-her-name and Kay Bid-dle. The two ladies who bonked Todd over the head with stage props—a kind of lantern and some sort of a sword—during an-other rehearsal. Ambulance, EMTs, the ER, the whole nine yards."

"Terri's last name is Colman, and how'd you hear about all that anyway?"

"Like George always says, I've got my sources."

"Let me guess. Names like Linda and Arlene? The English Department stool pigeons."

"Arlene's my second cousin," said Katie defensively. "She likes to share."

Mike sighed. "The main problem is that half the county is related to the other half and they all like to share. But, okay, maybe you having a finger in the English Department pie may pay off. Like now we've got spies in the lair of Danton McGraw."

"The scourge of the Drama School?"

"And then some. So keep the pipelines open. Though I hate to admit we're relying on Cousin Arlene for the juice. Not on anything solid."

Katie sighed. "I'm already sick of the college scene and it's only been a few hours."

"I was born sick of the college scene. Privileged little bastards. What's the matter with U. Maine anyhow?"

"Nothing," said Katie. "But Bowmouth's okay. Pretty good faculty, and besides, they give financial breaks to local kids."

Mike eyed her suspiciously. "Are you telling me something? Like you graduated from Bowmouth while all the time I thought you were a simple hometown girl who went to the Coastal Community College?"

"I did that, too. But I went the last two years to Bowmouth. Full scholarship for unusually talented person who was ravished with the idea of law enforcement. Now be quiet. I want to imagine Terri and Kay as a couple of homicidal females who wanted to wipe the floor with Todd Mancuso."

Mike nodded, silence prevailed, and the Bronco slid into place behind the state police office and the two deputies, arms loaded with boxes of statements from the Fine Food Mart, made their way into the state police office.

Meanwhile in an examining alcove at the Mary Starbox Memorial Hospital all hell was breaking out. Todd Mancuso was alive, alert, and kicking like a roped steer.

"He wants out," said ER nurse Hannah Finch to PA Ed Trapper.

Ed, a strapping six foot six, was the sort of physician's assistant that would normally silence any out-of-control patient—particularly one having what Ed called an ego fit.

"I tried to settle the guy down, but he keeps going on about some play where he's a feature attraction. Like the play won't function without him." Here Ed turned to the curtained alcove and shook his fist at it.

"And," Ed continued, "he wants me to produce this Vera Proozle or Proshak from the Drama School for God's sake. Says she'll spring him. What I think is she'll have a cow when she sees the condition he's in. Black-and-blue from stem to stern, bloodied up, fat lip, and sutures across forehead and chin. Couple of loose teeth."

"I think," said Hannah, "it's the 'show must go on' mentality. Especially if you're a star. Or one of the stars. Anyway, I called Vera Pruczak—that's her name. And she's hotfooting it right over."

"And here I am," said Vera, materializing like a genie behind Ed Trapper. She was wearing what must have been a durable rehearsal costume of a black turtleneck covered by a khaki cape, which hung over worn dungarees, followed by high-top sneakers. As a sign of her distress, her electric hair was even more than usually excited and only partly disciplined by a tiger print scarf. "I've got to see Todd. Get the real picture. See if this is humbug or the real thing."

"It looks pretty real to me," said Hannah. "He's a mess. We finally got an IV into him, gave him a sedative which I think he faked swallowing. And he wants out."

"Which he probably can do if he signs a release," said Ed. "Half-dead people can leave as long as no one else is in charge of them. And they're of age."

Vera shook her head. "This is what I get for canceling the rest of afternoon rehearsal. The whole cast was infected with some sort of Halloween bug, so I let them out to work off the steam. Of course actors shouldn't let outside events upset them, but these are a bunch of half-grown kids. 'Theatre discipline' is just another expression. Signifying nothing."

Ed grinned. "You mean," he said, sinking his voice into a deep, sonorous bass, "it's a tale told by an idiot."

Vera paused, looked him over, head to toe. "Would you like to try out for a small part in one of our spring plays?"

"It's an idea," said Ed. "I've been doing this medical thing, but I've been thinking about the Drama School." Then hearing a commotion, the sound of falling glassware, he turned and saw a slender nurse's aide scuttling out of the alcove with a tray on which soup, Jell-O, and teacup were awash from an overturned glass of juice. "Don't make me go in there again," said the girl. "That guy is out of his tree."

"Oh for heaven's sake," said Hannah, who was never given to stronger expressions, "Louisa, please go clean up that tray and I'll go in with you."

"You know I'm using the name Weeza," said the girl. "It sounds better for theatre work."

"Right now you're in a hospital," said Hannah. "And to me you're Louisa. And don't forget to check Mr. Mancuso's temp next."

"No, she won't," said Vera firmly. "First I'm going in and have a quick chat with Todd. Look him over. We really need him for Mercutio and if it's only a few bruises . . ."

"A few bruises!" exclaimed Hannah. "His face looks like hamburger."

"Probably nothing a little makeup can't handle," said Vera in a cheery voice. "As long as he's basically sound. I've called Dr. McKenzie to come over and give him a look because he's the doctor who checked Todd out before after the last business, the lantern, you know."

"I know," said Hannah. "I was on duty when he came in."

"And Weeza," said Vera, turning to the girl who still held the dripping tray, "be on time for tonight's rehearsal. The finale needs work." She turned to Hannah and Ed. "Weeza Scotini is one of our star dancers."

"I think," said Hannah, now irritated in the extreme, "that the Drama School is causing more trouble in the emergency room than the entire population of the town of Bowmouth. And you can't go in until I've checked Mr. Todd Mancuso's vital signs—with Louisa."

And Hannah grabbed the tray from Louisa-Weeza, slid it onto a nearby table, and escorted her into the alcove. After a certain amount of rustling and mutterings, the two returned, Weeza with wide-open eyes.

"That Todd," she said. "He can do every accent on earth. He was German just now, calling himself *'ein Wunderkind von Hamburg.'* He looks awful, but who cares if you can act like that? I've watched him do some of Mercutio and I saw him this summer and he's something else."

"He has talent," admitted Vera, "but we don't want it to go to his head. I need a serious Mercutio, not a film star." She turned suddenly, being afflicted, as her students claimed, not only with second sight but also with a working radar.

"There you are, Alex," she said. "We need you again. It's Todd Mancuso. Wouldn't you know. It's what I get for letting the cast loose. They go off to the supermarket and start a scene. Anyway, Todd swears he can get up onstage, which he probably can. We can limit the swordplay for the rehearsal. After all, he's only got cracked ribs and bruises. We can cover up the sutures with makeup. After all . . ."

"I know," said Alex almost angrily. "The blasted show must go on. I think you and Todd are raving mad. I'm not going to sign any discharge. Where are his parents? They should be called."

"They were," said Hannah. "But we only got the message machine. They're somewhere on a trek in Italy."

"Terrific," said Alex.

"And he's twenty-one. A senior."

"So on his head be it," said Alex. "And it may well be on his head. The scenery collapsing, someone tossing a lantern again, sticking him with a sword or two. Never mind. I'll go in and have a word with him. The admitting ER physician is ready to throw in the towel. Or throw Todd at me."

After which things moved with remarkable speed. Todd's vitals were pronounced satisfactory; Alex McKenzie, longtime sufferer from Vera Pruczak's fits and starts, was unable to overcome her influence and persuade Todd to stay put. George Fitts arrived at the hospital just as transportation of the victim was arranged in Vera's van to the Drama School. George announced he would follow behind them and for Vera to have a quiet room available in which Todd could be questioned. Vera then departed after reminding George that the interview with Todd must be a very short one, "Todd needs to rest and recover, and I don't want you and your crew to stress him."

This session, held in the Drama School faculty common room some twenty minutes later, proved a dead loss. The room was not well lit; the furniture was elderly and given to sagging. George sat at a small writing desk, Katie and Mike on a small sofa, and Todd slumped in an ancient armchair, fumbled with his facial bandages, alternated nods and head shakings with a muttered "yeah," or "nope," or "I dunno."

"He's being a complete asshole," said Mike to Katie in what passed for a whisper.

"He's being Marlon Brando in *On the Waterfront*," whispered Katie to Mike.

George looked up. "Do either of you two have questions for Mr. Mancuso? Questions unconnected with Hollywood."

But it was no use. No questions from any of the three were answered. Todd hadn't recognized the person who cornered him by the utility room. He'd been on his way to the men's room and someone called out his name. Yeah, it might have been a man. Or maybe not. Todd wasn't sure. "Yeah, it happened fast. Slugged, dragged, beaten up. . . . Yeah, inside the utility room. . . . Yeah, I'm sure. All those mops and pails and stuff."

"Anything remarkable about this person's appearance?" asked George, repeating this question for the third time.

"Nah. I already told ya. Costume. Everyone was dressed up, see. This guy—if it was a guy—had on somethin' black. Dracula maybe. Spider-Man maybe. You nevah know. And a mask. On his face, so who in hell was it? I dunno. And that's all I gotta say. So can I get outta here? Back to the theatre. Okay?"

George, usually the master of self-control, looked almost ready to pick up a lamp himself and hurl it at Todd. Instead, George inhaled and nodded.

Katie, who had been waiting for Todd/Marlon to come up with "I coulda been a contendah," turned to George. "That's it, isn't it?" she asked.

And Todd, a faint smirk showing briefly on his bruised face, rose stiffly, uncertainly, from the chair and inclined his head in George's direction. "Pleased to meet cha," he said.

And George pointed to Katie. "It's almost eight. Find Professor Pruczak and bring her here. Mike, go to the entrance and keep an eye out for Sarah Deane. We'll see if we can get a sensible statement from someone."

Sarah arrived by exactly eight at the Drama School, was pointed to the faculty common room, now populated by Deputy Katie Waters, Deputy Mike Laaka, and Sergeant George Fitts. There Sarah found Vera Pruczak ready to move on. And out.

"No matter what the police say, we can't do a joint chitchat," said Vera to Sarah. "That's what I've just told all these police people here." Here Vera rose, sweeping her cape over her shoulder. "They know what I know, and now they'll find out what you know and the devil take the hindmost."

"What!" said Katie. "How does the devil come into this?"

"An old expression," said Vera crossly. "It says what I'm thinking about this whole frightful business. And now, I'm too busy to talk anymore. As it is we had to put off the rehearsal until eight forty-five because of you people. I've sent Todd to rest in the Green Room and Terri Colman and Kay Biddle will be keeping an eye on him."

Sarah looked alarmed. "Vera, aren't those the exact people that put Todd in the hospital the first time? Aren't you asking for trouble?"

Vera waved trouble away. "Nonsense. They were all just a bit high. Todd had been annoying Kay and Terri for weeks, trying to get a rise out of them. Todd can go off into space sometimes, thinks he's put on the earth as a jester."

"There's another word for it," put in Katie.

"He went too far and he knows it. I've had a long talk with him after that incident and all is well. The point is," said Vera firmly, "that right now he's with two women he knows well, whom he trusts. Neither of those women took him into the utility room and beat him up."

"Just how do you know that?" asked George, fixing Vera with the George Fitts look, a look intensified by thick lenses in frameless glasses.

"I know my students," said Vera. "And if I were you, Sarah, I'd point out to Sergeant Fitts and Deputy Waters and Deputy Laaka that you saw no familiar faces from the Drama School lurking around that utility room. The thug who did this undoubtedly came from the English Department."

"Have you anything to back up that idea?" asked George.

"Look outside the English Department. The building is crawling with signs saying things like 'Kill the Drama School.'"

George nodded, scratched something in his notebook, and then eyed Vera again. "Those signs are very much like the ones being paraded around the Drama School. By Drama School students, I assume."

"There's a difference," said Vera. "Our students are doing it in a sense of fair play. To save their school. The English Department and some of its faculty, plus quite a few of their students, are the aggressors. Our theatre students are putting on a show of defiance in the face of threat. You do understand, don't you, that they are having a dialogue in the dramatic sense, but the English Department students, probably those who are doing a minor in theatre, are all worked up and being foolishly belligerent."

"Why do you say those doing a minor in theatre?" asked George.

"They have a foot in both places, but they are majoring in English. That's their real home. Therefore, I do not usually cast them in lead parts. Understudy parts, walk-ons, crowd scenes. They probably resent this."

"You're saying they aren't really actors in the true sense, the true psychological sense," said Katie, always ready for fodder to add to her evening psychology courses. Katie had dreams of someday forcing the likes of Mike Laaka and George Fitts to acknowledge that thorough knowledge of abnormal psychology is the first essential to understanding crime.

George looked at Katie with marked disapproval. "Your psychology courses have taken you off into space more than once. Stick to police procedure and proper interrogation methods and you won't have time to make wild guesses. Guesses unsupported by evidence."

"Katie is correct," said Vera firmly, "Actors are different. Very different. Listen to Katie and you might learn something." With which Vera swirled about, raised a hand in a graceful departing gesture, and closed the door behind her.

6

THE Green Room of the Drama School occupied a half of one of the bulges added onto the older part of the building, giving it a rounded wall and a straight one. Adding to the strange shape was a motley collection of furnishings including an overloaded bookcase; a discarded futon draped with a much-mended patchwork quilt; several straight chairs; a long table; and a collection of ill-matched armchairs. The walls, rounded and straight, were decorated with a number of scenes of past Drama School performances. These ranged from early—pre–Vera Pruczak—productions of a non-threatening nature (*The Merchant of Venice, Pygmalion, Harvey*) to the more recent works of the likes of Edward Albee, David Mamet, and Tom Stoppard. Now to the room's contents had been added the personal effects of those students participating in the *Romiette and Julio* production. Book bags, hiking boots, scarves, textbooks, scripts, and odd pieces of discarded costumes littered the room.

Todd Mancuso sat or rather slumped on the futon. His blood-ied costume had been taken for cleaning, and he was now dressed in someone's oversize black sweatpants and the ubiquitous Red Sox sweatshirt—this tribute worn by almost 80 percent of Bowmouth students. Todd's bruises had darkened, and despite hospital efforts, his face and head, with its sutures, surgical dressings, and adhesive strips, suggested a traffic victim, not a star performer.

Kay Biddle and Terri Colman sat in chairs adjoining Todd's sofa. Both women had given short statements to the police that afternoon at the Fine Food Mart, and both had denied seeing or hearing anything untoward. They had merely come to the store for a supply of eatables to see them through the long rehearsal. Later both had been called to the phone at the Drama School and been informed that they would be spending quality time on the police hot seat the next morning. After all, Mike reminded Katie, these two women were responsible for Todd's first visit to the hospital. Todd was *their* victim. So if once, then why not again? Now sitting in the Green Room, Terri and Kay, having been ordered by Vera to stay with Todd, seemed honestly concerned about effects of their earlier attack, and at the same time both hoped to talk some sense into the man. He should be discouraged from acting the stupid joker with the sort of foolishness that had practically forced the two of them into an attack mode.

Terri, dressed in an Elizabethan velvet doublet over jeans, kicked off with a short sermon mixed into a general warning on sensible behavior. But unlike past encounters with Todd, her speech was infused with a certain amount of sympathy.

"You see," she said, "we're very sorry someone beat you up."

"You mean beat me up again," put in Todd.

Terri ignored this. "The fact is," she said, "you've been behaving like a total asshole. A genuine Yahoo. Driving us both bonkers. Ruining our scenes. Cutting in front of our entrances."

At which Kay, in her turn, spoke up. "If you screw up any more scenes, my dearest Todd, I'll do more than slice your ear; I'll take your head off your neck." Here Kay leaned forward and shook her fist at Todd. "The fact that I like you and Terri likes you shouldn't encourage you to behave like a two-year-old. As an actor we think you're awfully good sometimes. Some scenes just belong to you. And Terri and I don't mind that. Fair's fair. Just leave us our space and let us have our lines. And offstage, try not to be such a goddamn fool. Okay? Understand? Got it?"

Todd sighed, the weary sigh of a ninety-year-old man about to expire from the extremities of old age. But even so, even with the pretense, the sigh sounded genuine. "You want the truth? Okay, I'm too beat up to pretend to you guys. I like, no, make that love, both of you. Kay, I wanted to go out with you sometime. As a person. Not part of this circus. Take a hike. Rent a canoe, a kayak. Make that three kayaks, because Terri, you've got to come along, too. You're as important as Kay. We all need to get away from this place. You can breathe greasepaint for just so long and then you have to have fresh air. A drink. Or a girl. Make that two girls. Or jump off a cliff."

Kay frowned. "What you wanted—whatever the hell it was—you went about it like . . ."

"You've already said 'asshole.' "

"Among other things," Terri broke in. "Maybe we overreacted. But maybe that knock on your stupid skull with the lantern is just what the doctor ordered."

Todd gave a small grin. "Dr. Freud?"

"I think," said Kay, standing up, "the sliced ear I gave you was also helpful."

"Put it this way," said Terri. "We were both overreacting. But it was for your own good. Now I think I'll go do something useful, and let you two work out whatever you want to work out."

"Oh, sit down, Terri," said Todd. "I need help from both of you. Kay, I'll try to behave because I think I need you for a friend. Or more. You, too, Terri."

Terri made a face. "Both of us as more than a friend? Triple threat. Ménage à trois?"

"But right now what I really want," said Todd, pushing himself into a straight sitting position, "is to get my hooks into whoever beat the crap out of me. You were both at the market this afternoon. Didn't you see anyone in the whole place who might have wanted to nail me? Someone who wanted my part? Was jealous. The trouble is I was hit so fast I never got a look at the person. Beyond a sort of loose black outfit."

A long pause followed. Terri tried running through the entire cast of *Romiette and Julio*. Who wanted a bigger part? Was jealous of Todd, all the big parts he'd played the past summer? Or more to the point, who wanted to play Mercutio? Or even Friar Laurence?

"Jealousy is a great mover and shaker," said Terri. "Someone wanted your parts."

"There wasn't a waiting line for Friar Laurence," said Todd. "But Mercutio is something else. Grover Blaine is my understudy for that part, and he probably hopes I stay down and out. Derek Mosely is understudy for Friar Laurence."

"First," said Kay, "you're assuming that one of those two did it, since I've heard they were both at the market, though I didn't see them. Maybe Grover because he's a bully and a wannabe rapist. A sexual predator who doesn't dare go all the way. I think he's your basic wuss in wolf's clothing. And if he really tried to force someone, he'd be out of college with the speed of light. And behind bars. We females are all on to Grover the Groper. We've even formed a sort of an alliance to take care of his type. We'll make you a member. But Grover is the dean's son's best buddy, so we haven't tried to clean his clock. Not yet anyway. But he's on the schedule."

"I don't remember seeing Grover or Derek there," said Todd. "But maybe it was some local thug. Or a spaced-out druggie thought I was his girlfriend's boyfriend."

At which interesting point, Vera thrust her head into the room. "Todd, we're going right to one of your Mercutio scenes, and I'm having your understudy, Grover, go through it. You should watch and make suggestions."

"Do you think Grover can really do the job?" asked Terri.

"What choice do we have?" said Vera. "Grover speaks right out, knows the lines, so he'll have to do. And Todd, you should be ready to go on as Friar Laurence." Then with an embracing gesture, Vera swept the two women out of the room, and then she stayed behind to assist Todd, should he prove faint.

Which he almost did. Stood up, teetered on his feet, reached for the back of a chair to steady himself. Finally, taking a deep breath, he managed to walk slowly to the door.

And met Dr. Alexander McKenzie, whose brow was dark with disapproval.

"Yes," said Vera, seeing Todd frown. "I asked him to come. Keep an eye on you. See you don't move around too much. Friar Laurence isn't supposed to be very active onstage, so lean against some solid scenery if you feel dizzy. Don't go all out with your voice. Keep your gestures small. Just for the rehearsal, of course."

"I'm here because of you, Vera," said Alex, speaking through tight lips. He turned to Todd. "Show me what scenes you're supposed to be in, what you're supposed to do for the real performance."

"Listen, Dr. McKenzie," said Todd. "I'm okay. So help me."

"I may have to," said Alex. "Find your script and come and sit down. I've got a seat in the front row on the side where we can catch the rehearsal. And if you start screwing around onstage without permission, I can probably find a straightjacket somewhere."

With which Todd left and headed for the stage. Alex and Vera followed.

"If he's really not okay," said Vera, "I'll pull him from the whole affair. I'm not a monster."

"Never thought you were," said Alex. "Just very focused."

"Priorities," said Vera, then, with a quick glance at the dark landscape beyond the window, "Are those protest groups still going at it?"

Alex nodded. "It's like a virus. It spreads. The Pharmacy School students, God knows why, are supporting the English Department. And the Dance School is boycotting Saturday's concert by Music School students. And what all that has to do with anything is beyond me."

"Dance students will usually support the Drama School, and the Music School seems to be on the side of the English Department, though heaven knows there aren't many rational musicians. It must have something to do with mathematics. Musicians are supposed to be good at numbers, and we know that Danton McGraw is a numbers person, a bean counter. It's nothing anyone can control; it's built into their nervous systems."

And with that Delphic piece of wisdom, Vera found a seat next to Todd, and Alex moved to the other side of his patient.

"Trapped," said Todd with a feeble attempt at humor, his face already frowning from the pain of walking and sitting down.

"Hush," said Vera. "And pay attention. We haven't got all night. I want you to watch Grover. If he's going to take the part we don't want him looking like some sort of gangster or drug dealer when compared to the good guys, Romeo, Benvolio, and Paris. In fact, Paris as Juliet's approved suitor should look fairly special. But Mercutio should always be an electric presence from his first entrance on. I may have to fasten a wire into Grover's costume. So, Todd, watch, and be ready with suggestions."

"Make notes and sit and clap," said Todd resentfully.

"You are resting up. Under Dr. McKenzie's watchful eye. While Romiette and Juliet—"

"You mean Julio." Todd reminded her. "Julio is a him-her."

"Sometimes I forget," said Vera. "But for now you'll be going on as Friar Laurence. The part won't take anything out of you physically. Be grateful I've cut half of his lines."

"I am not grateful. And let me at least do the Mercutio death scene."

"Not tonight you won't. If you're in good shape, you can get to play both parts on Wednesday. It's an easy costume switch; all Friar Lawrence has to do is pull off his habit and his wig and turn into Mercutio. But tonight Grover will do the fight scene and die."

"Damn," said Todd.

"Think positively and I'll let you die on Wednesday."

Todd twisted in his seat and faced Vera. "'A plague o' both your houses! They have made worms' meat of me,'" he proclaimed loudly.

"Hush," said Vera, "or I'll snatch Friar Laurence away and give it to your understudy, Derek."

"I really am worms' meat," said Todd. "That bastard did a job on me. And sitting here, I feel I'm going to explode. Like a 'dog, a rat, a mouse, a cat . . .'"

"Shhh," hissed Vera. "So you know your lines. Stop showing off and be quiet."

Alex turned to Todd. The boy needed a distraction. To stop

thinking of his part being usurped. "So how is Vera going to end the play?" Alex asked.

"Paris, Juliet's suitor, is killed at the end but comes out in a finale all decked out as a sexy Parisian courtesan," said Todd. "And half the cast come dancing back onstage and do a sort of jazz gavotte."

"So very upbeat," said Vera.

Although not in physical pain, Sarah found herself, like Todd, trapped. Trapped in the Drama School faculty sitting room where George Fitts leaned forward on a small table, his pen poised over his notebook, his rimless glasses and the pale eyes behind fixed on her. On the other side of her straight-backed chair sat Katie Waters.

But trapped or not, what Sarah was now was feeling was an overwhelming fatigue. The endless day had turned into an endless night. The idea of being grilled by George Fitts and then being made to sit through Vera's Shakespearean extravaganza was more than Sarah could imagine surviving. What she needed was a hot dinner, hot drinks, hot bath, heated blankets. Flannel nightgown. Soft pillow. All these comfortable pleasures while Alex did useful things to the fireplace in the kitchen. While he fed Patsy the dog. Fed the kitten. Oh my God, she thought, coming to with a jolt. The kitten! That new orange kitten. She had not yet come to terms with Alex about the kitten. Nor had she called the animal shelter. Oh shit. And now here she was, trapped. She glared at George. And at Katie.

"Relax," said Katie, the psychologist-in-training. "You just sit back, breathe deeply, and let all your muscles go loose."

Sarah gave Katie a look. "If I did that I'd wet my pants. Now let's get this show over with. I want to put in my appearance at the rehearsal and then get the hell home."

George tapped his pen. "All right, Sarah. We'll make this as short as possible. But we have a new bit of information to run by you. No matter what you think, or what I think, you happen to be front and center in this business."

Sarah shifted on the wooden seat of her chair, tried crossing her legs for greater comfort, and waited for George and his "new" bit of information.

"You've found the guy who beat up Todd?" she asked without much hope.

"We found a student, a grade-school student, who says his younger brother saw someone hanging around the utility room. Who went away and then came back and kept looking around over his shoulder. As if he was on watch for something."

"You mean you've got a witness telling his brother who told you . . ." Sarah began and then shook her head. "That's not much to go on. You call it hearsay, don't you?"

"Right now," put in Katie, "we take what we can get. And what we get is a eight-year-old schoolboy telling something to his ten-year-old brother."

"I'll bite," said Sarah, her voice tired, barely audible. She uncrossed her legs, which brought only a slight relief to a developing backache.

"Harry Potter," said George.

"What?"

"Harry Potter," repeated George. "Or one of the characters in those books. You know, castles and boarding school and witches and magicians and dragons."

"Yes," said Sarah, "I know." A true fact, because Sarah had read all the books and seen the movies and even listened to the newest CD recording of *The Half-blood Prince.* Then since George appeared to be waiting for a more complete response, Sarah added that she had seen at least four Harry Potters that afternoon at the Fine Food Mart. "You know, the black-rimmed glasses and the school uniform robe and a broomstick."

"The trouble is," said George, "that this younger brother said it wasn't Harry."

"Hermione? Ron? Mrs. Weasley?" said Sarah making stabs.

"We don't think so," said Katie. "Some other character. One of the bad ones."

"That could run into hundreds," said Sarah crossly. "Is that all you've got?"

"It, or he, was wearing a black robe," said George.

"Great," said Sarah. "Half those characters wear robes. All the Hogwarts kids do and so do the masters and teachers and some of those ghosts whizzing around."

"The guy—the boy said he thought it was a guy—was pretty tall."

"Almost like a giant?" asked Sarah without much hope. Someone the size of Hagrid would certainly be noticed.

"Think it over," said George.

"Yes," said Katie in her psychologist mode. "Let the whole shopping-market crowd run through your head, and you'll be able to sort some of them out."

"But not now," said George firmly. "Katie hasn't got her psychology degree yet, and besides, we don't have a couch in here. But when you're back home see if you can put together a tall figure in a robe who was one of the bad guys in the Harry Potter series."

"How about Snape? Severus Snape," said Sarah, amazed that she could come up with Snape's first name. And then warming up, "How about that awful Dudley Dursely, or Mr. Dursely? Or, I have it, Voldemort?"

George held up his hand. "That's enough. With all those characters in your head you can pick and choose and eliminate." He changed his expression to something mildly affirmative. "You can think of it as a police lineup. And now go back to the rehearsal. If that's what Professor Pruczak calls it. To me the whole production is like a circus run upside down. I imagine Shakespeare is restless in his grave."

Sarah couldn't resist. "George, don't tell me you worry about Shakespeare. Is he one of your favorites?"

George gave her the eye. "I have always enjoyed real, that is, genuine, theatre. Not Professor Pruczak's idea of theatre. But I have trouble with *Hamlet*. All that endless talking and not doing. But *Macbeth* is almost perfect. With a satisfactory ending."

And Sarah left and for possibly the fiftieth time reorganized her views on Sergeant George Fitts. She saw him restless at *Hamlet* and rejoicing at *Macbeth*, which in itself was pretty scary.

Sliding into her seat in second row center, behind Alex and Todd, she found that the rehearsal had moved past Mercutio's death (Grover filling in for Todd) and Julio (Kay Biddle) now was accepting the sleeping potion from a stooping and frail Friar Lawrence (Todd Mancuso).

"How's it going?" whispered Sarah, leaning over Vera, who sat in the first row, the script on her lap.

"So-so," said Vera. "I've reached the point of no return. Never want to see the thing again. Nor any of these students. But Todd's holding up even if he's playing Friar Laurence as if he's suffering from senile dementia."

"And me? You don't need me anymore, do you? No real costume changes until tomorrow night. Besides, I can't throw any light on what the English Department's up to."

"Actually, Danton McGraw turned up. Being Mr. Charming. What could he do to assist? 'So sorry about Todd. One of the town lowlifes, probably.' And he's sure he and I can work out our differences. Loves the theatre. Blah, blah, blah. But he is going to work with Grover on the Tybalt-Mercutio killing scene. Grover's footwork is pretty loose. He backs away in the swordplay part and keeps upstaging Romiette."

"If Todd has to skip the fencing scenes on Wednesday, maybe no one will know. After all, most of the actors wear masks and the same sort of male-female costume."

"We'll see. Wednesday is two days off. But McGraw even offered to take on Mercutio himself. Well, I certainly turned that idea down flat."

"Would he be any good?"

"Don't kid yourself, Sarah. That's what scares me about the man. With certain limitations that have to do with humor and an overinflated ego, the man is damn good. And now he's in harness with the dean. She even turned up to watch the balcony scene."

"Dr. Fosdick?"

"Herself. I think they're working together. Maybe she's putting her pretty little hands around his neck and squeezing a little. She may be the one who thought of the idea of gobbling up the Drama School. Who knows. Okay, it's time for the last scene. I've cut a lot, so now we have Romiette killing Paris, and Julio stabbing herself."

"Or himself," said Sarah.

"Whoever," said Vera. "And then the finale. A piece of work if I do say so. We've worked some of the moves with the Dance School."

"I'm going home," said Sarah. "I'll catch the whole thing Wednesday night. . . . Nobody's going to take over the Drama School before Wednesday night." She looked around. "Where's Alex gone? He was sitting right here."

"Dressing room. Seeing how Todd survived those scenes as Friar Laurence. Heart rate, blood pressure, all that jazz."

Sarah began sliding her arms into her jacket, gathering up her handbag.

"Wait," said Vera. "Here it comes. The finale. Right out of the Folies Bergère. Super cancan. Paris is super. That's Weeza Scotini. She's doing a minor in dance."

The music—now from the organ, later to be a larger orchestral unit—revved up. And Sarah, hearing familiar and irritating thumps of "Ta-Ra-Ra Boom-De-Ay!" held one hand to a throbbing brow.

And split.

Back home at the Saw Mill Road farmhouse, Sarah shuffled through the front door and was met by Alex.

Who was holding a small orange kitten in his arms. And stroking him.

Sarah blinked and stared.

"Hungry little devil," said Alex, moving the kitten to a place on his shoulder. "I think we should call him Piggy. He's had a whole tin of kitten meat. Which I picked up on the way home. And still beat you back."

"The Humane Society, the animal shelter," said Sarah, reaching an arm to the wall for support. It was a matter of minutes before she would collapse to the floor.

"Checked with the manager there. She's one of my patients. No calls in for an orange kitten. No orange kitten's got loose from his cage. They'll wait eight days and then he's ours."

"Ours? Both of us?" Sarah could hardly believe what Alex was saying. A man who had never mentioned being in love with cats. Or kittens. A dog man, she thought.

"I've always liked cats. Admired them. They're so basic. Know what they want and get it. On their terms. And he's a handsome one, too." Alex reached up and ran his hand down the kitten's head and along his back. "He likes backrubs," Alex explained.

Ten minutes later, after a bowl of mushroom soup and a buttered scone, Sarah sank into a hot bath, the water frosted with bubble bath, and began running over the entire cast of evil characters in the Harry Potter series.

But fatigue dulled her brain and even in bed, enfolded in Alex's comforting arm and trying to keep Piggy from crawling under the blanket, Sarah failed to unearth the name.

In fact, what with all the next day's distractions, it was not until All Hallows' Eve that the right name eased itself in a nasty slithering—make that Slytherin—way into her head.

7

TUESDAY, the day before Halloween, was a day to rejoice in. Early sun, kindly breezes, friendly temperatures, prevailed on this late October date. Ahead lay social engagements, parties, and a spunky (from all reports) theatre offering in the evening. Add to these delights the early dismissal of classes, ditto office hours. The famed (at least within a circle of fifteen miles) Bowmouth three-day Halloween hoop-de-do was approaching climax. So what more could an employee, a faculty member, a student of Bowmouth College, want?

Apparently a lot.

Take, for instance, Linda LaCroix, secretary-in-chief of the English Department. Things were falling apart faster than usual. Of the faculty members, who had been notified (make that ordered) by Professor McGraw to hand in their plans for the midterm exams by this date, only three had. Then Linda, intending to come in by seven forty-five that morning, was waylaid by an early-morning clutch of students rotating around Malcolm Adam Hall with large painted posters denouncing the Drama School. None of which added to the ambience of that handsome ivy-smothered building—a place that Linda had always been proud to point out to friends as her "office." The students, recognized immediately by the sharp-eyed secretary as being English majors, had waylaid Linda, flapping anti–Drama School posters in her face. This business had so slowed her progress that she made it into the office barely by eight. Adding to this annoyance, Linda's new cobalt blue slacks and tangerine fleece pullover had been splashed by a passing student stamping through a puddle left over from yesterday's rain.

The day did not improve when Linda found that the three mousetraps set around the edges of the office had been sprung sometime in the night and the cheese bait was gone and no mouse bodies present. All of which meant that perhaps more than one well-fed mouse was now loose in the area. Probably, thought Linda with a shiver, hiding under her desk. Or, worse, in the ladies' room ready to run around her ankles when she sat on the toilet. To these uneasy thoughts was added the fact that chief clerk Arlene Burr had not yet arrived. Then came a call from Professor McGraw saying that he would be over at the Drama School going over the fencing scenes and to please keep the department ship afloat.

And the ship was now being boarded. Students appeared asking the whereabouts of instructors—this instead of knocking on the instructors' doors—calls came in from maintenance people, from the library wanting the return of a certain bound manuscript borrowed by one of the teaching fellows in September. Then a ring from old Professor Silas Ulysses Morgan complaining that the heat was off in his office. Even Linda's pointing out to him that the outside temperature was unusually warm and that the offices were set for sixty-five did not appease him. "I'm old," croaked Professor Morgan. "I want you to do something. I can't get my lecture notes together if I'm shaking with the cold."

"Blast you, Professor Morgan," said Linda, after pushing the off button.

"Hello," said Arlene, appearing behind Linda's shoulder. "Are you picking on my favorite professor, Silas Morgan? What's he done?"

"He says he's cold," said Linda, "which," she added, "is a crock of shit."

"I'm glad you're not a nurse," said Arlene. "Old people feel the cold. But I've got some news that ought to shake a few feathers loose."

"There are already too many feathers loose. And where *have* you been? It isn't Halloween party time no matter how the rest of the college behaves. Dr. McGraw wants, in his words, 'to keep the ship afloat,' which I'm trying to do, no thanks to you. It's past nine."

"Stop trying to be McGraw's clone; the original is bad enough," said Arlene, slipping into place at her desk. In honor of the day she wore a black T-shirt with a large pumpkin whose grinning face was swollen in a lifelike way by virtue of her rounded breast works.

"Okay, so what *is* the news?" demanded Linda, who, despite her intention not to be distracted by the sort of trivia Arlene lived on, found her curiosity twitched.

Arlene smiled, ready to deliver her bombshell. "Like it's really a doubleheader. First it hits the Drama School. Second it hits the English Department."

"Spit it out. I've got work to do," said Linda.

"It's Groper Blaine."

"Don't let anyone hear you use that name. God, Arlene, we're supposed to be professionals. His name is Grover Blaine, and he's the best friend of the dean's son, Derek Mosely, which is something you should keep in mind."

"I don't think McGraw has started bugging our office, so I'll say it again. Groper. As in groping someone. Which I guess he has. Or at least a girl over at the Drama School has filed a complaint to the authorities. Arts and Sciences, maybe. Somewhere, anyway."

"Spit it out. What sort of complaint?" asked Linda.

"What do you think?" said Arlene. "Groping. I don't know if it gets filed under harassment or what. I suppose legally it's 'touching in an inappropriate manner.' Which is what groping is. I think."

"You mean just touching? Not raping. Maybe punching. I suppose there are different levels of groping. Squeezing, maybe. Or grabbing. Or holding down."

"Or none of the above," said Arlene. "But I guess the complaint will go to the usual committees. Something will be decided. I mean the guy could be expelled, suspended, arraigned by the police. Or he could just be reprimanded, made to apologize."

"Ouch. This will really sting the English Department. And the dean. And God knows who else. McGraw will chew nails."

"It happened over at the Drama School," said Arlene. "In one of the practice theatres. After the rehearsal was over. So Vera Pruczak will be on the hot seat, too."

"Because," said Linda, "it happened on her turf."

"To be fair," said Arlene, "it could be some hysterical kid. The guy pats her on the shoulder and she goes berserk. Maybe she's been a victim sometime. A victim would overreact."

"Leave it alone; the whole damn thing sounds bad enough as it is," said Linda. She looked over at the clock and shook her head. "Right now I've got this office to run, because McGraw's gone down to the Drama School to work on the fencing scenes and phone calls are beginning to stack up."

"You don't suppose he's trying for a peace plan with Vera," suggested Arlene. "A kind of truce. Schmooze a little, put on the charm. They can work out a plan and maybe get rid of this Grover while they're at it. Use the dean as a lever. After all, the attention McGraw's been giving her should count for something."

"If Grover is really guilty the heat will be on in both departments," said Linda. "Now get to work. We need a rough draft of the next semester's classroom assignments."

Professor McGraw was only too aware of the heat. His cell phone had gone off just as he stepped out of Malcolm Adam Hall shortly after eight that morning, right after charging Linda to keep a steady hand on the department helm.

The news had been unpleasant in the extreme. Not only was Grover Blaine an English major, but the news had come from Dean Alena Fosdick. And, she told Danton in a voice mixed with anger and distress, Grover was not the only student implicated; apparently her son, Derek Mosely, had been a bystander at the affair. But the girl—name not revealed—had recognized both students as two English majors. One groped; the other watched and did nothing to stop the business.

"I am," Alena said in a tense voice, "mad as hell. That Grover

Blaine is disgusting. You should have done something. Both English majors. And does Vera just let students hide out over there and do this sort of thing? I tell you I'm concerned. *Very* concerned. If the Drama School is taken over by your department you've got a double mess."

As if, Danton thought, I am in charge of every breath taken by English majors. He had tried to be calm, reasonable, but as Alena went on, it was obvious that she really did think Danton himself bore some blame. That he had promised to check on the boys, their progress. Keep their noses to the grindstone. Get them tutored. Encourage them.

"And," she added, her voice almost trembling, "we'll have to keep the lid on this. We don't want newspapers or the police coming around. It's all one of those stupid mistakes. I hope you can see that no false information leaks from your office. I'll be calling you after I find out more. But I have confidence in Derek. I'm sure he'll tell me the truth. If he says Grover was set up, then I'll believe him. And you should, too."

"Christ," said Danton under his breath as he stuffed his cell phone into his pocket. "Spare me mothers." And as to rumors or undigested information leaking out of the department office, okay, that should be watched. He had those two jabbering secretaries, and how about those big-eared students who hung around the office, swallowing every little item that turned up? Well, what did Alena expect? The whole college was a rumor mill. And here Danton was hit with a wave of nostalgia for the world of the U.S. Navy. Better yet, the confined world of the atomic submarine. Particularly when submerged.

And Alena Fosdick. She was way out of line. That talk about his watching out for those two boys, those promises he gave, happened only one day ago. He wasn't a miracle worker. But then he remembered, he actually *had* done something. He'd directed Professor Donelli and that other one, Sarah Deane—was that her name?—to keep an eye on the two. Make contact. Call those two students into their respective offices. Be warm and helpful faculty members. Because, by God, he'd done all he could. And even Mary Donelli and Sarah Deane probably couldn't do much, what with those crazy protest marches and Halloween screwing up anything resembling academic discipline. Did Alena think twenty-four hours and an office chat or two were going to make those two guys shape up overnight? But there again, the mother factor was at work.

But right now play the whole affair low-key, he reminded himself. And play both sides of the fence. English Department reaches out to the Drama School. First, go see Vera and calm her. Because, he reasoned, even without this Groper affair, she must already be worked up, what with her star Todd Mancuso beaten to a pulp only two days before the play. She should be open to overtures. He'd tried during rehearsal last night being a supportive colleague without noticeable success. So now try more of the same. A peace treaty. No, make that a temporary peace treaty.

Because of course Danton McGraw was not one to forget his number-one aim, but first things first. Put the Drama School takeover on the back burner and deal with Mr. Groper Blaine and Mommy's pet, Derek Mosely. Oil on troubled waters. Be sympathetic to Vera's dilemma, since the incident took place under the Drama School roof, in fact, almost under her nose.

With these matters being juggled about in his brain, Danton almost walked into a marching unit of students now engaged in an early-morning rally around the sacred walls of the English Department.

The first student he recognized, in fact, the one he had almost knocked down, was one Jason Fleury, a senior who was doing a special tutorial on maritime literature under Danton himself. The boy, a rotund bug-eyed fellow with sagging jeans, a white shirt on which was written in bold letters T-Shit, staggered and got his balance.

"You," bellowed Danton, reaching to steady him. "Fleury. What do you think you're doing?" And without waiting for an answer, Danton shouted to the group, now stopped in their tracks, placards at half-mast, "All of you. Do you think you're doing the English Department a favor by marching against the Drama School? Giving a helping hand to the College of Arts and Sciences? You're doing real damage and looking like a pack of idiots. You're behaving, all of you, as if you just got out of third grade."

"We're trying to support the English Department. You know, be sort of loyal," piped up a small female voice.

"Why let the Drama School attack us and just sit there?" demanded Jason Fleury.

"Because," said Danton, "if you ignored the stupidity of the drama students you might just be accused of acting like adults."

And he turned on his heel, strode off, and after taking several deep breaths arrived under perfect control at the back entrance to the Drama School. He should now really reconsider the Grover/Groper problem. To begin with, Danton had been hit with the same idea as had Arlene. Perhaps this girl was one of those hysterical women who in her past had been manhandled, touched, fooled around with—even raped, for God's sake, something bad anyway—and now if a man even looked at her, she went off the deep end. Or, this was barely possible, the girl might have been put up to acting a part. After all, she was a drama major. What better way to stick it to the English Department than to drag one or more of its students into the mud? Harassment, even assault, improper sexual approaches, these were hot issues. What a weapon!

Of course, Danton told himself as he reached for the Drama School door, the most likely truth of the matter, unfortunately, was that Grover Blaine and his buddy, Derek, had actually groped, pawed, done something disgusting to some poor student. A girl who could not get rid of them or somehow escape. And both boys were as tall as Danton was, which likely made them more formidable. Oh Christ.

Checking his watch, Danton stepped inside and headed for Vera's office. About twenty minutes to work on her and stitch together his (non-binding) non-aggression pact. Then take a look at the two fight scenes in the play. Would Grover the Groper be cut from the understudy part of Mercutio? Doubtful unless the disciplinary powers had met and found proof positive of misbehavior. Or Grover had confessed. Or Derek had squealed? Derek seemed to be the weak one of the two, the squealer type. Anyway, Todd might well be up and around today and demanding to get back on the stage, so the question of his understudy taking over was probably moot.

Vera seemed none too pleased to see the English Department chair at an early hour in her office.

"What are you doing here, Danton? Joining the protest march?"

"Vera, Vera. I have nothing to do with that. In fact, I just gave some English students hell for acting like fools. Look, I've come here with my peace pipe. Let's you and I be sensible and see if we can turn these students off. English students, drama students. Get them to simmer down."

"It's not those idiots who are driving me crazy," said Vera crossly. "It's this new business. Your two English majors—"

"Doing a minor in theatre," said Danton.

"Whatever," said Vera. "Both of them getting nailed for sexual harassment or whatever it was."

Danton tried for control. "Please bring me up to speed," he said, adding, "May I sit down?

Vera nodded grudgingly and indicated an uncomfortable steel chair, something left over from a recent contemporary play. Vera, on the one hand, was now dressed in her work clothes, overalls and turtleneck with random scarves tied here and there. Danton, on the other hand, was, as yesterday, not his usual trim naval self, what with rumpled shirt and loose tie.

"So," prodded Danton. "What gives? Alena Fosdick called me and she's in a real snit."

"A real tizzy," agreed Vera. "She called me this morning, too. Went on about unhealthy theatre atmosphere and random acts of violence. You'd have thought she was describing the Middle East."

"Alena," said Danton, "is very sensitive. Two bad marriages have left their mark. And this is about her son and her son's best friend. And she claims that Derek wouldn't lie about the thing."

Vera shook her head. "Since I've heard that one of her marriages involved abuse, you'd think she'd be sympathetic."

"You forget," said Danton. "She's—"

"A mother," finished Vera. "Yes, yes. I know. Anyway, the Arts and Sciences College disciplinary committee is having a preliminary hearing this afternoon."

"In the meantime . . . ," prompted Danton.

"I can't toss either boy out of the play until after a hearing. And the girl, she's been told to communicate only with her family, her family's lawyer, and later the disciplinary committee."

"No question of rape?"

"Absolutely not. Or there would have doctors and ER visits and the Bowmouth police. Maybe an arrest. No, it's simply a matter of touching. Or reaching. Or reaching and touching. Or neither of the above. That's all I know. Now get out of here and start rehearsing the fight scenes with Grover and cross your fingers we won't have to use him on Wednesday. And oh yes, make sure the fighters wear their masks."

"Fencing masks?"

"No, the mask masks. Like a Halloween mask or as worn at a masked ball. I've made everyone in a fight scene wear them for the last two weeks to get used to seeing around them. Peripheral vision was just a little bit compromised when the actors first had them on. But we've been doing the two street fight scenes in slow motion until this week. It's important that the actors can actually see what they're doing."

Danton stared at her. "God, Vera, at least enlarge the mask eye spaces so the actors can see what's going on. Those are foils they're using. Real weapons. If anyone's hurt, you'll have more than Grover Blaine to worry about."

"I have complete confidence in the fight choreography. You've worked out the proper fencing moves yourself. Now go."

"Peace, Vera?" Danton stood up and fixed his number one smile on Vera.

"We will see. After the play and when this Grover business is settled. Then, if you've still got your grab bag out, our artillery is ready and we're ready to go over the top."

The two fight scenes had been scheduled for rehearsal that morning under the critical eye of Professor McGraw, on one of the school's two practice stages. The brief swordplay in act 1 set in "a public place" on the streets of Verona required a short sequence of lunge, parry, riposte, counterparry featuring the firebrand Tybalt, the peacemaker Benvolio, and assorted extras from Vera Pruczak's recruitment of the Bowmouth Fencing Club. This scene was particularly tricky because citizens and "peace officers" arrive with clubs to subdue the swordplay between the Montague and Capulet factions.

Twice Benvolio stumbled and sent Tybalt staggering; once one of the peace officers fell over his own club and splatted down on the stage, pulled off his mask, and swore. Danton McGraw mounted the stage, pulled him to his feet, and had started to say something about obscenities when he found he was addressing a female actor.

"Damn Vera," mumbled Danton as he called for the scene to begin again. However, the act 1 scene was completed without more missteps, and the actors for act 3, scene 1, were called onstage. Vera, as she had been doing throughout the rehearsals, reminded the cast what was going on in that particular scene. Privately she wondered if a single one of her students had actually read the entire play; perhaps they had not even gone beyond glancing at Monarch Notes.

"Listen, pay attention," called Vera. "Benvolio is Romeo-Romiette's friend and helper. Tybalt is a Capulet nephew and Juliet-Julio's cousin. Tybalt is a fire-eater, and you, Malcolm Wheelock, when you play him, stop sounding so reasonable. Romiette for the sake of his love for Julio refuses to fight Tybalt. Mercutio can't understand why Romiette is behaving like a coward. Takes up the argument and gets himself stabbed by Tybalt. And is dragged dying offstage by Benvolio. Tybalt exits briefly and re-enters, as does Benvolio. Romiette, I want you to show real anger when you attack Tybalt after he comes back onstage. Tybalt, when you fall try not to roll off the stage. Just die quietly. Your scene is over. Now all of you try to show appropriate responses without trying to upstage each other."

At which, Vera stepped aside and beckoned to Todd Mancuso,

108

who had been sitting in the wings, to come onstage to demonstrate Mercutio's moves. This he tried valiantly to do, the result being that after a short advance, a feint, and a lunge he almost passed out. He was then firmly escorted offstage by Danton and told to sit still and pay attention to any changes in footwork and swordplay.

So now in the wings, on a stool, arms folded, eyes blazing, sat Todd Mancuso, his sliced ear an inflamed crimson, his face purple with bruises, and the head lacerations from the lantern assault still bandaged. In fact, anyone observing Todd at that moment would claim that he was the very picture of the furious but fatally wounded Mercutio himself.

Act 3, scene 1 finally got under way and Danton McGraw, shirtsleeves rolled, foil in hand for demonstration purposes, had a sudden insight into the character of Grover (aka Groper) Blaine, the Mercutio pro tem. When faced with Tybalt's foil the boy flinched; he ducked and his feet retreated when they were supposed to advance. He did not parry and riposte; he slashed wildly with his blade while backing up. All in all he turned the whole fight cast into an uncertain wobbling mass.

Over and over they went through a series of simple moves. "Advance, advance, extend, lunge," shouted Danton. But Grover could only get as far as "extend" and then his lunge died aborning and he retreated.

Why hadn't Vera seen it? She had told him that Grover's footwork was a little loose, but hell, it was worse than that. Grover was unfit for the part. Hadn't she rehearsed him in the scene at all? He knew the boy had taken fencing classes, but perhaps without his padded jacket and wire mask, he couldn't function. Well, Vera wasn't a fencer, but she must have noticed that the boy was screwing up the fight sequence, and Mercutio was as likely to die of being tripped up as having a sword thrust through him. In fact, the only thing Grover had going for him was his memory for his lines and his strong voice. Once down flat on the stage and presumably dying, he could handle the part.

And, thank God, Tybalt and Romeo/Romiette seemed to know

what they were doing. Danton, abandoning Grover as an active player, worked with these other two, and by forcing Mercutio to go through the moves standing still with his foil raised made the death stroke seem fairly plausible. Danton was glad to see that Tybalt (aka Malcolm Wheelock) was actually a male, in a more or less male costume, and since he was the captain of the Bowmouth fencing team knew how to handle a foil. And Terri Colman, although apparently not a fencer, was an agile person, a quick learner, and played male-female Romiette in his passive-aggressive mode without a hitch.

Mercutio's scene finally ended with Benvolio toting him off to die and was followed by a flashy bout between Tybalt and Romiette, which Danton ended after Tybalt was killed.

"Good," said Danton. "Keep it just that way. And remember, if Grover actually plays Mercutio, you have your work cut out for you. Surround him, keep him from backing up, and keep the moves simple: just a short lunge, a parry, and the thrust under Romeo's arms—"

"Romiette," corrected Tybalt.

"Oh God," said Danton, "it doesn't matter. Romeo was good enough for Shakespeare and it's good enough for me. What I'm saying is Benvolio will keep Mercutio from backing up so Tybalt can do the quick one-two just as you practiced."

At which point Todd Mancuso came off his perch in the wings and announced to Danton and the other actors that even if he were bleeding to death, even if in the middle of cardiac arrest, he would play the part himself, so forget about an understudy.

Assistant Professor Sarah Deane, with no classes to teach, no student appointments to keep, found herself drawn inexorably toward the Drama School. It was nearly noon and the marching squads around Malcolm Adam Hall seemed to have diminished in both size and verve. This was hopeful. Perhaps it was the fine, warm weather, so students had found better uses of their time, particularly at the luncheon hour.

The same proved to be true at the Drama School. Despite a

new splash of graffiti denouncing the English Department, this done in purple and red paint along the entrance portico, the sign holders seemed to lack their earlier enthusiasm. Also, since rehearsals would be going on all day and dress rehearsal was on the docket for the evening, members of the cast and stage crew were too busy to march; they were inside occupied with the upcoming production.

As Sarah was about to mount the front steps she became aware that a figure whose presence she had vaguely felt walking behind her was about to reveal itself—this by stepping directly in front of Sarah and stopping her in her tracks.

Sarah looked, blinked, and then recognized. A student in her Introduction to English Poetry class. Louisa, wasn't it? Called Weeza. Her last name—Sarah ran through a quick mental file and came up with Scotini.

"Hello there, Ms. Scotini," she said, remembering Danton McGraw's strictures on not using student's first names, a habit she found hard to form.

"It's Weeza," said Weeza. "Call me Weeza; it's a lot friendlier."

"Okay, it's Weeza. So are you in the play? Acting? Dancing."

"I'm sort of a double person. I'm Paris, the guy who wants to marry Julio, but in the end I turn into a woman. For the finale. I lead off with something out of the Folies Bergère. You know, a sort of cancan."

"Good for you," said Sarah, for want of anything better. If she ever got a handle on Vera's remake of the play it would be amazing.

"Only," said Weeza, slowing her steps, "I need someone to walk into the Drama School with. Would you mind?"

"No, not at all," said Sarah, wondering where this was going. Weeza had never struck her as someone overcome with shyness.

"You see," said Weeza, avoiding Sarah's eye, "I don't want to be pestered by anyone. It's been a sort of awful day."

"Oh, I'm sorry," said Sarah.

"My advisor is out of town, and I know you pretty well from class, and, well, it's like this, and I know I'm not supposed to talk about it. But," Weeza hurried on, trying to get the words out before she stopped herself. "But it's all over the campus anyway. You see,

111

I belong to a secret group, but I won't tell you our name. We're sort of trying to keep an eye out for anyone being harassed. Or worse. And it's been pretty obvious for a while that several students are way out of line."

"Male students?" put in Sarah.

"Yes. The point is, an incident was going to happen at some time or other, sooner or later, so last night I kind of let it happen sooner. To get it over. And then I put in a complaint early this A.M. to Professor Pruczak and to the dean. And there was a disciplinary committee meeting, and I had to appear and explain what happened. But there won't be any decision right off the bat. At least not today or maybe not tomorrow."

"Wait up," said Sarah. "Are you talking about . . ." Sarah stopped. Maybe there were two, maybe three, four, or more, Grover Blaines creeping around. Touching, feeling, maybe assaulting women students.

But Weeza finished it. "Grover Blaine. Make that Groper. It was time someone nailed him. He bothers the younger kids, the freshmen, and they don't know how to handle him."

"Has he actually . . ." Again Sarah paused. This was not a conversation she was supposed to be having.

"You mean like rape? Or assault? Or exposing himself? Nah. Frankly, I think he's a total jelly. The guy just gets so far and backs off. But you know cowards are bullies, so maybe he won't always back down. Anyway, it was time to stop him."

"Wait up," said Sarah. "You said you sort of let something happen? Was the harassment business planned? By this group of yours."

Weeza shrugged. "No, it wasn't anything like a committee plan. They know, but I did it on my own. And he really did go for me. I looked like easy meat, I guess. And now he's on ice. At least for now."

"You acted as bait," said Sarah. "A sort of sting operation. God, Weeza."

"Listen to me," said Weeza. "Something was going to happen. Something really gross. Better it happens to someone who's ready for it."

"Like you."

"Right. I can handle a bad scene. I've done the whole college a service. And even scared the shit out of Grover's buddy, Derek. I hope they throw the book at both of them. Derek just stood there. Like some kind of accomplice. Just grinning away. I'm short and small and I suppose I just looked like a perfect victim. But I'm a quick mover and I've done karate. So no problem." Weeza smiled up at Sarah and added, "But right now the whole thing's turning into big time, so I want to walk in with you so everyone won't goggle at me and ask questions. It's been tough to go through this, all the questions, and the dean having cat fits—Derek being her son—and she's talking about defense lawyers. But listen, it's something that should have been done to those two guys in the first week of school. Okay, let's go in. Right into the rehearsal."

Sarah's head now whirled with pictures of courtroom scenes and cross-questioning by a furious Dean Alena Fosdick and probably a maniacal Danton McGraw. And oh Lord, she certainly knew more than she should about Weeza's part in the business.

And Weeza seemed to read her mind. "Don't worry. What I did was really legit. What I told you is one hundred percent confidential—you know teachers are like lawyers, priests, and journalists, aren't they? They have to keep things to themselves even if they have to go to jail."

"I don't know about jail," said Sarah, "but I think a migraine is a possibility."

"Worth it to tell someone," said Weeza firmly. "And if you mention it, I'll deny the whole thing flat out."

They had now reached the top of the stone steps to the Drama School, and she reached for the door and turned to Sarah. "You know what?"

"What?" said Sarah, not really wanting an answer.

But she got one.

"To fix those two slimes, I'd do it all over again if I had to."

8

AS Sarah watched Weeza disappear in the direction of the student dressing rooms, she began turning over in her mind the conversation that had just passed. Did it require some immediate action? (Where, how, what?) Or the passing along of important information to the authorities? (Which authorities? All authorities?) Of course, whatever she said to anyone—Vera Pruczak, the dean, the disciplinary committee—would be denied just as Weeza had promised. And was anything Weeza had told her about Grover and Derek too different from other little pockets of nastiness that were to be found in any college? These were part of a college package not featured in the catalogues and included, besides sexual harassment, incidents of racial prejudice, the usual breakouts of vandalism, binge drinking, drug use, hazing by clubs and fraternities, not to mention episodes of stealing—cameras, radios, watches, laptops, stray pieces of jewelry left carelessly in bathrooms and gym lockers. Then there were, of course, academic misdeeds: plagiarism, term papers bought and sold, pulled off the Internet. As for libraries, it was open house. Librarians waged a continual war against sticky-fingered students as text- and reference books were lifted, and if the books had been protected with electronic patches to set off alarms, these could be tossed out of upper windows into waiting hands

Sarah arrived within Vera's orbit of operation without deciding anything. Except a plan of watch and wait. After all, the whole Grover/Derek and Weeza matter was now out in the open and in the hands of the Arts and Sciences disciplinary committee. And, more important, the central figures of the affair were involved in the current production and any new untoward activities would be caught by a multitude of witnesses.

Vera pounced on her. "Costume changes. Dress rehearsal coming up. Some of the actors have only a few seconds to change for a new scene. A lot of the extras are in the ball scene, in the two street fights, and then turn up as monks in the Friar Laurence scenes and again in the finale. Here's a list of scene changes. So go on backstage and check with the actors."

What Sarah found backstage, huddled behind a large moveable section of Friar Lawrence's domain, was Terri Colman, Kay Biddle, and Weeza Scotini all engaged in a hissing match. The three women were lined up, half in costume, half out, leaning forward and giving Todd Mancuso hell.

Sarah was about to creep away and find other matters needing attention when Weeza beckoned her closer. "Tell her what's happened," ordered Weeza. "She knows all about my reporting Grover and Derek. I filled her in."

Reluctantly, Sarah moved forward. What she gathered in the next few minutes of garbled information was that the disciplinary committee decision was still on hold and that Grover and Derek were to be considered students in good standing until a final ruling came in. "Which means," said Kay in a low but furious voice, "that those bastards can put on costumes and just be part of the cast, all buddies together."

Sarah turned to Todd, who was reclining on a large bench used in the garden below the balcony scene. He looked to Sarah's eyes like someone fit only for a hospital bed. His face was still discolored, his breathing heavy, his feet restless, one hand plucking nervously at his velvet Elizabethan doublet. But his voice was strong, his eyes focused and hard.

115

"What the hell is the matter with all of you?" said Todd. "This is a play. Get on with it. Never mind how crazy the play is, we have obligations. And never mind those two shit heads. They'll get theirs. Right now we have to pull together. And if I have anything to say, I'll be Mercutio tomorrow night so help me God. Grover can do Mercutio tonight in the dress rehearsal and then he's toast. Derek is toast. I don't need an understudy for Friar Laurence. Just listen to me. Those two guys are real losers, so don't waste your time on them." Here Todd fixed Weeza with a hard stare. "Okay, Weeza. Good work. Way to go. We're with you all the way."

Weeza gulped and nodded, Terri hugged her, and Kay pounded her on the back in forceful congratulations.

At which point Sarah began a retreat but was called back. "Hey, Professor Pruczak says you're to help with costume changes," said Todd. And before Sarah could speak, he went on about the complications of getting Mercutio redressed as Friar Laurence.

"It's not too hard, but it has to be quick. I get my boots off and put on sandals. Slip my habit right over my Mercutio's doublet and ruff and get the wig—it's a tonsure—on straight. Makeup with my face all banged up is a problem, but I think a dark complexion is okay. Friar Laurence can be Ethiopian. No reason why not. In this play anything goes."

Sarah, having pulled a notebook from her trousers, jotted down that Todd's makeup was to be kept ready not in the dressing room but just offstage. And then Kay and Terri discussed certain small changes in attire while Weeza pointed out that she needed major help in turning herself from Paris the suitor of Julio/Juliet to Paris the chief cancan dancer—female—in the finale.

The dress rehearsal began promptly at seven thirty that night, and strangely enough, considering previous events, all went as smooth as glass. The prompters had little to do; actors remembered their cues and did not falter over their lines or seem confused over change of role or sex. The curtains rose and fell as intended; the scenes were changed with rapidity and with a minimum of noise

116

and delay. And props appeared when called for, and the costume changes, with Sarah and other stage crew members pressed into service, went smoothly.

The audience, made up of faculty members who would miss the Halloween performance, assorted clerks, registrars, students from other departments, maintenance and grounds and security people, all seemed to enjoy the production or, being unable to take in what was going on, were numbed into dazed silence. This reaction, Vera remarked later, was most apparent among several members of the local Bowmouth Committee for Civil Improvement who had turned up en masse to check out the rumors they had heard of a disturbing theatre event.

"I think," said Danton McGraw to Alex McKenzie, sitting off to the side in the front row—Alex had been pulled in again to check on Todd Mancuso—"Vera's going to pull it off. For now anyway. The whole gender-switch business is as confusing as hell. But she won't get away with it forever. The town will wake up and suddenly remember what they've seen."

To which Alex only shrugged and changed the subject to his patient. "I don't think Todd should even think about doing the fight scenes," he told Danton.

"But," Danton objected, "we have a very questionable Mercutio understudy, Grover Blaine. He has real problems with some of the action."

"And I have heard," said Alex, "that Grover is under something of a cloud. Along with Derek Mosely."

Danton sighed. "I suppose the whole college knows all about it. And of course," he added, as if suddenly remembering, "your wife teaches in the English Department. And those two are both English majors. It's publicity we didn't need."

"What no one needs," said Alex, in a markedly acidic tone, "is two men harassing women in the college."

"If the charges are true," said Danton. "Anyway, let's wait and see. The investigation isn't complete. I hope it's just a case of two juvenile students playing smart-ass but not really hurting anyone."

"Fine line between smart-ass and hurting someone," Alex said.

"Wait for the verdict," said Danton. "In the meantime, I hope you can give Todd the go-ahead for tomorrow night. His first scene is easy and we can slow the action in Mercutio's death scene."

"But then he has to go on as Friar Laurence," Alex pointed out.

"Friar Laurence is a piece of cake. Anyway, you'll check him out an hour before curtain?" asked Danton.

To which Alex nodded, reflecting that Halloween and theatre were intruding on what he had hoped would be a day of avoiding all forms of tricks and treats and could be spent in a canoe off on some lake checking out late duck migrants.

That Tuesday night, the smooth-running rehearsal—ominously smooth, Sarah called it, remembering the tradition that bad dress rehearsal equals good opening night—finished sometime after eleven thirty. Now Sarah and Alex were settled in the kitchen over herbal cinnamon tea (Sarah) and a pallid-looking whiskey and soda (Alex). The kitchen, an everlasting work-in-progress, showed signs of trying to be two things at the same time. This was due to Sarah's desire to keep something of the old country kitchen alive: wood stove, soapstone sink complete with pump, rocking chairs, wintering geraniums, coral berry bushes, and juvenile avocado trees (started from seed), and underfoot a number of small hooked rugs. This décor ran against Alex's wish for state-of-the-art refrigeration, stove, dishwasher, disposal, plus counter space, and safe transportation—the hooked rugs even with rubber pads slipped and slid in an alarming manner. To add to the general sense of conflict was the collection of Irish wolfhound Patsy's tartan sleep pad, his water bowl (elevated), his dinner dish (also elevated), plus his chew bones and stuffed play toys scattered here and there. However, the scene was apparently to the liking of the new orange kitten, now permanently named Piggy for his appetite. He had settled down in front of the wood stove as if he had spent his life there.

However, tonight was no time for getting into the home decoration argument. Or even to discuss whether the household *needed* a stray cat added to it. Both Alex and Sarah were on the very edge of sleep but needing a bit of nourishment before giving in. And for Alex there was a strong need to ask a few questions.

"First," said Alex. "Your boss. This Danton McGraw. I gather from you and all the lower orders of the English Department that he's a complete ogre. Attacking the Drama School head-on. A Naval Academy officer larger than life. Everything spit and polish."

Sarah looked up from her steaming mug of tea. "You've got that about right."

"Maybe he's playing a double game. I sat next to him tonight during rehearsal and he seemed entirely normal. Reasonable. Concerned about Todd Mancuso."

"You mean concerned that Todd won't make it up on the stage without fainting dead away."

"Well, yes," said Alex. "But that's to be expected. I gather Todd is a star performer and McGraw has been working on the fencing scenes. McGraw's ego may be tied in with that action. Anyway, McGraw doesn't have much faith in Grover Blaine as an understudy."

"You mean because Grover may have built himself a criminal record?"

"He didn't say 'criminal.' Didn't imply it. Said the evidence is still out and no decision has been reached. Said it was too bad that Grover and friend Derek are both English majors."

"More interested in the department's reputation than in whether those two creeps did something nasty."

"Who's prejudging?"

"Me. They have a record of bothering women students, though up to now it's really been in the gossip column. No one seems to know if anything's ever been proved. But there's something about them. The way they look at you. Or away from you. And they both have the same expression when they sneer at you."

"You, the instructor?"

"I get a modified sneer. Fellow students get the full-force sneer."

"Don't ever climb on the witness stand, my love, or you will be sliced up like cold chicken."

"Thank you so much. But I do know if something's wrong about someone. And those two guys don't add up to honest, forthright young men. And they look like someone I've seen somewhere. Only I can't remember who."

"Go to bed. Patsy's yawning. It's past his bedtime."

But Sarah, leaning over to ruffle the gray wiry hair on the top of the dog's head, wasn't finished. "You see, this kid's younger brother saw someone from the Harry Potter books hanging around the utility room at the Fine Food Mart. Not one of the good guys but one of the bad ones. I'm a Harry Potter fan, and I've counted all the evildoers, but all I come up with is Professor Snape. But neither Grover nor Derek looks in the least like Snape. At least not the way he's described in the books or looks like in the movies."

Alex put down his glass and stood up. "I haven't read the books, and I don't have a fix on those two students except seeing them around the Drama School theatre. But to me they both look rather like a mean albino-type fox. Or weasel."

"Exactly!" cried Sarah. She jumped up, slipped on the small rug under the chair, and grabbed at Alex.

"Goddamn rugs," said Alex, twitching the rug forward, rolling into a ball, and heaving it in the general direction of the trash bin.

"Weasel, fox," repeated Sarah. "Albino or blond. I've got it."

"And?"

"Malfoy. Draco Malfoy. That's the one they look like. Draco's the evil boy in the Harry Potter series. I just couldn't think of his name. Of course, Derek is closer to Draco than Grover because Grover is a little heavier. But both look like Draco, or at least like the actor who plays him in the movies."

"Okay, they look like Draco Malfoy," said Alex. "And Draco Malfoy was hanging around the utility room the afternoon that Todd Mancuso got beaten up."

"Only it was a Malfoy look-alike," said Sarah. "The kid who saw him is a Harry Potter fan. He doesn't know about Grover Blaine or Derek Mosely."

"But you do. So this might pin the beating of Todd on one of those two birds."

"Or both," Sarah reminded him. "They could have worked together. One hangs around watching; the other does the beating."

"Oh Christ," said Alex. "It's bedtime. You're just talking yourself into something. We can't just call the police and say we've got a Harry Potter character who beat up Todd."

"George Fitts never sleeps," said Sarah. "He can start looking for hair or bits of saliva or DNA from the utility room."

"If that whole room hasn't been scrubbed clean," said Alex. "And if Todd's clothes haven't been thrown away. The hospital would have stripped him in the ER and may have incinerated his things. They were blood soaked."

"But," Sarah protested, "the police were in on the scene. Todd was obviously the victim of a beating. Wouldn't they have gone over the utility room? And made sure the ER kept anything that looked like evidence?"

"Yes," said Alex, "That's what should have happened. But I wouldn't bet on it. Anyway, go ahead and give George a buzz. It's all you can do."

Sarah gave a weary nod, sighed deeply, and reached for the phone.

Ten minutes later, after a conversation that revealed George as fresh as a daisy and Sarah increasingly confused and incoherent, the two humans and one wolfhound and an orange kitten crawled upstairs to bed. And such was the fatigue of the humans that Patsy was able to gain the entire middle of the bed and the kitten the center of a pillow without any objections from the weary householders.

George Fitts, a man for whom sleep, as Sarah had said, seemed to play little part in his investigative life, got into action. First he roused Mike Laaka and repeated Sarah's suggestion that a Draco Malfoy type who resembled both Grover Blaine and Derek Mosely was of great interest to the police.

"Draco who?" asked Mike in a thick voice. He had been asleep for the past hour.

George explained, as if to someone who lived on another planet, that Draco Malfoy was an important character in a series of books by a Scottish writer called J. K. Rowling and that Mike should check one of the books out. With this explanation it became obvious that Mike thought Sarah and George were, in his words, "completely out to lunch."

"You're calling these two guys suspect because they look like someone out of some kid's book? And your witness is some little kid who told his brother."

"Harry Potter and the other characters in the books," said George, "are probably better known to most kids than their own teachers. Probably their own families. Besides, it's all we have to go on. I'll check with forensics to see if anyone took samples from the utility room and went over Todd Mancuso's clothes."

"Why wouldn't they have done that?"

"Don't argue, just check. Tell Katie Waters to go over to the ER pronto. Your job is to find out how soon after Todd was taken away to the hospital the Fine Food Mart people cleaned the place. Our people were all tied up that afternoon chasing down witnesses, taking statements. Some maintenance guy may have slipped into the utility room with Lysol and a scrubbing brush."

"To kill any lurking DNA?"

"Murphy's Law. Let's hope it didn't happen. After all, the beating was only Monday—that's yesterday."

Mike's groan was audible on the phone. "You want me to get going now?"

"Now, as in eleven forty-five. Tuesday night."

"And call you whenever. About whatever?"

"Keep in touch," said George, and hung up.

Katie Waters had, like Mike Laaka, been asleep when Mike's call came in. The idea of rushing over to the Mary Starbox Memorial Hospital emergency room to see if the crew there had hung on to some torn and bloody garments worn by one of Monday's ER visitors was not pleasant. Why wouldn't the clothes have been turned right over to forensics? Answer: because maybe no one had called forensics. Because no one from the small-town police force or from the sheriff's department had tailed the ambulance and demanded surrender of the clothes. Because perhaps Todd had been thought to be simply a victim of a student brawl. A person of no importance. Caught up in an event of no importance.

Katie debated with herself. Call the ER, that was the easy way. Or get on her horse and try to find someone from the ER who would know what had happened to the clothes of one battered patient (there may have been several) brought in on Monday.

She opted for the face-to-face approach simply because she could almost feel the hot breath of Sergeant George Fitts on the back of her neck. He would not accept investigative work that didn't involve the up close and personal system.

The ER was alive and busy. Two cardiac cases had turned up just before midnight; three teenagers whose car had nailed a tree in Appleton had been brought in bloodied, unconscious, smelling of liquor, and altogether in doubtful shape. And the waiting room was filled with those who had come in with lesser ailments: the colicky baby, the person with a cracked ankle, the student with a broken nose, a senior citizen who felt all "weak and dizzy." Well, priorities were priorities, and it all meant that Katie was not going to be allowed to so much as ask a question until things settled down. Her hopes had been centered on Nurse Hannah Finch, who had been present at Todd's arrival. But Hannah unfortunately wouldn't be turning up for duty until six thirty in the morning.

Katie made an executive decision. She left her cell phone number with the ER desk and returned to her car. Locked the doors, curled up in the backseat, shoes off, her jacket rolled as a pillow, her all-purpose travel blanket pulled close around her, put her cell phone close to hand. And slept.

And woke. And turned and twisted and resettled. And slept again.

And at five minutes to six on Halloween morning reassembled herself and retreated into one of the hospital's visitor bathrooms to refresh herself. Then out to the cafeteria for a mug of coffee and a glazed doughnut. This all in twelve minutes—Katie was a quick mover.

Then back to the ER and to a successful nailing of Hannah Finch just coming on duty a few minutes early. Hannah, a normally cheerful woman given to wearing cotton jackets with bird designs (today it was tree swallows), was not pleased to see Katie. The nurse had tangled with the deputy last summer during a particularly nasty in-house homicide and wanted no more of her.

"Busy," said Hannah firmly hanging up her coat and stowing her handbag. "The place is full of the night shift's leftovers. And two ambulances are on their way in."

Katie made it short. "Todd Mancuso. The guy who was beaten up, brought into the ER Monday afternoon. Left in the evening. What happened to his clothes?"

"He discharged himself," said Hannah with disapproval. "Absolutely no sense. He was a wreck."

"But his clothes? Do you remember what he was wearing?"

Hannah made a face. "We first thought he was some sort of weirdo cross-dresser. He wore bloomers. Striped ones. And one red stocking and one green. High-top black sneakers. With pointy toes. But then that drama teacher, Vera What's-her-name, came charging in and said she needed his things, the costume parts anyway. I told her the clothes were all bloody, but she said they were needed for some college production."

"And," prompted Katie.

"Todd was stripped after he came in on the stretcher. But the costume things were held for him in a plastic bag, and this Vera took them away with her. Now I've got to go."

"And Todd's underwear?"

"She didn't want that. And don't ask me what happened to it. I haven't a clue. We were too busy to go around rescuing anyone's bloodstained underwear." And Hannah draped her stethoscope around her neck and walked off toward a curtained alcove.

"But," called Katie after her, "what do you usually do with that stuff? If it's ruined."

Hannah spun around and glared. "If the patient doesn't want it, we throw it into a red plastic bag marked Bio-Hazard and get rid of the stuff."

Katie sighed, reached for her notebook, noted time, place, and

informant, and then looked around for one other ER person involved, the physician's assistant called Ed Trapper.

This gentleman, his night shift over, his eyes bleary, his scrub
shirt worse for wear, was found headed for the employees' restroom.

Two minutes' conversation proved that Ed himself had stowed
Todd Mancuso's blood-soaked underwear in the Bio-Hazard bag.
Then shortly after that Ed had seen the bag, along with other such,
sent off to the nether regions of the hospital where such undesir-
able materials were then disposed of. As to possible police intervention, the presence of someone from forensics: "Forget it," said
Ed. "Unless we've got a homicide coming in or some major
manslaughter affair, or a car wreck involving alcohol or drugs, no
police types turn up. This looked like just another college thing.
Around Halloween, there's always some idiot getting chewed up.
Tonight will be a major scene. I can't wait."

"Neither can I," said Katie crossly.

She headed for the double doors, the parking lot, her car and,
once settled behind the wheel, pulled out her notebook and
scratched in Ed's information. Or, she thought, more properly non-
information. Next in line, a call on Vera Pruczak to see what had
happened to the pieces of Elizabethan costume she had rescued
from the ER. This interview to be followed by finding Weeza, the
on-site hospital aide and also an actor in the production. But before any of these another mug of coffee and two doughnuts.
Dunkin' Donuts was the proper stop. From there she would call
George Fitts and report her negative findings. The trouble is, she
thought, everyone is so dependent on DNA evidence that they can
hardly figure out anything without it. Even blood typing and fingerprints took a backseat to the magic of deoxyribonucleic acid.
And that's what George Fitts always wanted. Some piece of clothing covered with hairs or blood or sputum or semen that came up
with the DNA of the attacker.

Katie discovered Vera Pruczak prowling backstage with Sarah
Deane trailing behind her like lady-in-waiting to royalty. Because
Vera *was* looking royal. She wore a sort of purple caftan with a
high-standing collar that suggested wings and what appeared from

beneath the caftan to be a pair of silver shoes on the order of the ones in which Dorothy traversed the Deadly Desert. Sarah, in tune with her servant status, wore jeans and a sweatshirt with Kalamazoo College on its chest, a product of a summer yard sale.

Katie hailed them both. "I'm on official business," she announced. And then, unable to help herself, she said, "Vera Pruczak, you look gorgeous. Is it because of Halloween?"

"Nonsense," said Vera. "I always wear this on the day of an opening. It's more than superstition. It keeps me focused on what is necessary. And these shoes . . ." Here Vera kicked up a leg and displayed one of the silver slippers, which, seen closely, showed signs of considerable wear.

"I played Dorothy in eighth grade," said Vera. "My first lead role and I haven't looked back. Although," she added, "I've had to have the shoes stretched."

"But," said Katie, "Dorothy wore ruby slippers."

"No, she didn't," put in Sarah. "That was a Hollywood trick. The book says silver slippers, right, Vera?"

"Absolutely. And now, Katie, to what do I owe the honor?"

Katie flipped over a page in her notebook. "The hospital people said you took Todd's costume with you when you picked him up from the ER. So what happened to his things?"

"Good God," said Vera. "Do you think I took them as souvenirs? I did what was proper. I saved them from going down the hospital incinerator. That velvet doublet fits Todd perfectly. Exactly right for Mercutio. The two-tone stockings, too. We call them 'doublet and hose,' proper Elizabethan dress."

"And those funny pants, sort of bloomers."

"Those 'bloomers' are called 'slops,'" said Vera.

"You're kidding."

"I don't kid about costumes. The correct term is 'slops.' Anyway, I took the whole bundle over to the dry cleaner's and had a rush job done. Our costume department can't afford to lose anything. And we'll be doing more productions from that period again."

"But blood," objected Sarah. "Dry cleaning wouldn't get the blood out, would it?"

"I thought of that," said Vera, with satisfaction. "Before I took the things to the cleaner's I went after the blood with cold water. You don't want blood to set for good."

"I think that's exactly what George Fitts would want," said Katie.

"Well, I didn't. However, with lots of soaking and rubbing and then the complete dry-cleaning job, the clothes are just fine. Of course, we had a little mending to do, but now the whole costume looks perfect."

"Terrific," said Katie in a bleak voice. "Thanks and good-bye."

"And good riddance," said Vera cheerfully. "Sarah and I have work to do. Give George my love and say you and he and Mike should all come tonight."

"I can't think of anything," said Katie, "that would guarantee mayhem more than if you have all three of us in the audience. But I wouldn't put it past George to send us all to hunker down at the theatre just to send out bad vibes."

Mike Laaka was having as little luck as had Katie Waters. Mike's interrogation of the Fine Food Mart personnel had yielded the depressing fact that even as Todd Mancuso was being loaded into the ambulance late on Monday afternoon a maintenance crew armed with buckets, brushes, strong antiseptics, and sprays had hit the utility room and given it the works. This information Mike passed along to George. And George, who had just received Katie Waters's report of the hospital disposal of underwear and Vera's dry cleaning of Todd's costume, decided on action. He summoned the two deputies to meet at noon to go over, in person, their respective unproductive reports. If there were holes or omissions, George wanted to squeeze them out.

They sat in George's office, a space that Katie had described to associates as something less welcoming than a solitary confinement cell. The entire décor was done in beige around the walls and rust-colored linoleum under the feet. Two photographs of the Maine State Police headquarters hung on one wall; an enlarged road map of the three touching counties took over the second wall. Behind George's olive metal desk hung an array of clipboards, charts, Maine State Police notices.

"The only thing we have going for us," said George to the two deputies, who sat on two identical metal folding chairs facing him, "is this Harry Potter character Malfoy that Sarah Deane believes looks like both Grover Blaine and Derek Mosely."

"Wonderful," murmured Katie.

"They will both be involved in the Halloween play tonight," said George. "As understudies for two big parts. So will Todd Mancuso as a principal player of one or two roles. And, in case you've forgotten, Kay Biddle and Terri Colman are also in the play."

"So two and two make four," said Katie. "Those two students nailed Todd Mancuso with a lantern and a foil. Are you expecting a rerun?"

"Try to keep an eye on those two women if you possibly can," said George. "But Grover Blaine and Derek Mosely have priority."

"Those guys already have a black cloud hanging over their heads," said Mike.

"The cloud," said George, "will stay there. But the harassment charge against those two isn't our affair. The college is handling it. And will continue to do so unless official charges are brought against the two men by the woman who filed the complaint."

"What are you trying to say?" asked Katie.

"That we should be interested in those young men because of the attack on Todd Mancuso in the utility room. So I think we go to the play tonight, spread out, and see what we can see. Katie, it might be useful for you to look in backstage from time to time. I hear Sarah Deane is helping with the costume changes, and you know how she attracts trouble."

"Sarah would really give you the finger if she heard you say that," said Katie.

"Let the record speak for itself," said George. "And Mike, you watch from the side of the auditorium but also at intervals check backstage, the offices, the dressing rooms. I'll be in the audience and move around during intermission."

"For Christ's sake, George," said Mike, "don't you have any

other hot law-and-order stuff on your plate? Something more important that this Harry Potter caper."

"I have no homicide on hand right now," said George stiffly. "And the beating of Todd Mancuso in that utility room will involve an assault charge. Possibly an assault with intention to maim or kill. A felony."

"What you're doing, George," said Katie in a decided voice, "is asking for it. I told Vera Pruczak that if any of us turn up at the theatre we're going to be the cause of even more trouble."

"Thank you, Katie," said George. "But you both have your orders. I'll see you tonight at the theatre."

"What," said Mike, "about Halloween? Katie and I usually patrol during the trick-or-treat period."

"You can still do that early on," said George. "But you know the sheriff's department has planned to double up on the evening patrol and the state police will be standing by. Get to the theatre at least half an hour before the curtain goes up. Which is nine o'clock tonight. And one more thing," George added in a severe voice.

"What's that?" said Katie, eyeing the sergeant suspiciously.

"You're both going to your offices right now and make up your reports of your evidence collecting at the hospital, the Fine Food Mart, and here at the theatre."

"You mean reports of our not collecting evidence," said Mike.

George, who always tried to avoid answering Mike's side remarks, tapped his finger on his desk. "I want those reports by five tonight. Then get going on your Halloween patrol. And don't even think about stopping for dinner. Not even a fast-food pit stop. You won't have time."

9

HALLOWEEN, Wednesday the thirty-first of October, went its merry and sometimes unruly way. The weather had turned warm, almost balmy. Toddlers, often mere babes dressed as bunnies, miniature cowboys, or tiny angels, appeared in the arms of proud parents as soon as the sun slipped over the yardarm. But as the shadows deepened, the nursery-school crowd gave way to the grade-school crowd: Spiderman, soldiers in tan camouflage complete with frighteningly real-looking plastic rifles, Boston Red Sox uniforms, the New England Patriots ditto, plus assorted royal types from princess, to king, to variations on Frodo, Shrek, Darth Vadar, Harry Potter, and the like.

Sarah, taking a needed break from Vera's theatre world, found that she needed some everyday adult experience and drove up to Mary Donelli and Amos Larkin's house. This house was set on an extension of Bowmouth Drive just over the hill from her own and Alex's old farmhouse. Mary welcomed her, handed her a large bowl of candy, and told her to be ready for doorbells.

"Our son, Terrence, is off being a ten-year-old pirate at some school party, and I thought we'd have peace because we should be too far away to get the hungry mobs," said Mary. "But apparently parents are willing to drive miles to fill up their little ones with rotgut candy."

"Army types are big this year," said Sarah. "And several trolls, but I'm not sure from what source, movie or TV. Or even a book."

"You can't keep up," said Mary. "But Dracula is still around. Pointed white wax teeth and ketchup dribbling down their shirtfronts."

Then after a short intermission of dealing out small sacks of fudge cookies, Mary turned off the welcome light on the front porch and returned to Topic A in the English Department.

"I hear that Danton the Terrible has been infesting the theatre. Does Vera let him in of her own free will?"

"He's Mr. Fencing Master," said Sarah. "And he's even been rehearsing the understudy in case Todd Mancuso falls apart at the seams. Todd's pretty shaky and how he can pull off a fencing scene, even a few moves, is beyond me. Alex thinks Vera's crazy to let Todd try. He's going to be there as Todd's personal physician. As a favor to Vera. And I'm supposed to be helping the actors change costumes, especially Todd, who's got to come to life as Friar Laurence after he's been killed as Mercutio."

"And Grover the Groper is the understudy," said Mary. "Even after he's been caught being a foul fellow. By Weeza Scotini, I hear. Went right after her. And Derek Mosely, the dean's little boy, stood there and watched."

"There are absolutely no secrets in this college," complained Sarah. "I think the entire English Department information bureau is managed by Arlene and Linda. The CIA should mail them to the Middle East and get them out of our hair."

"I think Amos is of your opinion. Although he'd send Danton along with them. Probably bound hand and foot. So, any more news on the beating of Todd Mancuso?"

"Nothing except some kids . . ."

"I know that, too. The Malfoy connection."

"You see," said Sarah, "nothing can be kept quiet. But that didn't come from Arlene or Linda, did it? Only George Fitts and Mike Laaka know it."

"Wrong. I have a better source. Terrence is in the grade school class with the older brother of the little kid who claimed to have seen this Malfoy clone hanging around the restrooms at the Food Mart. But no one told the boys to keep a lid on, so it's all over the grade school that Draco Malfoy beat up Todd Mancuso."

"Oh God," said Sarah. "I wish I'd never made that connection with Grover and Derek. I should have shut up. It was bad enough finding Todd beaten to a pulp without my thinking those two guys were part of the scene. I don't like them, I think they're really sleazy, but I suppose there are about fifty students in Bowmouth who look like someone out of the Harry Potter series. Or a character in *Star Wars III* or some hot new TV show."

"Relax," said Mary. "It's in police hands now. Just do your bit in the costume-changing job. Amos and I will be going, although he says it'll be over his dead body. He even thinks that Danton Mc-Graw has a point when he says that Vera is going too far with this gender-switch business.

"I didn't say that," said a voice. And Mary's husband, Amos Larkin, appeared in the front hall. He was in shirtsleeves, his glasses perched on top of his ruffled red hair. "Not the drain, but there'll probably be a shrinkage in the donations. I hate like hell agreeing with anything McGraw says, but I think Vera's pushing it just for the sake of making trouble. Not in the interest of really good theatre. I'm all for satire. And burlesque. Takeoffs. Farce. But from all I've heard, this Romiette thing is just a bizarre mishmash whose sole purpose seems to be to get a rise out of the English Department."

"Which is easy enough," said Mary.

"Granted. And like Vera, Danton is great at getting a rise out of other people."

"Like you," Mary reminded him.

"He got in my way. Trod on my turf. Lectured me on classroom discipline. But even so, he has a point, maybe a minor one, about Vera being gung ho to put a fire under the tails of the townspeople. She lives in a community, like it or not. A rural community. God knows I've been burned in effigy—almost—by teaching Jonathan Swift at his most graphic. Chamber pots, hideously old women with fake body parts, bedroom scenes, etcetera. But Swift was a genius. And literate. I'm not sure about Vera being literate."

"Oh, come on, Amos," said Sarah. "She's very with it. And she has done some legit stuff. *King Lear, Ghosts,* a few years ago. And Gilbert and Sullivan. Tom Stoppard, yes, but he's accepted generally. I think with *Romiette and Julio* she wants to wake people up. Mix current issues into a Shakespearean setting."

"And causing total confusion while she's at it. But my real beef will be if the scholarship awards are cut back after the fund drive falls apart. Because of this play. Half my best students are on scholarships."

"Enough of that," said Mary. "How about supper, Sarah? With Alex, if you can find him. Is he on call?"

"At the hospital until eight. Some conference. Then on call with Vera at the theatre so that he can monitor Todd."

"Saint Alex," said Mary.

"Hardly," said Amos. "But he probably thinks that if he doesn't keep an eye on Todd no one will. Vera will want Todd to play the part because he's so damn good. And Todd, he's as stubborn as hell, will be onstage tonight as long as he can breathe."

"Which he may not be able to do," said Sarah. "And yes, I'd love supper. I want some normal life away from the police and from Vera. And the theatre, even if it isn't up to Amos's standards."

"Damn, Sarah, you make me sound like a total snob."

"Which you are, Amos," said Mary. "You want the best of the best and can be a real pain in the tail about it."

"And there speaks the student I managed to help graduate with highest honors. And before Mary says it, here I stand the old drunken professor rescued from his sodden ways by the great love of Mary Angelina Elvira Donelli."

"Angelina Elvira!" exclaimed Sarah. "I didn't know. Impressive."

"Come inside," ordered Mary. "And I'll give you both a very unimpressive supper. We have a busy night ahead. Murder and mayhem await."

Judging from the crowd that jostled its way into the theatre that evening, murder and mayhem were uppermost in the minds of the arriving audience. The students, almost to a man, had chosen variations on the dark and evil look. Protests and placards had given way to horned helmets, witches' robes, fangs, and splashes of blood. Many wore their costumes from an early-evening party or from escorting younger brothers and sisters on their trick-or-treat tours. Only the faculty from the various Bowmouth departments managed to give a sense of sobriety, although even a few of these wore witch cloaks or sweatshirts with a bat motif printed on them.

Sarah arrived in time to go over the costume change list. Now it was necessary to check on the whereabouts of Friar Laurence's makeup, his monk's habit, his sandals, and to see that the foils were collected on a rack ready to be taken out for the fencing scenes. Also, a real costume challenge would come at the end of the last act after Weeza Scotini, in the part of Juliet's suitor Paris, had just been slain by Romeo. The minute the final curtain rang down, Weeza had to be stripped of her male Elizabethan costume and zipped into her scanty Parisian outfit. Then as the music broke into the familiar "Ta-Ra-Ra-Boom-De-Ay!" Sarah had to complete Louisa's metamorphosis by lacing on her dance shoes, equipping her with a large feather fan, and slipping the jeweled silver mask over her face and then push her onstage to lead the dance.

Now, at exactly nine twelve, the Music School's orchestra struck up an overture and a medley of Elizabethan melodies featuring a bass rock continuo that blasted the restless audience into silence. Five minutes later, with many of the elderly holding their ears, the curtain rose on act 1.

On came the chorus of three androgynous persons dressed in a combination of ruffs, doublets, farthingales, feathered caps, and curled wigs chanting in falsetto the theme of the evening:

> "Two households, both alike in dignity,
> In fair Verona, where we lay our scene,
> From ancient grudge break to new mutiny,
> Where civil blood makes civil hands unclean.
> From forth the fatal loins of these two foes
> A pair of star-cross'd lovers take their life."

Sarah, watching from the wings, had the leisure to watch act 1 progress. So far, so good, right through scene 3. But scene 4 meant the checking of face masks, the equipping of the torchbearers with torch flashlights, and then worrying about Todd Mancuso. She hadn't seen him except for a glimpse before the overture. But it was a big scene for Mercutio, and she couldn't even imagine Grover Blaine being able to carry it. But no, here came Todd accompanied on each side by his pals Benvolio and Romiette. Vera had explained that these two were to keep close to Mercutio lest he begin to show signs of faltering. Or, worse, collapsing on the stage.

But no. Todd carried it off. He even maneuvered himself free of his two companions, and although he faltered for a moment, he was able to steady himself and in his strong baritone delivered the Queen Mab speech in fine style. However, his last speech of the scene lost some of its earlier resonance, and Sarah began worrying about his long appearance in the third scene in act 2.

Her worry was justified. The scene, set in "a street," afforded little in the way of physical support, but Todd did his best. He used the one bench to sit on, lean on, and hang over the back. Vera had long since decided that this object might be a real lifesaver for Todd, and so it proved. But Mercutio had a real verbal challenge; his part was full of repartee, puns, jokes, quips, and ended with the song of "An Old Hare Hoar," which Todd, sitting on the bench, sang in almost a musical whisper. It was effective, but Sarah doubted whether anyone past the fourth row could hear.

Somehow Todd got through a short appearance in the sixth scene as Friar Laurence, although Sarah never thought he could manage it. Todd was obviously fading fast. He had trembled as she slipped the monk's habit over his doublet and red and green hose. But on he went, Friar Laurence in a state of shuffling old age and speaking in a tremulous voice. And just as the scene began, Alex appeared at Sarah's elbow.

"I'm pulling him out. Vera said I'm to decide and I have. No way can he do that fight scene. I've told Danton to get the under-study ready."

"This is a short scene," said Sarah. "And Mercutio goes right on for the beginning of act three."

"I know," said Alex. "And here's McGraw with Grover. Right on time. So Sarah, come on and meet Todd with me when he exits on stage right. I'll sit him down behind the backdrops and tell him the verdict. He'll probably be angry and disappointed. You'll be helpful in talking to him. As one of his teachers and someone he's familiar with. He thinks I'm just a spoiler, an overprotective physician. After he settles down, I'll look him over and see if he's fit to do the rest of the Friar Laurence scenes."

"Not much time. Only half a scene followed by a long scene with Juliet or Julio. Then he's on again."

"Okay. Now let's get over and be ready to meet him."

And Alex, followed by Sarah, moved silently along the assorted props, lanterns, paper vines and flowers, clothing racks, scenery flats, until they were in place for meeting Friar Laurence.

Todd came off. Alex took him gently by the arm and told him that it was no-go for Mercutio. But if Todd checked out, it was possible that he could finish the play as Friar Laurence.

Todd to Sarah and Alex's surprise did not explode. Or protest. He simply nodded in a resigned way. "I thought you'd say that. I know Vera's been giving you orders. So I'll rest. I'll be all right. I'll go on playing Friar Laurence as a doddering old geezer and not move around much."

"Come on behind the backdrop and sit down," said Alex. "I have my trusty blood pressure outfit with me, plus my trusty stethoscope, so we'll see how things go."

"Does Grover want my costume?" asked Todd in what Sarah thought was a remarkably quiet voice. The boy seemed to have accepted his fate.

"No," said Sarah. "Vera's got a substitute costume ready for him. People won't notice little things like variations in an Elizabethan doublet."

Todd nodded. "But look, take my red and green stockings and give them to Grover. I don't need them for Friar Lawrence anyway, the habit covers my legs."

"You know, Todd," said Alex, offering his arm for the trip behind the backdrop, "you have more sense than at least three-fifths of my patients. I thought you were a hothead in the hospital, but I take it all back."

Todd shrugged. "Maybe some sense began to leak into my head after Terri and Kay got after me. I've given both of them a hard time all fall. And I'm disappointed as hell at not to finish with Mercutio. I think he's the best thing about the play. But never mind. And if I could just have some orange juice or something like that."

Alex smiled. "If this were really Elizabethan times, I'd give you a flagon of ale."

Todd gave a weak answering grin. "Make it a cup of sack. Falstaff's favorite."

Sarah, finding herself not immediately needed, tried to see from the wings how the fight scene was going. But to her regret, the angle was awkward and she couldn't get a full view of Mercutio's last moments. The stage seemed full of busy masked figures, although Mercutio—or understudy Grover Blaine—stood out as the tallest of the group. Sarah had expected Grover to be as awkward as earlier described by Vera, but he seemed to have pulled himself together, spoke fairly clearly, and put up a credible performance of thrust and parry until finally succumbing to Tybalt's thrust under his arm. In fact, as Sarah squinted along the stage, it seemed as if the whole crew, including those cast as First Citizens, was taking pokes at poor Mercutio. Anyway, the blood splatters were very effective—ketchup, was it, or some real-looking theatrical compound? But now Benvolio and another masked actor were helping the dying Mercutio offstage. She had thought this was to be Benvolio's solo job, but hauling a staggering deadweight across half the stage was obviously too much for one person.

And as Mercutio was dragged out of sight, Sarah noticed that yes, Vera had come up with something close to Todd's costume, but she must have not had time to pull on Todd's donated red and green stockings, because Mercutio wore black stockings. Or tights. But now Terri Colman as Romeo/Romiette had thrust his/her foil through Tybalt and a second body lay on the stage. More blood spatters. And a blood-tipped foil.

Then Sarah had to get back to her original station, check her notes, and get ready for the last act, which would be a great jumbling together of all the events in act 5. She must prepare the flask of sleeping potion, poison, the dagger, and the costume for Weeza Scotini, aka Paris. Sarah also had the added job of dusting off and smoothing the costumes of Romiette and Julio so that the starcrossed lovers would pop up wholesome and tidy for the finale. Of course, Vera had pointed out, not everyone could be revived. Not Mercutio and Tybalt, because enough was enough and Shakespeare should at least be granted a few authentic moments with his characters.

Act 5 featured a somewhat rehabilitated Todd Mancuso (had Alex given him a quick snort of something? Sarah wondered), and the action bobbled forward in a mix of frantic entrances, exits, confrontations, and love moments until Friar Laurence had revived Romiette and Julio, and the cast, led by Weeza, jingled and jangled and pranced to victorious and fantastic conclusion.

Then it was over. Six curtain calls followed, the cast members raised their hands and blew kisses, and someone from the Music School presented a huge bouquet of roses to Vera. And Sarah watching it all from the stage left wing felt a wave of relief wash over her. It was done, it was over. They could all go home, to bed, and start living normal lives.

Except there was something amiss with the curtain call actors. Kay Biddle and Terri Colman had vanished shortly after the second call. And Danton McGraw must have felt it was beneath him, or somehow inappropriate considering his role as Drama School enemy, and had not turned up at all to share the applause after Vera called for the directors, choreographers, and set designers to take a bow. Also rather strange was the pleasure that Grover Blaine and his cohort, Derek Mosely, seemed to take in partaking of all the applause. Front and center wasn't perhaps the place for understudies, although Grover had done a fair job with Mercutio's death scene.

But these were small matters. Sarah, shaking off any untoward ideas, found Alex at her side. "Home," he said. It was not a question.

"Can't," said Sarah. "The cast party. On the stage. Big deal. Vera is having it catered. You can't sneak out."

"I most certainly can. And I notice that Professor McGraw has already sneaked. Smart man."

"He's probably had enough of the Drama School scene. And Vera. But at least the fencing went pretty smoothly. And the blood was amazingly real."

"I helped with that. Special formula the hospital uses in EMT training. Red food coloring with a flour and water base. Bring to a boil, stir, and there you are."

"Charming. We can use it for steak sauce. But you won't stay?"

"Can you get a ride home?"

But before she could answer, Vera was beside them. "Alex, you must stay. Sit next to Todd. I think he may collapse. He's shaking. I wanted to call the ambulance, but he said no. And asked for you."

Alex sighed and nodded. What was one more hour of an already lost evening?

The banquet was lively. A long table had been set up in the middle of the stage, and the cast members, still on a high from the performance, gave toasts, recited bits of the play, praised one another. One stirring moment from Vera's point of view was when a student, one of the Capulet family, raised his glass to praise the director's broadminded view of love and marriage. "Which shall be for all sexes, male, female, and in between," shouted the student. "I ask you to drink to gender-bending love and marriage."

"That," said Alex, "ought to cook Vera in some local circles."

"Vera is Vera. And I don't think a few local petitions and church sermons are going to change the woman. She loves to rattle cages."

"So did Gertrude Stein, but she was safe in Paris," said Alex. At which point Todd Mancuso, now in jeans and a sweatshirt, took an empty chair across the table from him.

"You look pretty good now," Sarah observed. "Vera thought you were at death's door."

"I think I've got my second wind," said Todd. "I guess Grover pulled off Mercutio."

"Much more aggressive than I was told he could be," said Sarah.

"He's gone off somewhere alone, because his buddy, Derek, is over there talking to Weeza," said Todd. "But I'll try and find him, do the decent thing and congratulate him,"

Sarah nodded, the feast went on, people came and went and returned, and finally the last toast was toasted and the last tribute to Vera was given. And the crowd, now showing distinct signs of fatigue, began to gather itself and make ready to depart. Tomorrow was another day.

Alex turned to Todd, who had returned from looking for Grover with no apparent success. "You're not planning to walk back to your dorm, are you?"

Todd nodded. "I can make it."

"You can make it with me. In my car," said Alex. "You'll be in the passenger seat, so don't argue. If you took off by yourself and collapsed on the way, someone would call nine-one-one and an ambulance would take you to the hospital, and I'd be dragged away from my warm bed and my warm wife and dog and cat and be forced to drive to the hospital and see you. So dammit, that's an order."

"We could use you as Henry the Fifth," said Todd.

"I'll go and find my jacket and handbag and follow you both," said Sarah. "If I stay any longer I'll slide under the table and then someone will really have to call nine-one-one."

These plans being agreed on, Sarah pushed herself away from the abandoned table with its jumble of plates, rolled napkins, and empty glasses and went backstage. Where had she left her jacket? Her handbag? Were they even together? Dressing rooms? The Green Room? Or hung up on a random piece of scenery? The backstage area, now with most of its lights turned off, the stage crew and actors gone, had a hollow, disheveled, almost eerie look. Most of the space was still encumbered with the flats, backdrops, and props for each set. Odd pieces of costumes, face masks, foils, jerkins, doublets, gloves, all the detritus of the finished play, hung on nails or over the corners of odd furniture or had been jammed onto a shelf. Well, she was not about to play housekeeper. Vera would chase the actors and stage crew down tomorrow to clean up the place. *Romiette and Julio* was now history, and in a few days' time Vera would be checking scripts and blocking out the moves for the next Drama School effort.

Sarah's steps now took her across the part of the backstage where the dying Mercutio had been dragged through a doorway. And there—ugh—was the blood. Even in the very dim light she could see dark streaks across the wooden planking. Honestly, she told herself, at least someone should have mopped up that mess. For all she knew this gory theatrical mix would stain the wood for years to come. And for heaven's sake why hadn't Mercutio stood right up, grabbed a towel, wiped himself up, and not allowed the blood to spread itself all the way back to that papier-mâché fountain used in the garden balcony scene?

Unless. Unless the door fastened into the scenery flat had stayed open long enough for the audience to see into the backstage area. And so Mercutio had to be dragged farther back. Back behind the fountain, safely out of view.

Sarah shook herself. Dried stage blood was not her business. She was looking for her jacket, her handbag. And then she heard it. A sort of mewing sound followed by the slightest of rustles. Then silence. Then again. Suddenly Sarah was back at the Fine Food Mart standing by the utility room. Listening to Todd Mancuso moan. Or cry. Sounding like a cat in distress.

But now silence. I've finally lost it, Sarah told herself. I'm having flashbacks. Was something odd in the fruit punch Vera served at the dinner? It was supposed to be harmless since half the actors were under drinking age. But Sarah wouldn't put it past some joker to spike the drink. Drop in some drug that made your brain go backward so that your ears heard cats crying.

But there again. The cat. Right behind the fountain. Louder this time. Less catlike. More personlike.

"Oh goddammit to hell," said Sarah, staring at the fountain. And then she moved. Followed the dried blood drops back, around the fountain. Nothing. Except a garden bench. With nothing on it. Or under it.

But behind the bench a long cloth. Some sort of drop cloth. Or a front cloth used in short scenes downstage. She could make out a design on its surface even though the thing was loosely rolled up.

With something in it. Or under it.

Something long.

With feet.

Feet with black high-top sneakers with pointed toes. Elizabethan sneakers.

"Shit," said Sarah softly. She shoved the fountain aside. Pushed the bench over. And kneeled down.

Carefully she unrolled the cover and revealed the back of a head, a shoulder covered in an Elizabethan doublet with a blood-soaked Elizabethan ruff.

Grover? The Mercutio understudy? Or who else? Not Derek certainly; he'd been dressed as a monk for his understudy job. Not Todd, because he'd been made to sit it out. Who then?

Even with these confused ideas racing through her head Sarah's hands had been busy. Slowly, carefully, inch by inch pulling down the cloth. She had to be careful because she remembered Alex talking about how well-meaning (by which he meant danger-ously stupid) helpers were apt to start ripping off clothes and thereby releasing pressure on wounds and so immediately starting a blood flow.

She had gotten as far as the man's waist—it was a male back and shoulder, she was sure—and had found no source of injury. No holes or torn cloth or seeping blood. Where was Mercutio sup-posed to have been stabbed? She couldn't remember, but now that she had reached the end of the spine without finding any wound the cloth—it felt like velveteen—was dry and warm. So now it was time to move around and see the rest of the head and the front of the man. Moving carefully on her hands and knees, she worked her way around the man's neck and head. Bending over, she saw the Mercutio face mask was still on but had slipped down over the nose and now covered the mouth and jaw.

At which point an even louder noise rumbled from the man's throat and then turned to a distressing gurgle. At which Sarah jumped, almost landing on the victim's outstretched hand. The light on the other side, the front of the body, was so dim as to be almost useless. But she couldn't leave him now just to fumble around looking for light switches or flashlights. Gingerly she moved the mask back up over the eyes, over the head, which had lolled toward the floor as if the man wanted to inspect it for splinters. Slowly, much too slowly, Sarah was adjusting to the lack of light, but she still could not see any conspicuous wound to account for the blood. Still she might be able to find the injury by touch. To be safe she reached into her jeans pocket, found, a miracle, a clean handkerchief, and wrapping it around her hand ran it lightly over the face, the hair, the head, and found nothing frightening. Except, she thought, using even a clean handkerchief I might be contaminating an injury. "Oh Christ," she muttered. "It's damned if I do and damned if I don't. But I can't leave a bleeding person, because he might be dead by the time I called for help."

Of course, she should have called 911, but her cell phone was in her missing handbag. And no one was still left onstage or backstage. Were they? It was time to find out before she did any more damage to this guy.

She began to get up, slowly pushing herself into a crouch. And as she did, the man's head rolled, as if run from some motor, from its almost facedown position back and toward Sarah.

And she saw the man.

Not understudy Grover Blaine.

Not the real Mercutio, Todd Mancuso.

But the chairman of the English Department.

Commander, USNR, Professor Danton McGraw.

10

MERCUTIO! Danton McGraw! Danton McGraw, whose eyes seemed pinched closed in an expression of extreme pain. But what was wrong? Where was he hurt?

Sarah in the dim light tried to follow the contours of his face, to his chin, below his chin. And then she saw it. A puncture wound in the neck that appeared to be allowing small bubbles of blood to seep slowly out of the hole, drip down below his jaw, and saturate a once-white Elizabethan ruff.

Oh God, how long had he been lying here? Slowly, slowly bleeding to death. How many acts and scenes since Mercutio had been hauled off the stage? It seemed like hours. And how to stop the bleeding—stop without contaminating the wound? And how at the same time stop the bleeding, get up, and leave the man to find a telephone? Or yell for help—if anyone was left in the theatre to hear.

She made a decision. Something had to be done about the bleeding even if doing it added hundreds of evil bacteria to the wound.

Sarah reached for the handkerchief, folded it twice, and patted it into place over the puncture. But it wouldn't stay there without help. She fumbled around for something to tie the makeshift bandage down. She pushed down the cloth cover away from McGraw's body to see if there was a belt connected with Mercutio's costume. No luck. But how about a stocking? Those black stockings. Was Mercutio wearing body tights or something held by a garter belt? She reached down, untied and snatched off one of the black shoes, and gave a mighty pull to the stocking toe. It resisted and then something snapped loose and down it came.

The stocking, wound around the neck, did the job. Of course, the trick was to hold the handkerchief down, keep pressure on it, but not have the stocking so tight as to strangle the man. Sarah felt an almost hysterical desire to laugh—or cry—at the idea of saving a person from bleeding to death and then throttling him with his own stocking.

But now he was safe, she hoped—for a few minutes at least—so she could find a telephone and call the rescue squad.

She stood up, groped her way back to a backstage door, and, almost stumbling, plunged down a small flight of stairs and found herself at the edge of the auditorium. Vera's office. There would be a telephone there. Sarah raced up the darkened aisle, across the lobby, and to the office, grabbed the door. Locked. She ran back to the auditorium. She'd try the Green Room.

And then she saw him. Halfway down in the darkened auditorium she made out the silhouette of a figure. Someone leaning over one of the theatre seats.

Her mind went into a defense mode. All she could think of was that bleeding man backstage and that someone had made him bleed. Like this man. A murderer.

"Don't you move a step!" Sarah yelled. And then, "I've got a gun and I can shoot." An untrue statement if there ever was one.

The man straightened. "What the hell," he called. "Who is that?"

Sarah knew she had to stay tough. "None of your goddamn business. Just don't move."

"Sarah? Sarah, is that you?"

A voice, a familiar voice. But you never knew. "No," she called. "I'm not Sarah."

The man walked closer. "For Christ's sake, Sarah. It's me. Amos Larkin." Remember? Married to Mary Donelli? And for God's sake if you have a gun drop the damn thing. Get over where I can see you and tell me what in hell you're doing playing sheriff."

Amos Larkin. Sarah felt as if a load of hot air had suddenly left her body, leaving her weak and shaking.

"Amos!" she cried. "It's so awful. Backstage. I think he's bleeding to death and I'm trying to call nine-one-one. But I can't find a telephone. Vera's office is locked. Maybe the Green Room. Or the conference room."

Amos strode forward, took her by the arm, and forced her down in an aisle seat. "Slowly. Tell me. Who is bleeding backstage?"

"McGraw. Danton McGraw."

"What!"

"Yes, and we've go to do something fast. Look, I'll take you back there and you hold your hand on the bandage. Keep pressure on it, and I'll find a phone somewhere. Or," she added, without much hope, "you don't have a cell phone with you?"

"No. Can't stand them. Take me right backstage; then you hunt up a phone. Bound to be at least five of them around. And where are the lights for this place? See if you can turn something on after I take over."

These plans were followed. On a run. Amos, squinting in the dark, found McGraw, still senseless, his breathing heavy and interrupted with disconcerting gurgling noises. Sarah put Amos's hand over the stocking that held the handkerchief to the wound, and then she took off. And by hitting every switch on a nearby partition was able to bring a modest light to the area where Professor McGraw lay.

Her first shot at finding a telephone was perfect. The small conference room not only had a light switch close to the door but also boasted a wall phone. And Sarah hit 911 and in a choked voice called for help, said someone was bleeding, and gave the directions.

The ambulance came with great speed, not astonishing, since the Mary Starbox Hospital and the theatre were on the same campus and within half a mile of each other. Sarah, feeling as if she had been in a particularly rough game of rugby lasting more than twenty-four hours, barely had the strength to climb into her car and follow Amos to the hospital. Once arrived, she found that the ER powers had seized control, the stretcher had been wheeled out of sight, and she sank into a waiting-room chair wondering what was to happen next.

Amos answered the question. "I've called Alex and said you were delayed. An incident, but you're fine. And that you're on your way home and would explain."

Sarah raised her head with great difficulty—Amos was standing over her like some ancient but fierce red-haired warrior. "I'm not on my way home."

"Yes, Assistant Professor Deane, you are. You've had it. You look like hell. And you can't do any good here. Nor Alex. He's not Danton's primary care physician, as they call them. You'll be having serious sessions with your police friends tomorrow, but if you stay up all night fretting about this business, you'll be no good to anyone. And you probably have classes to meet in the morning."

Sarah made a face. "I never understood how Mary could have married you."

"That's a puzzle to me, too. Now get up and while you can still turn an ignition key and step on the gas, go. And if there's any drastic news, I will call. Okay?" Here Amos reached over, grabbed one of Sarah's arms, and dragged her to her feet.

And Sarah went. And somehow, like a sleepwalker, she found her car, started it, drove to Saw Mill Road without meeting with a tree or a ditch, and found the downstairs blazing with light and Alex standing by the doorway. Fully dressed.

She crawled out of the car. Alex came forward and gently moved her to the door, to the kitchen, and handed her a cup of boiling something.

"Good for the nerves," he said. "Hot cider with a little additive in it."

Sarah took the cider, took a sip, grimaced, took another. Relaxed and let out a long breath. And faced her husband. "You sound just like Amos. Strong males straightening out the little woman because it's all too much for her, the sensitive little dear."

"Strong males finding a bleeding body might be sensitive, too.

It might even make them want to crawl into a hole and forget it. For you, my love, this is the second bleeding body you've gone and found. Of course, I'm not counting Todd Mancuso's first encounter with the foil and lantern."

"Which I somehow missed."

"What I'm saying to you, my dear idiot, is that it's late at night, it's been a long day, even without bodies, but finding your department chairman in extremis can knock the wind out of anyone."

Sarah nodded, then fixing Alex with a look, noticing that he was wearing a windbreaker, said, "Amos told me you shouldn't come. That Danton McGraw has his own doctor."

"Who appears to have gone out of town. I said I'd come in. It's a matter of dealing with shock, blood loss, preventing infection, and that's what the ER hematology people and the infectious-disease people do best. Me, I'll hang around and look helpful. Something I do need to do. You, please, please, hit the hay. Your half of the bed is already filled with one Irish wolfhound and an active orange kitten."

And Sarah, despite a wish to squash a male's pretensions of greater stamina, found it remarkably easy to give in.

Some time later, she became aware that Alex was returning, moving Patsy from his pillow, lifting the orange kitten to the foot of the bed, and climbing in next to her. He turned briefly to her, whispered, "He's stable. At least for now," and turned over and went immediately to sleep.

Thursday, the first day of November, brought with it a strong hint of winter. The temperature sank into the low forties; gusts of wind-blown detritus left over from the Halloween celebrations scooted around the campus of Bowmouth College, rolled over the faded grass and along the gravel walks that ran from building to building. But far more interesting to the student population was the sight of the Drama School, like the victim of some sort of contagious disease, strung about with warning yellow tape. The police had sent in the troops, stormed the gates, and seized control of Vera Pruczak's kingdom.

Vera arrived at the Drama School at seven thirty that morning, knowing nothing of Danton McGraw's accident—or death—rumors among the police and in the ER team were considering both possibilities. Vera found herself escorted by a Maine State Police trooper and told that, under his eye, she could take her briefcase, which held her class notes and schedule—after opening and showing the contents—and in an hour report to the dean of Arts and Sciences for rescheduling her classes in other buildings. But first she was wanted by Sergeant George Fitts, who was holding court in a just-arrived trailer on the starboard side of the Drama School.

For George the goings-on between the English Department and the Drama School had moved past being merely troubling; now an assault with an intent to kill Professor McGraw was on the police menu. And this event could perhaps now be added to the beating of Todd Mancuso in the utility room of the Fine Food Mart. And most possibly both these affairs might be tied in to the first attack by drama students Terri Colman and Kay Biddle on the same unfortunate Todd Mancuso.

Furthermore, both victims, Professor McGraw and student Todd, were connected with the warring English Department and the Drama School. And both were intimately tied into Vera Pruczak's production of *Romiette and Julio*. Todd as an actor in the production and Professor McGraw not only as a fencing coach and choreographer of the swordplay scenes but also now revealed as the person who, for reasons yet unknown, went onstage to play the part of Mercutio. The question here being, what had happened to Grover Blaine, who was supposed to take the part? Grover Blaine who, with his friend, Derek Mosely had recently, through hearsay from two schoolboys, been associated with the beating of Todd Mancuso. Also of interest was the fact that Professor Sarah Deane had discovered both victims. Moreover, she was a close friend of Vera Pruczak of the Drama School and had been assisting backstage during rehearsals and during the performance itself. And she was employed as an instructor in the English Department.

"It's like a crossword puzzle from hell," said Deputy Mike Laaka to Sergeant Fitts. The two men sat at two facing tables in the trailer surrounded by the usual electronic display of computers, telephones (many extensions), radios, fax machines, and copiers. George, on the one hand, in his sharply pressed civilian clothes gave his usual impression of a high-ranking military person who had chosen to go about incognito, while Mike managed to look human in his jeans, denim shirt, and disordered white-blond hair. He had been roused along with George shortly after the ambulance had reached the hospital. The result was, as always, that George appeared calm, cool, looked refreshed; Mike, rumpled, cross, and sleep deprived.

"And I hate crossword puzzles," Mike went on. "Those clues about movie stars of the forties and rivers in Bosnia and who struck out twelve times in the 1953 World Series."

"You're right, for once," said George. "What we have are clues, characters, and events, but none of them fit into the squares. Not yet anyway."

"Too many people are mixed into the thing. I know what you always want, George. One lone corpse in perfect condition, wearing a smashed watch showing the time of an attack, his clothes dribbled with saliva packed with DNA from some stranger."

George nodded his agreement with this and then pulled out a new notebook and scowled at the morning entries. "Since we can't have a perfect body, we are stuck with trying to make sense of these insane academic fights and territorial arguments. It's been fairly obvious since Todd Mancuso's beating that the English Department wants the Drama School—"

"To cry uncle," put in Mike.

"And that Todd Mancuso as a representative of the Drama School was beaten up by this Draco Malfoy character—make that either Grover Blaine or Derek Mosely—as part of this English Department takeover scheme."

"Or because they're a couple of lowlife thugs. Like to make trouble," Mike said.

"That, too," said George. "So we need someone from the fight scene who's decided to stab Mercutio. Right onstage since it's part of the action. And then help drag him off and knock him out with whatever was available and stash him behind that bench."

"Okay," said Mike. "But you'll need every person who had access to the backstage area. Someone might have seen McGraw being hauled away. And, hey, have you got a reading on the blood onstage? Onstage, backstage? Real or fake? Or both?"

"We're waiting on the lab for that." George looked at his watch. "Seven fifty. I left word for Vera Pruczak to come here by eight. We can clear up some of the stage action. Find out if she planned to have Danton McGraw as one of Mercutio's understudies."

A question that was answered by Vera on her entrance one minute later. Her appearance was suggestive not only of someone caught in a strong November wind but also of a person tumbled from the theatre world into the stranger one of real life: murder, hemorrhage, homicide on the hoof. Her usually loose clothing, scarves and vests, normally came off as a theatrical fashion statement. This morning she looked like something out of a rummage sale. To George's question as to whether Professor McGraw was part of her lineup of Mercutio understudies, she gave an emphatic negative.

"No way. It never occurred to me. Never. He was the fencing expert, worked out the moves. But he did once ask to take over from Grover Blaine because he thought Grover was making a mess of the part. I put my foot right down on that idea. I saw enough of the man as it was. A genuine troublemaker. I could tell you—"

But Vera was stopped in midstream by George with two pointed questions: "Which actor was supposed to kill or appear to kill Mercutio? Which actor or actors were supposed to help him through that door into the backstage area?"

Vera sat still for a moment as if trying to see the scene again. And then, turning pale, she said, "Tybalt was to kill Mercutio. Tybalt takes off. Then Benvolio, he was Romeo's—or Romiette's—friend, had to get Mercutio offstage. But not before Mercutio has two speeches, the last one about a plague on both your houses."

George made a note that he underlined twice. "So," he said, "could Mercutio have been speaking those lines before being stabbed? Or was the injury not enough right then to prevent him from saying his lines before he left the stage?"

Vera again considered the scene. "I think," she said slowly,

151

"that I was impressed by how well Mercutio said his last lines. He really sounded as if he'd been wounded." His voice turned a little faint. "I thought I'd misjudged Grover Blaine; he can really act."

"I'm waiting on forensics to let me know if there was real blood on the stage. Then we'll know that Mercutio got hit right on-stage in front of all of us."

"And maybe again after he was hauled backstage," said Mike. And then, suddenly alert, he fixed on the real question: "Which character was supposed to actually kill Mercutio?"

"I told you: Tybalt," said Vera.

"Who ran offstage after killing Mercutio," said George, who had seemed to have paid some attention to the action. "Tybalt could have waited for Mercutio's arrival and tucked him back of that fountain. Pulled that piece of canvas over him."

"No time," said Vera. "He has to be right back onstage for Romeo to kill *him*. Benvolio comes back onstage to tell them that Mercutio's dead, and right after that Tybalt enters. And Tybalt couldn't have dragged Mercutio anywhere later because *he's* been killed by Romeo and has to lie right there on the stage for the rest of the scene."

And Mike, listening, was interested to hear that Vera had re-verted to the masculine form of the character. Damn, he thought, I may have to read this stupid play. Aloud, he asked Vera, "How many people are supposed to take Mercutio offstage?"

"Only Benvolio." She was silent for a minute and George saw that her hands were busy wringing themselves and one of her feet had started tapping on the floor.

"But," she added, sounding shaken, "two actors did it. Benvo-lio and someone else. Shakespeare only used Benvolio and so did we. I don't know how this happened unless Benvolio suddenly needed help. I don't know where this other actor came from or who it was. Everyone wore masks for that scene. In fact, in most scenes. I thought it added to the whole effect. We called the play a 'Masque,' you know. Oh God, wouldn't you know. Maybe I'm too old for all of this."

Mike gave her a sympathetic nod. Here was the queen defied

by her rebellious subjects who had gone ahead and changed the rules.

George turned to Mike. "Find the actor who played Benvolio and see if he knows who helped him with Mercutio. Tybalt, too. I have a note that says both are on the fencing team, so try the gym first. Early afternoon. By then we'll know about the blood on the stage. But get to the autopsy on time."

As this police scene was playing out, another sleep-deprived person had arrived at close to seven forty-five at the yellow-taped Drama School. Sarah needed her jacket. Her handbag. She had just about decided that she had left both somewhere in the Green Room.

She was stopped by Katie Waters, dressed for work-and-search in jeans and a sweatshirt. She was on duty with several other deputies from the sheriff's Department, one Maine State Police trooper, and a team of forensic workers headed by the unflappable state pathologist Johnny Cuzak. Johnny had been present only last summer at a nearby planned-living community when Sarah, visiting Alex's parents, had stumbled on not one but two deceased residents.

Now Sarah was hoping not to see Johnny. She didn't need reminders of grisly past events, and besides, she had to be thinking about getting back to Malcolm Adam Hall to meet her business-writing class at eight thirty—a class that by its very nature was to Sarah a depressing one.

Sarah explained her mission, and Katie shook her head. "We haven't even begun to work through anything but the backstage area—all those flats and backdrops and costumes and props. What a jumble. So we can't let you go wandering around. If we come across your things, I'll give you a call."

Sarah protested, "Look, Katie, I need the handbag. I won't touch a thing when I'm looking. Never mind my jacket. But I do want at least my wallet. You can put on gloves and fish it out for me. I think I left it in the Green Room."

Katie hesitated. Then, "Walk right in front of me. I'll go in and look; you stand outside." She felt in the pocket of her jeans and produced a ring of keys. "Got these from Vera's office and she didn't even make a fuss."

In single file the two women walked down the hall away from the auditorium and to a closed door that stood between the large stage and a smaller rehearsal and practice stage. Some weeks ago one of the students with a warped sense of humor had tacked up a sign on the door saying: ENTER AT YOUR RISK O WRETCHED RASH IN-TRUDING FOOLS.

"Honestly," said Katie. "The Drama School is something else. What's that supposed to mean? That the Green Room isn't safe?"

"A student showing off that he's read *Hamlet*," said Sarah. "Go ahead and unlock the door."

Which Katie, after a moment of twisting the knob, did. Pushed the door partly open. Fumbled for the light switch, which she did not immediately find. So taking another step in, she extended her arm along the wall. And went crashing to the floor. Sat up, grasping her ankle.

And Sarah, in disobedience to orders, pushed the door wide open to let some of the hall light in, edged her way into the room, moved gingerly past Katie, who was trying to get to her knees, found the switch. And flooded the room with light.

And saw why Katie had fallen.

Almost across the threshold of the room lay a foil. Katie saw it and swore. Rose to her feet, wincing as she put weight on one foot, and then limped into the room. And Sarah, foreseeing future accidents, gave the foil a quick flip with the toe of her shoe and sent it out of the path of anyone coming into the room.

The oddly shaped Green Room, narrow at its entrance, bulged on one side toward the outer rim. Sarah could see that some effort had been made, perhaps just before last night's performance, to tidy the mix of personal effects that usually crowded the room. And yes, there hanging from the back of a chair was her handbag. She started forward. Was grabbed by Katie.

"Whoa. Back up. George Fitts will have my scalp if you step in here."

But Sarah had seen something. A red-and-green-striped something. Bent at an angle. From between two armchairs. She pushed Katie loose and took a step forward. And yelled.

"Katie! Oh God. It's a leg. And," she added her voice rising in almost a squeak, "it's got a foot."

And Katie saw it. Held Sarah back and limped slowly forward. Stopped. Looked down. Moved closer. Bent over. And then, "Oh Christ."

To Sarah: "Get back in the hall and stay put. Right there. Don't move. I'm calling this in." And Katie pulled out her phone and gave the alarm: "Code Red! A body. No sign of life. Drama School. Green Room. Get ambulance. EMT. Forensics."

And Sarah, standing outside the Green Room, leaning against the wall, was left to remember a red-stockinged leg and a green one. And memory filled in the rest. Hose, as in doublet and hose. The Elizabethan look. Todd Mancuso had worn green and red stockings but had stripped them off for understudy Grover Blaine. Danton McClure had worn all black. Sarah felt dizzy. Two bodies, dead or alive. Two Mercutios. One perhaps bleeding to death in the hospital, one very possibly dead as a doornail in the Green Room. Those red and green stockings. And memory handed her a candidate, a face. Pale blond hair. Pointed features. The look of an albino fox. Draco Malfoy aka Grover Blaine. Grover the "Groper."

Of course, Todd himself had been the first victim—found in the Fine Food Mart's utility room wearing those blasted stockings. But before Sarah could adjust her brain to three Mercutio victims, the EMTs and stretcher swept past Sarah into the Green Room. These followed by Johnny Cuzak and some gowned and gloved person, perhaps part of the forensic team. The door closed, and Sarah, glad to be away from the action, quietly made her way to the back of auditorium. Where she was seized by Mike Laaka, who came striding down the aisle.

"Sarah. Good God. You were there with Katie? I heard when the call came in. You look awful. Come on, sit down. Someone will get you something. Tea maybe. But stay put. We need you. This goddamn theatre business. Bunch of crazies. There should be a law." Then hearing steps behind him, Mike turned. "Hey, Alex. Oh brother, this is something else. Sarah's here. Looks like someone kicked her in the guts. You take over."

Sarah roused herself. "I'm okay. Honestly. I just feel a little sick. Alex, if you're supposed to go in and do something medical, go ahead. I'm still trying to figure out what's going on. Or what did go on."

Mike gave a rueful grin. "You and me, baby. And the whole Maine State Police."

Alex sat down beside her, put his arm around her shoulder, and gave her a quick kiss. "I saw the ambulance drive up to the theatre, and I knew you had gone to the theatre to pick up your handbag or jacket. Or something. Forensics doesn't need me. But I thought you might. Want to talk."

Sarah looked at her watch. "I've got a class. Business Writing."

Alex reached for his cell phone. "I'll take care of that." He punched in a number, said, "Hi, English office. Linda? . . . Cancel Business Writing. Sarah Deane. She's been held up. . . . No, not a burglary. But she may have to cancel another class, too. And keep the lid on this, will you? Thanks."

He faced his wife and pulled her close to him. "Want to tell me about it?"

"Don't you have office hours? Or rounds? Or something."

"I have some time to spare. And if you're interested, I called in this morning to the ER and Danton McGraw's still going. They're giving him IVs and four units of blood, so I think he might make it."

"Or maybe not."

"Think positively. He's a tough character. And now would you like to share? What have you found this time?"

"Katie Waters did. But I was there, too."

"I imagine you were."

"Alex, can you believe it? I think there are three Mercutios in this thing."

11

THE English office was in crisis mode. The chairman's office was empty. Word had arrived early in the office that strongman Professor Danton McGraw had been attacked and on this first day of November was teetering between life and death. Then, as the early morning wore on, rumors in various coats and colors arrived. Dr. McGraw was unconscious, in a coma, having seizures, a lung, two lungs, punctured, wounds head to toe, anaphylactic shock complete with rash, multiple fractures, concussion, complete paralysis from the neck down. These were only some of the reports filtering through the secretarial offices not only in Malcolm Adam Hall but through the other schools and departments as well. In fact, if it had been announced that the professor was suffering from mad cow disease, the diagnosis would have been thought entirely creditable.

However, since, as Danton McGraw himself might have pointed out, nature abhors a vacuum, the English Department's senior secretary, Linda LaCroix, stepped into the void. This situation was made for Linda, who hit the wires with a flurry of calls to the high-and-mighty in the College of Arts and Sciences. She started with Dean Alena Fosdick and worked her way by way of e-mails to assorted instructors and adjuncts and for good measure posted notices on the office door for students taking Professor McGraw's classes. In these endeavors, Linda was followed reluctantly by Arlene Burr. Reluctantly because Arlene had in the past few days been finding less and less difference between Professor McGraw and Linda herself. McGraw was a model despot, an organizational fiend, a compulsive collector of data on personnel, records, results, résumés, and interdepartmental memos. Linda was of a similar bent, a wannabe tyrant.

But Arlene, who had submitted to McGraw grudgingly, found herself in almost a state of rebellion with Linda. Take the current crisis. Linda seemed to think she owned it, was in charge of its management as well as acting a censor of all developments that trickled into the English office. She had worn today her most conservative but tight-fitting outfit—black pin stripes with high-necked shirt—her severest makeup with extra emphasis on the eyebrows. And even more alarming, she was now making frequent trips to the sacred space of the chairman's office, where once Arlene had found her actually sitting in McGraw's chair and punching in numbers on his speakerphone.

And here Linda was found by Professor Amos Larkin. He had just heard the latest rumor via an adjunct English teacher who had heard it from Arlene that Professor McGraw, who was not, as far as anyone knew Catholic, had just received the last rites of the Catholic church. It was time, Amos decided, to pass around a few actual facts, rather than let these rumors reach the point where they became the stuff of legend. He, having spent a good portion of the night at the hospital after seeing Sarah off, was now in no mood for trifling. His eyes were shadowed with fatigue, he wore his ancient Irish tweed jacket buttoned up, his necktie tight, and altogether he had a dangerous appearance. All we need, thought Arlene. Larkin throwing his weight around.

"Linda," called Amos in a sharp voice, "come out of that office and sit down with Arlene. And pay attention. First, Professor McGraw is resting fairly comfortably. His condition is stable. He is not suffering from some jungle disease, nor has he been attacked by an alien from Mars. If things move along as expected, he should soon be on the way of recovery."

"That's nice," said Arlene, looking disappointed.

Linda, feeling power slipping from her grasp, said nothing.

The telephone filled the gap. Linda answered, listened, said, "Yes," and then, "You mean right away? . . . But I'll have to find the file. . . . Yes, yes, I'll do it now.

"The police," she muttered. "About one of our students. They want to reach his family. The Registrar wouldn't cooperate. Honestly, I think someone's trying to destroy the English Department. She put down the phone, went over to a file cabinet, and began forking through folders. Returned to the phone. And said, "Yes, some people are here in the office. . . . Yes, I'll give you the information privately from Dr. McGraw's office." With which she disappeared into the chairman's office.

"Oh brother," said Arlene. "I can feel a cold shiver right down my back."

Amos walked to the door and turned and faced her. "Whatever you hear, keep it to yourself. Tell Linda the same. No matter how exciting this new message is, don't either of you go calling your best friends over in the History Department about what you've heard."

Arlene made a face. "Yes, surely. Of course, Professor Larkin."

Amos departed and Linda returned from the office looking puzzled.

"Now what?" said Arlene.

"Grover Blaine. His parents wanted. Right now. Home and business numbers. But there's a note in Blaine's folder that says his parents are away. Anyway, the police are involved."

"The police? Why?"

"How would I know? But someone's coming over. We're to stay put."

"Why? About McGraw? And which police?"

Linda looked annoyed. "I don't know which goddamn police. I've got an English Department to run. Afternoon classes to cancel. Get off my back."

"You," said Arlene, "may go directly to hell."

* * *

The identification had caused no problems. Wallet, IDs, personal identification, all took care of the matter. After the ambulance arrival at the ER entrance and the fact of death being declared, the body of Grover aka "Groper" Blaine was taken to the morgue in the basement of the Mary Starbox Memorial Hospital. He had been, as state pathologist Johnny Cuzak informed Sergeant George Fitts and Mike Laaka, a reluctant morgue visitor, dead for some time.

"Rigor's partly established," said Johnny. "But don't even think about asking for time of death. If that foil was really lying on the floor of the Green Room, the guy maybe was in the middle of some crazy fencing match. So two things to consider. Rigor comes on faster if the guy was really exercising. But the room he was found in was pretty cool, and low temperature can retard rigor. They told me the Drama School thermostat is set around fifty at night and this factor could cancel the other. So we'll have to wait on this question."

"Autopsy?" asked George.

"Three this afternoon," said Johnny. "We need time for the forensic guys to pick their way through the area where he was found. See if any little tidbits, vials of poison, venomous adders, are around. Make my job easier."

George sighed. Why had fate put him in harness with not one clown, Mike, but number-two clown Johnny? It was time to force the latter to focus on the business at hand. "In the meantime," said George, frowning at the pathologist, "you have this wound."

"So we do," said Johnny. "A neck wound, which looks like the proximate cause of death, but you never know. There's a slight head injury as if he'd been banged with something substantial. But we haven't finished taking the photographs, X-rays, scans. Tissue samples. Fluid samples. Gastric contents. Other preliminaries. So wait up."

"He bled to death," put in Mike. It wasn't a question.

"Among the other things he may have done," said Johnny.

160

"Don't crowd me. See you later. I'm going to prowl around this guy and have a general look-see. Wait for the lab. But, just out of curiosity, was that weirdo costume he had on part of the character he was supposed to play?"

George frowned. "He was dressed to take over the part of Mercutio if Todd Mancuso couldn't do it. But Grover didn't make it onto the stage for the scene."

"I guess those costumes were the last word in fashion in Shakespeare's day," said Mike. "Men in bloomers and skirts and long stockings. Real cute."

"It's barely possible," said George, "that Grover may have put himself in the fight scene as one of the crowd. Lost his job as Mercutio but decided to come onstage anyway. Who would know? They all wore masks. Of course, I would think those red and green stockings would have been a giveaway."

"Hey," said Mike. "I'll bet no one focused on stockings. Listen, Grover could have been in that scene and punctured McGraw's neck. On the stage. Or backstage. Who knows why; maybe he was failing English. After he gets McGraw backstage he bangs him on the head for good measure, like you said, Johnny. So there he is, out like a light and oozing blood. All Grover has to do is lug the McGraw guy out of sight and cover him up."

Johnny Cuzak grinned at Mike. "Every day I thank God that you never went into forensic medicine. But since you started the idea, how did Grover happen to turn up at the banquet and then in the Green Room? No, don't answer that. McGraw, despite losing blood, crawled on his hands and knees until he ran into Grover somewhere, challenged the guy to a duel in the Green Room. Which Grover lost. McGraw then crawled backstage dripping blood, passed out cold behind that bench, and there Sarah found him."

George, unable to keep his temper one minute longer, turned on his associates and said in a loud voice to "shut up, both of you. You're not funny and you're wasting time. At least my time. Mike, let's go. But for what it's worth, Johnny, we don't know yet if Blaine played any other part, or whether he put himself in one of the crowd scenes without asking."

"Yeah," said Mike. "The whole thing was off-the-wall. Very loosey-goosey."

George nodded. "Vera is a little vague on who was where in those big people scenes. I've asked her to bring a script and the director's notes, and we'll try and answer some questions. But this is sure: As far as anyone I've talked to knows, Danton McGraw was never supposed to be onstage as part of the performance. Grover Blaine was the one and only official understudy. Ready to go on dressed as Mercutio."

"Three this afternoon then," said Johnny. "Me, I don't care what my bodies wear. I want the skin and what's under it."

George released Mike from participation in the Vera Pruczak interrogation—this was no time for Mike go on about the idiocy of Vera's play. Not to her face, anyway. Instead Mike was sent to hunt down Sarah and try to get some sense of what the play was *about* into his head. "You're not going to be any help if you haven't a clue to what was going on," said George. "To figure out the murder, the assault on McGraw, you absolutely have to get some grip on the play. The real one and Vera's version. I've got a copy of the script. Look it over; check who is in what scene. And who plays what. And Sarah worked with the costume changes, so she has a handle on the exits and the entrances. She'll go over these with you. Very important. For once, Mike, you may have to concentrate." Here George paused and an almost evil smile twisted his thin mouth. "Let's see, it's Thursday, isn't it? And I know what's coming up."

Mike blanched. He had a secret life, a not so secret interest. And it had nothing to do with police work.

"The Breeders' Cup," said George. "Saturday. A full day of glorious Thoroughbred racing. But you, Mike, unless you work your tail off, will not have a chance to watch even one post parade during your ten-minute lunch break."

"George," said Mike, looking as if he, too, had had a foil stuck into his middle, "you are a sadist. A lowlife. A weasel. And you have no sense of the joy of seeing a horse cross the finish line. If it's the right horse."

George bent his mouth again. "I've been fortunate. I had winning tickets for the Preakness and the Belmont this year. Now go and find Sarah. Then meet me at one. I'm going to see what I can get out of Derek Mosely. Blaine's friend. Then maybe squeeze some other Drama School regulars. The stars."

Thanks to the efforts of Alex and the orders of George Fitts, Sarah Deane had been released from her first two classes. Now, she only had the afternoon Greek drama to worry about. Vera Pruczak also had had her academic and acting classes canceled, and a number of students taking English and/or drama classes but needed by the police to answer questions found themselves free not to finish assigned homework.

Mike discovered Sarah sitting in the English Department's faculty room. She was drawing little diagrams on a sheet of lined paper. Trying to make connections. Trying to draw lines from Todd Mancuso, to Kay Biddle and Terri Colman, to Derek and Grover, to Danton McGraw. Maybe include Weeza Scotini. What did they have in common—besides being part of an unexpectedly lethal version of an upside-down Shakespearean play?

In this business Sarah was interrupted by Mike Laaka. In his hand he held a copy of Monarch Notes and a Barnes & Noble item titled *Outlines of Shakespeare's Plays*.

"Hi," said Mike. "George says I've got to know my exits and entrances in this so-called play. I've got Vera's script and gave it a once-over. It's like something from *Saturday Night Live*. So I picked up these cheater outline affairs at the bookstore. But I'll bet you can give me a one-paragraph summary of the original and tell me what in God's name Vera thinks she's doing."

Sarah put down her pad of paper. "One paragraph? No problem. Two families feuding. Like the Hatfields and McCoys. Only these are Capulets and Montagues. Two kids, one from each family, fall in love. Romeo's friend Mercutio spouts poetry, makes puns and sick jokes. Juliet's cousin Tybalt kills Mercutio in a street fight. Tybalt and Romeo leave the stage but come back. Romeo kills Tybalt. Romeo and Juliet are married by a monk called Friar Laurence. She takes magic potion, goes to sleep. Looks dead. Put into family vault. Romeo finds Paris, suitor of Juliet, in the vault, quarrels, kills Paris. Believes Juliet dead. Drinks poison. Juliet wakes up and sees dead Romeo. Takes Romeo's dagger and stabs herself. Everyone unhappy. The curtain comes down."

"Wonderful. Sort of heartwarming. So, judging from the script I've had to choke down, Vera uses the thing as a springboard. Eliminates sex differences. Women play men, men play women, women love women, men love men, women even love men. And vice versa. A lot of people are killed, but almost everyone wakes up, comes to life, and there's this big dance thing at the end. And by the way, that Weeza student puts on a real show. Anyway, I think Vegas could use the whole affair."

Sarah nodded. "Or Hollywood could juice it up in time for the Oscars."

"Back to business, like old George says," said Mike. "I see you've been making notes. Where can we go for a one-on-one chat? George wants your brain picked clean."

"Would that you could," said Sarah, pushing herself to her feet. She stuffed her pad of paper into her briefcase, which was now doing service as a handbag, that article being held by the police along with everything else in the Green Room.

"I know a safe place," she said. "It's a little conference room. No one uses it much."

"Good," said Mike. "Let me run down to the cafeteria and pick up lunch. And I'll meet you there. Point it out."

Three offices past a supply room Sarah indicated a door marked with a brass plate proclaiming it the Margaret Scott Conference Room, this named after some long-gone but distinguished faculty member. Mike left at top speed, coming back almost immediately with bottles of Pepsi, two ready-made sandwiches, and a bag of chips.

The Margaret Scott room had a double window that oversaw the parking lot, a murky painting of Monhegan in a storm, a carpet of vaguely Oriental design, several chairs, and a long table. At this last Mike and Sarah sat, side by side, while she spread out her lists of names and collections of arrows pointing to one or the other or all of the names.

"There's no point in rehashing the feud between the English Department and the Drama School," said Mike.

"Except," said Sarah, "when it feeds into hostility between Vera and Danton. McGraw's grab at the Drama School seems connected with his idea that Vera was upsetting community feelings. That she was offending them by her sexually explicit productions last summer and now this topsy-turvy one. All in the middle of a major fund drive by Bowmouth College."

"We'll keep those ideas floating in the background. Now what have you got?"

Sarah pulled her pad of paper in front of her. "All the people attacked or who did the attacking had ties of some sort with the English Department or the Drama School."

"We only know two genuine attackers for sure. Kay Biddle and Terri Colman. With a foil and a lantern."

"You don't want to count the ID of Grover and maybe Derek Mosely with the beating of Todd Mancuso?"

"George sort of likes it. But with a kid's identification of a book character look-alike it would never make it into court. Eat your sandwich."

Sarah picked up a wax paper–wrapped bundle and discovered egg salad on wheat. Took a big bite, a drink of Pepsi, and then regrouped. "How about the foil connection? You've got a foil injury to Todd, his ear, a possible foil injury to Danton McGraw, and maybe the same for Grover Blaine."

"Johnny calls Grover Blaine's hit a 'penetrating wound.' "

"Go back to McGraw," said Sarah. "Besides the fake blood, was there real blood found on the stage when Mercutio—whichever Mercutio—got stuck?"

"George was waiting for the lab on that one," said Mike. But he pulled his phone out of his belt, punched in a number, and asked the question. Listened carefully. Then hung up and frowned. "Okay, the report is in. Real blood plus theatre blood onstage. Blood is Danton McGraw's type. More real blood beyond the door they helped Mercutio through. McGraw's hair in the blood. Seems he was bashed over the head with what we don't know yet. The trail of blood goes back to where you found the guy. And for what it's worth, the police have collected every weapon they could find in the whole damn Drama School."

"Why not every weapon in the college?"

"Don't rush us. We're getting to it. Now we're up to our ears."

"But the Drama School foils? None with blood on them? Or that foil in the Green Room?"

"So far not. But what idiot killer would leave a bloody foil around? The foil on the floor in the Green Room has Grover's prints on it. Partials, anyway. No blood on its tip, so Grover couldn't have hit whoever killed him. But there was no protective tip on it."

"Did the foils in the fight scenes have protected tips?" asked Sarah. "I didn't notice."

"Nope. They were supposed to look real." Mike picked up his sandwich—also egg salad—and took a bite that severed the object in two. He chewed, took hold of his Pepsi bottle, and with one swallow managed to reduce its volume by half. "I think," he went on, "it's lunacy to use unprotected swords, but who am I to complain? Our citizens run around with their own AK-47s and Uzis. Better they carry swords."

"Vera worked very hard on the choreography of the fights. To make them look authentic and be safe at the same time. So did Danton McGraw. In fact, he was number-one fight instructor. He worked on the moves."

"And look where it got him," said Mike. "But okay, the foil, any foil, is one connection that we can make. And here's a question for you: Did the guy who nailed McGraw and Grover have to be a fencer? Maybe a very good one."

"Good question," said Sarah. "Is McGraw able to answer questions?"

"Not so far. He's very groggy and has no memory for the scene. That's what a smack on the head and losing blood does to you. And he's much too weak for us to work him over."

"So you'll have to ask someone else. The guy who played Tybalt is captain of the Bowmouth fencing team. Name of Malcolm Wheelock. The coach is, guess who, McGraw."

"Okay, we'll ask this Malcolm. He's on the suspect list anyway."

"One thing we do know," said Sarah. "Is that Kay Biddle the one who sliced Todd's ear? Can you find out if she's done fencing?"

"George is getting a list of fencers, the college team and the ones taking lessons at college or at some club. But I don't suppose that clipping Todd's ear meant Kay knew how to fence. When she was questioned she claimed she grabbed a foil and ran onto the stage to help Terri out. Getting Todd's ear was beginner's luck, I'd say."

"But the foil business is still a connection. How about the charge against Grover Blaine? He and Derek Mosely have been troublemakers from way back. There's Weeza Scotini, who reported both to the disciplinary committee. But Drama School females have been lashing their tails about Grover for quite a while. And they've got some sort of protective group going. Is Grover being dead the result of something those people did? And here's one for you. My number one gossip person who shall be nameless—"

"Arlene the spy of the English office."

"I didn't say that. But Danton McGraw has been wining and dining Dr. Alena Fosdick and trying to get her on board for knocking out the Drama School. And one way he was going to get on her good side was to pay special attention to her son, Derek Mosely, and his pal, Grover. Danton even asked Mary Donelli and me to have little encouraging chats with the two of them, try to bring them academically up to speed. But that was Monday and, needless to say, other things have been happening."

"Vera told the police the reason that Grover was chosen as Mercutio's understudy was that he could fence, like all the men in the Drama School. They have to take fencing. Maybe McGraw didn't like Grover's style. Or McGraw wanted applause for himself."

"It might be like that," said Sarah. "Anyway, Grover took a bow with the rest of the cast. Came to the banquet. But left fairly soon. Before a lot of others."

"Did you notice who else left early?" asked Mike. "We asked

Vera, but she was on this theatrical high playing lady prima donna director, so I don't think she could've remembered her own name."

Sarah closed her eyes. Tried to picture the festive table. Some students still in costume, some changed to sweats, T-shirts, party clothes. Toasts. Cheers. And yes, some people did take off at irregular intervals.

"People kept getting up, moving around, coming back. Changed out of costume, returned. Terri Colman left. So did Kay Biddle. But I don't know if they went together. And of course Grover. But before or after the women I don't know. But his friend, Derek, didn't leave then. He was talking to Weezie Scotini. Then I think he and maybe Tybalt left before dessert. But don't hold me to all this. I wasn't taking notes."

"I wish someone had been. So how about Todd Mancuso?"

"I'm not absolutely sure, but I think he left to look for Grover but couldn't find him. Turned up later on and sat across from Alex, who insisted on driving him back to his dorm. I was to follow. But I did notice that Danton McGraw didn't show up for the curtain call when Vera called for the coaches and stage crew. And he wasn't at the cast party, either."

"Too busy bleeding backstage," said Mike.

"I guess so. What else do you want me to guess at? Because that's all I'm doing."

"Go back to Todd. He's in one of your English classes, right?"

"Yes. Greek drama," said Sarah. "But so what?"

"The students read the plays. They take parts?"

"Yes. Where's this going?"

"Todd's a talented actor."

"Everyone knows that. He can be anyone. Any voice. And whatever lines he reads in my class, well, he always does a terrific job. He's just a natural."

"Okay, let's think Todd."

"Todd! You're crazy."

"Hang in. Listen. Todd is one super actor. Todd is first attacked onstage by Kay and Terri. That we know. No, wait. Just listen. I don't think that first attack is connected to anything. I'll bet it's just coincidence. But then there's a major incident. Everyone for miles around knew about the rumor that either Grover and Derek or both might be the guys who beat the bejesus out of Todd in the utility room. Really hurt him. So Todd's mad. He's going to get even."

"He was a real wreck," said Sarah. "And he still *is* a wreck."

"Okay, he was beaten up. Let's say, though, he could stand up better than anyone knew. But, get this, he's decided to play the poor cripple. To get even. Nail Grover. Or Derek. Whoever's available."

Sarah shook her head. "You're saying Todd is putting on an act. No way."

"Putting on an act is what he does best. He discharges himself from the hospital. Makes sure he seems too weak and wobbly to play the fight scenes. Can only do the Friar Laurence thing. But not playing the fight scenes means that Grover will fill in. And he, Todd, can hang around and get Grover backstage. Or even, and this is pretty damn sharp. Todd had his Mercutio costume on, Grover has his own costume, and in that costume grabs a foil, puts on a mask—"

"Hold it. Todd gave his stockings to Grover."

"If he's one of the crowd, stockings don't matter. So there he'll be, on the spot, and can spike Grover in the Mercutio death scene."

"But that didn't happen. Professor McGraw got nailed," said Sarah.

"That's the only hitch I can see. Simple case of mistaken identity."

"Mike, Mike, you're reaching."

"Be quiet. McGraw goes onstage as Mercutio. For whatever reason. But Todd thinks it's Grover. After all, they're pretty much the same height and everyone has a mask. And there's this extra mystery person. Todd Mancuso. Who is one hell of a good fencer— that's common knowledge. Anyway, he sticks it to the wrong Mercutio—aka McGraw."

"But McGraw finished Mercutio's lines," Sarah pointed out. "Isn't that peculiar?"

"Nope. McGraw may not have even felt much. In all the action, the excitement, maybe he felt just a little sting. Listen, people who have been shot have been known to function for a little while before they drop. Anyway, Todd helps get McGraw offstage."

Sarah frowned. "The Benvolio character was supposed to do that alone. Wouldn't Benvolio have thought this extra help was peculiar?"

"In that play? Hell, everything is peculiar. Listen." Here Mike banged his fist on the table. "Benvolio and this other guy Tybalt have to go right back onstage, leaving Mercutio. Or McGraw, who must be feeling faint by now. And there's Todd waiting. Mask and all. He bangs McGraw over the head. Knocks him out. Or half-out. Drags way him backstage."

"Todd, so help me, was weak as a sick rabbit," Sarah insisted again.

"Todd can act. Revenge is a great motivator. So here's the interesting part. Todd along with the rest of the cast takes the curtain call. And sees Grover alive and well. Not bleeding. Not concussed. Big shock. But he's still got a job to do. When Grover leaves the party early, Todd follows him, catches him in the Green Room, and kills him. Neat job. Got one of those big blood vessels. Jugular or carotid. We'll find out at autopsy time. The whole Green Room project probably didn't take more than ten or so minutes from start to finish. Todd comes back, joins the cast party. Later on he joins you and Alex."

"I can only swear again that Todd Mancuso was a physical wreck. And he really *wanted* to do the fight scenes. Was unhappy when Alex and Vera told him no. When he came to join us at the end of the party he was even trembling. Wiped out."

"I'd be wiped out," said Mike, "if I'd put a foil into the wrong person, then had to get the right guy, Grover, by following him to the Green Room, kill him, move him out of the way, and zip back to the cast party." He stood up, finished off the last of his Pepsi with a gulp, and shook his head at Sarah.

"Sarah Deane, you've been suckered in like everyone else. That's what actors do to you. They're spooky. Weird. They can get inside someone else and turn into that person. Murderer, teenager, old man—look at that Friar Laurence performance—or make themselves into an injured and feeble drama student."

"You're hallucinating, Mike. Maybe there was something in the Pepsi."

"You wait. I'm going to wow George with this. Dealing with actors, you have to hallucinate a little. I'm pretty good because I like horse races. They make you think wild thoughts. Todd Mancuso. He gets my Academy Award."

"To be boring, a lot of the actors knew how to fence," said Sarah.

"Listen, I know the fight scene guys all took fencing. But they weren't real experts. Only Todd and the guy who played Tybalt, that captain of the college fencing team. And Benvolio, too. He's on the Bowmouth fencing team. We'll have them on the mat. Time exits and re-entrances after Mercutio is killed."

"Of course," said Sarah, "Tybalt is the villain of the play. Maybe it went to his head."

"Yeah," said Mike. "What's that thing called, 'method acting'? Where you turn into the person you're playing. If I can't pin it on Todd, I'll try for Tybalt."

"You leave Tybalt alone. Everyone says the guy who played Tybalt, Malcolm Wheelock, is an honor student. Neat guy. Everyone's friend."

"Yeah, and since when haven't neat guys and Boy Scouts and choirboys turned into your neighborhood murderer?"

"Good-bye, Mike. Go have a wonderful afternoon. Me, I'm going to teach *Antigone*, which is a very upbeat play. About death and burying your brother. Or not burying him."

"My wonderful afternoon," said Mike opening the door for her, "is going to the autopsy of Grover Blaine, and if you knew how I hate autopsies."

Sarah made a face. "You chose the wrong job then. What was wrong with fishing? Hauling lobsters?"

Mike grinned. "I spent a summer as a stern man for my uncle, but I hate killing animals. I used to throw lobsters back when his back was turned."

171

"So you turned to murder."

"And vehicular accidents and speed traps and cocaine and meth busts and breaking up street fights and picking up drunks and other good things."

"I feel guilty about lobsters," said Sarah. "But I eat them. We're all hypocrites."

"Speak for yourself," said Mike. "I haven't eaten a lobster since I was twelve years old."

12

AS Mike had expected, Sergeant Compulsive, George Fitts, had already made up a list of items for Mike and Katie to pursue. But first the two deputy investigators were to interview Benvolio and Tybalt—Mike was now thinking of them as owning these names in "real life." The deputies had been told to get a sense of the action in the Mercutio fight scene. Pick their brains for information on fencing equipment, protection, protocol. Also get a fix on fencing moves and the world of theatrical swordplay. "Give those sessions an hour or so," George had ordered, "but be on time for the autopsy on Grover Blaine." After the autopsy, both deputies were to get down to real work. Check on the fencing classes, practice sessions, participation in bouts by every student in the English Department and in the Drama School. Next—here Mike groaned aloud and mentioned "food."

"Next," said George, "check on local fencing clubs for information about Bowmouth fencers who participated in earlier fencing programs, matches. High-school years, middle-school years."

"Why skip elementary or preschool?" said Mike, glaring at George.

"A student who fenced during high school," said George, "may go on with fencing off campus. May fence with a club. He may not be interested in team sports at Bowmouth."

"Or *she* may not be interested," put in Katie. "I'll bet you didn't know, George, but women fence, too. They fence men. On the same level. It's skill, not muscle and brawn."

Mike looked down at her. "I'll bet on the men anytime."

"And someday you'll get a saber through your gut," said Katie.

The two deputies gratefully left George and walked briskly toward the Bowmouth Gymnasium, a sharp wind whirling about them, whisking the few remaining leaves from the maple trees and here and there loosening some long-holding oak leaves.

"Okay," said Katie, pulling her windbreaker closer around her. "Are we getting into all this fencing stuff because George thinks the foil is the number-one route to the murder? Or should I say one murder, one attempted murder?"

"Hey," said Mike, "it's the chosen weapon. Twice. If you count that the lantern and foil attack, it's a three timer. If we had a case with firearms, we'd be checking ballistics, testing gunpowder residue, all that crap. A sword is pretty simple. One, two, and in. No worrying about range and gauge. Or where some lowlife found a Beretta Cougar .32 automatic. So be grateful that it's a foil. That's what the actors used onstage."

"Don't make it that simple. What if one of the actors did it with a dagger? And didn't those Shakespeare types use something called a rapier? Or how about an everyday item like an ice pick? At least to hit McGraw. The actors were all crowded together and in that play—yes, I looked it up—this Tybalt was supposed to sneak his sword in under Mercutio's arm and kill him. The audience wouldn't notice an ice pick."

"But the other actors would," insisted Mike.

"Don't bet on it," said Katie. "Foil in one hand, dagger or ice pick in the other."

"Ambidextrous?"

"Why not?" said Katie.

"Forget ice picks. I told Sarah I've got the whole thing wrapped up. Todd Mancuso, expert foil guy, was lurking, got into the fight scene incognito, did the job, helped haul Mercutio out, conked him. Found he'd hit the wrong guy so went for Grover. End of case."

"Then call George and tell him you've solved the thing and let's go and have dinner."

"I wish. Here we are. The fencing-practice space is the old basketball court off to the left."

And in a cavernous space, filled with all sizes and shapes of students in motion, masked and dressed in assorted protective jackets, some white, some gray, brown, or black, a number of the fencers stood in lines extending their foils in unison. Others were fixed into bouts along linear strips of rubber, others hanging out on the bleachers, talking, pointing, making comments. Here on a nearby strip they found Tybalt, known in civilian life as Malcolm Wheelock. He was a tall, lanky fellow, dressed in white, attached to a wire and box, his weapon in motion. His opponent, female by the shape of the bustline—features being impossible since both wore wire masks—and he seemed to be in the middle of a bout. Katie and Mike took a seat on a bench cluttered with gloves, several masks, and a long canvas bag from which protruded the handles of several weapons.

The bout continued with much advancing and retreating, thrusting, blinking of lights, until finally Malcolm, with an extension of his weapon, a one, two, parry, *riposte*, and lunge, a blinking light, and it was over. There followed a salute, a lifting of masks, and a handshake. The girl said something to the effect that she'd get him next time, and Malcolm Wheelock unhooked his electronic tail and walked to the bench. Judging from his expression, he recognized Katie as the deputy investigator who had earlier taken his name, dormitory, and telephone number.

"What's up?" he said. Malcolm had a long face, a strong nose, and reddish blond hair that hung over his brow like a fringed lampshade. How could he possibly see what he was doing? Katie wondered. Walking, let alone fencing, seemed impossible.

"Just routine," she said. "A few questions. About fencing. The equipment you used in the fight scene. Mike and I don't know a foil from a battle-ax."

Mike scowled at Katie and said, "I've already figured out how the whole thing was done. But, never mind, we'll let Tybalt go over the scene from the beginning."

"Actually," said Malcolm, "I'm not crazy about being called Tybalt. He was one mean bastard. But I sort of enjoyed being in the play."

"Didn't you expect to be in it? You're a Drama School major," said Katie.

"Yeah. But not because of the acting. I'm interested in different stuff. Scenery design, moving stages. The engineering part. Lighting, special effects."

"So let's get down to it," said Mike. "First, where did the foils in the play come from? The fencing team?"

"No way," said Malcolm. "We wouldn't let those guys trash our stuff. The Drama School has its own supply. A lot of plays, early ones, involve some sort of swordplay. Instruction is required for the men. For women it's optional—like if they picture themselves playing Joan of Arc."

"So stage foils were all from the Drama School? No one brought their own personal weapon?"

"Not allowed. Everything, costumes, props, weapons, all came from the Drama School. Some of us drama students also take fencing as a sport, but that's different. We keep our own equipment in our dorms or at the gym. The guy who played Benvolio, that's Griffin Starr, he's on the college team. He does saber. So is Todd Mancuso on the team. He's épée."

"Would either of you have used a saber or an épée in rehearsals?" asked Katie.

"No, it was all foils," said Malcolm. He came over to the bench, stuffed his weapon into the black bag, and sat down, stretching his long white knicker-and-stocking-clad legs out in front of him. Then, frowning, he began describing the fight scene.

"It begins with Mercutio and Benvolio, he's the other pal of Romeo's, arguing about going or staying, and then in comes Tybalt, that's me, and then Romeo. Tybalt wants to start a fight with Romeo or Romiette—"

"Whoever," said Mike. "Go on. I don't care what you call them."

"Well, Romeo won't fight because he's in love with Tybalt's cousin, Juliet or Julio. Mercutio thinks Romeo's being a coward and starts fighting Tybalt himself. Benvolio and Romeo try to beat down our weapons, but Tybalt, that's me, nails Mercutio under his arm. Actually, right then, Benvolio squirts some theatre blood at Mercutio. Mercutio staggers and gives his last speech. Then Benvolio and this other strange guy help him offstage. Tybalt exits at the same time. Then Benvolio comes back and says Mercutio's dead. Tybalt re-enters and gets killed by Romeo. Romeo takes off and Tybalt stays on the stage lying in some more blood. Benvolio's in charge of adding more blood, which was a real sticky mess, got in my hair and all over my neck. Anyway, I lie there dead until the end of the scene."

"Lovely," said Mike. "So anything funny, out of whack, about the scene?"

"Well, yeah. Sure. That extra actor. Helping Benvolio take Mercutio offstage. That was new. But it didn't bother me. I don't know who it was because of the mask. All the people in the scene had masks. I haven't thought much about it."

"But look," Katie said. "You were offstage when Mercutio was taken out. By *two* people. Did you see anything happen to Mercutio—or Professor McGraw—when you were back there?"

Malcolm shook his head. "Didn't know it was McGraw, but I wasn't paying attention anyway. I had to keep an eye on Benvolio, listen for his cue to re-enter, because I go back onstage five lines later."

"Think," said Mike. "Anything else. Something different. Something more than this extra guy helping Mercutio. Did all the foils look alike? Did they have protective tips?"

"We rehearsed with tips. But Professor Pruczak wanted them off for the final performance so they would look real. Hey, it was safe. We knew all the moves, done them over and over. For the two fight versions. One with Todd, a real-looking fight. One with Grover Blaine where we slowed up the fight sequence a little. But all the same moves. But you know . . ."

"But what?" asked Katie.

"One funny thing."

"Yeah?" said Mike. "That's what we need. One funny thing."

"Well, the foils have a French grip and a small guard. But I sort of remember seeing a foil with a bell guard. That's a bigger guard than a foil has."

"Which means?" said Mike.

"A bell guard is usual with an épée."

Katie leaned forward, alert. "But no one had an épée because the Drama School only used its own foils."

"In this production they did. They've used other weapons in other plays."

"Never mind other plays," said Mike. "What's the difference between the two?"

"A foil is lighter. It's got a flexible rectangular blade. Maybe about thirty-five or so inches long. An épée is about the same length, but it's heavier. And it's stiffer. The bigger bell guard protects the hands from a hit. The foil only uses the torso as a target. The épée uses the whole body. Now the saber, well, I would have noticed a saber. It's got a really different hilt. And it's as light as a foil."

"Skip the saber for now," said Katie. "This épée business is getting interesting."

"You mean," said Malcolm, "it would make a difference if an épée was used in that scene?"

Mike turned to face Malcolm. "Foil or épée. What's your choice for giving someone a good poke with the unprotected tip of a weapon?" It wasn't a question, and a glance at Malcolm's expression or comprehension settled the question.

"So now where's this Benvolio character?" demanded Katie. "We'll need another opinion on what weapon did what."

But Benvolio, aka Griffin Starr, had left the gym in search of nourishment at the student cafeteria, so Katie and Mike headed in that direction, both their minds fixed on the possible weapon of choice.

"Which if it was an épée," said Katie, "is probably at the bottom of Bowmouth Pond."

"Forget ponds," said Mike. "You can find things at the bottom of a pond. Me, I would have dropped it off the coast. Oceans swallow things better than ponds."

"Imagine smuggling in an oddball weapon," said Katie, "and no one noticing."

"Because," said Mike, "they're not that different. The action, the dialogue, that's what everyone pays attention to. But listen, now we've got something to feed George. Maybe he'll buy us dinner."

"In your wildest dreams," said Katie.

Griffin Starr was a senior drama major and, like Malcolm, was a member of the fencing team. He was tracked down in the cafeteria at a large round table surrounded by a group of friends engaged in destroying a pile of hamburgers and chips.

Katie and Mike managed to shift Griffin to a more distant table and settled down for what they hoped would be a profitable conversation.

Griffin proved to be an affable sandy-haired boy with a snub nose, blue eyes, and a cheerful smile. A few minutes of questions proved only that he had used a foil provided by the Drama School. "No way ever I'd use my own equipment in a play," he said.

Katie got down to the point. "This person who helped you taking Mercutio offstage. You know who it was?"

Griffin shook his head. "Didn't know him—or her; some of the street scenes had men and women mixed up."

"Tell me about it," said Mike.

Griffin grinned. "The whole play was sort of a stew. But I don't know why that strange actor was there. Or why he was helping me take Mercutio out. But I wasn't going to make a big deal out of it, not there on the stage."

"And backstage, you saw the person? With Mercutio?"

"I don't remember anything special. Except a lot of stage blood came out with Mercutio. My fault. I overdid the blood thing. I've got this squeeze bottle and—"

"Never mind the squeeze bottle," said Mike impatiently. "What about Mercutio and this extra person?"

"I wasn't paying attention to anything since I was listening for my cue because I had to go right back onstage. First me, then Tybalt."

Katie tried her ace in the hole. "Did everyone use foils for the scene?"

Griffin looked surprised. "Yeah. Of course. We had to."

"You didn't notice anything different about one of the foils?"

"Nope. Listen, I was trying to do my fight moves and get ready with the blood all at the same time. I wasn't looking at foils. I might have noticed if something like a saber turned up. But everything seemed okay." And then as if he had realized that the two represented law and order and possibly news, he asked, raising his voice, "Hey, what's this about Grover Blaine? I heard he's sick. Or injured. Or even dead. I mean has a body been found? Not just Professor McGraw, but Blaine, too."

At which the crowd of friends at Griffin's former table sat up, opened their eyes, and stopped chewing.

"Voice down, please," said Katie, adding to herself, And you, Griffin Starr may be one of the ones on the hot seat for Grover Blaine. Aloud she said, "Don't spread rumors. If something's happened, you'll find out soon enough. And thanks for your help."

And with that Katie and Mike retreated. Time for the hospital morgue.

"Couldn't we have waited a few minutes?" said Mike. "I could have grabbed a hamburger. Or three hamburgers."

Katie shook her head. "Time and tide and George Fitts wait for no one. And we're already pretty late for the autopsy."

"Oh hell," said Mike. "Maybe it's good we didn't eat. If you knew how my stomach feels when I'm hanging around a stainless-steel table and watching Johnny use his saw and the scalpel and forceps and all those sharp instruments to make mincemeat out of someone's body."

"I don't want to know," said Katie. "More to the point, think about what Griffin Starr said. Only foils. He didn't see some oddball bell-shaped thing."

Mike nodded. "Doesn't mean that much. Griffin was too busy with his damn squeeze bottle."

"Anyway, I believe Malcolm Wheelock. He wasn't concentrating on fake blood."

"Yeah," said Mike. "And now George will have to round up the cast from that scene to see if anyone saw a peculiar weapon."

"Which means," said Katie, "it'll be midnight before we can get so much as a handful of peanuts. But I have two Mars bars in my jacket and I might just share."

Mike grinned down at her. "As long as you don't bring them out just as Johnny gets out his skull chisel."

Sarah survived her class. Just. Student interest in the plight of Antigone was at a low point. Rumors about the perilous condition of Professor McGraw and the possible injury and/or death of student Grover Blaine buzzed like angry flies around the class and left Greek drama in the dust. Only Grover's friend Derek Mosely, alone in the back row, sat silent, looking miserable. It was the first time that Sarah had seen him without his double, and she thought that Derek really looked as he'd been cut in half. But fortunately, there were three students who kept the ball in the air. Todd Mancuso, Kay Biddle, and Terri Colman, the Drama School wunderkinder, ignored the buzzing and read scenes with meaning and verve. Todd seemed somewhat improved in appearance and certainly had not forgotten how to put zip into his reading. Sarah was so grateful that she shortened the class by ten minutes—no Danton McGraw to catch her in the hall—and mentioned that by the middle of the month they would be attacking the works of Aristophanes. "Do a little reading in advance," Sarah told the class. "It won't hurt you a bit to get a jump on the assignments. And you might get a laugh out of the things that go on in his plays."

After class the three stars of the Drama School stayed behind.

"What about Grover?" demanded Todd. "I heard he was absolutely gone. Found in the Green Room. Is that true?"

Sarah, who of course had, with Katie Waters, found the body, shook her head. "I just know that the police are very interested in the whole play business. Who was where. And when. And who was at the banquet and who left early. Or left early and came back. That's all I can say, and that's just routine."

"You mean we're all going to be interviewed again?" asked Todd. "And have statements taken. This is worse than a bad movie."

"And Grover Blaine is alive and well and living in Maine?" asked Terri.

"I'm not an information booth," said Sarah testily. "You'll find out soon enough. What I do know, or don't know, it's my business. So go away. Read up on Aristophanes."

"Hey, Kay," said Todd. "You'll like *Lysistrata*. Women's rights. Control of men. Your scene. I was an understudy in the play. Summer theatre two years ago."

"With these Greeks," said Kay Biddle, speaking for the first time, "it would really have to be something to get me interested. I'm a contemporary-theatre fan. Twenty-first-century stuff makes sense to me. But women's rights in the dark ages, that's too far away."

"Most people," said Sarah, sounding to her own ears impossibly stuffy, "wouldn't call that time in Greece the dark ages." She reached for briefcase, still doing double duty as a handbag. "Now beat it. And don't go trying to pump someone. All you'll get is a lot of lousy information. Which if you spread it around will just get worse. And lousier."

"Is that a word?" asked Terri, grinning.

"It is now," said Sarah. And she marched out of the room, paused, and then made for the faculty lounge in hopes of tea, a biscuit, a comfortable chair, and time to think. About foils. Fencing. Skill required to pierce two throats. And to slice one ear.

By the time that Mike Laaka and Katie Waters made it to the hospital morgue, this situated in the basement of the Mary Starbox Hospital, the initial autopsy work had been completed, the preliminary Y-shaped incision made, organs removed for weighing, tissue sent off for lab tests. And now Johnny, with George Fitts at his side, had begun working on Grover's head.

Katie, with Mike standing somewhat behind her, received the expected glare from George, who looked pointedly at the clock on the wall. They were almost twenty minutes behind the time set. And they had used up even a few more putting on the masks and gowns that attending a postmortem involving death from unknown causes required. Why, thought Katie, gazing down at the eviscerated body of Grover Blaine, hadn't Johnny gotten right down to essentials? The puncture wound on the side of Grover's neck was so obviously the number-one place of interest.

But Johnny was not to be rushed. He nodded at the latecomers and, in a reproving voice, said that they had missed some of the fun. Examination of the face. He pointed to the victim's scalp, which now hung over the face, the front part of the skull being removed for examination of the brain. "No easily discernible damage in there," he said. "With the blow sustained to the head, I thought there might be, but not so far."

George, neatly tied into his gown, stepped closer to the table. "The victim apparently hit his head on a wrought-iron coffee table as he fell. We've recovered blood, hair, and clothing fragments from the table."

Johnny Cuzak shook his head sadly. "I think all wrought-iron furniture should be banned. They're agents of destruction. They shouldn't be allowed in a house. Or even on a patio. The number of victims who have struck their heads on wrought-iron tables is frightening."

"But that didn't kill him," said Katie.

"Doesn't mean they're not lethal," said Johnny. "Here's the real damage." And he reached with his latex-gloved hand and gently turned and slightly rotated the head of Grover Blaine so that the incised wound in the side of the neck was visible.

"Fairly deep penetration," Johnny said, pointing. Taking a slim pair of tooth forceps, he gently moved the outer skin layer apart and indicated the wound. "I've looked at some of the Drama School foils, but they almost seem too flexible to have gone in as deep as this. Hard to tell, though."

"The foil we found in the Green Room," said George, "showed smudges from probably ten other people on the guard. But also the victim's prints on the handle, partials, as I've said. My guess is that the victim used this foil."

"Foils were plenty available everywhere," put in Mike, who, as usual, had been standing as far away from the autopsy table as possible.

"You mean the foil with Grover's prints meant that he was trying to defend himself?" asked Katie. "Like they were fencing each other?"

George shrugged. "Maybe. Who knows? There may have been a challenge. Something like that."

At which Mike took several steps forward, his eyes briefly focusing on what was left of Grover Blaine's head. "We have news," he said.

"Speak," said Johnny, frowning at the perforation in Grover's neck.

"You can tell him, Katie," said Mike, now overcome with nausea and moving backward until he stood almost against the door.

Katie was only too glad. Perhaps the news might counter George's displeasure at their late arrival. "The strange actor in the fight scene. The one nobody knows. We think he didn't use one of the regular foils everyone did, the ones owned by the Drama School. Malcolm Wheelock—he played Tybalt—said he saw a special guard on one of the weapons and said it had to be an épée."

"Go on," said Johnny, reaching for a probe. "What's the difference?"

And Katie told him in detail, emphasizing weight and rigidity of the blade. "And," she finished, "only foils were allowed by Vera Pruczak. An épée would be forbidden."

George stared at Katie. "Why didn't we find this out earlier? I've got statements from everyone in the cast and no one mentioned an épée instead of a foil."

"I think that Malcolm Wheelock just remembered this odd thing when we asked him to think again about the scene. To be honest, we talked to the guy who played Benvolio, name of Griffin Starr, and he didn't think he saw an épée."

Mike, pulling himself together, walked back to the table, avoiding even a glimpse of its contents. "This Griffin," he said, "wouldn't have seen anything funny because he was concentrating on squirting fake stage blood on the Mercutio character."

"Katie," said George, "go back over the list of the actors in that scene and see if you can find someone else who saw the wrong weapon. Tonight. And see if one of them had any idea of the identity of this strange actor. We need that information as soon as we can get it. And Johnny, would you say that some fencing sword, épée or foil, would have made the neck wound, pierced the carotid artery?"

Johnny lifted his shoulders. "Could be. But I'm not going to swear to anything. It might be some sort of thin dagger."

"An ice pick," offered Mike, backing away again.

"Sure," said Johnny. "A dental probe. A knitting needle. An early Egyptian stiletto. So go on, all of you, find me a weapon with this guy's blood type and DNA match on the tip and a person's prints on the handle guard and I'll buy it."

Katie and Mike retreated, climbed the stairs to the first floor, and, followed by George Fitts, went out into the windy day, the skies now dark in the east, dimming in the west.

"All right, Mike," said George, who never forgot an assignment. "Katie has her job, so you go find lists of Drama School and English Department students who've had fencing experience."

Mike, feeling more like himself in the fresh air, found this job not as bad as it first sounded. Most of it, he felt, could be accomplished at a desk with a list of the college fencers, the team, the club, and those students taking fencing as a sport. He pictured his desk covered by these lists but also decorated by a large steak sandwich, a helping of fries, and an open bottle of Coors' Light.

"Call me by ten tonight with what you've found," ordered George.

"Or what he's not found," said Katie. She grinned at Mike and then took off at a run. With some luck she just might be able to round up all the actors in the fight scene and take a census on the number of foils seen versus the possibility of one uninvited épée.

Mike turned to George. "Frankly, I think looking for a fencing expert or even a fencing student is a big fat waste of time. Anyone with a good aim could get someone in the throat."

"It's a demanding sport," said George. "Hitting a target accurately, particularly if someone is alert about defending himself, takes a lot more than a good aim."

"A strong arm, a good aim, a stiff blade, plus an urge to murder a certain person, hey, that will do the trick any day."

George inhaled and blew through his teeth. "Look, forget motivation. That comes later. Now it's who and how. Obviously I haven't given you enough to do. After you've checked the fencing students, hunt up Katie. She'll be interviewing the actors about seeing an épée. Then you both try and put together a profile of this mystery fencer. Based on other actors' reports. Height, hair color, if the hat wasn't covering the hair. Anything about the person's face that the mask wasn't covering."

"That's two jobs," said Mike. "The lists of fencers plus the épée thing *and* the ID of the mystery person."

"Correct. Glad you can count." And George moved off in the general direction of the hospital.

"Hey, George. Wait up," called Mike. "We could all save ourselves a hell of a lot of trouble if we just asked Danton McGraw who was this extra guy."

"And why he decided to take over Mercutio," added George. "But that's got to wait. I'm going over to the hospital now. Not that I think I'll learn much. Professor McGraw is still groggy, has no memory of the event. They're still giving him blood. And keeping him hooked up to IVs. We've got a guard at his room, and I'm going to meet with one of his doctors to get a fix on when he's safe to interview. In the meantime . . ."

"Get my ass in gear and go to work," said Mike.

Katie Waters had an idea. After she'd met with actors about the épée, she wanted to go over again Sarah's memory of the backstage activity during the fight in act 3, scene 1, of Vera's production.

The two women met accidentally at the entrance to Malcolm Adam Hall. Agreed to find a booth in the cafeteria. The memory session to be assisted by large mugs of hot chocolate. After all, it was November.

Katie, armed, as usual, with a spiral notebook, had finally begun to have a good grip on the sequence of acts and scenes of the play. Fortunately, Sarah could remember most of the actors involved with the scene and those waiting to go onstage for the next scene. And despite masks and costumes she knew most of them by reason of their turning up in one of her English classes, watching the rehearsals, or helping with their costumes.

"Let's start with act three, scene one, a so-called public place," said Katie, checking her notes. "That's when Mercutio got his. Did you watch the whole scene from the wings?"

"Couldn't," said Sarah. "Vera asked me to keep an eye on Todd Mancuso, make him sit down, get his breath, before he had to go on as Friar Laurence. So I missed the first speeches of Mercutio."

"Did Mercutio seem any different to you? After all, it wasn't Grover Blaine."

"No, not really. Oh, I thought he was speaking with more authority than he'd done in rehearsal. But I couldn't hear all that well, and I didn't watch anything until the actual fight. And yes, I did see the two actors help Mercutio exit. What else? Well, there was blood on the stage—but it was supposed to be. But I didn't keep an eye on Mercutio after his exit because I went to find Todd a drink of water, and by the time I delivered that, Tybalt was dead onstage and Romeo had made his exit. Next I helped Todd Mancuso out of his Mercutio jacket—it was hot as hell back there and that doublet jacket thing was heavy with double sleeves. He'd worn that for the very first Mercutio scenes. And instead of a complete change, he had just pulled the Friar Laurence costume over it. I guess he still thought he might be allowed to do the fight scene. Anyway, after we got the jacket off, he had to get back into the monk's habit. And then he said that his tonsure was coming loose, so I had to fix that."

Here Sarah looked up at Katie, whose pencil had stopped moving. "Hey, Katie, are you going to sleep on me?"

"Yawn, yawn. It all sounds like a lot of nothing about nothing."

"Okay, you're probably right," said Sarah, taking a long satisfying swallow of bubbling hot chocolate with a heavy cap of whipped cream. "So go on out and help hunt down the fencing groupies. Maybe you can find a student who had secret fencing lessons with an épée. Keeps the thing under his pillow. Her pillow."

"Planning murder in advance?"

"Your job. Not mine. I'd find out how long Grover Blaine has been harassing female students. And if he's made someone mad. I mean really mad. Not like Weeza Scotini. That was a setup."

"So," said Katie, "what I should do is sneak around in an invisible cloak and go through dormitories looking for closet fencers. Maybe taking lessons somewhere off campus. George mentioned that. But I'm thinking about not fencing in public. Not at clubs and in recreation programs. Or taking part in matches."

"Somewhere by the light of the silvery moon. Out with the wolves and the vampires."

"If I tried going anywhere on my own or without a search warrant, George would have my head."

"Probably your liver, too," said Sarah.

Katie drained her cocoa, wiped a rim of whipped cream from her lip, and stood up. "In case you have any funny ideas of solo work, forget it. George is wary of you, girl." Katie paused and then lowered her voice. "Just in the impossible possibility you do think of something, or you stumble into some interesting crap, how about you tell me first. I can run interference for you, because believe me, old George, he doesn't want to find your footsteps leaving prints across his case."

Sarah nodded. "I will tiptoe."

13

SARAH, left with her own rather mixed ideas about assaults by sword, found those she did have ran somewhat counter to those of George Fitts and company. Her particular focus meant a visit to the English office.

However, she had only gone some twenty feet past the cafeteria when her attention was caught by the sight of Derek Mosely slumped against the door of the student lounge. Derek, staring into space, looked like someone who had gotten out of bed but had forgotten how to put on clothes. His sweatshirt was on backward, the gray sweatpants looked as if they had been through a particularly tough session of rugby, and his blond hair hung uncombed over his forehead. Sarah was about to move on when she looked more closely at his face. His expression was of such abject misery she found herself stopping.

"Hello there, Derek," she said.

He looked up at her briefly and then shifted his gaze to his shoes.

"I'm very sorry about Grover," said Sarah. It seemed a safe thing to say. She didn't know how much Derek had been told about the fate of his friend.

Derek raised a haggard face. "I know he really died. Not just hurt. He was killed. I just heard from the English Department office."

Sarah nodded. "That's really tough. I know you and Grover were together a lot. He was a real friend. And your roommate, wasn't he?"

"Yeah, he is. I mean he was. That Linda secretary wanted me to talk to someone. Some dumbo called a 'Grief Counselor.' Or a minister. Or something."

"Not a bad idea," said Sarah. "But how about your mother?"

"That didn't work. My mother is really mad at Grover and me because of that business with Weeza. You know, the discipline committee thing. Because I'm supposed to be some sort of an accessory although I just stood there. Kept watch. My mother always hated Grover, said he was no good. But you had to know him like I did. You'd think my mother'd care about us being hauled up like that. But all she thinks of is her job."

Sarah moved away from the touchy subject of Dean Fosdick. "Your father," she asked, "have you seen him? It might help to talk to somebody."

"Hell no. Not my father. Professor George High and Mighty Mosely. He's up there being a big cheese in the Chem Department at U. Maine. He hates my guts. Thinks I'm a total fool, which I'm not. Just because I hung around with Grover."

This line of thought seemingly at a dead end, Sarah tried a shift. "Are Grover's parents on their way here?"

"Yeah. I guess so. I don't really know them. Look, does everyone know he's dead?"

"It seems to be getting around. A lot of classes are canceled and the police have set up a mobile office outside the Drama School."

Derek nodded. "I've talked to the police. Twice. Yack, yack. That Sergeant Fitts thought I should know where Grover was during the cast party. But he left before I even noticed. Just took off. I don't know if he was with anyone. Or he was followed by someone. I was talking about about soccer. But I never saw Grover again."

Sarah felt that Derek was fast approaching breakdown. "How about something in the cafeteria?" she suggested. "The cocoa is great. Or coffee. Something hot. It might make you feel a little better. My treat."

But Derek shook his head. "I'm supposed to be seeing my advisor. Ten minutes ago. He'll probably try to set me up for counseling, too. Something stupid anyway."

Sarah produced a smile. "It doesn't hurt to talk. Give it a try. And my cafeteria offer still holds if you feel like it sometime."

Thinking this encounter over in her mind as she worked her way through the corridors to the English Department office, Sarah decided that Derek was really going to need some sort of help. But probably not from his mother. Dean Alena Fosdick, if Derek spoke the truth, did indeed seem more interested in distancing herself from the harassment charges hanging over her son than in offering any maternal solace. And the suggestion about his father had certainly bombed. In fact, the only positive thing Sarah could think of was to hope that Derek was not involved in his buddy's death, since he might never have left the cast party. As to his participation in the attack on Professor McGraw, well, who knew? Then there again was Derek's possible role in the beating of Todd Mancuso at the Fine Food Mart. All in all, Sarah decided, things didn't look good for Derek in the near future. Pulling him together would certainly take more than a mug of cocoa in the cafeteria. Well, maybe his advisor would suggest real professional help.

Sarah walked into the English office hoping that Linda LaCroix, the now-established Tyrannous Rex of the department, was doing important things elsewhere.

No luck. Linda stood in the middle of the English office. Her hand was raised and her voice was shrill. As Sarah stood at the door entrance and listened to what might be considered a minor tirade, Linda seemed to be delivering a lecture to Mike Laaka, who stood holding a pile of manila files and a briefcase and looking as if he wanted out.

"You can't just walk out of here with those records," shrilled

Linda. "Those are department records. Student records. English major students. I can't run this department with student files missing. Sign a receipt now and get them back by tomorrow morning, understand?"

Mike bent over Arlene's desk, pulled out a paper from the briefcase, flattened it on the desk, and signed it. "There you are, Linda," he said. "And you know, sweetie pie, that you are letting a little power go to your head. You need Professor McGraw to pull you down a few notches."

Arlene, bent over the screen of her computer, had been carefully avoiding the two but now moved her head a few inches toward center. "It'll take more than McGraw to do that job," she said in a low voice.

Which Linda caught the meaning of, if not the words.

"Arlene," said Linda. "Finish that committee write-up. I have to take it down to the meeting. In five minutes. And if you'd pay more attention to what you're supposed to be doing instead of making remarks to the police, we'd get along a lot better."

"Since," said Arlene with heavy sarcasm, "you're so busy running the English Department, why don't you go sit in McGraw's office and leave me in peace."

"Thanks, ladies," said Mike, shoving the folders into his briefcase, and then, turning to the door, nodded at Sarah. "See if you can get these two ladies to lighten up. We're talking homicide and assault and cooperation, and Linda wants to me leave a pint of blood for each of these folders. Now I'm off to the Drama School for more of the same, and I'll bet Vera will offer me a cup of coffee. Or something better. 'Hospitality,' that's the word you're looking for, Linda." At which he turned and slipped past Sarah, then paused. "In case you're interested in checking student fencing records, you can forget it. I've got the whole schmear. Safe in police hands."

At Mike's departure, Linda swiveled around. "Hi, Sarah, the office is closed. For today anyway."

"Did Mike walk away with the names of students who have something to do with fencing?" asked Sarah. She gave Linda a wide smile to indicate that an "old friend" was asking a harmless question of another "old friend."

Linda drew herself up in a royal way, head back so it was literally possible for a five-foot-ten woman to look down her nose at a five-foot-six other woman. "That, Sarah, I'm afraid is strictly police business. Police and English Department business. So what can I help you with? The exam schedules haven't been printed up. I've been much too busy."

At which Arlene, like a magician, rose and flipped two stapled sheets together under Linda's chin. "The committee report, Your Majesty. And you've got thirty seconds to get down there. Amos Larkin will have your scalp."

"Amos Larkin had better not say a word or I'll remind him of his life as a drunk when I covered up for him a hundred times." At which Linda snatched the two papers and swept from the office.

"Oof," said Arlene. "She bites, she growls, she snaps. And you know, we were really good friends."

Sarah grinned. "You know that old saying about 'power corrupts.'"

"I like it," said Arlene. "I'm almost praying that Dr. McGraw gets back on his feet soon and lets her have it. Puts her right back in her place, which isn't great, seeing her place is right next to my desk. For me it's a no-win situation."

"What do you hear of Dr. McGraw?" asked Sarah.

"Oh, Mike Laaka and Sergeant Nasty have been in and asking if he's been in touch with this office. Like secretly. I mean give me a break, because I hear he's really out of it. That thump on the head did a job on him. Which was okay by me except when Linda began acting like she's got a Ph.D. in management."

Sarah, although her hands were itching to grab a file drawer, decided on a little more sympathy. "It's really tough, I know. People get carried away."

"And guess what now," said Arlene, shifting into high gear. "Linda's decided that I have to wear more formal clothes, you know, dark suits with little white ruffled collars. But not too executive. That's for her. I'm to look like the worker bee. Nothing wild. Well, shit, I'm not going that route. I like comfort clothes." Arlene indicated her thick blue fleece sweater with a Patriots logo stretched out along her breast line. "If she's not careful," she added, "I'm going to switch to my jogging sweats, and it won't be a pretty sight."

Again Sarah smiled and then decided to go for it. "I have an idea," she said. "Still sort of fuzzy. But I need help. Not illegal help exactly, but the folders of some of my students who also take drama courses and were in the play."

Arlene looked at her suspiciously. "Just because I'm not Linda doesn't mean you can go waltzing off with student files."

"Not waltzing off. Looking through. Students in my class. English majors, some of them. And some of whom also happen to be Drama School students. I'm teaching Greek Theatre you know."

"Yeah, I know. Big fat excuse."

"Fifteen minutes. Right here in the office. Or across the room in the student waiting area. You can see me from there. Okay? It's in the interest . . ." Sarah paused, trying to think what sort of interest she could dig up. She began again, "It's in the interest of raising student averages and examining conflicting outside interests of kids who aren't working up to snuff. It has no connection with what Mike Laaka took away. And," Sarah went on, getting a second wind, "for writing classes. Using the past as a guide to the future. I thought if I showed students their entrance essays, it would be a sort of inspiration."

What a bunch of bull, she thought, listening to herself roll out the string of lies.

The snow job worked. Mainly because Arlene had lost interest in files, records, even the English Department (as run by Linda LaCroix), and wanted only to return to her new Janet Evanovich murder mystery, which lay hidden in her desk drawer.

"Go ahead. Go on," said Arlene. "I'm not here. I haven't heard a thing. But put the files back where you found them or Linda will make sure you never get tenure. And believe me, she could do that."

At which the telephone rang. Arlene punched a button, said, "Yeah, yes. . . . Okay. Just the copies. Hold your pants."

"Linda. Wants spring semester curriculum list. Student sign-ups for classes. Just in case McGraw can't teach. And I'll bet they're trying to find a fill-in chairman for the department."

This was interesting. The fill-in chair might be a shade kindlier and easier than the incumbent. "Who have they got in mind?"

"Don't know. I know who they don't have in mind. Mary Donelli's too new; Dr. Morgan's too old; Dr. Greenberg wouldn't touch it. Besides, he's going on sabbatical. Professor Lacey is a flake, and so it goes."

"How about Amos Larkin?"

"He can be as tough as McGraw. They'd nix him. Might go off the wagon. Disgrace the department. You know, once a drinker, always a drinker. And I heard that he makes Dean Fosdick nervous. Spouting off Swift, being sarcastic."

"I still think Amos is your best bet," said Sarah.

"Don't ask me. I'm only the servant woman around here. Now I have to bring down that list to the meeting." And Arlene bustled out with an armful of folders.

Sarah went to the file cabinet, the one just raided by Mike Laaka. She opened the file marked "Current Eng. Maj." Of course, Mike had already snaked out those students connected with Vera's production and who, under the "Sports Interest" heading, had mentioned fencing experience, a high-school fencing team, a fencing-club membership, or even fencing at a summer camp. Taking the bundle of files under her arm, she settled herself at Arlene's desk and pulled out a sheet of copy paper from under Arlene's printer. Sarah's ideas were beginning to gel, and she scribbled down the names of those student actors who had never mentioned fencing as even a fleeting interest. It was the negative approach. Leave the fencers, present and past, to George Fitts and company. She would try another angle. Something simple. Find students who do *not* mention fencing. Those who just might have had past experience with the sport but had given the whole thing up. Not interested anymore. No point in mentioning it for the school records since they have moved on. Taken up tennis, dancing, riding. Acting. Piano. Whatever. But the skill, the training, would be there, waiting. Collect the names of these non-fencers and go digging. Major research lay ahead.

One hitch, as Mike Laaka had suggested: the weapon assaults might just have been the result of strength, a good eye, and dumb luck. But three times the result of luck? Unlikely.

So back to students with no fencing records. Not an approach that the police would care for. Police don't like working from negatives. Sarah's list, when finished, was fairly small, but it did take in several of the more prominent actors in the play. Sarah jumped up from the desk, pulled open the file drawer, and began slipping the folders back in place. And as she did so, she began to wonder why the usual crowd of students wasn't pushing its way into the office. But of course, the death of a student, the injury to the department chair, these had probably had the same repellent effect as would a sign saying: Smallpox. Finished, she tucked her sheet of notes into her skirt pocket and pushed the file drawer back with a satisfying click.

And found her shoulder in the clutch of Linda LaCroix.

"Sarah Deane. What are you doing with those files? Files are off-limits. If you want some information on one of your students you have to ask. You can't just help yourself. Professor McGraw would have your scalp."

"You can have my scalp, Linda," said Sarah. "I'm just checking some statistics against my class lists."

"What did you put in your pocket?" said Linda, reaching.

"Dammit, Linda. Keep your hands to yourself. If you want to worry about your files, worry about Mike Laaka and the police. They might shred them by mistake. Forget about me. I'm harmless. Good-bye. I'm going over to the Drama School for a social visit."

Sarah's trip to the Drama School was quite successful. Vera was found in her office, a number of scripts spread out before her. Since the furor of the two attacks had settled down into a search mode, she was feeling that life could continue and she might even be able to read through and choose a script for the midwinter play. In this frame of mind she had been liberal with eye makeup, put a patch à la Marie Antoinette on a corner of her mouth, tied up her hair into a backward knot, and around her wrist hung several bracelets holding threaded coins that rattled with every move.

She welcomed Sarah by thrusting a cup at her, her middle finger decorated with the heavy ring that always reminded Sarah strongly of the sort of poison ring that the female Borgia members had used to great effect.

"Sarah. Darling. It's been too awful. Our wonderful play turning into a murder. And an assault. Blood everywhere. And poor Grover Blaine."

Sarah sat down and accepted the cup filled with a dark fluid of unknown origin. "Yes," she agreed. "It was horrible. His poor parents. Probably thinking college was as safe a place as any in the country. He wasn't crawling around city streets or dodging guns in the Middle East. Just living on a campus in rural Maine."

"And you found him," Vera reminded her. "That must have been terrible."

"With Katie Waters. It's the sort of thing you can't forget." And Sarah, as she said this, knew her view of Grover Blaine's body would be added to her memory bank, which, when least wanted, would deliver a sort of ghastly slide show of images.

"And then," said Vera, "there's Danton McGraw. He's been at my throat the whole fall semester. But he was so damn useful. Worked on the fencing scenes and seemed really concerned about putting all the moves together."

"So concerned that he took over Mercutio's part?"

"That's the mystery," said Vera. "All I can think of is that Grover's swordplay was inadequate, and Todd was too shaky to go on, so at the last minute Danton decided to fix things. By taking the part himself. He's an egoist plus a kind of perfectionist,"

"But he had to find a costume," said Sarah.

"Oh, that was easy. I had extra doublets, tunics, capes, stockings, and hats all over the backstage for the street crowd scenes.

He was the same height as both Grover and Todd. And with a mask and cap, well, who could tell?"

Sarah nodded agreement and then put in her request. "A few folders. Checking out past interests. Some of your drama students. And mine, too. A project I'm working on."

But she didn't have to go on. Vera waved at a battered wooden file cabinet in the corner of the office. "Help yourself. I won't even ask if this is legit. Almost hope it isn't. I keep remembering the old days when Alex found a body in an ice sculpture and someone drinking cyanide. And you getting a grip on the library heist and the whole bit."

"You mean the *good* old days?" asked Sarah.

"Other things, too. I wasn't very adventurous that winter. I hadn't had the job all that long. We did *Mikado*. You were Pitti-Sing. Or was it Peep-Bo?"

"Pitti-Sing, and it seems a hundred years ago." Sarah took a gulp of her drink, shuddered, the tea had something strangely pungent mixed in, and rose from her chair and attacked the files. Vera went back to her scripts and began making sketches on long white strips of paper. And except for an occasional opening door, the sound of scuffling feet somewhere in the building, the two women went about their business uninterrupted.

Sarah finished her notes, only seven students who qualified by being in the Halloween production and *not* ever having mentioned a past or present interest in fencing. She stood up, ready to go home, feed the orange kitten, and take her dog, Patsy, for a walk. Forget for at least one whole hour her probe into the lives of non-fencers.

But Vera, who had become restless during the end of Sarah's search, walking about, her hands in motion, her bracelets jangling, now stopped in front of her.

"Something I haven't told anybody about. Not even George Fitts. Or the disciplinary committee. It's a group of our women students. And a few concerned men. I think Grover Blaine may have inspired the thing. Not exactly a vigilante group, but a group to prevent unwelcome male intrusions into their lives."

"What a delicate way of putting it. You're describing male

groping and pawing, spiking drinks, making obscene suggestions. Acting as if rape was around the corner for some lucky girl."

"So far no rape. But some frightened undergraduates, some of them really babies."

"I know about Weeza and the sting operation she set up for Grover. And Derek, who apparently played Grover's watchdog. But Weeza said she more or less acted on her own. The group— she didn't tell me their name—wasn't actively involved. But was supportive."

"I wondered about Weeza, because she's too street-smart to let herself get cornered by Grover Blaine, of all people. With his rep."

"She said she was doing a community service. By the way, do you know the name of this group?"

"I haven't a clue. And I don't think I want to know. But for what it's worth, Terri Colman, Kay Biddle, Weeza Scotini are the top brass, plus about ten to fourteen other women. Then there's Malcolm Wheelock—Tybalt—who's a sort of advisor. And Griffin Starr—Benvolio. They're accepted because they're decent guys and generally admired by everyone. Not like Todd Mancuso, who until he got clipped onstage and then beaten to a pulp was a royal pain. Now that he's been tamed I have great hope for the boy. In fact, I heard he'd joined the group."

Sarah thanked Vera and departed, her mind now stuffed with this additional information about the Drama School's watchdog group. Was it action oriented? Did it make plans? Perhaps another talk with Weeza Scotini. Of course, in the light of events, the idea of a vengeful undercover group with fencing—or unacknowledged fencing—members was pretty scary. In fact, Sarah told herself, as she pushed herself out into the November wind, it not only was scary but also sounded like something to be looked into. Later.

Danton McGraw, having graduated from an ICU, was now being held on a skilled nursing unit—known in the vernacular as "Skew"—in the Mary Starbox Memorial Hospital, Room 56. Although he was weak and still receiving the last of units of whole blood, the essential McGraw personality remained intact.

This in the view of Weeza Scotini was unfortunate. Weeza in her triple role as Bowmouth student, part-time nurse's aide, and member of the underground protection corps of the Drama School regarded Professor McGraw with something like fear and loathing. In fact, as she trotted back and forth answering demands—the shade up six inches, the water pitcher filled, a new pillowcase, another cotton blanket—she had to draw on all her theatre training to smile agreeably, nod politely, and fetch and carry with speed and finesse.

Danton McGraw, although physically weak, with his hematocrit and hemoglobin at low levels, was still in gear mentally. Except, of course, for the memory lapse for his time onstage as Mercutio and his offstage encounter with a heavy object hitting his head. These gaps aside, Danton's brain was busy, and his hospitalization allowed a great deal of time to think. And to plan. If ever there was proof that the Drama School was lost to any sense of discipline and order, look at this homicide, plus the assault on himself. Here indeed was proof positive that the place was ripe for a takeover. It was time, to use naval parlance, since McGraw was a naval person, to circle the destroyers, put up the smoke screen, man the depth charges, and stand ready with a coordinated salvo. However, the English Department still needed the backing of its flagship, the College of Arts and Sciences. So it was time to mend any fences broken by harsh words he may have said about Derek Mosely to his mother, Dean Alena Fosdick.

And there was another weapon in McGraw's arsenal. In addition to murder and assault, many members of communities surrounding the college, the towns of Bowmouth, Union, Appleton, and Hope, seemed to have come belatedly alive to the fact that the production of *Romiette and Julio* was indeed a dangerous "gender-bending" production and as such should be condemned. And any support for the much-advertised fund-raising program for the college to be held up, pending changes in the Drama School's productions.

It was all made to order. McGraw, who at first thought that the "moral" aspect of the Vera's play would escape community notice in the excitement of Halloween and a lively musical finale, felt the thrill of vindication. He himself had no scruples one way or the other about gender-mixing theatre. But if he saw a tool lying close to hand for his project—make that a wrecking project—he was the man to use it.

Lying back on his two pillows, one arm extended to receive the contents of a unit of B positive blood together with an infusion of lactate ringers, Danton, his scalp covered by a bandage set at a rakish angle, used his other hand to scan the local newspaper, the six-page *Bowmouth Mirror*. Flipping past sports news and the rising price of gasoline, he settled happily on the announcement that the Reverend Nicholas Copeland of Fryeburg's Church of the Troubled Waters was to visit a community church on the coming Sunday in Bowmouth. The subject of his sermon was listed as "Theatre of the Devil." It sounded promising.

In this happy frame of mind Professor McGraw was unpleasantly interrupted by the appearance late on Thursday of Dr. Alexander McKenzie followed immediately by Sergeant George Fitts, complete with clipboard.

"Hi there," said Alex, ignoring the scowl on his patient's face. *His* patient since McGraw's primary care physician was still elsewhere—Alex was beginning to suspect not at a conference but on a golf course.

"Everything looks pretty good," said Alex. "Your hematocrit is creeping up. Slow but sure. We'll have you in for another scan to check your head injury, but right now I thought it was okay for Sergeant Fitts to ask a couple of questions."

"I do not, repeat: do not, remember what went on after I got onstage as Mercutio," said Danton firmly. "I sent word that I don't. I've heard more than I want to know about memory loss after a head injury."

George bent his head in brief acknowledgment, pulled up a straight chair, and leaned slightly over Danton McGraw's bed. "We'll accept that, Dr. McGraw," he said. "Now I'd like a before-and-after description of what you actually do remember."

Danton braced himself for a greater effort, fixed his eye on the half-filled plastic bag of blood dripping down its tube, and told George to speak up.

"When," said George, raising his voice, "did you decide to take over the part of Mercutio? I understand that Grover Blaine was the chosen understudy."

"Grover Blaine," said Danton, "was going to ruin the scene. I don't like to complain about the dead, but Grover got worse with each rehearsal. He could speak, he could be heard, but used no inflection. His movements were choppy. And slow. He backed instead of advancing. He was almost dangerous. I'd been hoping that Todd would be able to go on, but when I saw there was no chance of that, I moved in."

George nodded at Alex. Sometimes George, if he had a trusted person present at an interrogation, liked to pass the ball. The sergeant was only too aware that his own personality had the effect of a visiting refrigerator.

So Alex stepped in. "What did Grover say about you taking over?"

"It happened pretty fast. The Mercutio scene was coming up. He mumbled, said he didn't want to give up the part, but I said this was the way it was going to be. I told him his fencing was clumsy. I was afraid someone was going to be hurt. That's the truth. In the actual performance all those foils had their protective tips off. Vera Pruczak's orders. Damn foolish ones, too, I thought. But you know Vera."

Alex glanced at George. He was to continue. "Okay, so Grover stepped aside. Did you tell him to keep quiet about the switch?"

Danton nodded vigorously. "Absolutely. There was no reason for anyone to know. I knew the lines, the scene was short, the actors wore masks, and Grover and I are about the same height. I told him everyone would think he played the part. He was to take the curtain call along with all the other actors. And I'm told that he did that."

George frowned, made a note, and took over. "So that I have this straight. We know you don't remember your exit as Mercutio. Any idea how long before you came to? Were aware that you'd been hurt? Found yourself in pain, bleeding, lying covered up backstage?"

"I've told you. I don't remember details. Just remember feeling like absolute hell, a pain around my throat. I couldn't call out, couldn't do anything. Felt like I was dying."

"You could have been," Alex put in, "if one of your English Department people hadn't found you and put a pressure bandage on your wound and called for help."

McGraw opened his eyes wider. "I didn't know that," he said. "Who was it?"

"Actually," said Alex, "it was my wife, Sarah Deane. After the cast party was over she went looking for something she'd left backstage."

McGraw closed his eyes. "Oh yes, I do know her," he said. Then with a grim smile, he added, "Always where she shouldn't be."

"I know what you mean," said Alex.

"Thank her very much for me," said Danton. "But I'm no use to the police. I didn't start coming to until after I'd gotten to the hospital."

"One more thing," said George. "Do you have a sense that someone was out to get you personally? For any reason?"

McGraw frowned. "I've got a few people who would like to deep-six me, but I don't think they were students who wanted to be in the Mercutio scene for the sole purpose of slitting my throat."

"Not slit," said George, the perfectionist. "Puncture. It was an incised wound."

"The thing is perfectly simple," said Danton, now growing weary of the questions. He needed all the rest he could get. Every minute wasted in non-recovery activities, like this interrogation, meant that the English Department would be falling further into chaos.

"Simple?" said George.

"Obviously a case of mistaken identity," said Danton. "Someone out to get Grover Blaine. For whatever reason. I can think of several. But that's your job. And now I have to rest." He looked over at Alex, who nodded.

Danton closed his eyes, but leaving at the same time a down-turned mouth to indicate displeasure at the visit.

George and Alex left together, George to return to the police trailer. "I'm going to collect the names of people who had it in for Grover Blaine," he said.

"I think," said Alex, "they are legion. Mostly female."

"The harassment business?"

"Among others."

Alex turned toward the hospital parking lot. Time to move into a homegoing frame of mind. Not murder, but Sarah, supper, an orange kitten, and a large Irish wolfhound awaited.

With this domestic picture in his head, Alex swung his old Jeep out into the main college driveway and came within an inch of mowing down a figure going by him on a motorcycle hell-bent for leather.

The bike shot down the campus road, screamed out onto the highway, and, with the rider bent double leaning over his handlebars, turned at a sharp angle onto the main road, accelerated, swung dangerously around the corner of Saw Mill Road, and roared up the hill.

Alex usually liked to drive home at a leisurely pace, part of the decompression needed for the return from the hospital to domestic life. But now he pushed his foot hard on the accelerator. Ahead was an accident waiting to happen. That damn fool had no helmet and was driving literally fit to kill. Kill himself and probably somebody else in the bargain.

But then as the motorcycle reached the top of the first incline, the rider suddenly jerked the machine to the left, shot across the road, and sped at full speed up a small dirt road, turned again slightly, and aimed directly at a tall spruce tree.

Alex jammed on his brakes, stopped, and jumped out of the car. But there was nothing he could do but watch in horror. A suicide in action.

The route to the tree was by the edge of a field, rough with fallen leaves, brush, and weeds. The bike, like a missile, kept its straight course, the rider now lying almost flat on the saddle. Then at the last minute, the rider jerked himself upright and threw up his head as if to meet the trunk of the tree, literally, head-on.

204

And as if in response for this sudden movement, the wheel of the bike twisted sideways, became for a moment airborne, and then banged and bounced into the underbrush.

And the rider like a figure leaving a trapeze flew off the bike and disappeared into a dark space on the edge of the field.

14

AS the rider spun off the motorcycle, Alex started running. Across the road, toward the spruce tree the motorcycle had missed, and then to the fallen bike, which now lay under a tangle of sumac and alder. From there he tried to see down into the place the rider not only had landed but also had disappeared into something like a black hole. Alex climbed over the fallen bike, worked his way around the brush, and saw that the ground sloped sharply down into a marshy pond. A pond whose muddy and roiled surface showed that something had disturbed it, a something that was partly visible in the form of an arm and the back of a head.

Alex made it to the pond in three jumps, waded into the waist-deep muck, and got a grip on the arm. Pulled and hauled a dripping and weed-fouled person to the edge of the water. Alive and struggling for breath. Spitting water and dirt.

Laid out prone on a length of grass, the young man turned and struggled to sit up, and Alex, still trying to assess his condition, pushed him gently back to the ground. A quick look suggested no injuries, no obvious wounds, no evidence of broken legs or arms. No twisted jaws, missing teeth, or any sign of a head injury. His face showed only streaks of mud. A struggle for breath appeared to be the most obvious symptom of distress, and this seemed to be simply the result of having the wind knocked out of him when he fell smack into the pond. Alex felt his pulse, found it fast but not frightening. Pulled his stethoscope out of his jacket pocket and again was relieved. Nothing out of the way.

And after several minutes when the man again tried to sit up Alex supported him into a semisitting position.

"Hello, Derek," said Alex, who from his first view of the soaked and tangled white-blond hair and the sharp-featured face, filthy though it was, had recognized the son of Dean Alena Fosdick, a student he had seen during rehearsals of the Halloween play.

For a moment Derek stared at him, eyes opening, and then with a gulp of despair he threw himself facedown on the ground and began sobbing. And sobbing. And, at intervals, crying, "Jesus Christ, oh Jesus Christ. Oh shit, shit, shit."

Alex, his hand on the young man's shoulder, waited for the storm to subside.

Which it did finally, leaving Derek looking like something washed ashore by a surging flood.

"I think," said Alex, "that first I'm going to help you into my car and take you over to the ER. That was quite a scene just now. Then if everything checks out okay, I'll drive you home to your mother's house. I think spending the night in your dorm wouldn't be a good idea."

But the word "mother" sent Derek into a spasm. He shook his head, began to cry again, and then said in a thick voice, "If you do, I'll really kill myself. I loused this one up, but I'll do something else next time. And I won't go to the ER. I'm of age and I'm okay."

Alex bit his lip. This was clearly a case for psychiatric intervention. But some sort of compromise seemed necessary. "Okay, we won't go to your mother's, but I'll have to let her know where you are—when we decide where that's going to be. But if I don't insist on your mother—who is really the proper person—then you're going to go to the ER with me. I'll stay with you while you're examined. And—"

"I know, you're going to find one of those shrinks who's going to put on an act of understanding and I won't talk to him."

"Let's start with the ER," said Alex, "and go from there. Don't worry about your Yamaha. We can have that picked up later."

Another choked sob and a gulp. "It isn't even mine. It's Grover's. He let me ride it sometimes, so I had a key."

"To the car," said Alex firmly. He took hold of Derek's hand and hoisted him to his feet.

The examination of Derek Mosely in an ER, blessedly uncrowded for once, included not only a thorough going-over of the patient but also, for Alex, a private talk with a staff psychiatrist. This all took up the better part of two hours during which Alex called Sarah, explained what was going on, and to his surprise found her urging him to bring Derek to their farmhouse.

"For supper at least. I know how he feels about his mother. I saw him today, just for a minute. But I hadn't any idea he was that far over the edge. I feel guilty. I should have sensed something. Maybe we can think of something to do about him."

This agreed, Alex went back, found the psychiatrist, one Jonas Jefferson, extracted a promise from Derek to see the man in the morning, the promise based on the fact that Derek would not be pushed to go to his mother. Instead he would be driven to Alex's house for dinner; Alex would call Derek's mother. Then they would see. One step at a time.

After a shower and the presentation of a jacket from the lost-and-found and a set of clean hospital scrubs—his own clothes being sodden and stained with marsh mud—Derek was escorted by Alex to the parking lot and settled into the passenger seat. Then, as Alex headed the Jeep off toward Saw Mill Road, he glanced at the bleak-faced student sitting next to him and quietly locked the passenger car door.

The success of this venture in rehabilitation of a student devastated by the death of his best and possibly his only friend did not depend on the kindness and care of Alex. Nor on the sympathy of Sarah, who had added hot soup and ice cream to the evening menu. It depended first on the presence of Irish wolfhound Patsy. This knowing animal, always ready for more attention, moved in on the stranger, presented his shaggy head for a pat, and then allowed his paw to be held, his neck to be circled. After dinner, Alex watching from the porch window, Patsy allowed Derek to take him for a short walk by leash around the perimeter of the house. After this excursion, adding to these canine therapeutic efforts, were the antics, loud purring, and lap sitting by the new orange kitten, Piggy.

"You see," said Sarah to Alex as he brought the tray of dishes to the kitchen. "Animals do it every time. I think you could cut in half the number of psychiatrists in the country and substitute dogs and cats. And," she added, thinking of her beloved equestrian aunt, Julia Clancy, "a number of horses."

"In some cases," said Alex, remembering his animal-centered childhood, including an iguana, a guinea pig, a rabbit, a pet crow, a garter snake, "even a python would do."

"I draw the line at pythons," said Sarah. "But now what? Aren't you going to call Derek's mother about all this?"

"As soon as I use the word 'mother' he goes ballistic. But yes, I'm going to call her. Try and keep the peace. Derek has pointed out he's twenty-one, so no one can force him to go home. Anyway, I hope Mom will accept the fact that he's spending the night here."

"With Patsy next to him on the bed?"

"And Piggy on the pillow. Okay, you go in, keep an eye on him, see if he'd like to stay. Tell him I'm checking in with his mother. Then we'll take it from there."

It was arranged in minutes. Dean Alena Fosdick seemed glad to have the problem of Derek with all his unhappy disciplinary baggage moved to another arena. Away from her, yes, but to a place that, since it featured one of Derek's teachers and his physician pro tem, could cause no censure, no remarks about unfeeling parents. Alena ended the conversation saying she was sure it was all for the best.

"The best for her," said Alex with irritation as he put down the phone.

"Probably the best for Derek," said Sarah. "I'm trying very hard to see it from her point of view. Dean of Arts and Sciences with a son who is in major trouble. Nasty, messy trouble. A kid who is one major pain in the neck. Pal with that big bully Grover the Groper Blaine. And Derek tarred with the same brush. Mr. Aider and Abettor."

Alex shrugged. "Nothing we can do about all that. For the near future I can only see Derek standing in a big pile of shit. And that doesn't even touch this suicide business."

Sarah returned to Derek, who was lying on the floor next to Patsy, one arm over the dog's neck. He'd turned the television on and was watching a rerun of *The Simpsons*. A scene of peace—even if temporary. Twenty minutes later Derek—and Patsy and Piggy—had been stowed in the extra bedroom. Sarah herself had had a hot bath, soothed by Vitabath foam, and settled down in bed with a copy of *Barchester Towers*. The campaign against Mrs. and Bishop Proudie was just what Sarah needed after a very difficult day.

In bed Alex quizzed her about that day: "You've had some scheme up your sleeve. I can tell by your eyes. Not quite meeting mine. I've lived too long with a sneaky sleuth. You were put on earth to drive George Fitts crazy. Not to mention me."

"I haven't put a single finger on anything the police are doing. Mike says he's looking into fencers at Bowmouth. Ones in Vera's play, who mentioned fencing on their college applications, you know, where they list sports they have taken. Students who aren't fencing now but did it before college. Summer camps, high school."

"So what are you dabbling in?"

"Not dabbling," said Sarah. She pulled a pillow under her neck, turned, and faced Alex, her expression one of justified indignation. "I am simply interested in students who *don't* fence. Never mentioned fencing as part of their sports record."

"You're accentuating the negative."

"Right."

"And how does that work?" Alex turned around and put his face within six inches of Sarah's. "And have you stolen files from the English Department when Linda's back was turned?"

Sarah used an effective elbow. "Get away from me. Who asked you to play district attorney? You're supposed to be a compassion-

210

ate physician, not the Grand Inquisitor. I didn't remove any files. Just noted a few names. The non-fencers."

"Of whom one person whose past fencing experience of a gold medal won in the Junior Olympics has never come to light."

"Be real."

"This person," Alex said, ignoring the interruption, "has been planning a murder by épée. Has always hated Danton McGraw and/or Grover Blaine, applied to Bowmouth for purposes of revenge, keeping any past fencing expertise a secret."

"So comes to Bowmouth College, becomes a senior, but harbors this hate for three years, and then pow! That's what you're saying?"

"Something like that," admitted Alex. "But tell the truth. You, my love, like hitting from a different angle. En garde. Professor Deane is armed and her foil is extended. Or make that an épée. So you're looking for a student who kept his fencing career quiet?"

"More or less. I like the idea of someone who fenced before college, got bored with the whole scene, gave it up. Never mind long-range planning. Say an opportunity came to get rid of some enemy, Grover, and, as you say, and/or McGraw, well, go for it. The play, the perfect setting, everyone in masks, crowd scenes, costumes available. Fencing is probably like riding a bike. You may not be at the top of your game, but you can still wield a mean weapon."

"An épée which this person has concealed under his or her bed in the dorm."

"Some seniors aren't in dorms. They share apartments. The épée could be in a private bedroom. In the closet."

"A closet fencer?"

"Not funny. The weapon could be any old damn place. The trunk of a car, stuck in a golf bag. The trouble is I've spent a long time searching club records, match records. Summer camp records—although most camps are closed now, but some of the staff opened their files."

"How on God's green earth did you get anyone in an organization to open their files? No, don't tell me. You said you were a member of the Maine State Police working on a murder investigation."

"I didn't say Maine State Police. Nor the sheriff's department. I did use the word 'investigate' in a general sense. Anyway, I struck out. Which ought to make you happy."

"I never want you to strike out, but I wish you'd stick to baseball or something wholesome. Okay, tell me. What did you find out?"

"I went to headquarters. The U.S. Fencing Association. All fairly recent tournaments and the results. Clubs, schools. Different age groups, Junior, Cadet, and so forth. Tournament standings. I figured that this mystery person was good enough to get two people in the jugular. . . ."

"Nicked Danton in the jugular, speared Grover in the carotid."

"Just listen. This person might have been good enough to have won or at least placed in a tournament. It took forever. Our students, especially the drama ones, use nicknames. Probably have more zip. There's Terri Colman, real name Theresa Mary, then Kay Biddle, name Kathleen-Ann Biddle, and Weeza Scotini is Louisa. Then two Maddies who are Madison and a Joey who's a Jonathan. It goes on and on."

"And you drew a blank?"

"All over this country there are about two hundred female fencers named Kathleen, Katherine, or Katie. And Kay. Scads of Theresa Marys, and more Madisons than I could count. But none with the right last name. I'll go through the list again tomorrow, because I've probably missed a few thousand clubs and schools, but I'm a little discouraged."

Alex punched his pillow, pushed it over next to Sarah's, and reached for her. "I want a lovely lady who is a little discouraged. But is willing to sleep on the whole thing. And here's something a little positive for you to think about. We have in our possession one male student who was trying to smash his head into a tree and who failed, but not because he decided against it. Motorcycle malfunction. And now he seems somewhat stable. And some of your sympathy and good soup may have done the trick."

"I can't even take credit for that. Patsy and the kitten Piggy did the work."

"But in both cases you are the one who supplied those two

212

beasts. Now snuggle up and tell me what office you plan to steal from tomorrow."

On the morning of Friday, November 2, Alena Fosdick, dean of Arts and Sciences at Bowmouth, was in what has been called a state. This a compound of panic, fear, anger, nervous twitch, and a strong sense that nothing was her fault and so why was everything so screwed up in her life?

She had arrived at her office, even more carefully, beautifully, put together than usual, attired in Oxford gray trousers and a long jacket with a white neck tab vaguely suggesting someone in holy orders. Her face job was a work of great care, everything defined that needed definition, everything soft and blushed in order to radiate health and, if not exactly youth, a sense that youth was not too far back in her past. She greeted her secretary, a cheerful woman known as Muffin, with calm dignity and then retreated to her office, firmly closed and locked the door. The last thing she needed was a sympathetic approach by Muffin, who had in the past given signs that mothering was a top priority. Tiptoeing across the carpet, Alena pulled out her padded office chair (fabric by Martha Stewart) and put her head down on her desk. She didn't cry; she had too much self-control to ruin her makeup. But she couldn't start acting the administrator, the dean, when what she wanted was to be shipped somewhere else, somewhere like a sunny beach in the Caribbean, wearing a thong and being lovingly tended by some caring male of the godlike variety.

Since this scenario seemed a remote possibility, she finally raised her head and began to consider strategies for returning to a place of domestic and professional security. To somehow extricate her son, Derek, from the mess in which he had landed himself—and by association his mother. Her son known to be the best friend of murdered Grover Blaine, the loathsome student whose unsavory reputation had recently spread not only throughout the College of Arts and Sciences but also perhaps through the whole blessed college. Of course, Derek had always just stood around and let Grover do what he felt like doing. And what he felt like doing made Alena feel like throwing up. Derek, the follower, Alena was sure, hadn't actually *done* anything to any female student. Or beaten up anybody. He just wasn't constituted to take the lead in anything aggressive. But who could prove that? The disciplinary committee action, possibly coupled with a police charge, would start up again. Derek was, it was widely rumored, a student who had assisted, if not actively participated, in a number of unsavory adventures, now possibly including assault in a food store and murder. And with no Grover Blaine to throw the book at, there was only one defendant left. Her son, Derek.

Okay, she had to find a sympathetic, but not too costly, lawyer to represent the boy so that she wouldn't end up being known as the dean who had a kid in jail. On recent events, the mills of the gods were already beginning to grind. Repeated interrogations of students, faculty, and staff, the taking of forensic evidence, in addition to that damn harassment charge, still to be decided, and the lord knew what else. And that call last night from Dr. Alex McKenzie had really shaken her. So much so that she had retreated into an angry defensive posture of defending her job and abandoning Derek to a physician she didn't really know and to his wife, this Professor Deane, one of her son's least important English teachers. Alex had explained that Derek had not wanted to go home and that it was better perhaps that he didn't. Alex hadn't gone into details, except to say that Derek was quite upset but was settling down and he would check with her sometime in the morning. Well, so much for domestic worries.

Professional worries were another matter. But the domestic ones now impinged on the professional. On her job. And regarding that job she now had to consider one Professor Danton McGraw, currently serving a term in the Mary Starbox Hospital Skilled Care Unit. She regretted the hot words that had passed between them. Danton exploding over two English majors—her son and his buddy Grover bringing a dirty cloud down on the English Department by playing sex games with that drama school woman, Weeza What's-her-name, who for all anyone knew might be a sex predator herself. Of course McGraw's rage was partly directed at the out-of-control Drama School, but he had hinted that word was around that Derek and Grover were under suspicion for beating up Drama School student Todd Mancuso at the Fine Food Mart. "Talk about a total foul-up." Alena, hissing to herself, almost said "fuckup" but caught herself. Dignity at all costs—costs to Alena spelled J-O-B.

A plan. She needed a plan. She couldn't just sit here and suffer and let Muffin start letting in the usual complainers for all over the college. That new French teacher, Madame Carpentier, was already creating tornadoes in the Language Department, and Alena was not up to tornadoes. Okay, go for it. She needed an ally. And the only one she could think of was this same Danton McGraw. They had hit it off so well a few days ago. Both agreeing about the ultimate fate of the Drama School. What was needed now was for her to come as a colleague bearing an olive branch. McGraw, who had come to academe from the U.S. Navy, would be gratified by apology and submission. She could play that game.

Alena punched in her secretary's phone extension and asked Muffin to call the hospital and find out if Dr. McGraw was seeing visitors and, if so, to say it was quite urgent that Alena see him for a few minutes. It concerned the Drama School. His ideas were wanted. Ask if he needed anything, books, magazines. Or something from the English office. Files, schedules, notebooks.

The answer came from a nurse. Yes, Dr. McGraw would see Dean Fosdick. For a very short time only. He did not need any supplies, books or magazines. "He suggests you come around eleven thirty, just before the lunch trays turn up."

This response didn't suggest enthusiasm, even gave a hint that Alena was going to be considered as a sort of premeal snack. Or one of his medications. But once she was in the door, a wedge would have been inserted, and then later, tomorrow perhaps, it could be driven in deeper. Alena informed Muffin that she would be out of the office after eleven thirty and then settled at her desk to plan her attack.

First, express sympathy for his injury and horror at the death of Grover Blaine. Second, hit on the obvious role that the Drama School had played in these events. Third, mention the community revulsion at the gender-mixing aspect of the play. This, up until that morning, Alena Fosdick had not been in the least sure of. In fact, the laughter and applause that the production had provoked seemed to have argued against any community objection. But the local *Courier-Gazette* had reported that a well-known clergyman, who happened to have seen Vera's play, would be coming all the way from Fryeburg on Sunday to preach on the recent theatre production. This, Alena told herself, was indeed hopeful.

Last, Alena would get to the matter at the heart of her visit: her troublesome—no, make that "disturbed"; it sounded more humane—son, Derek. "Think, Dr. McGraw," she would say. "Didn't some of the odium of the harassment charges of two *English majors* properly belong to the English Department?" She would remind Danton of the promise to find a mentor for Derek—and the late unlamented Grover Blaine. Obviously this idea had not had time to be put into action, but it gave her a chance to put Danton on the defensive. The bottom line was that Danton must exert his influence and put Derek back in good standing so that his misdeeds, if they were really such, would be seen with forgiving eyes.

Thus Alena made her way to the hospital, to the Skilled Care Unit, received a nod at the nurses' station, and arrived at Room 56, which was now hung with two signs. One said: Absolutely No Visitors. The other identified the room's occupant as Dr. Danton McGraw, his physicians as Dr. Eugene Santaro (he now absent somewhere) and Dr. Alexander McKenzie.

Alena paused, considering her entrance; it would have been so much easier if she had carried flowers, books, magazines. Something distracting, giving her arrival a sense of purpose. But one thing in her favor: McGraw would be lying in bed wearing one of those unbecoming cotton wrinkled hospital gowns with little ties behind and perhaps an equally wrinkled, and non-matching robe over the gown. No one in those costumes could ever look as if they belonged to the world of management. Also, he would undoubtedly be encumbered with an arm stuck with needles and adhesive tape and tied to plastic bags on poles dripping something into him. Best of all, she would be looking down on the man. She would be in charge of the interview.

Alena braced herself, knocked on the door, and stuck her head around the edge. In front staring at her an empty bed. She stopped cold. Where was he? Dead? The way things had been going lately, this seemed perfectly possible.

A voice from the side of the room. Next to the window. Sitting upright in a high-backed vinyl chair. Dark hair neatly combed, clean shaven, face not pale, as it should have been with all that blood missing. Moreover, he wore not a ratty old hospital gown but a dark blue number with U.S. Naval Academy writ large on the pocket. It was almost a uniform.

"Come in, Alena. I won't bite. You have something on your mind?"

Alena, her vision of being in a position of strength fading fast, walked into the room, hesitated, looked for a chair of equal height, and, not finding such an object, decided at all costs to stay standing. She could still loom. And he couldn't stand up easily. It would be an awkward business with that IV apparatus attached to his left arm.

"For God's sake, Alena, sit down," said Danton. He waved his free hand toward what was the flat top of a long heat register that ran under the room's window. And then when the dean took a step forward, he shook his head. "I can't stand people who hang over you like some sort of messenger of doom. Sit down. Please."

And Alena Fosdick, moving a magazine and a copy of the *Courier-Gazette* aside, sat down. And found her head some ten inches lower than that of the English Department's chair.

"We don't have much time," said Danton. "Lunch trays and then medications. Lab work. The usual routine. I suppose you want me to do something about your son, Derek. Who if I may say so—and you probably know all too well—is up to his ears in a lot of legal crud . . ."

Alena, feeling herself reduced to half her normal size, nodded unhappily. "I did want to talk about him. You know that Derek's friend Grover—oh, it's so terrible about Grover. I mean it's terrible about you, too. But Grover. Murdered, they think, and you almost . . ." Alena stumbled on until Danton lifted a cautionary finger.

"Slow down, Alena. I can see you're upset. With Grover gone, Derek is of great interest. I'm very sorry about it, but we can't interfere with the police, can we?"

Alena rallied briefly. "You could point out that Derek was just a follower. To the police, I mean. That Grover Blaine was a rotten egg who just pushed Derek around. And maybe you can talk to the disciplinary committee."

Here Alena took a deep breath and then played her only trump card: "You know, don't you, that I do want to work with you on the Drama School matter. Doing something about Vera Pruczak."

Danton nodded in a distant way and then his gaze had shifted from her to his bag of dark red fluid. He looked as if he was counting the drips.

"Are you getting a lot of blood?" she asked. "I mean they do it in units, don't they? So you must be feeling better." Really, she thought, I can't even put a sentence together.

Danton turned his eyes back to his visitor. "Blood? Oh yes, I lost quite a bit. After all, with a foil stuck into your jugular you're bound to feel the effects."

"A foil?" squeaked Alena. "You mean one of those fencing swords?"

"I haven't been told in so many words that it was a foil, but that was the available weapon. But if I'd been doing it myself I would have chosen an épée. But to go back, you want me to stand up for Derek to the disciplinary committee?"

Alena hesitated. "Well, perhaps say he's been a good student, an English major with nothing on his record."

"'Nothing' about describes it. But I'll say he *is* an English major. And unless they press me I won't say his work is uneven and his grades are in the basement. But I can't present him as an example of student rectitude. He spent too much time fooling around in classes with his pal, Grover, something other teachers have mentioned."

Alena, digesting these sad truths, swallowed hard. But she wasn't about to give up. "Can't you saying anything helpful?"

McGraw seemed to consider this, looked up again at the slow-dripping blood, and then returned to Alena. If the Drama School was to be made an appendage of the English Department he would indeed need her help. A small gesture was needed.

"I can say," he began, "that Derek appeared to be completely under the thumb of Grover Blaine. That he was a follower who didn't initiate any moves himself. That in the sexual harassment charges filed by Weeza Scotini he was described as an onlooker. Doing sentry duty."

"And," interrupted Alena, "I've heard from Derek and the police that he's more or less accounted for during the period when Grover was killed. He claims he stayed at the cast party the whole time. That, of course, will be checked."

"I wouldn't have considered him as a possible murderer of Grover. Unless there had been a sort of lovers' quarrel between them."

"Lover!" exclaimed Alena. "Not a lover. I mean those boys were just friends."

"That's probably what many parents say," observed Danton. "Don't be upset. I don't know a thing about their relationship beyond knowing they were always together."

Alena shook her head. "Not lovers. Dead wrong. Absolutely dead wrong. Because Grover and Derek shared everything it doesn't mean they were lovers. They talked a lot about spending time hunting down girls. For dates, parties. I think it was a sort of spiritual thing for Derek. Derek almost worshiped Grover. And I admit that Grover gave me the creeps."

Danton looked at his watch. "Lunch is coming. I heard the food cart rattle. Look, I'm not going to suggest to anyone that Grover and Derek were lovers. That's only a guess, and it's none of my business. But I will testify that Derek is a student in good standing—never mind his grade average—in the English Department. Frankly, my suspicions regarding Grover's killer point toward of one of those hellcat females in the Drama School. Thanks for coming, Alena. When I get out of here we'll talk about our special project. By that time the police should have someone behind bars."

With which Alena Fosdick had to be content. She could only hope that Danton's promise regarding Derek meant something. Otherwise Derek might be joining the mystery murderer behind bars. As for her son being a lover of Grover Blaine, Alena shuddered. She didn't, thinking it all over a little more calmly, so much mind the idea of Derek's being gay; in that area she considered herself enlightened, and she had grown up close to two wonderful gay cousins. But what stuck in her throat was the terrible fact that his chosen partner was that odious slime Grover.

15

SARAH and Alex had eaten a hasty breakfast with guest Derek Mosely, whose entire conversation seemed directed at or concerned with the two resident animals. Then the machinery of the day had begun to grind: Alex would escort Derek to his appointment with the psychiatrist, Dr. Jonas Jefferson. After this session Alex would meet with both doctor and patient in order to see what the next step would be in the "rescue" effort. Sarah, for her part, got peacefully through her first two classes by dint of sending each class in a body to the library to get a grip on reference hunting. This space in her schedule allowed her to spend some serious time thinking about the future of Derek Mosely, a student who had always been, with his friend, Grover, at the bottom of her list of worthy students. Now, at twelve thirty, she met Alex for lunch at the former Spring Chicken Diner—renamed the Spring Chicken Café. The owners of this nearby eatery had tried hard to erase the memory of past names (Spruce Tree Diner, Maine Meal Diner) by giving an upscale ending to their establishment.

She found Alex settled in a booth studying a menu shaped like a large egg. From its three-page size it seemed to be presenting chicken in every form known to science.

"Where's Derek?" she said. "I hope—"

"All is well. At least for now. I think the session with Jonas went pretty well. Derek said they talked about dogs. And cats."

"And that did it?"

"Probably some other issues were aired. Better yet, Derek is willing to go back for a session tomorrow and is going to his classes today. Soccer practice this afternoon. I told him I'd rescue Grover Blaine's motorcycle and leave it to be repaired. And if he decided not to go back to his mother or to his dorm, he could come to us again. I called Alena Fosdick, but she was out of her office. But all in all, Derek seems much more together."

Sarah grimaced. "He's going to need to be together when he faces what's coming the next few weeks."

Alex nodded, and they both picked up their menus and began to sort through the chicken offerings, Sarah settling for Chicken Laredo and Alex for something called Tufted Chicken Legs, which he admitted was a gamble.

Despite their intention to have a sensible ten-minute adult conversation not centered on recent events, after four minutes featuring the state of Maine, the economy, and weather predictions, murder and assault moved back to center stage.

Sarah began it. "When I haven't been stewing over Derek, I've been rehashing the whole Danton McGraw and Grover Blaine business. McGraw wasn't Mr. Favorite Professor, but that didn't mean that he was a candidate for murder."

"Unless by Vera Pruczak or one of her minions."

"I'd say that by now everyone for miles around must have figured out that spearing McGraw was a mistake and Grover was the real target. After all, Vera's minions—and that's most of the Drama School—saw McGraw as an enemy, but it probably wasn't personal. But they really, really hated Grover Blaine. Especially the ladies."

Alex, who had been frowning at his just-arrived Tufted Chicken, poked it tentatively and tried a mouthful. Chewed and nodded. "As I thought. Fried chicken. Just like the Colonel's. Anyway, I think everyone mixed in with the production knew there was a pretty good possibility that understudy Grover Blaine might be taking over the Mercutio part."

"But the decision to give Grover the part was pretty much a last-minute affair."

"So are you suggesting that the real target was Todd Mancuso?"

Sarah put down her fork and stared at Alex. "I can't believe that Todd was the real target. I mean, come on. Todd, not Grover. Not Danton McGraw. Or maybe all three were on the hit program. So it didn't matter who played Mercutio. They were all possible targets. It's like the Marx Brothers."

Alex considered this triple possibility. And rejected it. "Forget Todd as a target. At least during the play. Even if the final decision was a last-minute one, everyone knew Todd was in bad shape and might be taken off the part. And there was understudy Grover Blaine all dressed and ready to go on the stage as Mercutio."

Sarah, her eyes watering from her first taste of Chicken Laredo, put down her fork fanned her mouth, and reached for the water. Drank slowly. Then agreed.

"Todd's two known enemies, Kay and Terri, have made up with him. In fact, I think Kay might have a very soft spot for the guy. Todd's other possible enemies, the two who might have beaten him up in the Fine Food Mart, are Grover and Derek."

"So back to square one," Alex said. "Our two favorites."

"Here's an idea. I'll bet that one person beside Grover knew about Danton taking the role."

Alex nodded. "Easy. Best Buddy Derek would have heard from Best Buddy Grover—or Best Bully Grover—that McGraw was taking over the Mercutio job. Grover would be mad at having the part snatched away and he'd want to sound off. To Derek."

Sarah took a minute slice of Chicken Laredo, scraped some of the fiery sauce from its surface. Then she agreed. "Those guys were almost clones. Although Grover was the Alpha dog."

"Lovers, you think?" asked Alex.

"Who knows? I've never thought much about that angle, though now you mention it . . . well, maybe. They certainly stayed glued together. You're suggesting that maybe Alpha dog Grover pulled a fast one on Derek. Found another best buddy. Or even a girl. Someone who might replace Derek as number-one stooge."

"Could be," said Alex. "Derek might have come apart if he found he'd been kicked aside for a new male lover. Or female lover. So are you talking about Derek with a foil in his hand playing the mystery fencer? Lover's revenge?"

"It's a wild guess. But it would have been easy enough for Derek. He could easily get hold of a costume—they were hanging all over backstage. And he can handle a foil."

"But get his mitts on an épée?"

"No problem," Sarah said. "Even if only foils were allowed in the play, Derek's doing a minor in drama, so he has to take the mandatory fencing classes. They must get instruction with foils, épées, sabers, probably battle-axes and broadswords."

"Then Derek finds out the wrong guy was stabbed because there's Grover alive and taking a bow at curtain call. So he hunts him down and nails him in the Green Room."

Sarah took one more spicy bite of her chicken, doused the fire with another swallow of water, and was silent. Thinking. Trying to remember. "But," she began, "Derek told me that Grover left the cast party, just took off without telling him. That he never saw him again."

"You'd have to go over the police timetable on that one. And they may not even have a grip on it. There were a lot of comings and goings."

"I saw Grover myself at the party early on. Then he was gone. Danton McGraw never turned up, which for me was a relief. I remember thinking good riddance to both Grover and McGraw. The cast party was better without them."

Alex pushed a gnawed chicken bone aside and turned his attention to his salad. And for a few minutes attention was paid by both to finishing a somewhat dubious meal.

Then Sarah suddenly said, "Did I tell you, Mike Laaka has the whole thing solved. Todd Mancuso was putting on an act of being weak. He thought Grover was the one who beat the shit out of him at the Fine Food Mart, so he went onstage as one of the crowd, nailed Mercutio, who he thought was Grover." And then Sarah related Mike Laaka's rather tangled explanation ending with how Todd, having hit the wrong guy, lured Grover away from the cast party and killed him in the Green Room.

"The only thing going for Mike's plot," Sarah finished, "is that Todd is an ace fencer."

Alex abandoned his lunch. Shook his head vehemently. "Please ax that idea. Todd was in no shape to nail anyone. But before we go back to the real world, what about your research into non-fencers? The ones the police aren't looking at."

"It's boiled down to a small collection of names from the Drama School. Some in the production, some who might be doing a minor in English. But so far it's a non-starter. I've been hunting, but none of the first names match the last names. I've looked at the lists of some major fencing events under 'U.S. Fencing Association' and names from clubs and camps and schools. And I suppose some fencing genius could be hiding at some obscure 4-H group or church or international summer school, but I haven't found him. Or her. As you suggested, I'm hoping to find a person who gave up fencing before coming to Bowmouth but when the time was ripe was ready for action. Anyway, I'll keep swatting away at it."

"But you won't let Mike disturb you?"

"Of course not. What else is an overworked English teacher to do? I don't think I'll get another chance at the English Department, but I'll hit the Drama School again. See if I've missed something. I have a sense that there's an odd bit I've missed. Some files I looked at weren't filled out quite right."

"Linda will have you in chains."

"Next to her," said Sarah, "McGraw begins to look quite mellow."

"Take care, my beloved, if you're caught with hot files in your hand. Somewhere a mystery fencer is lurking. Possibly equipped with an épée up the sleeve." Here Alex reached over and took both her hands in his and fixed his wife with a stern eye. "What I'm trying to say is please, please watch your back."

"You mean my neck, my carotid artery or my jugular vein. Or both."

"This is no joking matter. Goddamn it, Sarah, I mean it."

"I wasn't really joking. But I hate being lectured to."

"We're talking murder. Remember?"

"Yes, I do. And I intend to be very careful," said Sarah. "And now I'll change the subject. Have you heard about the sermon on Sunday?"

"Sundays usually have sermons," said Alex.

"This one seems to be a reaction to Vera's *Romiette and Julio.* The Reverend Nicholas Copeland from Fryeburg. He's preaching in the Bowmouth Community Church about the play, and I'd guess Bowmouth College won't come out smelling like a rose. Or at least Vera and the Drama School won't."

"You've got that right," said Alex. "McGraw may find it easier to digest the Drama School than he thought. Okay, enough. Back to work. My patients are probably stewing in the waiting room, complaining about last year's *National Geographic*s. And you, again, please take care."

"But how about Derek? Do you think he might try the same thing again? Or something like it. Not motorcycle. But pills. High windows. Carbon monoxide?"

"We're doing what we can. At least Jonas is. With Derek's okay, he's talked to Alena. Result is that the mother wants out of the whole affair. If she puts her head in the sand maybe someone will come along and rescue the kid and the whole nasty thing will go away. She's thinking of having McGraw go to bat for him. Anybody but herself."

"Jonas doesn't think Derek is ready to try the suicide thing again?"

"Not right away," Alex said. "But we should be ready to have him as a houseguest for a while."

Sarah nodded and made a note. A trip to the Fine Food Mart for student-type foods for a particular long, lanky, bony depressed student. Carbs and spices and things like ribs and burgers and jerky. Nothing healthy. But not until after her last class. And not until she'd made a quick strike on a file cabinet. Even two file cabinets. And rifled through those few folders again. Because, like a burr, hidden for a while under the press of events, little oddities had begun to scratch at her brain.

Sarah arrived at the English Department office after her last class—during which Derek had been silently present. There she found her friend Mary Donelli, a woman usually of great calmness, having a major face-off with diva Linda LaCroix. Linda had found that faculty and student demands were sucking her life's blood. More and more she felt an affinity for Commander McGraw. He knew how to keep the lid on people like Mary Donelli, who had come waltzing in demanding that her midterm exams sheets be copied the very next day.

"Just cool it, Linda," said Mary in a sharp-edged voice. "If you go on like Simon Legree you'll blow a fuse and then the office will really fall apart. You're making me mad—which I can take—but you've made Amos Larkin mad, and that's like poking a crocodile. Telling him that you can't run off that syllabus for a week."

Linda, briefly out-argued, turned on Sarah. "No, Sarah Deane. You may not look at any more files. They're not there for you to rummage around in playing detective."

And Sarah, in her own way, became dangerous. "Linda, you know goddamn well that sometimes I'm in the middle of an accident, like this Halloween business, and I try to help. And I'm teaching in this college and I should be able to see my students' files."

"Not okay," said Linda. "Privacy is a big deal. You know that. I'm here to see that things stay put until Professor McGraw gets back. Mary, you'll get your exams but not tomorrow. Right now I've got to get back to work." At which she marched to the chairman's door, opened it, stepped in, and closed the door with a firm click.

"So there," said a voice from the back of the office. Arlene. She turned away from her computer screen and grinned at the two women. "Linda has spoken and it's up yours."

Mary blew through her teeth. "I just hope I can keep Amos from coming in here and throttling the life out of her."

Arlene indicated the chairman's door. "She's really moved in. Uses his desk. His water jug, his phone, computer, the works. The only thing she doesn't dare touch is that black desk chair with the U.S. Naval Academy seal painted on it. Actually, for my part I'm happy she's in there." Then seeing that Sarah had an expectant look on her face, Arlene shook her head. "No, no, no. You can't touch those files. Never again. My job is worth a lot to me. Even if I found six dead bodies in the files I wouldn't tell you."

"How about me?" said Mary, winking at Sarah. "I'm not playing detective. I just might want to check grade averages. Winter term sign-ups."

"Forget it. Nobody goes near those files. And Linda has a new lock on the outside office door, and when she goes out she locks up. And yes, I have a key. It's around my neck and it's worth my life if I don't use it to keep the varmints out. I think Linda has sort of zoned in on McGraw's brain and is taking directions by ESP."

Sarah gave in, nodding to Arlene. And Arlene in turn melted, ever so slightly. "If something about a drama student taking English classes turns up that is absolutely wild and dangerous, well, I might let the police know. Maybe you later. If I get the chance. When Linda is in the loo. Or flying around stinging people."

Walking down the hall with Mary, Sarah asked, "Do you think it's beyond reason to hope that Amos could take over the department? For now. There needs to be someone in charge of the place. Besides Linda."

"The faculty wouldn't touch him. And Amos wouldn't touch the idea. He hates administration in any form. And no one wants the job. Not with this murder business smelling up the department. Take hope. I hear McGraw is on the mend."

They parted and Sarah found herself instead of heading for the parking lot moving toward the dark blue police trailer that stuck out as an unnatural appendage next to the white circular Drama School. Maybe, just maybe, Katie Waters might lend a helping hand. Or a sticky finger. A file lifter. Mike, of course, had come for the files, but Sarah doubted that Mike would know an odd personal item if it bit him. Mike liked black-and-white facts, as did George Fitts. But Katie had an eye for the peculiar, an item out of sync.

And as fortune would have it, Sarah ran smack into Katie, who, head down, windbreaker flapping behind her, was marching toward the parking lot.

"Katie," shouted Sarah.

Katie looked up. Grinned. And shook her head. "The answer is no," said Katie.

"No what?" said Sarah.

"No to whatever it is you want. I'm not an assistant to civilian snoops."

"A minor request. Something you—and Mike—like to do. And Linda can't stop you."

"Which is?"

"Look through the files of English majors. Students doing a minor in drama or involved in Vera's play. The non–college fencers. If you find anything that strikes you as having been changed, erased, looks peculiar, could you let me know?"

"No. No. No." But then Katie hesitated. "But I might do it for my own information just for the sake of making some progress in this stupid case. And maybe"—she smiled widely—"being one up on Sergeant George Fitts."

"And you won't share."

"Anything I hand to you will prove dangerous to my health, or the sheriff department's health and the state police's health."

"It's nothing dangerous. Just a tiny little hunch I want to follow up."

"Here's a thought for you," Katie said. "I happen to know that you can get your hooks on Vera's files. Probably already have done it, because Vera runs a loose operation. And you know what, I could, with a very clear conscience, rat on you."

"But you won't?"

"Don't push me. But I have one speck of news. Which may be public pretty soon, so it's okay. The police called in the younger of those two boys who claimed they saw the Harry Potter character hanging around the utility closet and rest area at the food store. Showed them photos. The younger one made an ID of Derek Mosely as the one hanging around the place for quite a while. Then, after a lot of lip biting, thought that he might have seen Grover Blaine for a short while together with Derek. In the same area."

Sarah stared at her. "Both those guys. Todd Mancuso, too?"

"No, we can't have everything. But it'll bring charges against Derek Mosely a little bit closer."

"Oh shit!"

Katie in her turn stared. "Why 'oh shit'? Do you have some warm cozy feelings for those goons?"

Sarah ran her hand over her head, ruffling her already-untidy short brown hair. "It's not warm and cozy feelings. It's more like seeing a goddamn mess."

"Your turn to share."

"We trade?"

"You," said Katie, "are still a civilian. I am still police. I can't give. But you can because if it's pertinent to the case you might be withholding evidence."

Sarah thought. Pertinent to the case? Not exactly. Except sidewise. Tangentially. Not the suicide try. But the lovers' quarrel idea? Derek the avenger. She hesitated, pushed her foot into a few dry leaves. "Okay, this is off-the-record—if there is such a thing. I'll deny anything I've told you. It involves Derek's sanity. Maybe his life. And things are being taken care of. By Alex and the psychiatrist Jonas Jefferson. And Derek's mother knows."

"Whatever you're talking about is something everyone but the police knows."

"If I tell you, will you try and keep Derek off the griddle?"

"Christ, Sarah. I can't do that. But you have to tell me what's going on with the guy or I'll get on my horn and call in the troops."

"Hold off." Sarah almost shouted it. "I'm calling Alex. See if he can be part of this. It has a lot to do with Derek's stability. Or even sanity." At which Sarah rummaged in her briefcase and came up with her cell phone and called. And, to her surprise, connected. Alex was on the way home. She would be picking up Derek, wouldn't she?

And Sarah explained about the hornet's nest into which she had now poked a hole. "We're down by the Malcolm Adam Hall parking lot. Could you meet us?"

"Cafeteria," said Alex shortly.

"And bring Jonas Jefferson if he's loose."

"Wait," called Katie. "Let's do this kosher. Police trailer."

And by urgent use of radio transmissions, cell phones, ordinary telephones, a small convention was called to meet within thirty minutes in the police trailer. The cast from the law-and-order branch included the olive-drab George Fitts, sweatshirted Mike Laaka, and blue-jeaned Katie Waters, and from the medical branch Dr. Alex McKenzie, elderly herringbone tweed jacket, and Jonas Jefferson, non-threatening sweater and khakis, and from the academic world Assistant Professor Sarah Douglas Deane, disheveled but decent in jacket and slacks. The only notables missing were Derek Mosely, presently occupied on the Bowmouth soccer field, and his mother, Dean Alena Fosdick—who when asked if she wished to attend the meeting answered in the famous words of Bartleby the Scrivener, "I would prefer not to."

The hour of much back-and-forthing of contradiction and agreement in the confined, slightly overheated trailer produced the following.

From Dr. Jonas Jefferson: Derek Mosely was currently in a fairly stable state. But the doctor could not predict the result if his patient had to face new police charges added to the harassment ones already in place. However, without invading Derek's privacy, Dr. Jefferson did say that the boy seemed much more upset about his friend Grover's death than worried about the college or police investigation.

From Mike Laaka: Derek didn't seem like the aggressive sort. He acted like Grover's stooge, was maybe his lover. Had he been stood up and lost it? Actually took the offensive? Or was he really thrown flat by Grover's murder?

There was a slight increase in attention when the word "lover" was spoken and several eyes switched to Jonas Jefferson. Whose face remained properly impassive.

From Alex: He couldn't predict from moment to moment how Derek's state of mind would change. But for what it was worth, he, Alex, and Sarah would be willing to let him stay at their farm and drive him to the college for his classes. To which Sarah agreed, adding that Derek's relationship to Grover, whatever its exact nature, was a remarkably close one. Whatever one did the other did also, and this included sports, taking the same classes, sitting together, and signing up for the Drama School play.

From Katie Waters: Was Derek, as things stood now, a danger to others or to himself? Should he be confined to a psychiatric unit of the hospital?

Dead silence at this remark. Then George Fitts: "We'd be more comfortable having some sort of control over Derek's movements. Where he goes, where he stays. We might be able to delay the bringing of charges for the Todd Mancuso beating. After all, Derek was playing lookout from what we can tell. And Derek's lawyer is bound to challenge the testimony of an eight-year-old boy witness. And he would make mincemeat of the ten-year-old brother who got the ID of this Draco Malfoy look-alike through hearsay."

Alex: A compromise. Derek to stay with Sarah and himself by night. Have an escort for him by day. To classes, to sports, to meals. If he didn't accept this idea, then perhaps a room in the hospital psychiatric unit.

Jonas Jefferson: "Sounds okay to me. Shall I put the question up to him?"

Agreement by all. Jonas to the soccer field to intercept Derek. Sarah following Dr. Jefferson to hear Derek's response to proposition. If he said yes to the escort idea, she'd go on to the Food Mart and return to pick up Derek. Meanwhile, the soccer coach would be asked to keep Derek in view for the remainder of practice.

Departure of all but George Fitts and Katie Waters, the latter having been fingered for an assignment: Derek's escort.

"Why not Mike? Or anyone," Katie demanded.

George shook his head. "Not a chance. You're the best for this sort of thing. Mike isn't known for tact. You stick to Derek. Any trouble, call pronto. When he's in class you can stay outside in the hall after you've asked the instructor not to excuse him without reaching you."

"I'm to go potty with him," said Katie irritably. The assignment was not to her liking.

"You know the drill, so don't argue. You can watch the soccer from the sidelines."

"And catch balls that go out-of-bounds?"

"You're lucky," said George. "Fresh air guaranteed. Very healthy."

"Shall I carry?"

"Don't let Derek know unless you have to restrain him. All the usual precautions. And catch up with Sarah at that food place and coordinate tomorrow."

"And that's an order?" said Katie, knowing the answer.

George, who had returned to his notebook, didn't bother to look up. "This job," he said, "requires sympathy without softness. Dr. Jefferson spoke highly of your interpersonal talents."

"Dr. Jefferson doesn't even know me."

"Wrong. You and he testified on a case of an abused minor about three years ago. He has a photographic memory. He said you seemed very sensible and not easily flustered. Okay, if Derek agrees to the Dr. Jefferson's proposal—which is also ours—you can coordinate times with Sarah Deane; she's going off to the soccer field right now. And I fervently hope she'll keep her hands off any part of this case."

"You wish," said Katie, pulling her windbreaker on and zipping it up the front. The late-afternoon breeze was cutting sharply through the trees, and the skies were threatening.

All went as planned. Derek was withdrawn from soccer practice. Dr. Jefferson offered Derek the choice of escort plus night house stays with Sarah and Alex. Or a stay in the psychiatric unit.

To the first Derek quickly agreed. He looked somewhat more wholesome at the moment. Soccer practice had forced the long, pale, lanky Derek into a real physical effort—something many people, including Jonas Jefferson, felt had a positive effect on depression. Sarah, arriving after this agreement, felt that at least one step had been taken toward dealing with a miserable situation. And so, she thought to herself, with Derek under wraps, maybe something could be done about assault and murder with an épée And the checking of oddball student files.

She mentioned this last to Katie as Derek returned to the soccer field. And Katie told Sarah if anything odd turned up in a file she would tell her. "Without," said Katie firmly, "giving you any details. So there. Go away. I'll be going back to the English office to-day, or what's left of today. Tomorrow I'm Derek's nanny. Call me tonight to set up meeting times. English office maybe."

This was agreed, Sarah adding, "For God's sake don't say you're his nanny. Think of something else. Try girlfriend. Cousin from Detroit."

"That was a joke. I think 'Deputy Investigator Katherine Waters' will do just fine. It's time this Derek began living in the real world."

Sarah's trip to the Fine Food Mart was uneventful. No cries, moans, nor signs of battered customers locked in utility rooms. In fact, the only thing that caught her eye as she shoved her loaded cart around was a number of large posters featuring a tall figure with hawklike eyes standing in front of a sketch of a church steeple. This announced in bold type the forthcoming appearance of the Reverend Nicholas Copeland of the Church of the Troubled Waters, who would be delivering a sermon at Bowmouth Town's own Community Church. The use of the word "devil" had been dropped, and his subject was now listed rather ambiguously as "Questions for Maine's Theatres." It added that refreshments would be available later in the Parish House.

Vera had better arm herself for this one, thought Sarah. And suddenly she had a vision of Vera, dressed in her usual costume of scarves and beads and dangling bits and pieces, standing up before the sober and serious church congregation. She would gesture grandly and in her penetrating stage-trained voice projecting to the last pew go on about the freedom of the arts, the integrity of the dramatic impulse, and the truth of the imagination—here she would refer to Keats and leave her listeners shaking their heads. All in all, Sarah feared for the future of the Drama School.

Then she shook herself and pushed her cart forward and, concentrating on guest Mosely, grabbed a pound of hamburger, a gallon of Ben & Jerry's Cherry Garcia, a case of root beer, an extra bag of dog biscuits for Derek to feed Patsy, and, with gesture toward health, a bag of crisp apples and a quart of fresh-squeezed orange juice.

Sarah found Derek in conversation with the soccer coach, who welcomed her—he had a freshman son in one of her classes. "Just telling Derek that his footwork is good and to really push it when he gets control. Go for it, take it in if he can. Not always passing it. Some guys hog the ball, won't pass. Derek is too nice. He passes it."

Or gets rid of it as dangerous, Sarah thought. That might be in keeping with his whole personality. Aloud she said to Derek, "Soccer's a great game. Glad you're playing."

Derek nodded, and after another trip with Sarah to his dorm room to pick up more clothes and some of his textbooks, his laptop, a radio, the two headed out of town toward Saw Mill Road and the old farmhouse. And dog Patsy and kitten Piggy, both of whom, Sarah trusted, would continue to work their rehabilitative magic.

Katie Waters did hit the English Department again. By luck, she found only Arlene getting ready with key and lock to leave for the day. A few firm words from Katie in her deputy mode and an agreement from Arlene, who just wanted to get the hell out of there, it was late, for God's sake, brought Katie an armful of the desired files. "Back early A.M. or I'll have Linda boil you for dinner," said Arlene. "And by God she'd do it."

Katie nodded and hastened away to the library, having no desire to be caught by her fellow investigators with folders in which Sarah Deane had shown an interest. George would not only boil her for dinner; he would also barbecue, fry, roast, and pickle her.

16

SETTLED in the police trailer at a table chosen for its distance away from George Fitts, Katie began looking over the folders of English majors stacked by her right elbow. By the other elbow she had placed the playbill of *Romiette and Julio*, which listed those involved in the production from director and actors to stage crew and theatre volunteers.

The first folder she picked was not in proper alphabetical order—had Linda or more likely Arlene given up on such dull tasks? Never mind. Onward and upward. Katie began flipping through the rest of the collection.

One after another, a complete bore. An Alison, a Meredith, a Colin, a Diego, a Julia, an Arnold, an Ali, a Jacques. Not a fencer in the bunch. Just the non-fencers who, from Sarah's point of view, might be hiding or ignoring this past interest so that no history of skill in swordplay would come to light. "But forget it, Sarah," Katie murmured to herself. Of these non-fencing English majors, not one had been involved in the theatre production. As to the drama students doing a minor in English but who had not mentioned fencing, Katie put only six aside. These six she decided contained a number of changes, erasures, or scratch-outs and so might be considered somewhat suspicious. Since George had never ordered a search into non-fencers, she would make a note of these names until such time as they might prove useful. And she would tell Sarah that the six disfigured files from the English Department might be duplicated in the Drama School files belonging to these same six students. Anyway, it would give Sarah something to play with. Reaching for the phone, Katie caught Sarah, cell phone in pocket, standing watch outside Derek's dorm room and gave her the news. Or non-news.

"This is all I can say. Look for rubouts, erasures. Patchwork. Additives. Some of these files are a real mess. I know Vera will hand her files right over for you. She has no sense of protocol. And since George hasn't ordered me to look up non-fencers, the drama students are all yours. But keep your mitts off anything in the English office."

"Do you think," said Sarah slowly—it was something she'd been turning over in her mind—"that some of these women students have been married and have changed names? Or were married and went back to maiden names?"

"Go for it," said Katie. "Maybe the college allows married students. Or divorced students. Or civil-union students. Students with concubines. God only knows, so trot down to the Drama School and find out. Good-bye, I'm busy. Over and out."

But Sarah, now doing escort service with Derek, would have to leave that bit of scouting for later. But married students? Well, although the admissions office was closed, any of the longtime faculty regulars should know about married undergraduate students. Of course, graduate students, many of whom were married, sometimes took undergraduate courses. What a headache.

As for the Drama School files, after Derek had been fed and Alex was put on watch, she was planning to go back that evening and do a bit of hunting. First the non-fencers. Follow Katie's information and see if blots and changes had concealed something notable. And also, and increasingly interesting, find out from someone, Weeza Scotini for instance, about this protective, and possibly proactive, Drama School special forces group. Maybe some serious steps had been taken by one of those.

The evening went smoothly: dog and orange kitten did their parts; Derek scratched his way through a history essay, read a few pages of *The Scarlet Letter*, and then turned the television on to a *Star Trek* rerun. Watching him from a far corner of the living room, both Sarah and Alex, without discussing the matter, decided for the time being their role should not smack of tutor or house parent and so left Derek to his own devices.

From the kitchen Alex made a call to Alena Fosdick, brought her up to speed on recent plans for Derek, whereby Alena thanked him for calling, for the trouble he was taking with her son, and wished him good night.

Sarah followed this with a call to Mary Donelli about married students.

"Undergraduates?" asked Mary. "Not bloody likely. It's not verboten, but the whole undergraduate social scene doesn't support the idea."

"But have there been married students?"

"Well, sure. Every now and then. Seniors and juniors often live off campus and here and there we have a couple. Not just bedmates. Real wedded couples. But these don't mix it up much with the other students. Take their courses, do their homework, and go home and play house."

"And," Sarah said, "women getting married often keep their own name."

"Depends," said Mary. "Sometimes if their family name is Skjinskyovnia they might want to swap it for Smith or Brown."

"And some students may have married, applied to the college under their married names, divorced, and gone back to their maiden names."

"Sarah," said Mary in exasperation, "don't you have papers to correct? A class to get ready for? This will get you nowhere except being arrested by George Fitts for obstruction of an investigation."

"But George isn't investigating non-fencers."

"Don't nitpick. You'll more likely end in jail for invasion of student privacy. Okay, good night. You just go on, pick locks, climb up walls, and peek into windows. But keep clear of Linda."

"I'll try," said Sarah. She hung up, grabbed a windbreaker—a light rain had been added to a now-increasing wind—waved to Alex and Derek, muttered something about missing student papers, and headed out. Derek, she was glad to see, was looking a small fraction more animated. After his TV watching had finished, he had just been offered a chess game and had just taken Alex's knight.

The Drama School was well lit. Vera, using the practice stage, had started readings for a series of one-act plays to be presented at the end of the fall term. And as if it had been planned in advance, the office was open, the tall file case with drawers unlocked, so all that was needed, like Alice's underground bottle, was a sign saying: Read Me.

Sarah settled herself at a table with a number of files belonging to the non-fencing students, which meant those not hustled off by the police. The majority of these suggested no oddity such as the mention of a married name or the return to a maiden name after a divorce. But as Katie had warned, some files of Drama School majors contained rub-outs, cross-outs, and, in two cases, stickers covering something over the name and address location.

The blotted and marked files included a student, Manja, who always dressed in a handsome sari, a German student, Greta von Somebody—her application written in German with a penciled translation and the last name smeared. But the two were not involved in Vera's production for the simple reason that they had been at a foreign student conference in Boston for the past week. Next on the pile the three familiar Drama School stars of Vera's production: Terri Colman, Kay Biddle, and, in a folder marked Drama Major–Dance Minor Weeza Scotini, who was interesting because she'd taken the important part of Paris in the play. And that, except for the finale, she would have been masked and dressed as the male, Paris, and so had access to crowd scenes before she had to morph into a female dancer in the last scene. Sarah remembered Weeza's vibrant high-kicking performance with admiration.

Weeza of course was memorable for being the sting operator who had nailed Grover and Derek with an harassment charge. However, a quick scan of Weeza's application and class records revealed, beyond the fact that her first name was Louisa—which everyone knew—there were no indications of interest in fencing, a desire to take lessons in the future, or having taken them in the past. She had listed her sports interests as field hockey and cross-country running.

So much for Weeza-Louisa. Number four was a Seth Nussbaum, whose folder had a pink slip marked "excused from fencing class—see medical note."

But beyond a reference under "Health" to childhood asthma, Sarah was unable to fix the excuse. But maybe asthma was enough. Or Seth was using it to get out of the required fencing class.

The sounds of voices and approaching footsteps sounded an alarm. Sarah, loath to give up her treasures, shoved the four into her briefcase and headed for shelter. Shelter meaning any unoccupied space. This turned out to be the visitors' lounge, a small ill-lit chamber near the main door. To this Sarah retreated and some thirty minutes later had decided that Terri, Kay, and Weeza, besides showing no interest in fencing, were also known haters of Grover Blaine. Number-four suspect, this Seth Nussbaum, remained the odd man in the group, and for all Sarah knew Seth may not have known Grover. Have actually liked him. Or detested him. This would have to be looked into. But in the meantime, she, Sarah, would have to go back to her fencing research and see if she had somehow missed one of these. Or two, although the idea of two murderers who were secret fencers was a bit frightening.

Seth Nussbaum's file was as clean as a whistle, but files on the other three were patched with changes and cross-outs. And someone, the student or the Drama School secretary, had done too good a job in concealing the original notation. Terri Colman and Kay Biddle both had several small white stickers pasted randomly over such items as name, address, phone, and previous schooling entries. Weeza Scotini had inserted her "Weeza" over the scratched-out "Louisa." But there were other erasures on hers, too. What was being hidden on these three files? A name? A past fencing trophy or title? But how does one safely lift off such stickers? Sarah had tried lifting by fingernail to no avail. Tearing the things would probably end in ruining whatever was underneath. Under normal circumstances she might have called Mike Laaka or Katie Waters for help, since the task seemed to have "police lab" written all over it. But in the present hostile police environment to laymen that route seemed closed.

How about Alex? He could hit the hospital for her, because there must be some product in the supply rooms that could lift sticky material. After all, medical people must constantly be confronted with dressings and adhesive tape sticking to sensitive skin. Okay, that was the route to take. Sarah sprang to her feet, tucked the four folders into her open briefcase, and made it to the door. Made it to the now-wet top step of the entryway. To the second step. And slipped. All the way down the handsome granite staircase. Bump, bump, bump, bang. Splat!

Wind knocked out. Elbows and knees throbbing. Head spinning. Briefcase flung on the ground spewing out stolen folders in every direction. The sharp wind catching them, sending their paper contents spiraling, flying east and west.

"Oh no, no," gasped Sarah, reaching helplessly for her briefcase, its jaws wide-open, empty.

Help came. Four students finished with rehearsals, stood for a second at the open door, grasped the situation, and pelted down the steps. The first, Weeza Scotini, stooped to help Sarah to her feet and then joined Terri and Kay in a wild chase over the Drama School grounds after the files. Some twenty minutes later these three, now aided by Todd Mancuso, Malcolm Wheelock, and the newly met student, Seth Nussbaum, presented Sarah with a heap of bent and damp file folders and their limp, sodden contents.

"Don't know if we got 'em all," said Kay. "They blew all over like crazy."

"You may have to wait for daylight," said Terri. "Or get a flashlight."

"And they're pretty wet," said Todd. "Listen, I think you'd better get them inside to dry off pretty fast. Some of the name labels look loose."

"Yes," said Terri. "And they look like our folders. I mean I saw Weeza's name and Seth's. What's up, Dr. Deane?"

Sarah, unable to snatch the bundle and run away, had to scramble. "Working on a new English class. A sort of independent roundtable thing. For some of you people who don't take fencing. Vera's idea. To fill that time slot."

"Hey," said Kay. "That thing you call a time slot is what we call a break. We need that time slot."

"It's just an idea," Sarah said. "Informal. No homework, just sort of brainstorming sessions over certain plays. Unusual ones." God, she thought, now I'll have to come up with a list of unusual plays.

"I think," said Kay thoughtfully, "you'd better count me out. I'm over my head as it is."

"The class is just in the planning stage," Sarah said. "And I think Todd is right. I'd better get these folders home and dry them." And tell Vera what I've done, she added to herself.

At which, limping slightly, her knee hurting from the fall, Sarah headed off toward the parking lot. To her car. Through the college gates, driving more slowly than usual through the rain and wind, trying not to think about consequences of her most recent falsehood. And then, by concentrating on nothing more than the blurred passing scenery, she was home.

And at home she found it was close to ten o'clock and that Derek had retired with a dog-training manual, together with Patsy dog and Piggy kitten. And Alex, she was glad to see, deep into some article on changes in this year's flu vaccine. Result, Sarah had a warm kitchen in which to dry folders and files and time to find out if anything worth the effort of lying and stealing lay hidden in the collection.

Reward. Well, sort of. The damp weather had done the trick. In two ways. In several cases the ink entries seemed blotched beyond repair. But also several stickers had loosened, curled at their edges, and could be peeled off. Three items worth attention emerged. A pair of first-name changes, Weeza-Louisa and Terri-Theresa being items she already knew about. Another showed a last name on making application to Bowmouth College, another version given at the end of the freshman year. No explanation. The third oddity: a note from a physician explaining that in view of this student's recent serious case of hepatitis it was advisable that fencing or other physically demanding sports should not be undertaken until he had a medical clearance. Name: Seth Nussbaum.

Okay. Count four suspects. Terri, Kay, Weeza, and now this Seth Nussbaum. Yes, perhaps "suspects" was a little strong, but at least these provided fodder for future exploration. Back to the U.S. Fencing Association and all those camps and clubs and school fencing programs. Oh God. But tomorrow at least was Saturday. No classes. Go to bed and sleep on it, get up at dawn, and hit the computer and the telephone.

But as Sarah climbed into bed, moving Alex away from a diagonal position that ate up a large portion of her side, she was struck with a depressing thought. One more character had been added to the stew. This Seth Nussbaum, hitherto unknown, had now been revealed as not only having had hepatitis but also fencing had been particularly mentioned as something he must avoid. Ergo this Seth was a fencer. Had he been in Vera's play as a crowd member? Or handled the lights? Prompter? Cancan chorus member? Curtain puller? Had he been on the playbill? Well, she didn't have one handy, nor could she remember seeing his name. But she didn't need another non-fencer who might turn out to be an accomplished swordsman. And then drifting asleep she tried to remember what he looked like when he was busy rescuing her folders. Why had she never noticed him before? Probably because he was just your fairly tall brown-haired, brown-eyed very everyday-appearing student wearing jeans and a sweatshirt, with no special quirks or distinctive marks. And of course, he was one of the Drama School students who were *not* in any of her English classes.

And Sarah drifted off to dream of foils and épées and sabers and harpoons and kitchen knives and toasting forks, all wielded by not three but four armor-clad Mercutios clashing and circling around the top of a high cliff that looked over a sunlit sea while she lay immobile on a rocky beach and tried to cover her ears.

Saturday morning, November the third, saw Dean Alena Fosdick in a state of despair. She had always lived a careful life. In the beginning her parents had seen to it that their beautiful only child had meals on time, her bed had an eyelet lace canopy, her Victorian doll's house had been furnished exactly as shown in the finer children's magazines. Also her mother had made certain that Alena's clothes were never on the high edge of child style nor were too retrograde to provoke her friends into laughing at her. She had been sent to a proper, i.e., conservative, private school (after a nasty roughhousing experience in a public-school kindergarten), and all in all she marched into adulthood equipped with ready-made taste, subscriptions to the sort of magazines that could best furnish her house, dress her person, and encourage a cautious view of the world. This last characteristic had suggested that she avoid a controversial doctoral subject in English. Her advisor at the obscure Windamere University had suggested Flannery O'Connor, but Alena, sure that O'Connor would probably fry her brain, had opted instead for the Raggedy Ann dissertation. After all, Alena had reasoned, what was wrong in writing about feminine stereotypes in popular children's literature? Sadly, this choice, as mentioned, had furnished some colleagues at Bowmouth College with a hearty laugh.

Also, to add to her disappointments, her life to early adulthood had not equipped her with "husband choice" expertise. Having survived two abusive marriages, she had emerged a much more cautious, careful, and wary woman. A fly in the family ointment of course had been her son, Derek, who, as the years went by, had not provided her with the solace that she thought a son should give. But even so, they had muddled along pretty well until Derek had attached himself to the regrettable Grover Blaine.

Of course the idea of Derek and Grover being lovers had been bubbling somewhere in Alena's brain, but she always shoved it down. Almost any male student on the campus would have been perfectly acceptable as her son's partner except the horrible Grover. She also had an unmentionable worry, one that she would try to keep at bay. The odious Grover and Derek looked so much alike and Derek took so closely after his father, George Mosely, in appearance that there was an unnerving possibility that George had somehow impregnated Grover Blaine's mother—whoever and wherever she was. This was a dark pit Alena did not intend to descend into, but the very idea gave her shivers.

Alena had first received the news of Grover's murder with only one emotion. Profound gladness. Thanks to the powers that be. But these feelings were almost immediately contaminated by the reflection that Grover was now past blame for the beating of Todd Mancuso, and the sexual harassment charge brought by Weeza Scotini still hung over Derek's head. And then there was the dreadful idea, the same idea that had occurred to the police, that Grover's death might have come at the hand of Derek as a sort of lover's revenge. Things now seemed so black that there were moments in which Alena felt she could never leave her house again. Or go to her office and play at being dean of Arts and Sciences. Oh hell, hell, hell. She looked around her perfect living room. The Governor Winthrop desk, the red and gold Chinese carpet, the large oil of the Owls Head Lighthouse, the Hepplewhite side table, the tastefully framed Wyeth print of Ground Hog Day.

And now there was Derek, living at someone else's house, under police escort, and all she had done to help the situation was pretend it had nothing to do with her. If she hadn't known that Dr. Jonas Jefferson was in charge of the boy, she might have sought an appointment with him to help put her own head together.

"Oh hell," she said again, this time loudly to her living room. She sat absolutely still for a moment, revolved unpleasant options around in her addled brain. Then reached for the telephone book. Dialed.

"Sarah Deane?" queried Alena to the voice that answered.

"Yes," said Sarah. "Is that you, Dean Fosdick?"

"I'm Alena, please. Look, could I come over to talk to you? Just for a few minutes. About Derek. I think, well, it's possible I'm being too harsh. Or not sympathetic."

You certainly aren't, Sarah told herself. Aloud, she said, "How about in an hour?"

Alena agreed, took down directions to the Saw Mill Road farmhouse, and then got up and made herself a stiff drink of scotch with very little water.

Sarah for her part said, "Hell`," loudly. She was only about an eighth of the way through the U.S. Fencing Association's records, seeking mention of her chosen students. Of these, the hitherto unknown Seth Nussbaum from Buffalo, New York, came up as her first find. He had been a whizz-bang at saber and épée, winner of assorted school and club titles. But as to a relationship with Grover or Professor McGraw—zilch. Frankly, Sarah told herself, this Seth character was simply a distraction. An oddity. But still.

She returned to the Web site of the U.S. Fencing Association and punched in the next name and began crawling through a series of tournaments and rankings.

And the telephone rang again. Mary Donelli.

"Hey, Sarah. We've got a date."

"We have?" said Sarah in as discouraging a tone as she could muster.

"Sunday. Church. Bowmouth Community Church. The Reverend Nick Copeland. We can't let Vera down completely. He's probably going to skin her alive. She'll be turned into the devil incarnate, the source of all evil."

"As Chairman McGraw would undoubtedly say, she's a troublemaker for the sake of troublemaking and she's ruining the fund drive."

"That ain't the way the Reverend Nick is going to put it. So I'll pick you up at eight thirty sharp. Service at nine thirty, but half the county will be there."

"Okay, okay, but I think Vera should stay away."

"What! And miss a chance to go on about the meaning of art? Freedom of speech? Never. She'll be there with bells on."

"Poor Vera, that's what I'm afraid of," said Sarah, and hung up. Free time for research was dribbling away, and any minute Alena Fosdick would be at the door for family hour. This of course was a positive development. Perhaps the woman did have a heart and wasn't so obsessed by her job and her reputation that she couldn't see that her son was in deep trouble. Had Alex actually told her that Derek had tried to kill himself? If not, perhaps it was time for someone to stop tiptoeing around the matter and tell Alena the truth. But without Derek's permission? No, he was twenty-one, an adult, so the job belonged most properly to Dr. Jonas Jefferson.

Sarah looked at her watch. Fifteen more minutes for fencing research. A quick zip through a few more lists. Okay, try clubs, schools, and camps. She had just hit the Web site for Camp Merrilark in Union, Maine, when the doorbell sounded.

And there was the lovely Alena in her fashionable informal outfit straight out of the casual clothes sections of *Vogue* and *Elle*. But her face contradicted the outfit; it was contorted, blotched, worried.

Fifty minutes later Alena's face had smoothed. A burst of tears in the middle of her trying to justify her no-hands-on approach to the current crisis had contradicted everything she was saying.

Sarah's sympathy and Alex's late entry to the scene bringing his best bedside manner (not always on display) did the job. Alena agreed to have dinner with them that night, providing, said Alex, that Derek agreed.

He did agree. Reluctantly. Truculently. But through a dinner of comfort foods the air warmed, and Derek was able to say that he was sorry for the trouble he was in (no admission of blame) and Alena to say that she, too, was sorry, that she knew Grover's death was a blow (this said with tightened jaws), and that she hoped that she and Derek could see more of each other. And that she'd been in touch with a lawyer who seemed friendly.

"Isn't that an oxymoron?" demanded Derek.

Sarah looked at him, surprised. She'd never suspected that he could handle more than a two-syllable word.

But Alena laughed. Alex laughed—lawyer jokes were always pleasant—and so the evening wore down in fairly good humor.

And by nine thirty Sarah was able to return to her research channels.

Eleven o'clock, a strike. Actually two strikes. The second, a not too compelling one, went to a student who in her proper name had attended a summer camp that offered fencing. But when roused from her bed, the assistant director pointed out, the camp didn't keep track of which campers signed up for what. Unless they had won something and so had their names put on a plaque in the camp dining room. Run-of-the mill performers had been simply noted in the letters sent home at the end of camp: "Cathy has tried very hard in soccer"; "Harry has improved his sailing skills"; "Mandy loves archery." And no, the name Sarah mentioned did not ring a bell, said the assistant director, yawning audibly.

The real strike in Sarah's opinion was a winning hotshot fencer. One with a notable name change. The student's secondary school had been the Lawrenceville School in Princeton, New Jersey. Was this student now a closet fencer? Or a fencer who for reasons unknown had given up the sport and gone on to pastures new? Whatever, this former fencer was now snuggled right down among the students of the Drama School. Doing a minor in English. Having had a notable part in Vera Pruczak's production of *Romiette and Julio.*

Sarah, just to enjoy her possible triumph in this second case, hit the site for Lawrenceville School. Goodness sakes alive, as her grandmother might say. A strong fencing program there. And her secret student fencer had cleaned up. Featured. State and school championship. Medals, citations, cups galore. Skill with foil and épée. And, to cap it all, this talented fencer was one of the students who had expressed fear and loathing of Grover the Groper Blaine.

But now what? The police? That seemed, at the moment, a bit on the drastic side. After all, a fencer who no longer fenced wouldn't shake George Fitts into action. Give him another day or so and he would have discovered this fact himself.

Sarah needed more confirmation. More details. Or should she go directly to this ace fencer and say something like, "Excuse me, but have you got an épée under your bed?" Or, since tomorrow was Sunday, the day of the coming church event, perhaps a short watch period was in order. Then she would have to see. Perhaps Katie Waters would be the way to go. Or Mary Donelli. Not Alex, because that led directly to the police. But someone anyway, because a backup, a consult person, was needed. However, right this minute Sarah was very tired. It was time for bed. Perchance not to dream. At least not of weapons and blood and bodies.

Sarah was lucky. That night her dreams transported her years back to the coast of Texas, where she had first met an acerbic but handsome physician named Alex McKenzie, and there he was in the dream trying to bring the details of the ivory-billed woodpecker to her attention. "The bird is extinct," she told him. "Not anymore," he said. "I have identified it. They're all over the place. A positive nuisance."

And then peace until morning.

17

SARAH woke on Sunday to find Alex abroad and the smell of bacon filtering into the room. Sunday, she told to herself, bouncing out of bed. A proper day for reckoning, for conclusions. A clearing to be made in the jungle of information crammed into her head. But how to begin? I can't, she told herself, go screaming into the world saying, "Look what I've got. Four students. One who competed in fencing tournaments and then stopped. Another student who might have fenced—without distinction—at a summer camp. Number three, Weeza Scotini, a dancer and so physically coordinated that she could probably put a foil wherever she wanted. And last, a talented fencer who had suffered a bout of hepatitis."

But Sarah's earlier excitement had faded. What did it all add up to? Assault and murder? Well, hardly. Suspicious past behavior, no. Unless hating Grover Blaine was in itself suspicious. But that feeling would take in most of the English Department. Solution? Let things simmer and focus on her own sins of omission and commission. This last could be done appropriately during the coming church service. Then get hold of Mike or Katie and hand over what might be no more than second-rate information.

But the thought of church turned Sarah to think of Vera Pruczak. Poor woman, she would be shredded and held up to the community as a variation on the scarlet woman busy corrupting the world of Youth. But no. Wrong description. When in adversity and under attack Vera's skin had in the past proved to be made entirely of rhinoceros hide.

The Derek problem of that Sunday had been solved. Instead of turning him over to Katie—who was duly grateful—Alex decided to take Derek along in a birdwatching expedition along the coast. That Derek didn't know a robin from a sparrow was of no concern. "He'll get fresh air, a certain amount of sympathy, exercise, and he even might learn something," said Alex. "I'll lend him your binoculars. He can play with the focusing."

Sarah decided even if her binoculars didn't make it back from the expedition in one piece, the removal of Derek for such a healthy reason was worthwhile. Alex was being rather saintly, she thought. He usually used his birdwatching time not only for the joy of tramping outdoors and seeing birds but also for the pleasure of doing something alone, something that had absolutely nothing to do with medicine.

Mary Donelli arrived promptly at eight thirty in her second-hand newly acquired green Forester. "I can see out better," she claimed. "And it can handle the snow and mud."

Sarah, after some thought, dressed in a churchgoing outfit of dark red wool slacks and a black jacket topped with a high white collar. "I feel ecclesiastical," she said, climbing into the front seat. And then, looking at Mary's bright red cape and navy skirt, said, "You look like a cardinal. We'll both fit in just fine."

As Mary turned the car toward the center of Bowmouth, the subject turned not to assault and murder but to Vera Pruczak, the "defendant," as Mary put it.

"If Vera's lucky, she'll still have a job. Vera might just get her walking papers. She doesn't have tenure and has only an MA. Never mind those romance things she writes. The academic fathers turn purple when they're mentioned. Vera's play is costing local public support. I've even heard from admissions that they're deathly afraid of a falling off in applications."

"That's nothing new," said Sarah. "Admissions is always deathly afraid of something."

Mary slowed the car; a traffic buildup showed down the main road to Bowmouth village. "Everyone's going to the church," she said. "We may have to sit on the steps. But what I'm saying is that Bowmouth doesn't exist in a vacuum, and that it's a big feature of the community. And I'll bet that the Rev. Nicholas is going to put a lit firecracker under that community's tail."

"You're saying the community can't handle a little production which wasn't much more than a noisy satiric comedy. Vera was just having fun. Sexy high jinks."

"Satire, comedy, and sex make some people very nervous. Never mind, maybe the Rev. Nicky will save us all from whatever it was that was endangering us."

"You wish," said Sarah.

"Listen," said Mary. "If Vera hadn't been so in-your-face with the production, toned it down just a little, then the whole dose might have slipped happily down the public throat. Soft-shoe sometimes works better than hobnailed boots."

"You're mixing metaphors, Professor. Anyway, being soft-shoe isn't Vera's style. And once we had those two events there was no way of putting a lid on the thing."

Mary shook her head. "The postmistress said to me yesterday that there must have been something really bad going on in the play to have provoked those attacks. She said she was really 'shook'—her word—when she saw Romiette up there on the balcony being wooed by Julio." Here Mary turned the wheel hard and slipped in ahead of an oil tanker. "We're going to have to push it to make the last pew."

"Cross your fingers," said Sarah, "that Vera doesn't play Cleopatra in her barge."

"That role was made for her," said Mary.

The Bowmouth Community Church was a typical New England church building with its white clapboard, steeple, and uncomfortable wooden pews. But this church boasted the added glory of two

252

stained-glass windows, one on each side of the nave. One showed a colorful rendition of the loaves and fishes being dealt out to the people—a scene that reminded the regulars of their fund-raising bean suppers. The other in darker tones portrayed Jesus rebuking the wind and raging water, an appropriate choice for a community set close to a frequently roiled Atlantic Ocean.

Today the church was full, Bowmouth citizens, college students, faculty, and staff, plus additives from all over the county and beyond. When these were fairly settled, Vera Pruczak made her late entrance, a queen looking for judgment. She came flowing down the aisle, beads clicking, her feather boa floating behind her neck. Then she stopped, appeared to turn herself into something taller and fiercer, and stepped into a third-row pew—the space apparently saved for her by a bevy of Drama School students.

And next—it all rivaled a star-studded Hollywood premier, Sarah thought—down the aisle, slowly, steps hesitant, his arm supported by Linda LaCroix, his face pale and drawn, came Professor Danton McGraw. He was assisted into a seat next to the English Department's chief clerk, Arlene Burr. Next to Arlene sat Dean Alena Fosdick, serious in a Sunday outfit of dark claret with a lace jabot.

"Wow," said Mary, digging Sarah in the ribs. "Lights, camera, action." The two women were wedged into one of the last pews, almost crushed by a three-hundred-pound giant from one of the local lumber companies.

"How did Amos get out of this?" whispered Sarah.

"Amos would rather drink hemlock than find himself trapped in the English Department–Drama School brawl. In church yet. Hush, hear we go."

And go they did. Greeting. Invocation. Hymn "The Son of God goes forth to war / a kingly crown to gain / His blood red banner streams afar / Who follows in his train?"

"Sets the tone," said Sarah, closing her hymnbook.

"We ain't heard nothin,'" said Mary. "Here comes the rev. And hey, isn't he the handsome devil."

"Devil?"

"A common expression."

The Reverend Nicholas Copeland had what is known as "presence." Six feet three or four, tall, dark hair, a long-boned face with a prominent nose down which sharp eyes peered. He was clothed in an academic robe with black velvet arm stripes and a hood with red, yellow, and green bands suggesting to the academics in the congregation that the reverend held a doctorate from an unidentifiable university.

Now like a giant and fearsome raven, the reverend doctor raised both black sleeves, stretched out his arms, and said in a voice of thunder, "Let us pray."

Sarah from that point began to lose her grip. Perhaps it was the voice. Baritone, sliding down to bass and rising again. The words, having to do with heaven and blessing and family and love and charity, rose and fell. The hands, large, with a single signet ring that every now and then caught a light, waved, gestured, or were folded in sadness over the Reverend Nicholas's chest. Bit by bit, Sarah felt her eyes growing heavy. She was sliding, sliding, into a glorious pit of red and green and blue stained glass.

"Wake up," said Mary, kicking at one of Sarah's feet. "I think it's *Aida*."

Sarah shook herself and tried to focus. Listened for a minute and shook her head. "No, more like what's-his-name, Sarastro." she whispered. "You know, *The Magic Flute*."

"Whoever it is, he's holding his audience."

"Congregation."

"Audience. This is a major performance. Vera could use him."

"Be quiet," grumbled the large man next to them.

But it was almost over. The Reverend Nicholas again stretched his hands in an act of supplication. "Are we," he pleaded, now a baritone, "to allow foolish, hateful nonsense that makes a joke of love and life and family to disturb our wonderful community? Our great state. Our beloved nation. To allow a corrupt and snide adaptation of one of the world's great playwright's finest plays to destroy the love we hold for art and theatre?"

He paused, eyes lifted, and listened—and got—a rising chorus of "No, no, no."

And then Vera rose, moved to center stage, just below the three steps leading to the altar, and in turn waved her hands.

The Reverend Nicholas bowed. This was obviously a planned response.

"I welcome," said he, "Madam Vera Pruczak of the Bowmouth Drama School. She has asked for a few minutes of comment and I'm sure we wish to grant her just that."

Madam Pruczak went to town. In a voice of partly stifled scorn she pointed out that if Shakespeare's *Romeo and Juliet*, in its original form, was to be used as a pattern of behavior, then it seemed to support family feuding, street violence, civil disobedience, filial disobedience, jealousy, murder, and, with the connivance of the clergy, a secret elopement, marriage without parental consent—Juliet surely was underage—and a double suicide. And she, the Drama School director, had given the play a happy and joyous ending. Almost everyone of note had risen up alive. "The joy of dancing, triumph over death," called Vera in a voice that probably reached outside to the town hall. "And furthermore," said Vera, "remember the Elizabethan theatre used young boys to play women's parts. Gender change is a time-honored custom." From there, Vera went on about art and freedom of speech and the great tradition of the theatre and the need of the young to question the old. Diversity was all. "Oh, you people," cried Vera, rattling her bracelets. "Diversity, diversity! And may God bless you every one."

"Tiny Tim," murmured Mary.

"I, for one," whispered Sarah to Mary, "have had it. Enough already."

"You just hush up," said the man next to them.

But then it was time for Professor McGraw to rise to his feet, grip the back of the pew, and in a hoarse voice applaud the remarks of the Reverend Copeland and regret those of Miss Pruczak, and hope in the future the town would not be disturbed by thoughtless theatrical productions. He personally would try to make this a certainty.

And it was over. The congregation rose, milled, greeted one another, and filed out. Or on to the Parish House for refreshments.

And suddenly Sarah, shaking herself out of her trancelike state, remembered her mission, one involving the folders of four possible suspects. And right up there in front of her were those four. Surrounded by others of the Drama School. They moved down the church steps, seemed to be arguing over something, and then halted and clustered on the lawn by the "All Are Welcome" Bowmouth Community Church sign.

Sarah in some desperation grabbed Mary by the arm and pulled her into a corner of the entrance hall. "We've got to do something. Fast."

"Huh?" said Mary. "What are you talking about?"

"You know I've been looking into non-fencers."

"I don't know anything of the sort. Except that you'd been sniffing around."

"Three non-fencers who were really fencers. And another person who's very agile. I think they'd all qualify as persons who could stick an épée into someone. Someone the police might not be looking at."

"Oh my God, Sarah. What in hell have you dug up now?"

And Sarah described her findings and ended by saying, "One fenced at a summer camp, another did fence but can't do it now for health reasons—he's a guy I can't even remember seeing around during the production. Then there's a super fencer who cleaned up in New Jersey. The other one is a physical wonder, a terrific dancer."

"Your point being simply that the police should take a second look at these four. So, okay, I'll drive you over to the police trailer and you can spill the beans."

Sarah looked ahead at the group of students who seemed to still be arguing, gesturing, raising their voices. She shook her head. "I feel like a damn fool. The information may not be so great, and the police will probably be digging the same stuff up in a few days."

"So you're ahead of them. Go dump it in their laps and enjoy a day off."

But now the group of drama students seemed to have resolved something. They set off en masse toward a battered tan Dodge van. Sarah counted seven of them. Including, to her surprise, Malcolm Wheelock and Todd Mancuso—Mike Laaka's favorite suspect—

and then, as the expression goes, "the usual suspects." Terri Colman, Kay Biddle, Weeza Scotini, and the newcomer to the suspect list, Seth Nussbaum.

Mary got into the act and called over to them, "Hey there. Where are you going?"

Several students turned back, surprised or laughing.

"Blowing this berg," called Todd Mancuso. "Bowmouth Founder's Day is tomorrow. No classes. Did you forget? We students need fresh air. The big city. Ocean breezes."

And as two more students wheeled around to face Mary and herself, Sarah caught the eye of one. And held the gaze. And knew. And knew, the other student knew, too.

And before Sarah could even breathe the name to herself, the group hustled themselves into the van and took off.

"Oh hell," said Sarah. "What am I going to do? Did you see that look?"

"No, said Mary. "I didn't see any look. Let's get you to the police trailer."

"It's the sort of look that told me that the fact I took a bunch of folders from the Drama School might really mean something. To repeat, I feel like a fool."

"You said it, I didn't."

"I've no real evidence. But I wonder where they're going. Six of them. Do you think it's a conspiracy? A cover-up?"

"What I think," said Mary, "is that you need is more classroom assignments. But since I haven't anything to do right now, we'll follow them. Set this whole thing to rest and get you back into a state of sanity. They'll probably be driving right down the coast to some cute little harbor for wine and crabmeat. And won't we feel like idiots."

Sarah nodded, yes, that's exactly how they would feel. But she told Mary to make for her parked Forester with all possible speed.

"And to make you feel better, I'm calling the police right now and telling them what I know." She paused, hunted around in her handbag, and said, "Damn. Left my cell phone home. Thought it might disrupt the church service."

Mary unlocked the car and pointed. "Use mine. It's right there. But hang on. That old van is pulling away. Headed for Seventeen, I think. Warren or Waldoboro."

Sarah, after a certain amount of fumbling with a strange cell phone, finally connected to the police trailer. Connected with one Trooper Mitchell Morris. Was informed that Mike Laaka, Katie Waters, and Sergeant George Fitts were elsewhere. And then Trooper Morris rather reluctantly received the information that the four students she would name had to various degrees done some fencing or had particular skills and she, Sarah, thought the police should know.

"Hey," said Trooper Morris after hearing the names, "the police are probably on to all of them."

"But," protested Sarah, "they think that three of these people are non-fencers."

"Okay, okay. I'll make a note."

"And," added Sarah, determined now to be 100 percent upfront. "A bunch of Drama School students are off in an old tan van heading somewhere. Maybe toward Route Seventeen. And the group includes Todd Mancuso. Mike Laaka might really like to know that."

"Tan van? Make? Year? License number?"

"I don't know," said Sarah. "Except it wasn't new. Lots of dents."

"Okay, I've go that," said Trooper Morris. "And your name please."

Sarah yielded up her name, her address, and her relation to Bowmouth College. And hung up.

"Why the Todd Mancuso bit?" asked Mary as they swung toward Route 17, the tan van disappearing over the hill ahead of them.

"Oh, that's Mike. He's worked the whole thing out. Todd did it. In disguise. On stage. Backstage. It's far-fetched, really stupid. But Mike's hanging on to it. Mostly I think to rattle George Fitts's cage."

"That's hard to do," said Mary, stamping on the accelerator.

"Look ahead. Those guys are really pushing it. Maybe they'll be picked up for speeding and save us the trouble."

"Not trying to lose us, are they?"

"They don't know the car. I just got this baby Friday. Only three years old. A sweetie."

"But they might have seen us climb in."

"Nah. They were all loaded when we got to the car."

"Visibility from a van is possible."

"So shut up and duck down. Let them think there's one driver. This is a narrow road and lots of twists and turns. I'm going to have to close up a little. You can start thinking about what in God's name you want to do when we catch them, or park next to them—wherever it is they're going to end up. I mean have you got hand-cuffs and a warrant in your pocket."

"I haven't worked it all out," said Sarah. "Honestly, I can't think beyond perhaps confronting some of them and asking questions."

"And you have a foil handy to defend yourself with?"

"I thought we could have a sensible talk. You know, like sensible adults."

Mary shook her head violently. "Listen, we're talking murder here, sweetie pie. Grover Blaine dead. Murder is a capital offense. That assault with intent to kill Danton McGraw is a felony. And you think we're going to have a 'sensible talk.'"

"In a public place. Maybe even tell the attack person, or persons—it could have been two of them—to turn themselves in. That I've called the police with information."

"You've missed your calling. Now you're playing stool pigeon. Protect me."

"Let's hope I don't have to."

"No, I'll have to protect *you*, and that scares the shit out of me."

"Look out," said Sarah. "They're turning off Seventeen."

"I'm not blind," said Mary in a cross voice. Then added, "I'll stay a few cars behind the van so you can sit up. It might help clear your brain."

But Sarah's brain seemed to have settled on dead center, and so for lack of any useful thoughts she tried to absorb the passing landscape. Bare maples, windblown spruce, a few surviving oak leaves falling as she watched. Stands of tired-looking drooping birches. Depressing to the extreme. What had happened to autumn and the season of mellow fruitfulness that Keats had gone on about?

All the while Mary, concentrating on keeping those three or four cars behind the van, blamed herself for a certain lack of sympathy. And also for not understanding what Sarah had in mind beyond a confrontation that seemed both foolish and dangerous. But what are friends for but to follow blindly where others fear to tread? Nevertheless, it behooved Mary, from time to time, to suggest caution.

"If one of those guys had the nerve to stage a double attack in the middle of a play with hundreds of people milling around, he or she—"

"Or they—"

"They wouldn't have much trouble dealing with two nosey English teachers who think they can talk someone into confessing. That scene wouldn't even make a very bad movie. Oh God, Sarah, deliver me. I only want a quiet little life writing about Jonathan Swift along with Amos. And sometimes teaching a class or two."

"That's all I want," said Sarah. "Except not Jonathan Swift. Hey, watch out; they're heading right through that turnoff."

"Christ," said Mary. "Not Route One. Then they're probably off to Portland. Or Boston. Or points south."

"They'll have to stop for gas. Those big vans guzzle a lot."

"And a pit stop for restrooms. Even grab food."

And so it turned out. The two cars, Dodge van pursued by Forester, bounced down Wottons Mill Road, turned south on Route 131, left it and wiggled their way through a number of obscure tracks, hit the Old Augusta Road and with another twist or two somehow ended on good old Route 220, took a quick turn, and came to a halt at the combo gas station and restaurant, boasting a large sign decorated with a huge wagon wheel and the name The Squeaky Wheel. The van opened, and its passengers disembarked. However, none of the van crew turned around to watch the green Forester pull in and park some distance away from the van. Instead they disappeared inside the building and were swallowed up by several people leaving and a family arriving, perhaps to pick up snacks and soda, pay for gas, and use the restroom.

"Now what?" said Mary, turning off the ignition.

"It shouldn't be too crowded. It's after normal country lunchtime, one thirty."

"Don't you want it crowded? So no one pulls out a sharp instrument?"

"Just a few people around. Plus the people running the place. We should be safe as churches."

"Are you referring to *Murder in the Cathedral*? As an example."

"Mary, you can stay right in the car and listen to the radio. I'll do this on my own."

"Whither thou goest, I shall go," said Mary, undoing her safety belt. "And," she added, "regardless of how stupid thou art."

"Wait up," said Sarah. "Let's let them get settled."

"How do you know they're going to settle? Maybe just go pee."

"They'll be hungry. Long church sermon, no food. I'll bet on it. Give them ten minutes and then we'll go in."

"You mean saunter in whistling, not a care in the world? Or storm in saying, 'Hands up, no one move'?"

Sarah glared at her. "Just walk in," she said in a commanding voice, "as if we, too, needed lunch. Which actually we do. We might even get a table with them, all together."

"I'm going to write a book about this," said Mary. "It will be a bestseller. An example of lighthearted crime fiction. Ho, ho, ho. Kindly social chitchat and then, whambo! Crunch! Ouch! A little splatter of blood here and a little splatter of blood there."

"Right now," Sarah said, "kindly social chitchat is what we're aiming for. And we'll try to skip the whambo."

It all went exactly as Mary had pictured in the novel now shaping in her head. Sarah, followed by Mary, walked in, looked around, saw the Drama School group settled at a large round table. Put on an expression of surprise. Mary did the same. Exclamations from the two women such as, "Well, look who's here?" And, "Where did you all come from?" "What a coincidence!"

Expressions from the Drama School students such as, "Hey, it's the faculty." "The English Department trying to take us over." "Dr. Donelli, Dr. Deane, what are you doing here? Spying on us?" And from Todd Mancuso, "Shove over guys. Make room for the bigwigs."

It was all so natural. The students, dressed rather more soberly than usual, today wore dark slacks, trousers, shirts, and turtlenecks—these no doubt due to their recent church attendance—now moved themselves closer around the big Formica-topped table, reached for two extra chairs, and waved a welcome. Sarah and Mary picked up a couple of bottles of soda from the nearby refrigerator and, neither having any solid plans for attack, nor defense, nor even ones involving a meaningful conversation, gave in, smiled, and sat down. A waitress in jeans and a T-shirt decorated with the face of Elvis arrived with several cartwheel-sized pizzas with assorted toppings. Sharing was now urged by the students: "Too much for all of us, help yourselves. Our treat, and we'll expect an A in any of your courses." Laughter all round.

Sarah and Mary, feigning ease and good humor, promised the students that they would take care of dessert. And then during the early phases of munching looked around. The restaurant—a sort of funky byway café with two gas pumps—had made efforts at decoration. Pictures of moose in ponds, gulls on the wing, deer in forests, had been rendered on velvet and hung on the walls. Signs at irregular intervals welcomed travelers to the Squeaky Wheel "That Always Gets the Feast," warned against smoking, and celebrated—in advance—the Squeaky Wheel's Thanksgiving Family Dinner featuring "Our Own Wild Turkeys Roasted to Perfection."

Talk gradually developed, between mouthfuls of heavy-duty pizza, and there was a general relaxing. Sarah gathered from various remarks that the Squeaky Wheel was a favorite drama student stopping spot. After a few general remarks on the possibility of snow mentioned in a forecast, the conversation swung around to the Reverend Nicholas Copeland and his sermon—Did anyone actually listen?—and after this subject had been exhausted, Weeza Scotini brought up Vera's play.

262

"Oh, leave it. The play's history," said Kay Biddle.

"No, it isn't," said Weeza. "I mean what do you really think? All of you. Was it just over-the-top sleaze or was it useful satire? Or what?"

"I hate the word 'useful,'" said Terri Colman loudly. "But satire, isn't it meant to show up the negative so people will see the positive?"

"Simplistic," said Weeza. "Satire is much more complicated."

"Think of Jonathan Swift," put in Mary, more for something to say than a desire to get into a lecture mode.

"Old hat," said Kay. "I go for contemporary stuff. Slam-dunk satire. Hit 'em where it hurts. But Vera's play was just a spoof. Totally harmless."

"Go tell that to the Reverend Nick and half the town of Bowmouth," said Seth Nussbaum. "They're still twitchy over the thing."

Sarah saw the opening. She turned to Seth, who was dealing with a piece of pizza almost the size of an airplane wing. "What did you do in the play? Did you take a part or do something technical? Lighting or props?"

Seth chewed violently for a minute and swallowed. "Hey, you know I tried to get into your Greek play class, but it was filled. So maybe I can take it next term. Anyway, I helped set up the lighting, but I didn't handle it for the show. Vera needed me for a couple of the crowd scenes. Even the one where Mercutio got stabbed. The police raked everyone over who was in that scene about what we saw, but the answer was zilch. We didn't see nothin'. No one did. Too busy keeping out of each other's way."

"That whole scene went so fast," put in Todd. "I was watching from the wings and sweating like a pig in that Friar Laurence monk's costume."

But then, with a nudge from Mary, the conversation veered back to general campus topics, for which Sarah was grateful. Because here was Seth saying he was front and center in the Mercutio scene. Mentally, she put him on hold along with Mike's favorite, Todd Mancuso. Right now, she had to consider her approach to her number one candidate, the super New Jersey fencing whiz. Maybe Sarah could manage it before dessert. The ladies' room perhaps. Away from the table anyway. And if nothing happened, then what? But it had to happen because there they all sat, in the right place at the right time.

The idea of the ladies' room came up naturally. Kay and Terri said they had to go; Kay would pick up the key from the cashier. Sarah said that was a good idea. She'd follow. But why the key? This wasn't a gas station pit stop.

"Precautions, precautions," said Kay. "They don't want any incidents. Lot of places are doing it. Safety first. Especially for women, but the men's room uses them, too. And when they remodeled the place last year they put in decent doors. Not stupid wooden swing things."

"Yeah," said Todd. "Nothing's safe. You can't even make a joke about anything without getting a lantern on your head and a foil on your ear. Right, Terry? Right, Kay?"

And Sarah couldn't help it. Memory kicked in. The foil slicing the ear. Before she could stop it, her head jerked around and stared at Kay and then Terri. Dropped her gaze and crossed her fingers that no one had noticed.

"You can come to the john," said Kay to Sarah, voice cool, looking unruffled—maybe she hadn't noticed anything. "When the Squeaky Wheel put in the new doors they added two toilets. Now they've got a three holer for the ladies."

Sarah fell in behind the two others. Kay put the key into the new lock, the three stepped in, and the heavy door fell silently shut behind them. For a moment, Sarah thought they would finally face one another and have the Talk. But instead Terri went into the first stall and Kay said, "Oh damn, I've forgotten my lip salve," and left. Sarah waited a minute or so and then went into the second stall. And had hardly pulled down her flannel slacks when she heard the rush of flushing, then the first stall snap open, and then departing steps.

Immediately followed by the door almost silently swooshing open and more footsteps. Sarah, flushed, opened her door, expecting now to see Terri.

Not Terri. Mary Donelli. Standing in the middle of the restroom. Looking perplexed. Worried. And then, seeing Sarah, shook her head.

"That was pretty obvious. Asking me to come in as if we needed to have a secret conference. Saying you needed me."

Sarah stared at her. "I didn't say that. Kay Biddle went to get something and Terri just left. Maybe it's a mix-up. You're sure—"

"You're damn right I'm sure. Now let's get the hell out of here. They're all probably taking off laughing like hyenas."

"You mean," said Sarah, puzzled, "big joke? Or," she added, "big getaway?"

"You have criminals on the brain," said Mary. "I think we got a free lunch and they're just taking off, shaking us loose. Who wants the faculty hanging around? Suspicious faculty asking nasty questions."

"So what are we waiting for?" said Sarah, striding toward the door. "Let's see what's going on."

She reached for the new metal doorknob. Turned it. Frowned. Turned it. Rattled the door.

Looked back at Mary. "What's going on is we're locked in."

18

MARY stared at Sarah. Then shook her head. "Stop the clowning. Open the door. Or let me at it."

Sarah gave a final twist of the knob and then backed up. "Be my guest."

Mary attacked the door handle with vigor. Turned, shook, twisted. And, at last, put her shoulder to it and gave a great shove. Not even a tremble.

"Security," said Sarah. "A door that no one can break open. Great."

"Come on, give me a hand. Or a shoulder. It's probably just caught somehow."

More push, shove, and finally in exasperation, from Mary, a good, sound kick.

"Ouch!" said Mary, holding the toe of her shoe.

"My turn," said Sarah. "It may not be as solid as it sounds." She began a systematic series of thumpings up and down the door's surface. And then backed up and scowled. "I think the Maine State Prison could use it," she said.

"Listen," said Mary, "it's probably a reject from the prison. Too heavy." She looked around the room. Two washbasins, three stalls, one paper-towel rack, one sanitary napkin dispenser, one trash bin. "And no window. At least that I can see."

"No window," agreed Sarah. "Just that narrow ventilator up high on the wall. You couldn't even slip a cat through it. Goddamn those guys. Is this some sort of practical joke? Or . . ."

"Or did they all catch on to what we're up to—although I sure as hell don't know what I'm up to and you don't seem much clearer yourself. What was it you said about sensible conversation? Little face-to-face chats."

"I jumped when Todd Mancuso brought up that attack on his ear," said Sarah. "Just a reaction that I couldn't stop. And I think both Terri and Kay got the message. That you and I know something."

"Speak for yourself. I don't know a damn thing," said Mary. "So now what? Should we yell for help?"

"We can try," said Sarah. "But I wish this door wasn't so thick. Or that they put the restrooms closer to the table area. Okay, let's beat on the door and yell. Really yell."

This plan was followed. Yells, thumpings. Pause for breath. Repeat. Pause. Repeat. Response, in Seth Nussbaum's word, "zilch."

"Don't give up," said Sarah. "We're just not making enough noise. And the café people had the radio going during lunch."

"So how do we make more noise?" said Mary.

"Let me think."

"While you're thinking, consider this. That gang in the van might have spotted us right from the beginning. And a couple of them probably had an idea that you were up to no good. Had vibes or warning signs. Did you," Mary said accusingly, "let on at any time that you were looking into the so-called non-fencers?"

And Sarah remembered the scene on the Drama School steps. Her fall. The rain. The oh so helpful students—these very students—who scurried around rescuing her armful of folders and files. And that they had not missed the fact that these files had their names on them. And they had probably not entirely believed Sarah's made-up story about a special class.

"Oh God," said Sarah loudly.

"I agree," said Mary.

For a minute silence. Both women looked about the restroom but found no solution on the bare white walls, the washbasins, the toilet stalls. And then Sarah came to. "Get your cell phone out. Call the Squeaky Wheel and tell them what's going on."

Mary looked around. At her feet, on her arm. By the two sinks. Then groaned. "I left my handbag on the table. When they said you wanted me right away I thought maybe you'd had a fainting fit or something."

"Those fiends," said Sarah angrily. "What in hell do you suppose they thought they were doing?"

"Two guesses. One, it's a cute little joke for a cold Sunday in November. Two, a little end run around two stupid females, one of whom thinks she might be closing in on a murder. Who seems to have gotten hold of some extra information."

Sarah took a deep breath. "I think I should tell you about an accident I had. Outside of the Drama School. With my arms full of student folders and files. I fell. And it was raining."

"Shall I finish the story?" said Mary. "You're down flat on your face. The files scatter and these helpful students picked them up, took a look, and drew conclusions. Put a plan together in case you got active. Didn't you say there was a sort of protective group that Weeza Scotini told you about?"

Sarah nodded unhappily. "I don't know what they call themselves. But they try and keep an eye out for types like Grover Blaine. Like watchdogs. Weeza's a member. And some of the men are, too."

"And so these so-called watchdogs catch sight of you climbing into my car, or see you—whatever—and lead us on a chase."

"But," Sarah objected, "why? I mean the Squeaky Wheel is a place they apparently go to all the time. What are they trying to do?"

Mary shook her head. "Shall we guess. That it just might be connected with the attacks on Danton McGraw and Grover. And those guys don't want you messing with that scene. Or scenes."

Sarah, who had been leaning against one of the washbasins, straightened up. "Come on. Start pounding again. And shouting. Someone has to hear us."

But after a major orchestral effort from the percussion efforts of the two, nothing. Not a footstep or an answering thump or call. Only the very distant sounds of a radio playing far far away.

"The trouble is," said Sarah, running cold water over her abused fists, "that the restrooms are around the corner from the dining room setup and the entrance and the music is muffling everything. We're probably only attracting rats."

"Someone," reasoned Mary, "is bound to want to go potty. Sunday lunch is still in the time frame. Let's settle down next to the door—we can sit on paper towels. I'm tired of standing up. We'll listen for someone coming and then make a hell of a lot of noise."

It actually worked out exactly as Mary had predicted. A futile rattle of the doorknob was followed by an irritated female voice. Then footsteps. More rattles. A man's voice, "Damn. Those Bowmouth students, they must have gone off with the key. You wait here and I'll get the spare."

Mary and Sarah, who had with a single movement propelled themselves off the floor, now began to bang and shout. The female voice called, "Who's there? Have you got the key? Are you coming out?"

Mary, whose voice projected through solid doors better than Sarah's, boomed back that they were locked in. "No key."

"Oh dear," said the female voice. Then, "Never mind. Greg will get you out. He's the manager. He'll have a key."

At which Greg arrived; mutterings followed. And then a man—who must be Greg—called out that the extra key, the spare, always on the hook by the cash register, was missing. "That's never happened here before," he added, and his voice, muffled as it was, sounded puzzled.

"Locksmith," called Sarah.

"It's Sunday," called Greg. "The nearest shop is in Rockland, and it's bound to be closed."

"Police," shouted Mary.

"No way," said the voice. Then, "Look, I'll get hold of someone to take the door down. As fast as I can. So sit tight. Okay?"

Sarah glanced back at the toilet stalls and found herself laughing.

"Not funny," said Mary. She cupped her hands and called in her loudest voice, "Will you make a phone call for us?"

Greg agreed, took Alex's cell phone number, and promised to call and say that there would be a delay. Alex was then to call Amos and let him know. Be told there was no reason to worry.

"Will Amos worry?" asked Sarah.

"Only," said Mary through tightened lips, "if he finds out I'm with you."

But unlike the best-laid plans of mice and men, everything went smoothly. A local builder was reached, he and a friend arrived with tools, the door was opened, and Sarah and Mary stepped forth free women.

But the table at which the two had shared pizzas had been swept clean. And Greg, a stout, affable man with a shaven head and large ears, now that all was well cheerfully offered them free coffee, free dessert, a box of doughnuts to take along.

But Mary pointed out that she'd left her handbag on the table. Greg, his peaceful face now clouding, said that no such item had been left. The students had paid for their lunch, gathered their things, and taken off. "Seemed in kinda a hurry," said Greg. "Something about a bus. Or a car rental. Or a ride. I didn't really listen."

"Damnation," said Mary. "That's my cell phone, my license, my everything."

"Probably a mistake," said Sarah without conviction. "We're not dealing with thugs, you know."

"No, not thugs. Possible murderers, yes."

"*What* did you say!" shouted Greg.

"Just kidding," said Sarah, giving Mary a pointed toe to the ankle. "Mary's like that. Big joker."

"Yeah?" said Greg, looking at Mary as if he'd just seen a particularly repellent insect.

"Thanks for everything," said Sarah. "Listen, Mary, let's move it. We're late already."

"Late? Late for what?"

"You remember. The Sunday school party," said Sarah firmly, propelling Mary toward and then out the door.

Safe, shining in the late-afternoon rain, a rain in which a few snowflakes were now mixing, sat the dark green Forester.

"But," said Sarah, remembering, "your car keys? Weren't they in your handbag?"

Mary looked smug. "For once I'm ahead of you. I hide an extra key under the rear bumper. In a magnet box." At which Mary poked under the rear bumper, produced the key, unlocked the door, and she and Sarah scrambled into place.

And a voice behind them said softly, "Don't turn around. It'll be okay if you do exactly as I say."

"Who," squeaked Mary, "in hell are you?"

"Don't turn around," said the voice. A familiar voice. A woman's voice.

"Weeza," shouted Sarah.

"Keep it down," said Weeza. "I have something in my hand that I don't want to use. Now do as I say. Turn back to Two-twenty and head for the coast. Pull in when I tell you. Pretty soon you both can go home."

"Weeza," said Sarah. "What do you think you're—"

"No questions. It'll all be explained. Later. Just get this thing rolling. Not too fast, not too slow. We don't want the police to get excited."

And Mary got the Forester rolling, turned out of the parking lot, and tried hard to concentrate on the job of driving. And to force her mind into a neutral gear.

Sarah, whose own mind had shifted into high gear, tried to imagine a move that would not cause a weapon to go off, would cause the car to come to a safe stop, would allow Sarah to take off her seat belt and vault to the backseat, would . . . would what? No, when in doubt, when danger is breathing on the back of your neck, stay perfectly still. At least for now. But keep thinking.

Some thirty minutes or so later, as the voice behind had in- structed, Mary pulled into a small two-pump gas station and parked to the side. And not remarkably, this spot turned out to be directly behind a familiar, dusty, somewhat battered tan Dodge van.

"Here's what Dr. Donelli is going to do," said Weeza. "She'll get out of the car and get into the van. She won't put up a fight. Big mistake. But no one is going to hurt you—either of you. You're two of our favorite instructors. This is something we have to do. Okay, Dr. Donelli, your handbag is waiting in the van. But leave the keys in the ignition. That's it, good work"—this as Mary climbed out, walked slowly to the van, where a hand reached out and assisted her into the middle seats.

"Okay, you stay put," Weeza said to Sarah. "We're just going to shift passengers around. Borrow this car for a short run. Don't worry, you'll be going home. And keep looking straight ahead."

Sarah stiffened her neck but by slightly rotating her eyes was able to catch a glimpse of Malcolm Wheelock—ace fencer and captain of the Bowmouth fencing team. He was walking toward the car escorting a figure in jeans who had pulled a dark jacket over its head. The back door of the Forester opened and Weeza tapped Sarah on the shoulder.

"This will be pretty easy as long as you go along with what we're trying to do. If you behave you'll be home before that old wreck of a Dodge van can make it. Now we're putting on a new crew. Malcolm will be your driver. So sit still and stay cool."

At which there was a rustling and Weeza now appeared by the passenger's window and made a sign for Sarah to press the roll-down button. Which she did far enough for Weeza to stick her face in the space.

And for a mad moment Sarah considered attack by car window. A simple push of the up button might have a serious effect on Weeza's breathing apparatus. But what about the hooded figure in the back? Again caution was the better part of valor.

Weeza smiled. "I'm trading jobs. Your new back passenger wants a serious talk with you." At which Weeza called over to Malcolm, "Okay, Mac, let 'er roll."

And Malcolm did just that. "I love this model Subaru," he said cheerfully to Sarah. "My dad has a Forester, too. Now I'll get us going and turn the chat over to the backseat. But like Weeza said, eyes front. Just like the army."

Sarah, looking ahead, saw that enough snow had fallen that

the road's surface was white and snowflakes were whirling around the windshield.

"Not great weather for driving," said the backseat voice. "Nor even for flying if it comes to that."

Another familiar voice.

The snow was coming in from the Northeast. Down the cold Arctic Atlantic, from eastern edges of Nova Scotia to New Brunswick, and then blowing in on the ragged coast of Maine. It began arriving along the banks of Camden's Megunticook River in a few soft drifters by three o'clock that Sunday afternoon. By four the snow had begun to take itself more seriously and the flakes turned harder and came down faster.

Alex McKenzie and his sometime reluctant companion Derek Mosely, out for a hike and a bird-watch, agreed that it was time to hit the road, stop for hot chocolate and some other heavy-duty carbohydrate in the form of doughnuts and Danish.

"I'll take a couple home for Sarah," said Alex as the two finished their coffee.

"But I don't call her Sarah?" said Derek.

"Not unless she asks you to," said Alex. "And at the college you'd better stick to what the other students call her, Doctor or Professor."

"I don't know if I'm going back to college," said Derek. "I've been thinking."

"And?"

"What's the use? I mean it's just going be one big rap and another big rap."

Alex paid the bill and the two returned to the Jeep, now with a light mantle of snow on its top and hood. Once they were settled in their seats, Alex turned to him. "Can I suggest a medical way of looking at it?"

"Sure," said Derek. "Whatever."

"Suppose you have a small tumor. Not actually dangerous, but quite painful. You can live with the thing, but you'd never be happy with it there in your body. It might even grow and get more painful. But you could have it taken out. Surgery. A nasty procedure, going to the hospital, getting carved up. But you're put back together. Getting better very slowly. Periods of misery. But the tumor is gone. Think of yourself as the patient. You're getting well even though it seems to take a hell of a lot of time."

"That dumb story means my tumor is like what I did with Grover. Helping him out. Watching out for him, and then getting stuck with that harassment business."

"Okay, and what's the surgery part?"

"Sticking my neck under the guillotine, going to the police—and my mother—and telling them everything we did. Some of the things Grover tried to do with women were, well, they were pretty rancid."

"Dirty? Mean? Dangerous?"

"Yeah, I guess you could say that."

"Rape, assault?"

"Hey, I never helped out with that stuff. If Grover really did those things. But I think maybe he was mostly showing off, talking big. You know, like boasting. But not actually doing anything. And how can I go through this lousy confession routine when Grover was my best friend?"

"Grover is dead. That's a fact. He can still be a best friend in your memory of him, but tonight and tomorrow you've got that boring business of being alive and facing life."

"And facing life is like having surgery?"

"Sometimes it certainly is."

"Let's go," said Derek. "I'll think about it. My life right now is plenty fouled up."

They drove in a not too uncomfortable silence, reached the old farm on Saw Mill Road, walked in, and found the kitchen telephone blinking red.

Three messages. All from an increasingly irritated Amos Larkin. They added up first to the possibly late return of Mary and Sarah, second to the passage of time with no appearance of both women, and the last call suggested touching base with the police

274

trailer to see if Sarah had enticed Mary to some idiot snoop scheme that had prevented a return.

Alex swore. Turned to Derek. "Do me a favor. Feed Patsy and check Piggy's kibble and see that they both have water. I've got some phoning to do."

"Trouble?" said Derek. He seemed undisturbed by these messages; perhaps he even enjoyed the fact that there were others about to be given a dose of the same.

"Trouble" seemed to be the key word at the police trailer. Alex got hold of Mike, who relayed the fact that Sarah had called, that she'd left a garbled message about four students the police hadn't investigated. And mentioned a tan van, the license and make of which she wasn't sure. Also that Todd Mancuso was another student in addition to the four.

"Has Amos Larkin called you?" asked Alex.

"Five minutes ago. Said Mary and Sarah went together to the church service and Mary was driving a green Subaru Forester. But for us to wait before doing anything."

"The tan van?"

"Found that one," said Mike. "Older brother of Malcolm Wheelock's. Student at the med school. Van is on loan to brother. A Dodge with a Maine plate. We've sent out an all points."

"For the whole state?"

"Not yet. Knox, Washington, Lincoln, and Sagadahoc counties."

"Let's add the Forester."

"Have to clear it with George. And don't those two spaced-out ladies have cell phones? They should check in."

"Sarah's is here on the kitchen table."

"Amos Larkin," said Mike, "says Mary had hers in her car and so why hasn't she called? Listen, stay put, and I'll let you know what we're doing at this end. George has put an alert for Drama School students at bus stations, Portland's Down Easter Train station, and the Augusta and Portland airports."

"How about the Owls Head airport?"

"Come on. Be real. That airport is just around the corner and this gang hasn't traveled just a few miles to drive us all nuts. And for what it's worth, some favorite drama students didn't turn up for a reading set by Vera Pruczak late this afternoon. The guys in the tan van, I'd guess." And Mike hung up.

Alex always preferred action to waiting for phones to ring. What he really wanted to do was climb into the old Jeep and go raging around the countryside, in the futile hope of catching sight of a green Forester or a battered tan van. Since such an idea was obviously insane, he decided on cooking dinner for Derek and bringing in some wood to stack by the fireplace. In which latter task he would employ Derek. Good for his body and certainly useful in giving his sad, self-absorbed mind a different direction.

A phone call in the middle of a meal of raw carrots, hot dogs, and baked beans (straight from the can but nicely warmed) brought Alex fast to his feet. It was Mike.

"Think we've got a fix on that Dodge van. Being followed—no, we're not chasing them at eighty per. I know how your mind works. Should be cornered at Seventeen where One-thirty-one kicks in. Report says the van is stuffed with people. All apparently alive."

"And a green Subaru Forester?"

"Nothing. But once we've got our hooks on the van we can see what they know about Mary's car. With Mary and Sarah in it, we think."

"We hope."

"Think and hope. Okay, that's it. Be in touch later. Hey, and don't lose sight of that jailbait you've got, Derek Mosely. He'll be moving into the oven pretty soon."

"Compassion is your middle name, Mike."

"Make that Common Sense." And Mike dumped the phone down with thump.

An hour later, with Derek, dog, and kitten settled in front of the television watching a *Seinfeld* oldie, Mike returned.

"Van back. Drama School kids, all okay."

"And? I can tell by your voice there's more."

"Mary Donelli came back with the van. Says Sarah, and two drama students are off somewhere in the Forester. And yes, when last seen all were in good health."

"Oh Christ!"

"Yeah. But give it time. There's an all points out for the car, Maine and New Hampshire. If nothing turns up in the next hour or so we'll stretch it to Vermont, Massachusetts, and the Canadian border. George is debriefing the van gang now. One by one. Want to turn up?"

"I've got Derek Mosely here, remember."

"So bring him along. George is using the college private dining room. The cafeteria is next door and he's using that as a holding tank. Derek can be stuck off in a corner with Play-Doh and a coloring book where a deputy can watch him."

Mary Donelli, with Amos smoldering on the sidelines, gave a complete description of what she thought did happen and was still happening in her Subaru and was allowed to go home, to be recalled either later that night or early in the morning.

The debriefing of the Drama School students reminded Alex how difficult young persons can be when they are truly focused. The students strongly resembled a set of clams who had sworn to some higher enemy power to refer to no more than their name, rank, and serial number—in the latter case, their driver's license, college ID, and Social Security number. No one gave out with anything useful. One by one the following developed:

Yes, it was a spur-of-the-moment idea. Sunday with the next day off. Bowmouth Day. The Squeaky Wheel. Favorite place. All friends. Hang together. Lots of times. Do the same things. Visit around. Yarmouth or Falmouth, Freeport, maybe one of those. "Or was it Kennebunk." "Old Orchard." Or Portsmouth. Didn't pay attention. Professor Deane? Oh yes. She borrowed Dr. Donelli's car. Maybe to give Malcolm Wheelock and another student a lift. Partway.

"With Dr. Donelli's consent?" demanded George, who throughout the ongoing stonewalling remained his ice-cool self.

Consent? "We don't know." Maybe. Maybe not. Weren't paying that much attention. Borrowing Dr. Donelli's car? You mean that green Subaru? Well, those two were friends; why not?

"Did any of the conversation," asked George, "concern the play put on by Ms. Pruczak?"

Oh, it might have. "Since we were involved." You know, the usual back-and-forth. But hey, nothing serious. "Just the usual crap."

At the word "crap," this spoken in the solo testimony by Weeza Scotini, the last to be interviewed, George, his face set like New Hampshire's former Great Stone Face, called the crew together and informed them that they were to various degrees liable to a number of serious charges, all too numerous to recite at the moment.

And then as the students began to move toward the cafeteria door, George leaned forward and in a penetrating steel voice said, "What about this club you've got? Playing watchdog?"

Only a moment of surprise. Alex, listening, reminded himself that the student of theatre learns early the necessity of ad-libbing, of quickly filling in when an actor blows his lines. These "watchdogs," if Todd Mancuso and his accomplices were to be believed, were an honorable pack of students sworn to uphold civility, decency, fairness, fight prejudice of any sort, ditto harassment, ditto bullying. "Thank you so very much for listening, Sergeant Fitts," said Todd smoothly, slipping into the part of a former Eagle Scout, now honor student of high repute who had just been tapped for Phi Beta Kappa.

What a future that boy has, thought Alex as the troupe—perfect name for the bunch of them—filed out, straight-faced, butter not melting in any mouths.

They departed, shoulders straight, heads up, faces without expression. Alex stood up, ready to leave, and Mike allowed himself the relief of a long string of four-letter words that probably did wonders for his present state of fury. George Fitts leaned back in his chair, held up his notebook, empty of notes.

"Nothing said worth wasting paper on," said George. "Some adolescents—"

"Hell," said Mike, "these are seniors. Adults. About to leave the nest."

"Adolescents," repeated George. "Older ones, but still wet behind the ears, usually get themselves in a real tangle when they're interviewed. Screw up on details, contradict themselves. Get defiant. Or blubbery. Mix lies and truth. I hate taking depositions from them. But these guys, they take the prize. The Drama School and Vera Pruczak deserve a pat on the back. They'll be a success. The military could use them. You'll never get a solid word out of any of them in a POW camp."

Alex nodded. He'd been very impressed by the performance of the young actors. "Call me anytime," he said. "Now I've got my own older adolescent to take home."

"Tell that Derek," said Mike, "to come clean. He's well rid of Grover even if he doesn't know it. It'll go easier for him if he does some talking. Otherwise he's going to be nailed for everything Grover Blaine is supposed to have done."

"I'm working on it," said Alex grimly. "But in my own way. Not with a blackjack or a cat-o'-nine-tails."

"I'd love to try the cat on that guy," said Mike with a grin.

"Shut up, Mike," said George. "Someday you're going to have a citizens' protest on our necks claiming the police are abusive."

"So, Alex," called Mike. "What did the cat-o'-nine-tails actually look like?"

But Alex had departed for the cafeteria and Derek. It was high time to go home, pace the floorboards, and listen for the telephone.

Of course the voice was familiar. It was Sarah's first choice for the hidden expert fencer. One who could slice the tip off a man's ear, find the vulnerable places in a neck—make that two necks—a leading member of the watchdog pack, and right now one who had the gall and the guts to pull off whatever this particular caper was going to turn into.

"Hello, Kay," said Sarah to the back passenger.

"Thought you'd figure it out sooner or later. The police are certainly slow. Going only for the fencing types. You can turn around. No point in concealing anything. That was Weeza's idea. She's into cops and robbers."

Sarah swiveled around in her seat and faced Kay. Kay, calm, dressed for anonymous travel in a dark jacket, dark turtleneck, her dark hair pulled back, a navy blue scarf tied around her head. "I suppose it was my falling down and scattering all those files, having them get soaked, the stickers getting loose."

Kay sighed. "That sort of did it for me. I could tell by the folders that you were going to do major research. It was my old name, wasn't it?"

Sarah nodded, adding, "That was what I was looking for. All those fencing schools and camps, the U.S. Fencing Association, couldn't pull up a Kay or a Katherine or anything like that connected with a Biddle. Terri Colman had done some fencing, but I couldn't find out that she was special. Seth Nussbaum was good, but he'd had hepatitis so no very recent record. Weeza's an amazing dancer and she could probably pull off a fencing move. Todd Mancuso could have done it, but he seemed very sick. Anyway, you were number one. As Kay or Kathleen you cleaned up. But with your real last name, Bungle, you won camp and school tournaments, won a New Jersey State Championship. Foil and épée."

Kay groaned. "Can you imagine going into theatre work, acting, with a name like Bungle?"

Sarah shook her head. "No," she said. "Bungle wouldn't help your career much."

"I suppose," said Kay, "it must have been something in Hungarian or Finnish—they're on both sides of the family way back. But someone in the family shortened it and never got it fixed. So I changed to Biddle the beginning of my sophomore year. A great-aunt's name. But that Linda in the English office, she snickered about the name but wouldn't retype or erase. Just put a sticker over it."

Sarah sat still. She couldn't believe they were having this ordinary conversation about the need to change one's name when the subject properly was murder.

But now Kay tapped Malcolm on the shoulder. "The turn should be up ahead. Then look for the Dunkin' Donuts store. You can hop out there. Remember our plan. The bus should be coming along in about thirty minutes."

"What," said Sarah, trying to keep any hint of emotion out of her voice, "are you going to do? We've got to get Mary's car back to Bowmouth. Right now. The snow is getting really heavy. And people, probably the police, are going to be looking for us. For this car. For you. For me. For Malcolm. By now Mary will have told them what's going on."

"I'm not sure she really knows. And right now with the snow coming down and this being a Subaru, we won't be conspicuous. Subarus are the universal cars in Maine. What you and I need is a serious talk. I hope you're going to go along with what I say."

"And if I don't. Or can't?"

Kay shrugged. "Then the talk will get very serious."

19

LISTENING to Kay Biddle/Bungle, her tone of voice, and remembering that Weeza had mentioned a weapon, Sarah began thinking of escape. Considered waiting until the car slowed at the next curve, or halted at a stop sign, came to a T in the road; then she would pop the passenger door open and toss herself into space.

She pictured it. Silently remove the seat belt, inching her fingers slowly across the strap. Letting it slide quietly back into space, the action covered perhaps by the hem of her jacket. Then she would hunch up and imitating some sort of ball—a basketball would be right—roll out to the road. Roll until she hit the verge, get up, then run like hell, hoping the thickening snow would shield her. Find a place to hide, if bushes or woods offered themselves. Or a hilly countryside, a group of houses with backyards, gardens. Convenience stores and cafés with signs saying Open.

Of course, since Malcolm was going to be dropped off at a bus stop she could leap out then. But it was Sunday. Often these bus stops operated as quick departure and pickup places. Damn. That was no good. Besides, Malcolm, athlete that he was, could probably grab her in two strides.

"Okay," said Kay. "Here's how it's going to be. I'll be dropping

Malcolm off, and he'll be heading back to Bowmouth. You and I will drive to a quiet place for conversation. Correction. You drive and I'll give directions. Don't say you can't drive this car, since I've seen you in a Subaru. They're probably all alike."

Sarah took a deep breath. The car was going too fast for any escape efforts. Stick to talk. "Kay, look, why fight it? They're going to find you. Go back and face what you're going to have to face sometime. I'm not saying you're guilty of anything. I don't know. And the police know everything I do. I made a call before Mary and I left to follow you."

"And what exactly was your idea when you went to follow us?"

"The same as it is now. To talk. Calmly. Sensibly. Not getting mad. Mary came for support. My idea was to talk to all of you. You were all involved somehow in what happened during the performance. Watching, helping, covering up."

"We were together on one very important thing. Which you seem to be missing."

"Which is?"

"Our absolute agreement," Kay said, her voice like a razor blade, "in loathing Grover Blaine. Trying to put a stop to him. And if we had to, end him."

Sarah tried to digest this last sentence. Then struggled to get its meaning clear. "Do you mean 'end' as in murder? You always had murder in mind?"

"Did I say murder?" said Kay. "Terminate is more like it. Stop his sleazy attempts to intimidate, harass, paw female students, to almost rape them—although for all I know he pawed male students, too."

"Hold up. What do you mean, *almost* rape them?"

"Malcolm," called Kay. "Turn right up there. It works as a shortcut."

And Malcolm Wheelock turned sharply at a small intersection, drove down a badly lit street, swung right at a two-lane town street, shot forward, and came in on the backside of familiar Route 1 in Waldoboro. And there stood a Dunkin' Donuts store with a small Bus Stop sign attached to the side. The store, as Sarah had feared, was dark. One potential passenger, a bent-over white-haired man, sat on a bench outside, a suitcase gripped between his legs. Well, this was obviously no time to try an escape, to fling herself on the mercy of this fragile-looking human.

"Now, Sarah," said Kay, "listen carefully. Malcolm is going to give me the ignition keys; then he'll get out. You slide into the driver's seat. I come over and sit next to you. Just like Weeza, I have a small firearm in my pocket. Better than an épée any day. I'll hand you the car keys. You start the car and turn back from Route One on the road we just used. I know a fine place for our conversation."

At that, Kay suddenly gave a soft call, and Malcolm, who was just stepping away, turned.

"Just thought," said Kay. "Since Sarah's called the police, they may be checking bus stops."

Malcolm turned and grinned. "Thought of that. But I've got a cousin half a mile from here. I'll call and get picked up or hike over there. Then I'll evaporate for a while."

"And leave the whole gang at the college to face the heat?"

"Just for this evening. Until I can find a car. I'll be at Bowmouth by tomorrow morning. What's the saying, 'All for one and one for all'? Favorite book as a kid."

Kay nodded, waved. "Good luck, Mac." To Sarah: "Okay, let's split. I'll call out the turns."

Which Kay did with great precision, and after a left, a left, a right, and into the small town, she pointed out the white clapboard square shape and spire of the All Saints Baptist Church. The snow was coming down faster. It now was thick and hard and seemed to mean business.

"This is the best place to park that I know. People leave you alone in church parking lots. Hospital parking lots are good, too, but I don't know a nearby hospital. Okay, turn off the car lights and the ignition. And let's have it out. Where were we?"

"I asked you about Grover Blaine's almost raping someone. Or more than someone."

"That's a good question," said Kay. "I have a theory about Grover. A real slime and dangerous. But when it came down to it— I've gotten this from victims—he can't manage the rape part. He terrifies them, pulls at their clothes, shoves them around. But no final action. I guess a psychologist would have a label for him, but I'd say it's the bully-coward syndrome. Or he's impotent. Or both. Anyway, he was a disgusting specimen. But no one caught him until Weeza set him up."

"Weeza told me how that worked," said Sarah.

"It was going to be the safe way of getting rid of him. Trouble is there's Derek Mosely on watch, and there's Dean Fosdick, his mother, lurking. And the student harassment committee dithering and flopping around."

"So you decided to try something else."

"I didn't get a real group okay. They waffled just like that dumb committee. But something had to be done. Grover Blaine was a disaster waiting to happen. Sooner or later some nervous little freshman female would get it. She'd be pawed or manhandled or worried into drinking or jumping off something. Or breaking down and quitting school. Oh yeah, I grant you there are others around acting like rats, but Grover was numero uno."

"And *Romiette and Julio* was there waiting," said Sarah, trying to keep her voice level, keep any tone of reproach down.

"The staging of that play, the costumes, the crowd scenes, were made for eliminating, injuring, killing, crippling, someone. Taking care of the problem of Grover."

"And nailing Todd Mancuso on the ear gave you the idea. That's the place I began thinking. Everyone called it an accidental hit. I wondered."

"Smart Professor Sarah Deane. You are so right. That business wasn't planned. Terri and I both had had it with Todd's little tricks. But Todd was never in Grover's class. A jerk sure, but he's a decent person basically, damn good actor, but he had this star complex and ran away with the idea of teasing the bejesus out of Terri and some of the other women. Me, too. Thought he was some sort of Groucho Marx maybe. Terri grabbing that lantern was impulse and so was my reaching for a foil. Terri nailed him on the head and I made an extension, lunge, and touché. Off comes a neat little piece of ear. And Todd's been Mr. Nice ever since. Learned a real lesson. Actually, I sort of love the crazy guy."

"You're both of proud of that whole business," Sarah said.

"Listen," said Kay. "What really hurt him was having the hell beaten out of him by Grover in Fine Food Mart. That was brutal. And news gets around like crazy in a college, so I do know about those two students making a pretty good ID. Not many students around are look-alikes for Draco Malfoy. Grover was the bigger Draco, and pal Derek was the thinner version. But they did look like brothers."

"And the beating was another black mark for Grover. And Derek."

"Jealousy, I'd guess, on Grover's part. Todd the star actor. But Derek never got in the action. Not the action type. He played Rottweiler. Correction, make that faithful hound dog. You see, Grover was Derek's friend, only friend actually. Derek the geek."

"When you were planning to nail Grover playing Mercutio, were you just trying to injure him, wound him a little? Or slice his ear? Or?"

"Or kill the goddamn rat? It didn't matter which. If I'd wanted to slice his ear, well, I could have done just that. I went for the neck. Jugular, carotid, it depended on the angle I got him. Awkward as hell. I'm there in a mask and a wig, part of the Mercutio crowd, the visibility was lousy, and I'd only watched the scene, never been in it. So I had to have some luck. Which I did. I mean I got the neck. But it wasn't the right neck."

"It certainly wasn't."

"I almost passed out when there was Grover Blaine perfectly healthy taking curtain calls. I was sure I'd gotten Grover. He was in the whole Mercutio outfit. Doublet and hose. But the hose, the stockings, they confused me. When Todd played the part they were supposed to be red and green. The understudy was supposed to match. But I thought it was a slipup, no big deal. After I'd gotten him with the épée he was in no condition to fight back. I dragged him well away from Tybalt and Benvolio, who were listening for entrance cues. Then I bopped him hard over the head and he went down face-first."

"Did you use the same lantern?" Sarah felt compelled to ask this question.

Kay shook her head. "Found a wooden mallet just sitting

286

there, I don't know why. Anyway, he went down and I never looked at him as I lugged him way backstage and covered him up. As I said, the guy's size and the costume were mostly right."

"You didn't think he might bleed to death back there?"

"Oh, I thought someone would find Grover when the stage crew went to clean up after the party. I didn't worry. Grover dead or Grover bleeding. All the same to me."

Sarah tried to suppress a cold shiver. Kay's voice was as frigidly unconcerned. She might have been talking about swatting a mosquito and wiping the blood from her arm.

"But when you found out it was McGraw."

"Like I said. A shock. I mean I'm not wild about Spit-and-polish McGraw, but I didn't plan to stick a sword in his neck. But now I had to get Grover. Before the party was over. I saw him get up and leave, and for once Derek was talking to someone who wasn't Grover. I tracked Grover down, moved him away from the party scene, and said some really horrible insulting things. Almost spat in his face. It worked and he reacted just like I thought he would. Began to bluster and swear. I challenged him to a fencing match. He took me up on it. We went to the Green Room after he'd picked up a foil over in the practice room."

"A foil, not an épée?" exclaimed Sarah.

"No épée. I'd gotten rid of mine. It had bloodstains."

"But why didn't you just nail him like you did Professor McGraw? In some dark corner. A fencing match might have gone the wrong way."

"Then he might have been found too soon. I had to leave the theatre fast after I'd nailed him. As a come-on I told him it was going to be a real bout. A duel. He bought the idea. I knew it would be taking a chance. Not a big one, but even if he wasn't the world's greatest fencer, he might have gotten lucky. Anyway, we both had foils with the buttons off the tips. There's enough space in the Green Room. We turned on the lights, moved a few chairs out of the way. No masks of course. We even saluted. Then *en garde.* He advanced, I retreated, he advanced again, extended, lunged, and I parried. I could see he was plenty awkward and that it was going to be easy. I advanced, did a *coupé* over his blade, he parried just in time. I advanced, extended, feinted, slipped under his foil, and made the touch. In the neck. Just where I wanted it. He went down like a log. I pulled him to the end of the room, closed the door, and got out. Left the party. And so did Terri and some of the others. None of us had planned to spend too long there anyway."

Sarah listened in silence. Appalled. It was exactly as if Kay, in the role of a dispassionate sports reporter, were describing a not very important fencing match. It reminded Sarah of the unemotional, flat way that BBC announcers sometimes described tennis matches.

"Are you listening?" demanded Kay as Sarah stared at her.

Sarah breathed through her teeth. "That was no match. That was murder," she said. "Attempted murder for Danton McGraw. The real thing for Grover Blaine."

"Murder! The hell it was. I even had to give that degenerate bastard Grover Blaine a chance. More than I gave McGraw. And McGraw almost deserved what he got. What in God's name did he think he was doing taking over Grover's part? What an ego! But now he's okay. You heard him stand up today in church and yak about immoral theatre."

Another silence. Sarah tried to digest what she had heard. Kay, arms folded across her windbreaker, looked across at her with an expression set in concrete. Then a lone car, covered with a thin white blanket from the falling snow, slipped into the church parking lot, made for the end of it, stopped. In the dim light from the single lamp post, Sarah could just make out a couple of figures who reached for each other and made one profile.

"Whoa, that gave me a scare," said Kay. "But they're just a couple of nestlings. Too busy to look around. So now, Sarah Deane, what are you going to do? Are you going to join with us in keeping quiet? Now you know what I know, more or less. Our group—we call ourselves the Terriers—"

"Terriers!" exclaimed Sarah. "Is that name meant to sound like 'terrorists'?"

"No way. What a gruesome idea. Terriers are dogs who stick to their job. Stubborn. That's us. Loyal and very stubborn."

"So go on," said Sarah grimly.

"I knew you had a grip on some details, not on others. But ever since we collected those folders that were blowing around, I knew that you would find my real name under that stupid sticker. And you'd probably make an informed guess. The ability to hit a target area with an épée, or a foil, isn't something you're born with. The police, especially that Mike Laaka, seem to think fencing is a sort of weird game that's done by sort of an elite corps of rich students. Like pretend knights. What I'm saying here is we hope you don't want to add anything else to what the police already have."

"I don't know what the police already have. They don't share," said Sarah. "I told you before, I gave them the names of four people they hadn't pegged."

"What I'm telling you is we're all hanging together on this. We hope when they ask you about talking to me, you say you heard nothing you didn't already know. That's what Professor Donelli will say. She has to, because nothing was said when she was there at lunch. We all just had pizza and she was given a ride home—yes, over her objections—and that's because I wanted to talk to you. Alone. Explain a few things."

"I've told Mary that there were three people who knew how to fence and you were the favorite. The top fencer."

"Just guesses. Listen. Here's your choice. You can drop me off somewhere and drive home. You give me your word, and I'll trust you to stick to what you've already told them. On your honor as a proud assistant professor at ancient Bowmouth College."

"Is this turning into some kind of joke?" Sarah demanded.

"I couldn't be more serious. We, me, our group, think you can tell the police that I wanted this talk with you alone because I wanted to keep my fencing career quiet. And that's the truth. It wasn't a secret really, but I decided to shut up after I clipped Todd Mancuso's ear. Tell who asks you I didn't want to be hassled by the police, didn't want them sitting on my tail, following me around. Terri and I are both under the gun because of that scene. More absolute truth."

"And the other 'events'? Dr. McGraw and Grover Blaine?"

"Right now the police don't have evidence. Almost anyone in that play could have put on a costume. Or was already wearing one. Joined the crowd scene and drilled McGraw and Grover. No fingerprints, I wore gloves. And I haven't dribbled any DNA sputum around. And my hair and dandruff along with most of the cast's is sticking in every cap and cloak and cape and ruff and farthingale in the costume room. Unless they've already sent the things to the cleaner's. Vera always does that right after a performance."

"You're saying there's no case against you. Unless I sound off. Or one of your fellow Terriers does."

"Right. The Terriers may suspect me, be sure of what I must have done. Since none of them did it themselves. Actually, only Malcolm Wheelock and Todd Mancuso had the skill to pull it off. And Seth Nussbaum. But I'm pretty damn sure not one of those guys will cooperate with the police in saying when they saw me. Or where they saw me. So what about it? You're a good instructor. I've enjoyed your class. You're always pretty fair with everyone. Even the Dereks and the Grovers."

Sarah looked at Kay. Long, hard. And straight on. "What do you think I'll say?"

"I think you can go both ways. Lady Straight Arrow. Or Lady Simpatico."

"And if I'm Straight Arrow?"

"I'll be sorry. Then we part. And I'll make it hard for you. Not kill. Not pump lead into a good English teacher. But make it very tough for you to get home. I'll need the time to disappear. It's not going to be easy. I'll have to move fast. I'm a damn good actor, and I think I'll disappear and turn up as someone else. So, your decision. Time's wasting."

Sarah closed her eyes. Pictured life as an honorary Terrier. A buddy to the Drama School students. Perhaps somehow being made a faculty advisor for a few of them. Supporting them against Danton McGraw's takeover plans. Waving at them on the campus. Sharing pizzas on trips to the Squeaky Wheel. Thought again about Grover Blaine and her deep disgust of the man.

And turned to face Kay Biddle née Bungle. And said, "No."

Kay nodded and said simply, "Start the car and take the first left after you hit the main street."

The route chosen was no route. For a few miles it twisted and turned around North Pond Road, curled south on Western Road, and went down and turned back on something called Vaughans Neck Road (a complete stranger to Sarah), then followed a series of turns and reverses so that even one familiar road name would be passed twice, in a different direction. And the snow, now beating on the windshield, forcing the wipers to go at top speed, had begun covering the fields, topping the hedges, blanketing the roofs of small barns and distant houses. Even worse from the driver's point of view, the snow was now covering the white guiding lines along the middle and edge of the road. Here and there she caught the name of a road: Crawford Hill Road, Eastern Road, Graylock Road. But more and more as she drove, these signposts, the intersection stop signs, became blurred or covered over by white patches as if some giant hand had been throwing snowballs at them. Sarah leaned over the wheel, peering into the whirling, beating snow, listening to Kay bark out orders. Next left by that barn, right over the bridge, take right by that fence. The snow buildup on the roads was now causing the car to fishtail slightly at each curve, and when Sarah arrived at what seemed like a fairly large intersection she crossed it almost blindly and drove for a distance and then braked and pulled to the roadside.

"I can't see a bloody thing," Sarah said. "Do you know where you're going? Or where we're going?"

"We aren't going anywhere. You are. I am. But not together."

Sarah turned to Kay, took a deep breath. Time to give it one more try. "Come on, Kay. Please. Think about it. They'll find you. The police. You know that. Maybe not right away, but sooner or later. Midcoast Maine isn't like trying to escape into the Everglades or down in some canyon in Utah."

Kay gave a grim smile. "The White Mountains might do."

"Listen, Kay," said Sarah, almost desperately trying to make her voice warm, compelling, but not overdo it with long argument. "How about gritting your teeth and heading back to Bowmouth. Get a lawyer. Make the case for self-defense with Grover."

"And stabbing Professor McGraw?"

"I don't know how that would go," said Sarah. "But at least he's alive."

"If you're trying to try that old message about facing the music, that's not my thing," Kay said. "I'm guessing I won't be found. I'd bet on it even. Doing in Grover Blaine was, as I keep saying, for the good of the community. Bowmouth should give me a medal."

"But it was . . . ," began Sarah.

"Don't say it. But I agree with you about one thing. The driving's pretty tough. There's a dirt road up ahead. Turn right and go down to the end. There'll be a place to turn the car around. Then I'll take over. Lucky I know where I am, used to spend summers near here. I can do it blind."

Sarah drove cautiously, braking around narrow curves. The road was pitted and rutted; there were no street lamps, although every now and then she caught sight of a dark mass that must be a building of some sort. The road after a couple particularly tight turns rose suddenly and then dipped down to a wide level and the car's headlights caught what seemed to be a tipped-over canoe by the side of a rough fence.

"Turn around here," instructed Kay.

And Sarah, after considerable backing and turning, kept her mind busy with ideas of giving Kay a push and racing away into the snow-covered brush. Or tossing the ignition keys out the window. Something, anyway.

"Stop," ordered Kay. She turned toward Sarah and suddenly her hand shot out like a striking snake, turned the ignition off, and pulled the key free.

"That," said Kay, "was in case you had any crazy idea about throwing the keys away. Okay, here it is. End of the line. Hop to it. Get moving. Fast. I don't want to be tempted into doing something bad. I'm usually not this decent when it comes down to saving myself. Well? What are you waiting for?" This as Sarah frantically tried to drum up one more strategy for saving both of them: Kay from police, trial, prison, herself from very likely freezing somewhere in the wilds of midcoast Maine.

"Get the hell *out*," shouted Kay. "I mean it. Now."

And Sarah hit her safety belt release and threw herself at the door, opened it, and almost fell on the ground. She scrambled to her feet, began to run down the far side of the road, ducked behind a bush, heard the Forester accelerate behind her, saw it pass her and disappear into the night.

She stopped suddenly. Just stood there, her breath coming in gasps. In an almost clinical way, she told herself that this was a panic reaction.

"So stop it," she said aloud. "Stop it right now. And start walking. Somewhere. Anywhere. Keep warm. Move."

But these instructions didn't result in action. Instead she took two steps and then saw blurred in the snow a large tree on the road's edge and leaned against it. And panted. And then, forcing herself to count her breath, she gradually slowed herself to a point where thinking became possible.

First, she had not been shot, run over, or attacked by an épée. Nor had she been pushed into a pond or river or down a gully. Second, she had eaten recently and was not hungry. In fact, right now, the idea of those pizzas was causing a degree of nausea. Third, at least she was on a road and not in the middle of some swamp.

She looked around trying to make out something through the dark and swirling snow. From the character of the unpaved road, the scattered cabin-size shapes of buildings with not a single friendly light showing, she guessed she was in some sort of seasonal community from which everyone had departed, back to towns and cities, south to the Carolinas, Georgia, Florida. A summer only place. Witness that turned-over canoe next to the fence just ahead of her.

A canoe! As in shelter. If worse came to worst she could crawl under the thing, roll herself into a ball, think hot thoughts, and hope she could make it until daylight. The trouble was that instead of her usual weekend costume of jeans and sweater and windbreaker, knitted hat, and gloves, she had dressed for church. Her trousers were lightweight, but thank heavens at least for wool. Lightweight jacket. Proper shoes for church but highly improper for tramping around in the dark on a dirt road. And improper socks, make that thin stockings.

But okay, a canoe meant someone had a camp, a cottage, a dock. Somewhere. If she could only see, but with the falling snow it was as if she were stuck inside one of those globes that when shaken produced a whirling white storm. She narrowed her eyes and tried through sheer force of will to see beyond the first ten feet. Nothing. No path, no driveway. Nothing.

No, wrong. She had tire tracks. The Forester had left tracks. Now growing fainter with the snow, but still tracks. Follow them out, shouted her brain.

But it was so damn cold. Never mind. Just get her engine going, her legs moving. She'd been crouched behind the steering wheel for what had seemed like centuries. Now stiff and shivering she had to exert herself. One step, two steps. Walk faster. She forced her feet into one of the tire tracks and marched. She heard her grandfather's deep baritone voice when, as children, she and her brother, Tony, stomped around the Camden Hill trails after him: "Hi ho, hi ho, it's off to work we go," "Onward Christian Soldiers marching as to war," "Tramp, Tramp, Tramp the boys are marching," "Hay foot, straw foot, belly full of bean soup." "Left, left, I left my wife and forty-nine children. Right, right, right in the middle of the kitchen floor. Left, left." "Over hill, over dale, as we hit the dusty trail"—make that "snowy"—"Anchors aweigh, my boys, anchors aweigh." That was Grandpa's favorite; he turned teary eyed when he heard that one. Even after having his ship blown up at Okinawa, he'd stayed in the navy for six years more. And "Eternal Father Strong to Save" had just about knocked Grandpa out.

Sarah was now striding automatically, stepping along in the middle of an increasingly faint tire track. She could march only as long as she could see. And the blasted road twisted and turned so that once she had even gone off into the woods and stepped into mire.

The heat from her body was melting the snow on her shoulders, and she could feel the damp coming in around her neck, down her back. And a wind was rising.

"Damn it to hell." This shouted out loud. A defiant noise to the unfriendly weather. And a second later she again slipped off the road and found herself clinging to a fence. A wooden fence that perhaps, just perhaps, led to some snug camp whose careless owner had left the door unlocked.

She found the camp at the end of the fence, which ended almost at a short flight of steps to a snow-covered deck. But fortune smiled. Or at least grimaced. Several pieces of furniture sat on the deck, shrouded by tarpaulins. Tarpaulins, yes! The perfect substitute raincoat. She snatched one free from what felt like a wicker rocking chair. And in doing so knocked several objects from the chair's seat. Fumbling on the floor, she felt an object that from its wide, flat blade suggested a putty knife. The next item appeared to be a screwdriver. And the last a small long, round object that from its shape and terminus almost screamed the word *flashlight*. And it still worked. Not a brilliant beam but a soft, almost acceptable round yellow spot. Good. She hoped for an hour or more of light.

Now the decision. Try to break into the camp and spend the night wrapped in blankets and take off in the morning. Or go back to the road and by this tiny flashlight find her way to the entrance. Perhaps not onto a main road but at least, she hoped, a paved one. And, as she had driven with Kay, Sarah remembered that before she'd been ordered to turn, she'd seen scattered an occasional building. A barn, a house. Buildings with lights.

Just to check out her options, she gripped the flashlight and crawled around the camp, or cottage, or whatever it was. Front door, back door locked. Windows, ditto. Careful owners—even if they left tools and a flashlight around. But now the idea of actually breaking a window and climbing in began to lose its appeal. She felt somehow she had to keep moving. Okay, she had a tarpaulin raincoat and a light. She would walk. No, change that, she would march.

And march she did. The little light did its job, so there was no more tumbling into swamps and marshes. But after a while her marching march turned into slightly uneven, uncertain steps; Sarah's knee began hurting. That stupid fall down the Drama School steps. But just as her progress was about to slow into a real limp, she came out onto a main road. The real thing. Snow covered, but pavement, not like the slippery, bumpy track she'd been trying to walk on. And there below a knoll to her left across the road she saw a light. One single clear light on a massive building, a barn perhaps.

She just made it. Across the pavement, along another long fence, post and rail, which turned down along a steep drive. Directly to the barn with its single welcoming light. At least she hoped it was welcoming. The last few steps were misery. She dragged one leg after the other, and when she reached the door of the barn she gave it a push. It opened, slammed closed behind her, leaving her standing in a dim entrance space.

And immediately following the door closing came explosions of strange sounds. A sudden snort. A heavy stamp. A thump, thump. Followed by a whickering sound as if something was blowing through a big mouth, through big teeth.

Where in hell was she? She raised the little flashlight and saw a dim row of bars and doors across from her. Horses. Horse barn. She waved her flashlight, now growing fainter and fainter, at the stalls. A brass nameplate fastened to the door of a stall straight ahead caught the light. *Plum Duff.* Oh God, that was the name of her formidable aunt Julia Clancy's favorite horse, Plum Duff, affectionately called Duffie. Duffie, a sixteen-hand bay gelding, who had often been responsible for tossing Julia from the saddle. But always described by his owner as a "perfect sweetheart." Now, by some weird turn of fortune, Sarah stood in Aunt Julia's barn. And all about her Aunt Julia's horses, roused by the banging barn door, snuffled, snorted, and stamped in their stalls.

Sarah, now completely unstrung, sank to the barn floor, a floor most fortunately lined by several bales of hay. Hallucination? Sleepwalking? Or just plain old-fashioned unbelievable good luck.

But why in God's name would Kay Biddle leave her within striking distance of her aunt's farm? Had Kay had a twinge of conscience, a sudden impulse to do a kind thing? Answer: No. No sign of that. Sarah was here because Kay, although familiar with the area, probably didn't remember that a farm sat almost across that long, twisting dirt road. Might not have even seen it, down in a hollow as it was, because of the snow. And, most important, Kay un-doubtedly didn't have a clue that she, Sarah, had a close relative—and a favorite one at that—within miles.

Sarah rose unsteadily, tottered to the telephone mounted next to Duffie's stall, pointed the light on the dial buttons, and pressed the one marked House.

And the little flashlight, having done its utmost, flickered and went out.

20

THE voice that answered was thick with sleep but carried an undercurrent of alarm. Elderly farm owners are not used to receiving calls from the barn after lights-out.

"Julia Clancy," said Sarah into the speaker. "Aunt Julia?"

"Who is this? Who's down there?" Now Julia's voice added a crackle of anger. In the background two dogs began barking. Tucker and Belle, Julia's English setters and bedtime companions.

Sarah began again. "Aunt Julia, can you hear me?"

"Whoever you are, of course I can hear you. And I've just pushed the bell for my stable manager. His security team will be right there. And don't you go near any of the horses." And the telephone slammed down.

Security team? wondered Sarah. Poor Julia, that wasn't much of a defense. Julia's security team was one man, faithful Patrick O'Reilly. By day the security team swelled to an assistant manager and student riders and aides.

What to do now? If Sarah went up to the farmhouse, Julia would probably meet her with a shotgun, a weapon she had probably never learned to use properly.

So try again. Sarah pushed the House button. No answer. But

lights came on in the farmhouse, and then down the sloping path came Tucker and Belle, barking their silly heads off.

These were old friends. Sarah opened the barn door and embraced them, was licked and slobbered on. And then just as she was settling back on the bale of hay to await further developments, a pickup truck roared into the drive, its door opened, followed by the sound of fast steps, and suddenly a huge beam of light hit the window above the barn door. Then the side barn door was pushed open; the beam hit Sarah full in the face.

"Ah Jesus Christ and Mary in heaven," shouted Patrick, lowering the light. "Sarah Deane, what in God's good name are ye doin' here in the middle of the night?" Patrick, although long an American resident, when agitated found his tongue reverting to the auld sod.

"Patrick, oh, Patrick, I'm so glad to see you." Sarah shook off the setters, stood up, and threw herself into Patrick's arms. "I was afraid Aunt Julia would come down with that old shotgun of hers and blow my head off. She thinks I'm a burglar."

Patrick, always embarrassed by displays of emotion, plus having his employer's niece finding him in red flannel pajamas, bathrobe, and rubber boots, set Sarah gently back on her feet.

At which point, Julia Clancy pulled open the door and stood in her bathrobe and nightgown pointing an antique shotgun. "Hands up," she shouted. "I've got you covered."

Patrick, shaking his fist, roared, "Julia Clancy, don't be a damn fool. Put down that gun. It's Sarah Deane. Your own niece. And she's shivering and wet an' what she's doin' here is beyond me."

Julia started, lowered the gun, stared at Sarah, whose face was lit again by Patrick's torch, and then sprang forward and embraced her niece.

"What in God's name . . . ," she began. But with Sarah bursting into tears, Julia brushed aside the two excited dogs and took her niece in her arms.

Afterward Sarah thought the whole last hour could somehow be made into a one-act play—no, make that a farce—and probably make any reviewer write that even as a farce it went much too far over the edge.

Alex, still restlessly moving about the Saw Mill Road farmhouse, took the call at about eleven o'clock that evening. It was Julia Clancy announcing that his wife, cold, dripping wet, but safe, had turned up in her barn and scared them all to death. And Julia didn't have the faintest idea what in blazes was going on.

Alex swore, calmed down, and in a level voice asked if Sarah was able to speak.

"She was shivering so hard by the time I got her into the house that I've put her in a hot tub. I said I'd call you and say she's all right and everything is fine."

"Everything," said Alex between clenched teeth, "is not fine. When she's out of the tub, ask her to call me. I can't come and get her right now. I'm babysitting a student. Someone she knows about."

"She'll be spending the night right here," said Julia firmly. "But I'll have her call."

Which Sarah did. It was one of those telephone exchanges in which relief and anger were so mixed that the party of the first part couldn't tell how to feel or respond to or even answer the party of the second part. Enough to say that the following facts were established.

1. *Sarah was unharmed. Safe. And yes, it had all been a little bit scary.*
2. *Alex was glad that she was unharmed and safe. Yes, he imagined that whatever happened had been a bit scary. And he loved her.*
3. *And he was also as mad as hell.*

Sarah exchanged similar ideas, and then fatigue overwhelmed her, and saying she'd see him when she saw him and it was Kay Biddle who had wounded Danton McGraw and killed Grover and her real name was Bungle. With which she hung up the phone and fell into her aunt's guest-room four-poster bed as if she had been felled by an ax.

300

* * *

Mary Donelli on her debarking from the Dodge van earlier that
evening had been debriefed by the police, this unsatisfactory because Mary really had no grip on what was going on. Furthermore,
she was upset at what appeared to be the possible loss of her car.
She had been picked up at the police trailer by her husband, Professor Amos Larkin, who had questioned Mary so fiercely on the
suitability of continuing an obviously hazardous friendship with
Sarah that Mary, although almost agreeing with him, folded her
arms, looked away, and refrained from speaking for the better part
of the next hour.

Mike Laaka and George Fitts, as reported, had had an equally
unsatisfactory conversation with the student group that had returned in the Dodge van. Nothing could be gotten from the drama
group on later interviews, even when the students were grilled
separately. They stood, as Malcolm had said, "all for one and one
for all."

Alex, after his talk with Sarah, called the police at about
eleven thirty that Sunday evening. Sarah had been dumped in the
woods, somewhere close to the Warren-Union town line. She was
okay and had found the house of a relative nearby. Told him Kay
Biddle, or Bungle, take your pick, had confessed to assault and
murder and, leaving Sarah in the middle of a snowstorm, taken off
in Mary Donelli's green 2002 Forester.

"Christ Almighty," exploded Mike. "Can't leave well enough
alone. Can't keep her sticky fingers out of other people's business.
Who does she think she is? I've warned her."

"At least," said Katie Waters, "she's unhurt. That's unusual after a perpetrator has spilled the beans to someone else. In a murder case yet."

"Okay, okay," shouted Mike. "But I say we throw the book at
her. Interference, unlawful . . ."

"Unlawful what?" asked George in a mild voice. "Having pizza
with Drama School students?"

"Looking at Drama School folders and files. Student records,"
yelled Mike.

"Records we hadn't got around to looking at," said Katie, who had decided to defend Sarah on the general principle of always opposing Mike Laaka when he was raging.

George Fitts, for once looking tired, reached for the phone. "I'll extend the look for the Forester to the rest of New England, New York, New Jersey, and Pennsylvania. And keep train and bus depots in those states on the alert."

"Sheriff and the state police," said Katie.

"Of course," said George. "And town police departments. And farther along the Canadian border. But right now we'll work on the Dodge van gang."

"Nice name," said Katie. "They may go professional."

George looked irritated. "It's not enough for Sarah to talk about this Kay Whatever-she's-now-called confessing. We need more. Right now those drama students are feeling noble. Protect their own. Grover Blaine was a louse, needed smashing. But of course they say they have no ideas about his murder. Or who did it. But they'll begin to crack, especially if we keep having them in one by one."

"Alone and friendless, you mean?" said Katie.

George lined up his notebook tidily athwart his telephone list and stood up. "Relief coming in about five minutes. I say we regroup here at six thirty A.M."

"You mean at oh-six-thirty," Katie reminded him. "You sound like a civilian."

Mike shoved his chair back. "You all sound like civilians. I say call in Sarah Deane and roast her feet over the fire."

"Shut up," said Katie, "or I'll roast your butt over a fire if you go on like this."

"Children, children," said George. "We probably have our murderer. Now it's a matter of reeling her in. And putting the squeeze on her buddies. So simmer down everyone. You, Mike, go and have a cold shower. Or go roll in the snow. The ground's completely covered."

Monday, November 5, Bowmouth College's Founder's Day, broke with clearing skies overhead and almost a foot of new snow underfoot. Released from classes, those students remaining on campus for the long weekend indulged themselves in sleeping late, eating huge mid-morning breakfasts, and trying out cross-country skis or playing pickup basketball. Some students, reverting to childhood pleasures, threw snowballs at one another and fashioned snowmen.

Sarah had returned home as a passenger in Aunt Julia's farm truck and en route had been lectured on the subject of irresponsible behavior and frightening people in the middle of the night. However, by the end of the journey Julia had softened sufficiently to offer Sarah a chance to brush up on her riding skills (these mostly nonexistent) during the Christmas break.

Once home, and after a short nap, Sarah walked Patsy and then delivered Derek Mosely to the soccer field. An out-of-town game against Bates College would ensure that Derek would be taken care of for most of that day. She had learned from Derek and Alex, who had breakfasted together in the student cafeteria, that it was all over campus by morning that Kay Biddle had not returned with her friends. And that these same friends claimed complete ignorance of where she had gone. Derek showed a spark of interest in this fact because here was the name of an actual person who just might be linked to the death of his friend, his best friend, Grover Blaine.

"After all," Derek said as Sarah was driving him to the soccer field, "if Kay Biddle left with that group, all her best friends, and they won't say why she didn't come back, well, don't you think she might be involved? In those attacks and Derek's murder?"

Sarah didn't encourage this line of thinking for the simple reason that it was right on the nose. But it was also a bad idea for Derek to be thinking about the identity of someone who may have killed his friend. God only knew where that might lead.

But now with Derek in safe hands, Sarah had to report to the police trailer. George and Katie were both present; Mike, it appeared had been sent on a mission involving a search warrant so that Kay's dormitory room could ransacked by the forensic team. Sarah told her tale, emphasizing that Kay had seemed very sure of herself, that she sounded entirely credible and had related calmly the sequence of attacks on the wrong Mercutio and the successful duel against Grover.

"And," asked Katie, "just how did you get out of that scene all in one piece? Did you make a deal we should know about?"

Sarah described the invitation to join the Terriers, her refusal, and being left intact, unhurt, in the woods. "I don't know. Luck maybe. Maybe Kay thought I might just die quietly of hypothermia and wouldn't be found until she was in another country."

"Soft spot," repeated George. "Do you know whether Kay Biddle had any soft spots for anyone else? Favorites? A lover, or two lovers? Particular friends or enemies?"

"The enemies," said Sarah, "I think were pretty much limited to Grover and Derek. That type, anyway. But I think Kay thought Derek was really pretty much of a stooge. She said she wasn't crazy about Professor McGraw but said she didn't want to kill him. Or hurt him. She was very close to all those Terriers. They really hung together."

"Liked one more than the others?" persisted George.

Sarah nodded slowly, remembering a remark here, a look there. "I think she really liked, even more than liked, Todd Mancuso. And he was wild about her. Always trying to attract her attention. Terri, too, of course, but mostly it was Kay. Or is Kay now. That clip on the ear and the beating he got at the Food Mart seemed to have made him have serious thoughts on his past behavior and led to him making it up with both women."

"And Kay was the favorite. You're sure about that?"

"Don't push me on it, but I think so."

George was silent and Sarah could almost hear his cerebral machinery ticking. Then he looked at his watch and said thank you, she could go in a minute. After which he announced that an all points was out for Kay Biddle-Bungle and that the media would be giving the search publicity. Radio, television, the papers. "And," added George, "one last question for you, Sarah. What characteristic do you see that binds these so-called Terriers together? Not their aim at preventing harassment. But personal qualities."

Sarah didn't even have to think. Again she heard Malcom

Wheelock's refrain, "All for one, one for all." "Loyalty," she said. "Faith that they would stay together and support each other. Kay emphasized this when she asked me to come in with them. She knew they wouldn't talk, and I was to swear not to tell anyone about her confession."

"Interesting," said George.

"It sounds like they've joined the marines," said Katie. "Or some secret society that wears funny hats, meets underground, and swears allegiance."

"Whatever it is," said George acidly, "it's not helping the police solve two felonies." He paused, looked over at Sarah. "I wonder," he said thoughtfully, "if Mike isn't right after all. About how the whole stage business went."

"What!" exclaimed Katie. "Todd Mancuso!"

"I didn't say that," said George. "I've just been considering another angle."

"Mike might be right?" said Sarah in a shocked voice. "But how on earth? I believe Kay. She couldn't be covering up for Todd. I mean come on."

"You said it yourself," said George. "Loyalty was the key. Although I'd hate to admit that Mike was right."

Katie, shaking her head violently, repeated, "No, no, no. No way."

"Think about it," said George. "We owe Kay that. And Todd. Or there may be someone else we've pushed aside. I'll be seeing the whole Dodge van group shortly. Sarah, thanks, and good-bye."

Sarah, in a state of much confusion with her mind repeating Katie's denial of any idea coming from Mike Laaka, took her leave.

George and Katie then cleared the decks to deal with the Terriers. But as time would prove, a good chunk of the day would be devoted to questions and nonanswers and demonstrations of the fine art of stonewalling. Each student passenger of the Dodge van had been, as promised by George, called in one by one. Even Malcolm Wheelock, who arrived by bus in the early-morning hours, had been interrogated. But this face-to-face approach ended in failure. Nothing was learned except about the art of noncommunication. However, there were other strategies.

For instance, there was the crowd strategy. George would have all the drama students in together to face George himself, Katie Waters, and Mike Laaka, when he had finished with the business of the search warrant. George thought this group approach might turn up the heat on the "Terriers" by putting them through scattershot questioning. Perhaps some of the students would start to duck, would shy away from certain subjects, mix up their answers, contradict themselves or their friends.

But by two in the afternoon, sustained only by a bag of potato chips and bottles of Moxie, George and crew gave up on group interrogation. The students held together as if by chains, and despite suggestions, provocative remarks, and head shaking by the forces of law and order, they all stuck to simple "yes," "no," "maybe," and "don't remember."

"You aren't really thinking about Todd Mancuso as the guy?" asked Katie after Mike had at last been sent out for food and fluid.

"Just a stab in the dark," said George. "Actually, with that business of masks plus the fencing skills we've got established—"

"Sarah has established," Katie put in.

"She was about a day ahead of us on that one," said George in an annoyed voice. "And look what it got her. She's damn lucky not to be lying in some ditch with a foil through her throat."

"And we would have been ever so cautious and Kay would have made it to Boston without a confession and probably would right now be on a flight to Tibet."

George frowned at Katie. "There is a proper way of doing things which amateurs like Sarah would never understand in a thousand years."

"Go back to Todd as the perp," said Katie. "I can't believe he'd just stay with the bunch and let Kay be his stand-in, his scapegoat."

"So think about it," said George. "And consider how pleased Mike will be to see we're actually listening to him."

The session ended with the arrival of sandwiches and a collection of soft drinks. Mike accepted praise from Katie and George on the subject of Todd Mancuso, aka the new murderer suspect. "It took you long enough to come around. Me, it was right on the money from the start. Todd Mancuso, actor and fencer, taking his revenge."

"Don't get carried away," said George dryly. "There are other options. Scenarios. And suspects. Todd is just one."

"So you won't call off the bloodhounds?" said Katie. "I mean because of Mike's idea. You're still going to be looking for Kay Biddle."

"Absolutely," George said. "By news time the wires will be jumping. Local stations, CNN, and Fox. Even Maine Public Radio and Television."

"You'll get those big media guys excited because this is a unique case?" said Katie.

"No. And it isn't unique. But right now there's no big new murder on the horizon, no Michael Jackson or Martha Stewart or a White House biggie being roasted, so the media will spring for a nice college murder to fill up the empty spaces."

George rose from his desk and pointed at the door. "Mike, you go look in on the forensic team, see what they've found, so far, in Kay Biddle's dorm room. Katie, get to the Drama School and pull all the files on Kay Biddle—which I hope Sarah returned in one piece—then hit the Registrar for any additional info. Check on her other instructors, see what they have on her. And I'll be running down any prior arrests, incidents. Meet me here around eight tonight. We can check through media coverage then."

The media coverage was more than adequate, if not entirely accurate. Beginning by the four o'clock news, after the major networks had finished with international issues of war and peace, disaster in near and far places, and had given a nod to touchy subjects coming before the Supreme Court, they fell for the interesting attack and murder in a proper New England college. With little actual information, with wide divergence of opinion on the name of the actual play, descriptions were given of events that took place in a "wild" production of *Romeo and Juliet* or an "obscene" production of *Antony and Cleopatra*—opinion was divided on the name of the play.

At five o'clock that afternoon Alex had gone to meet the soccer team returning by bus and would drop Derek off for an hour's visit with his mother. This civilized plan was one thing the dinner party had accomplished. But as Alena had explained, it was best for both mother and son to keep the meeting to an hour; she would call Alex's cell phone at the end of that period. And she would try to avoid the subject of Grover's death. With which plan Alex had to be content. It was at least a tiny step in the direction of family unity, if not in understanding.

Sarah, now left in peace and more or less recovered from a rough night, found herself needing fresh air and a little exercise in the new-fallen snow. More and more she found herself rotating the idea of Todd's possible guilt in her mind. And more and more firmly she rejected it. However, after a short walk around the farmhouse, together with Patsy on his leash, she found she had a need to be on campus. Check her mail, look around in her office for any notes shoved under the door by students. Was it possible that tomorrow would just be another day of teaching, having meetings, going about the usual routine, talking about the possibility of more snow or a thaw, sleet, or none of the above?

She completed the mail check in a few minutes, and then with Patsy heaving his weight against the leash, this despite hours Sarah had spent studying a dog-training book, she found herself stamping along the partially shoveled path to the Drama School. Why she wasn't sure, because surely she had no desire to revisit any recent scenes there. But her approach was stopped short by the sight of Todd Mancuso. He was marching along as if in time to some internal drumbeat and heading straight for the police trailer. Sarah waved a hand in greeting and called out.

Todd stopped, shook his head as if he had been interrupted in some tremendous mental task, and then waved back. And halted.

Sarah joined him and, for lack of anything else to say, asked if there were any plans afoot for a new Drama School spring production.

Todd looked at her as if she had suggested a bus trip to China. Then he shook his head as if coming back from a faraway place. "That's not on my mind right now," he said. Then, after staring at

Sarah for a minute, he added, "You know, I think I'll start with you. See how it goes."

Sarah frowned. "See how *what* goes?"

"What I'm about to tell the police. I'll bet they're not ready, but I am."

"Whatever you want to say, I don't want to know. If it's police business, I'm staying out of it. I'm already in their black book."

"No, wait," said Todd. "Please listen. Kay isn't the only one to tell a good story. Mine is better. And true. Halloween night I went onstage after making everyone think I was too feeble to go on. Put on a mask and looked just like the crowd. I got Professor McGraw in the neck, thinking he was Grover, who was supposed to be my understudy. It was easy. I'd rehearsed Mercutio over and over and I knew all the moves. But then when I found out I hadn't got Grover, you see, I had to do it again. Find that rat and finish him off. After he left the cast party I followed him backstage."

"Wait a minute," Sarah shouted. "Stop it. You don't know what you're saying."

"I damn well do," said Todd with a tone of absolute certainty. "I killed Grover Blaine. In a duel in the Green Room. I even gave him a chance to defend himself. More than he did me when he was beating the shit out of me at the Fine Food Mart. Anyway, it's over and done and I'm glad I killed him."

Sarah tried for a voice of reason, tried to hold back any sound of emotion. "Listen, Todd," she said carefully. "You know I went off with Kay. After the Squeaky Wheel scene. And Kay was very clear about what happened. She described exactly how she managed the whole thing. She even asked me to join in with your Terrier group and keep my mouth shut. And I refused. I told her that this is murder and not some secret-society hazing or trial by fire. Or some stupid reality show."

Todd shook his head as if in sadness at Sarah's confusion. "Of course Kay was convincing. She's one great actor. She can convince an audience that she's some woman of ninety who knows how to fly backward. But I'm not letting Kay take the rap for what I did. I listened to the news. CNN on TV. And a local radio thing. The announcer broke into a music program to talk about it. The

309

media and the police are going after her like a bunch of hyenas. I'm not going to let that happen, so I have to tell the truth." And Todd again looked hard at Sarah.

Sarah felt that Todd was waiting for a response to this but only found herself mumbling something about the yes, there was great value in truth. But . . .

"No 'buts,' " said Todd. And began again. "Kay, she's a very strong person, but she's got this weird noble streak. Like she'd be willing to sacrifice for a cause. And I'm afraid I might be the cause. I've told her I love her. And I think she loves me. And I think she's doing this to prove it."

With that declaration, Todd Mancuso strode to the door of the police trailer and beat loudly on the door.

Leaving Sarah in stunned silence.

21

TODD Mancuso, paying no attention to Sarah calling after him, pleading with him to come back, gave the police trailer door a second and then a third hard thump. It opened, and Todd, without looking back, stepped inside and disappeared.

Sarah stood as if her feet had been frozen into the new snow. The winter sky was now darkening and the same seemed to be happening in Sarah's head. A hundred dim ideas, denials, and the sense of something insane ran circles in her brain. Todd the murderer. Kay the murderer. Both together as a team. And then, why not add Malcolm Wheelock and Weeza Scotini and Terri Colman and Derek Mosely? Couldn't they all be murderers? Action en masse by the Terriers. Foil—or épée—masked and tucked into velvet doublets and silken hose and ready to strike. And why stop there? Benvolio, what was his name? Oh yes, Griffin Starr. And of course, Seth Nussbaum. Why leave him out? How about Vera herself? Good idea! Vera might not be able to fence, but she could probably use a hat pin, that favorite of murder-minded Victorian ladies, to advantage. Vera might get real satisfaction in taking revenge on her enemy Professor Danton McGraw—whom she had perhaps caught backstage changing roles with Grover Blaine.

And then, of course Vera would have to kill Grover, who *knew all.* So off she goes to the Green Room to do the job. The hat pin again, or perhaps a knitting needle. But never mind the weapon; that was a mere detail.

At which point Sarah gave herself a shake and returned to present time and space. Her snowbound feet were freezing. It was time to move on. But where and what next? Should she hurl herself into the police trailer pleading, but pleading what? Todd's innocence or Kay Biddle's guilt? Or the guilt of both or the innocence of both? Or none of the above? Better she should quietly drive home and attend to the everyday needs of guest Derek, husband Alex, dog Patsy, and cat Piggy. But Sarah wasn't up to devising a dinner menu, so why not Chinese? She would stop off and pick up a selection from the Pagoda Palet, known best for its Szechuan scallops and shrimps. Maybe some Oriental spice would clear her head and, as a bonus, give Derek Mosely a small kick that might partly offset his depression. As for Alex, he would eat anything if it had a sufficiently strong bite.

The arrival of Todd Mancuso in the trailer caused a moment of silence from the police trio: George Fitts, Katie Waters, and Mike Laaka. Then Katie and Mike returned to entering data into their respective laptops, and George faced the newcomer with slightly raised eyebrows.

Todd, stamping the snow from his feet, took two steps forward and began. After a throat clearing, a checking to see if his audience was attending, he began by confessing to the stabbing (by mistake) of Professor McGraw. However, George held up a hand and stopped Todd in the middle of his first sentence.

"But," protested Todd, "don't you want to hear what I have to say? I'm the one—"

George kept his hand in the air and shook his head. "Not so fast. Take that chair"—he indicated an uncomfortable metal folding chair—"over there and sit down. Thank you," this as Todd, feeling somewhat slighted, sat down on the edge of the indicated chair.

"Let's just follow procedure here. Katie, will you set up the recording. Take off your jacket, Mr. Mancuso—Todd. It gets really hot in here. Katie, ready? Mike, take notes. Now let's see. Tea or coffee, Todd?"

Todd, increasingly annoyed at this casual approach to a felon about to confess, plus the use of his first name without asking, mentioned that the police were supposed to be reading him his rights.

George nodded. "Yes, Todd. You're quite right. Always stick to the subject. Thank you for reminding us. We'll pass on the refreshments. For now. But you know it was an interesting case. *Ernesto Miranda versus the state of Arizona*. The Supreme Court ruled in 1966 that statements made to police couldn't be used as evidence since Ernesto had not been advised of his rights. Unfortunately, Mr. Miranda was held on other evidence and was eventually convicted. But as a result of the court ruling, suspects are given a Miranda warning, so afterward you can tell all your friends you've been Mirandized."

By now Todd had reached a state of high irritation. He was being treated like a child. But he was a trained actor, and when such a person steps onto the stage—or into a police trailer—to give a soliloquy on the subject of his committing a capital crime, he deserves . . . well, he deserves respect. "Okay," he barked. "Read me the thing."

George nodded, remarked that he knew it by heart and didn't have to read it, and then in a serious voice told Todd that he had the right to remain silent, that anything he said would be used against him, that he had a right to speak to an attorney—

At which Mike, who felt invested in the process—this was *his* suspect—spoke up. "Hey, George, aren't you going to read him the longer form? Ask if he understands."

George glared at him, his expression seemingly made of equal parts of cobra venom and heated steel, and proceeded with the reading.

Todd waived his right to an attorney. "I just want to keep this simple. I did it. Wounded Professor McGraw by mistake and then hit Grover Blaine in the school Green Room. It was planned and intentional.

"Of course," added Todd, sitting upright in his chair, shoulders back, defiant. "And," he added, "you can call off that search for Kay Biddle. Now that you've got me."

"Ah, not so fast," said George, and a strange expression slipped over his face, an expression of possible understanding mixed with the faintest tinge of amusement.

"What I'm saying," Todd went on, "is you'll straighten the TV people out. The media, the radio reporters. Spread the word. Say you've got the right guy."

"Oh, of course," said George. "I will certainly do that. And we will suggest that another one of our suspects—there are quite a few on the list—has confessed to the crime. But that doesn't mean that we wouldn't want to spend some quality time with Ms. Kay Biddle. After all, her so-called 'guilt' depended only on hearsay evidence from someone else. We'll need to straighten out that business."

"You don't get it," Todd almost shouted. "Kay is innocent. She's just doing this act, you know, leaving a false trail. To take the heat off me. She's into sacrificing because we have a thing going."

"A thing?" queried George mildly.

"You know. I mean I love her and I think she loves me—that sounds like some sick dialogue from a low-grade movie, but it's true. Kay knows I killed Grover, but she's being, what I told Professor Deane just now, sort of noble."

At Sarah's name the sergeant visibly twitched. "What does Professor Deane have to do with this?"

"I tried this on her. Just now, outside. To see how it went."

"You mean to see how it sounds. An audition?"

"No. Oh, for Christ's sake, I committed a murder and you're not paying attention."

"But now I will. We will take you in custody and later you'll be seeing a judge. Mike, will you be good enough to cuff our friend here, arrange to have him booked—the works, prints, photo, call the county jail about a new customer, and get me the district attorney's office. Katie, please try and track down Professor Deane. She's probably thinking about a full-time career in law enforcement. If she's at home, tell her to stay put."

Katie, who had been listening to the exchange between

George and Todd-the-felon with great interest, pushed herself away from her desk. "Now, you mean?"

"As soon as you type out a statement for the media people. About our most recent event. Make that 'capture of a confessed felon.'"

Todd swiveled so quickly that a partially attached handcuff fell to the trailer floor. "Capture," he exploded. "I came in here by myself."

"Just an expression," said George. "Katie, say that Mr. Mancuso gave himself up. To the police. After confessing to an alleged assault and murder."

"Alleged," shouted Todd.

"Calm down," said George. "And start thinking seriously about what you're doing. Consider an attorney. If you don't, the court will probably appoint one for you. Katie, off you go. I'd like the information about this affair to get to the media as soon as possible. The early-evening news. Then when you get to Sarah's place, tell her, tell Alex, that you and I want to call on them this evening."

And so the machinery of the law cranked into motion, and Todd, after being appropriately "booked," appeared before the judge, his arrest was duly justified, and he was denied bail. Following these formalities, and wearing a cotton jumpsuit and a pair of paper slippers, he took up residence in a small cell in the county courthouse, comforted perhaps by a presence on his bunk of a one-volume copy of five plays by George Bernard Shaw, this in paperback, since a hardback book might have been considered a dangerous missile. Todd had for some time thought that he might be perfect for the part of Professor Higgins in *Pygmalion*.

Sarah and Alex and Derek worked their way through a variety of highly spiced Oriental meals, and then Derek removed himself, as had now become his custom, to the living-room floor in front of the TV set along with Patsy and Piggy. Derek's cheerfulness had continued since more and more he felt that his own case now paled before the media spread on the newest developments. The six o'clock news on all major networks had given the subject coverage. If things went on like this, Derek had said to Sarah, Grover's murderer might soon be locked up and later maybe executed. And he, Derek, might be forgotten. None of these ideas did Sarah support, although she only pointed out that Maine did not execute its prisoners.

Now glad for a few minutes of privacy, Sarah and Alex began cleaning up the Chinese banquet, and Sarah told her tale of Todd's confession and her disbelief in the whole thing. Into this scene of domestic tranquillity Katie Waters appeared. Was ushered in, offered the remains of their dinner from the white cartons, which Katie, being starved, accepted happily. "Poor Mike," she said. "No food since breakfast. He'll be impossible."

Alex, knowing that sheriff's deputies didn't arrive by accident on one's doorstep, asked to what they owed the honor.

"Sarah can tell you," said Katie. "I heard that she had a preview. Did you tell Alex about Todd's statement?"

"I told him just now. Let me shut the door to the living room and leave Derek out of this. He's pumped up at the idea of friend Grover's killer being nailed."

"Yeah," said Katie. "Right now Todd Mancuso is certainly numero uno for interest."

"Todd actually confessed?" demanded Alex. "*Okay*, if you need a witness, I'll testify that his physical condition was so bad that I don't think he could have hurt a rabbit."

"George," said Katie, "seemed kind of funny through the whole thing. He chatted, very casual, and even went on about the history of the Miranda warning. He doesn't usually act like this. He sounded like a high-school teacher. But I'm to say that he's coming over to see you both and please stay put."

"We intend to stay put," said Alex. "Very put. But I'd like to call off George."

At which point the doorbell jangled, the knocker was employed, and Alex found himself letting the enemy over the drawbridge and into the fortress.

Wine, beer, tea, coffee, were offered and George accepted tea—to Sarah's surprise. She always drank tea and couldn't believe that she and the chilly sergeant had even one thing in common. Except, of course, the dogs. They both loved dogs. Or did George actually love anything, even those Westies of his? Perhaps they were part of some search-and-rescue or drug-sniffing training program.

However, she must produce a mug of tea and try for civility. The door to the living room remained closed, and Derek for the moment was out of sight, although the protesting barks of Patsy could be heard. Patsy liked to greet visitors by literally standing up, placing his paws on their shoulders, and washing their faces. But eventually, the four settled at the kitchen table with tea for two, coffee for one (Katie), Heineken for Alex. Ready, Sarah wondered, for some sort of enlightenment. Or more obfustication. Or, very unlikely, just a friendly meeting after a long day.

But George rarely had use for the "friendly meeting" option. "Todd Mancuso has confessed to assault and murder," announced George. "Something," he added, "Sarah already knows. But I'm interested. Did Todd say anything to you about just why he's decided to do this?"

"Love," said Sarah. "Good old love. The great motivator."

"Even so," said George, "he could love Kay Biddle and also have killed Grover Blaine. And wounded McGraw."

Sarah sighed. "I don't know what's going on. Kay sounded absolutely certain. Firm. And mean, too. Cold as an icicle. She described killing Grover, move by move, all those odd, coupé, fencing terms ending with lunge and hit."

George nodded. "I'm sure she did. And I'm just as sure that Todd could do the same."

"What you're dealing with," Alex put in, "is a different species. Actors. Good ones. The kind that can twist themselves into any part. Play Richard the Third enjoying every kill, the next day Robin Hood or the Marquis de Sade or Saint Francis of Assisi."

"And Kay Biddle, too," said Sarah. "Joan of Arc or Lady Macbeth." She added this with reluctance because she had really believed Kay, felt that the whole scene, driving through the snow, hearing that matter-of-fact voice, well, it had absolutely convinced her.

"Change your mind about Kay Biddle?" asked Katie Waters, watching Sarah's troubled expression.

"At this point I'm willing to bet on a conspiracy of seven or eight or how many of those so-called Terriers are around. But Kay is still my number one."

"But you're putting out the word," said Alex to George. "To the news world. That someone has confessed."

"Not just someone. Todd is no minor and he has a name. But I hate confessions. The defense always makes chowder out of them. Goes on about police using force and intimidation. I'd rather get this guy, or guys, the old-fashioned way."

"Hunt and peck," said Sarah.

"Hard work and hard evidence," said George. "But one more thing before I go. Alex, do you swear by the memory of Asclepius that Todd was too sick to mount a double attack, first by épée, an effort which included dragging the victim backstage, and then win a foil duel in the Green Room."

"Not by Asclepius," said Alex. "But by my own sense of the man's condition. Pulse, heartbeat, tremor, sweating. He was pale, and looked like he was going to pass out. I thought even acting the part of Friar Laurence might do him in. Never mind any other activities."

"Thank you, Alex," said George. "I've always been interested in Asclepius. Maligned by some, praised by others. But that's always the way it is. Think what happened to poor Ignatz Semmelweiss." With which George rose from his chair and nodded to the company at large and took himself out.

"You know," said Alex thoughtfully as the door closed behind the sergeant, "George Fitts is turning out to be something like a family friend. Think of knowing the first name of Semmelweiss."

"Think of even knowing the last name," said Katie Waters, getting up in her turn. "George Fitts is this sort of collection of odd and probably useless facts. Like knowing all about Ernesto Miranda. His brain must look like a junk shop."

"There's nothing useless about knowing about Ignatz Semmelweiss," said Alex. "Go home and look up childbed fever and say thanks that you're mother is alive and well after having children."

"Seven of us like we were going out of style," Katie said, grinning. And departed.

Sarah looked at Alex. "If George Fitts is turning into a family friend, I'll . . ."

"You'll what?"

"Do something. Give me time and I'll think of it. The man freezes my spine."

"Speaking of which, the wind is starting up and the weather forecast is calling for more snow. And maybe a melt and then an ice storm."

"Groovy," said Sarah. "Now let's go and see if Derek is still alive. Or whether he's spent the evening with his ear stuck to the keyhole. I don't think I'd put it past him."

"Negative thinking again."

"It's the George Fitts curse."

But Derek was found sprawled on the rug, sound asleep, an arm stretched over Patsy, and Piggy the kitten curled in a ball behind his knees.

"See," said Alex. "Thou unbeliever. Get thee . . ."

"To my bubble bath," said Sarah.

And the busy evening wound down leaving assorted participants in the day's events with a false sense of tranquillity restored.

The next day, Tuesday, November 6, Bowmouth Founder's Day plus one, found students in a general state of reluctance; those who took long weekends appeared ragged and hungover, those who stayed on campus resented that they had done so, and as for the co-conspirators known as the Terriers, they found themselves caught between the need to go to their classes and the police need to interrogate them.

"I call them the AA group," said Mike Laaka after George had dismissed Griffin Starr, formally Benvolio, from an hour's session.

"As in?" prompted Katie, turning off the recording apparati.

"Aiders and abettors," announced Mike. "This cozy little nest of liars and deceivers. Think they're so damn smart. Bunch of snob college kids who don't have to earn an honest living like having to actually work. Oh no, these guys are going on the stage or to the movies. Bright lights and glamour and getting cash from Ma and Pa."

"Mike, oh, do shut up," said Katie in a tired voice. It was only eleven thirty A.M. and there were to be at least four more interrogations. In depth. At least an hour per student.

Katie looked at her watch and at Sergeant Fitts. "George, tell Mike that thinking that the entire college is made up of rich party snobs is counterproductive to getting their cooperation or learning anything from them. Mike's the real snob. He's trying to act like some simple, honest peasant who's being trodden on by evil spoiled college types." She turned to Mike. "I say screw you, Mike."

Mike grinned. "Sure thing, Katie. Just say when."

"Oh Jesus," said Katie. "Let me out of here." She looked over to George, now bent over his desk and peering into his computer screen. "Okay if I go and pick up the local papers and see if they gave Todd's confession a spread? And kept it up about Kay Biddle?"

George nodded, adding that he was checking the Net for out-of-town newspapers and TV reports. "I hope they give our two suspects some black print."

"They can't compete with the big stuff," said Katie. "You know, war, famine, and Hollywood sex." She rose, leaned over George, who was frowning at page 1 of *The Boston Globe*, which was not featuring anything of Maine and Bowmouth College interest.

"Try the comics page," she said, and slipped out the door.

"What is going to happen," said Mike, "is you're going to be holding something like five or six drama school students for obstruction, or collusion, or perjury—something good anyway—while Todd Mancuso will be crowned local murder king and Kay Biddle will be murder queen consort and the county jail will be stuffed to the gills with all those so-called Terriers. And the whole thing will be a sort of crazy joke. Right now two confessions, later maybe a lot more. Confessing is catching."

"As I said before, I don't like confessions," said George. "Take you down a very slippery slope. And we have two confessions for the same crime. I remember a case where the confession read like a fifty-page novel, every detail, and the prosecutor made mince-meat—"

But Mike never heard the end of this sad tale. A thump on the trailer door interrupted the flow. And then another thump, a fainter one this time. As if the thumper was having second thoughts.

George drew a long breath and then turned to Mike and said, "If that's Todd Mancuso who's been let out, say we're busy. And to go back to jail."

But it wasn't Todd. Mike rose and wrenched open the door and found Derek Mosely standing on the threshold. His face was pale, and he looked as if he wanted to turn and run. Except that right behind him stood Alex McKenzie. With an Irish wolfhound on a leash.

"Hello," said Alex. "Derek here says he wants to talk to you."

George looked over at the figure at the door. "That true, Derek?"

Derek turned back to Alex, but Alex remained silent. The ball apparently was now in Derek's court.

"Yeah," he said in a thick voice. "I guess so."

"Guess so?" said Mike. "Either you do or you don't."

George rose and stepped in front of Mike. "Come on in, Derek," he said. "Would you like Dr. McKenzie to come in with you?"

Derek turned and looked at Alex. As if for help, for a decision. But Alex remained still, his face impassive.

Derek bit his lip and took a deep breath. "I'll come in alone," he said. "Not with Dr. McKenzie. Not with the dog. I should do this myself."

"Dogs are always welcome," said George, expressing a view that no one for miles around had ever heard from the sergeant's lips.

"I'll be around outside," said Alex. "Give a shout when you're finished."

Derek, holding Patsy's leash, advanced into the trailer, was pointed to a chair, the same chair that Todd had used for his recitation, and sat down on its very edge, while the big dog sank down next to him and began to chew on a snow-covered paw.

"I want to say something," said Derek.

"Take your time," said George while Mike turned restlessly in his chair. Mike hated making suspects comfortable and happy, and with dogs yet. Go to jail, go directly to jail, do not pass Go, do not collect one hundred dollars, could have been engraved on Mike's shield.

But now there seemed to be an impasse. Derek moved his feet uneasily, leaving great clots of melting snow. Inhaled several times but said nothing.

George looked at him, reached down from his chair and ruffled Patsy's hair, and then said, "An English major, aren't you?"

"Yeah, sort of," said Derek.

"How sort of?"

"My best friend, Grover, was—you know he's dead, don't you?"

George nodded. He certainly knew.

"Grover, I met him at the end of my freshman year, and he wanted to go into English and do drama as a minor."

"So you did, too?"

"Yeah, I guess so. I hadn't made up my mind about a major. But my mother—she was an English major—she was all for it."

"Do you want to go on with that program?" said George in the same patient voice, a voice Mike had heard only rarely.

"I'm kind of thinking of science now. I like math and biology and then maybe I could switch to over to a prevet program because I like animals. And I've never been allowed to have one. Even a cat. Mother says they mess up things and need litter boxes. And dogs shed on furniture and pee on things and can get real mean when they're old. Like bite people who come to the house."

"I see," said George. "Well, good veterinarians are always in demand." He paused, looked seriously at Derek. Enough was now enough. "Tell me," he said. "What brought you here? And no, I don't mean Dr. McKenzie, though I suppose he had something to do with it."

"He hasn't pushed me. Suggested maybe, but didn't make me. It's my own idea."

"And?"

"I want to tell you about my having watched out for trouble

322

when Grover got hold of Todd Mancuso and dragged him into the utility room at the food store and beat him up. I was supposed to stay outside the door and give the alarm if someone came around. And then help Grover get away safely."

George studied Derek for a full fifteen seconds and then nodded. "Okay, Derek, I'd like to give you something called a Miranda warning. Do you know what that is?"

"Yeah, sure. They do it all the time on TV. Go ahead."

Thus, for the second time in twenty-four hours, the Miranda was duly given. Mike hit the recorder button and muttered a few words into the speaker concerning time, place, and identity of speakers. Then George returned to the subject.

"At the Fine Food Mart, you watched for Grover and helped him escape safely?"

"Yes," said Derek unhappily. "Grover was my best friend, so I pretty much went along with what he wanted."

"Is that what you did when Grover was caught by Weeza Scotini? Being watchdog while Grover tried to harass her."

"Yeah, that, too," said Derek miserably.

"And other times, too?"

"Yes, a few times."

"I think that we'll take a quick break," said George, "because I want you to think about getting a lawyer."

"I don't want a lawyer," said Derek almost defiantly. "That's what my mother is always saying. 'Never do anything without a lawyer.'"

"But it might be in your best interest. Do you know a lawyer you might like to have?"

Derek hesitated. And then, as if he suddenly saw someone standing in front of him, said, "I did see this one woman lawyer two times in court. Grover and I were hauled in for his speeding once. And once for having alcohol in his car. Nothing serious. This lawyer, she was a Val someone. A tall blond woman. I heard her talking to some judge. She seemed really decent."

George nodded. "I know her. Val Sheparda. What do you say, Derek? Would you like to be in touch? Tell her your side of the story."

Derek, frowned, then said, "Yes," in a low voice.

"Mike," ordered George, "will you make the call and give the phone to Derek."

And Mike, sighing deeply, put in the call. By his count there were now at least seven drama major students and one English major student (or two if you counted the dead Grover Blaine), apparently eligible for spending time behind bars. That probably meant at least eight lawyers would be made happy.

22

SINCE well before the Halloween theatrical extravaganza at Bowmouth College, it was not uncommon for certain academic entities
to spin out of control, leave their proper orbit, and collide heavily
with one another. But from music to medicine, from business to biology, a certain amount of interdepartmental turbulence was seen
as something common to any large organization. But in the annals
of push coming to shove, nothing in recent memory could beat out
the particular case of the English Department's and Drama
School's active hostility to each other. The result had been injury,
death, and a host of suspicions and accusations all affecting the
functioning of both departments. And these disturbances did not
even take into account what seemed to be an epidemic of confessions from a number of senior students. The result of all of the
above had ended in what seemed to be a permanent police presence infesting a small trailer athwart the Drama School's fine new
building.

One of the most troubled was Dean Alena Fosdick. She had
been going about for the past few days with a fixed frown on her
face, walking like a well-dressed robot. In the course of any se-

mester she usually had enough on her plate to cause perturbation and often real indigestion. But now Alena not only faced two major crimes occurring within the warring divisions of her kingdom, but added to these was the distress of having an errant son who not only had consorted with? Loved? Followed? Assisted the unsavory miserable activities of Grover Blaine? And worse than Grover's murder, in Alena's eyes, was the fact that Grover's death had apparently caused her only son to try to kill himself with a motorcycle. Drs. Jonas Jefferson and Alex McKenzie had tried to soften the story of the event but could hardly hide Derek's intention. And now, with the whole academic community watching, her son, Derek, showed a decided preference for the company and house of strangers, the counsel of a psychiatrist, the attentions of a dog and a cat, to his own mother. And this state of affairs, Alena felt, meant that the members of this community could almost be heard muttering "bad mother" under their breath as they passed her in the halls.

How to repair the damage? How to become a "good mother"? Answer: very difficult, since Alena had no wish to go to all the trouble of becoming a good mother. Such a mother might have to plan little dinners with her son, cook for him, have his friends over. Even, God help her, stand on the sidelines on a freezing fall day and watch him play soccer. Was she even fond of the boy? She didn't know and was too confused to try to find out. But at least, from the turmoil of the last few days, one solid positive fact remained. Grover Blaine was very dead, and if it could be proved that Derek had no part in his death—the lover's revenge scenario—then she might pull herself together and try to at least score a C+ in motherhood. That grade was at least a passing one.

Unfortunately for her peace of mind, she was hauled—her word—before George Fitts on the Wednesday morning two days after Bowmouth Founder's Day and asked to explore for the police the possibilities of Derek as murderer of Grover. For this Alena had clutched at her family lawyer, who sat with her monitoring the questions. For instance, did Grover own an épée? But Alena didn't know an épée from a turnip. Had he wanted to act in the crowd scenes? Alena had not the least idea; the subject had never come up. Had he come home to have his costume—doublet, hose, mask, stockings—washed and had there been anything like bloodstains on the clothes? To this last her lawyer objected, and the subject wasn't pushed. After a few more uninformative answers, George in his mildest voice said that Derek would probably tell her himself about the part he had played in the beating of Todd Mancuso as well as his other "watchdog" duties. George then pointed out that Derek had come of his own accord to the police to discuss the matter and this was commendable. Calmed by this positive note, Alena had been escorted out of the trailer together with her lawyer, who assured her that she had said nothing that could have injured her son in the least.

The net result of the interview from Sergeant Fitts's point of view was to place Alena Fosdick on a shelf reserved for nonessential elements in the case. To be dusted off if necessary but otherwise let alone.

"I think," said George to Katie Waters, after Alena's departure, "we can separate Derek's personal problems from the theatre assault and murder scene. Last night I talked to students from Grover Blaine's classes, from his dorm and his soccer team. The general agreement was that yes, Grover was a no-good bully, but no one had an idea that he was about to take a lover in place of Derek. In fact, many denied that Derek was Grover's lover. The majority opinion held that Derek was Grover's slave. A gofer. Someone to shove around. They thought maybe Derek loved Grover, but Grover was a user and a spoiler. Always on some power trip and incapable of loving anything. Except himself."

"Okay," said Katie. "I'll accept that for now. Me, I'd say that Grover couldn't get it up in the sex department and bullied girls because of it. A sociopath."

"Forget your psychology courses," said George. "Grover's gone. Let's work on the live ones. Stick to facts we actually have. For instance, how's the media coverage going?"

"Flat out," said Katie. "The idea of two confessions is popular. It's lucky there isn't any other crime sensation going on in most of New England. Boston, Providence, and Hartford, of course, but that's to be expected. But Bowmouth gets the attention for rural crime. So what's your next move?"

"I'm going back to try my group interview. Have those Terriers in for another visit."

"Except for Todd."

"For which I'm very grateful. A cell is a good place for him right now."

"Okay. But I thought you said the group approach was no good."

George gave Katie a wintry vestigial smile. "If you don't at first succeed . . ."

"Which means you don't have any other tricks up your sleeve," said Katie, grinning. She did like to find George almost admitting defeat. Or at least having to reserve gears and return to a previous strategy.

"And," continued George, "I am going to ask Sarah Deane to sit in on the interview. She knows these people from many scenes, including that recent trip to the Squeaky Wheel and her abduction by Kay Biddle. And, for what it's worth, Kay Biddle's possible confession."

"Was it a real abduction?"

"A firearm was involved. What would you call it?"

"I'd call the whole thing questionable. But anyway, we can't confuse Kay's confession with Todd Mancuso's confession."

"Or anybody else's confession," said George. "It's only noon and we've got time to receive other students who would like to plead guilty. I'm clearing my desk just in case."

"And for me?"

"I need that complete inventory of what was found in Kay Biddle's dorm room. Any lab results that the team picked up from the clothes in there."

"You won't get DNA results that fast."

"I know. But bloodstains for typing would be useful. Particularly showing a type that isn't Kay's."

"How about two blood types not Kay's?" said Katie. "Like a type for McGraw and one for Grover Blaine."

"Exactly."

"So what's Mike up to?" asked Katie, thinking perhaps Mike had managed to sneak off for a nap. Or been sent off to do some easy job.

"Mike," said George with satisfaction, "is picking up every fencing tool, sword, épée, saber, or similar weapon, bagging the whole cache, and turning it over to forensics. Yes, I know they've gone over the Drama School and the fencing team equipment, but half the team keeps its equipment in dorms, in cars, at a friend's or relative's house. I want every last weapon they can dig up even if Mike has to raid the ladies' rooms and the bursar's office. Although"—here George gave a resigned shrug of his shoulders— "the actual murder weapons have probably left the county or were dumped in the Atlantic Ocean."

"The way things work, they're probably buried right under our noses," said Katie. She got up, peered out of the fogged-up window of the trailer, grabbed her winter jacket, jammed a woolen cap over her head, thrust her arms into a pair of gloves, and left for the excitement of the forensic world and their dealings with every item in Kay Biddle's dormitory room.

Professor McGraw's part-time return to the English Department office—against the advice of his temporary physician, Alex McKenzie—had not been an occasion for general happiness. At least not for secretaries Linda LaCroix and Arlene Burr and, oddly enough, judging from his behavior, not for the professor himself. He was pale, walked slowly, and kept himself wrapped in a heavy wool jacket over which he had a pulled a quilted ski vest. He acknowledged the presence on his desk of a small pot of African violets from Linda and a Get Well card from Arlene with a curt nod, asked Arlene to fill his thermos with coffee, closed the door to his office, and for a full two hours did not emerge either to order, chastise, complain, or see other faculty members—these last turned away at his request.

"What's going on?" asked Arlene to Linda. Although the two had almost ceased speaking, the return of their strangely behaving boss had caused a temporary truce.

"I haven't the faintest," said Linda, scowling at the closed door. "After all that I've done, keeping the department running, keeping students out, putting the lid on all those faculty demands. Well, you'd think he'd at least try and say thank you."

"I've tried three times to call him," said Arlene, "to see if he wants lunch brought in, since he looks pretty feeble, but his phone's been busy every time."

"I know one thing," announced Linda. "We can't keep the faculty away forever. Mary Donelli says if he doesn't approve her exam schedule she'll make up her own. Professor Lacey wants to take his poetry class to Portland for heaven knows what reason. Probably some lowlife café he's found that has some ding-dong poet doing readings at the lunch hour who's a special friend of Lacey. Some female he's got on his string."

"And the whole trip to be charged to the English Department," added Arlene.

"Speaking of which, what's happening with those harassment charges against the dean's little darling?"

"Listen to this. I've got it straight from a friend in the ER that Derek Mosely turned up there a while back. Messed up and muddy. And that shrink, Jasper or Jefferson, spent a lot of time with him. And that he's not back in his dorm. To sleep, anyway."

"Sergeant Fitts needs you. Arlene Burr, the snoop lady," said Linda.

'Well, don't ask me questions. You want the answers but want to keep your lily-white hands clean. And here's another tidbit you'll have to deal with. Unless you can get McGraw out of his cave. Mike gave me a heads-up about Grover Blaine's family. I gather they live in Hawaii somewhere and just made it here. They want to pick up Grover's body and have him cremated."

"And just how did you find this out?"

"Take that snarl out of your voice. The father called here. Sounded like one tough bird. They've found a funeral director to take care of details, but also wanted some stuff from

Grover's dorm. Any stuff the police haven't already swiped or sliced up."

"Good luck," said Linda. "The forensic people have already vacuumed the place."

"The family only wants personal things. Photos, music albums. Some books or journals. Things like that. To remember their dear one."

"If his family does turn up here, you be civil, Arlene Burr," said Linda. "And, if I'm out of the office, you make sure McGraw sees Grover's family. It's possible they even loved the creep, and they deserve to see the boss."

And on that note both ladies returned to their computer screens.

And remained so for at least seven minutes without speaking. Remained until the door of the chairman's office opened and Professor McGraw walked slowly out, speaking to neither woman.

"What the hell," said Linda. "I spent ten bucks for those violets. I've a mind to put them on my own desk."

"McGraw's had all that time in the hospital to think bad thoughts," said Arlene. "We'll both probably be canned. But he really pisses me off, acting like we're made of plastic and run by switches."

Linda sniffed. "I'll swear he's up to something. But let him try to touch my job and I'll hit the red button and cause major trouble. He'll be sorry he didn't smile and say good morning and tell me what a great job I've been doing."

"And the great job *I've* been doing," added Arlene. And then, turning, saw the door open slowly and a man in a heavy naval greatcoat take a step inside. Some sort of officer, Arlene thought, judging from gold decorations around his cap. "Oops," she whispered to Linda. "I think we've hit the jackpot."

And the man stepped up to Linda's desk, this being the nearest to the door, and said in a gruff voice, "I'm Commander Blaine. Grover Blaine's father. I'd like to see the chairman of the English Department."

"Professor McGraw has just stepped out," said Linda.

"Well, suppose you find him," said the commander, "and have him step back in."

Arlene looked up. "He may be gone for the day," she said. "He's had an accident. Just out of the hospital."

But Commander Blaine was studying the name inscribed on Professor McGraw's office door. "Did you say 'McGraw'? Danton McGraw?" he demanded.

Linda and Arlene nodded in unison.

The commander shook his head. "Son of a bitch," he said.

"What?" said Arlene while Linda looked mildly shocked.

Commander Blaine shook his head. "Never mind. Just find him, will one of you. The college isn't that big."

"Actually, I think he's living in the hospital rehab unit for a few days," said Arlene. "One of the nurses mentioned—"

"Never mind one of the nurses," said the commander. "Just find him."

Like peas in a pod, thought Arlene, who felt she should be saluting. She lifted the telephone and made a call, punched a few numbers, and then held the phone away from her ear. "He's at rehab all right. Just went into his room."

"Tell whoever you're talking to that Commander Professor Danton McGraw is going to have a visitor and his name is Blaine. Arthur G. Blaine. Or say 'Spotter Blaine.' Class of Seventy-one."

"This," said Arlene, after the door had closed behind Spotter Blaine, "is getting better and better."

"Or worse and worse," said Linda.

Arlene threw her head back and sang loudly, "Anchors aweigh, my boys, anchors aweigh. Farewell to college joys, we sail at break of day-ay-ay-ay."

"Shut your big mouth," said Linda.

"College joys," said Arlene. "Think of that."

And Linda raised her copy of *Webster's New Collegiate Dictionary* in one threatening hand.

* * *

George Fitts had decided that the police trailer was entirely too confined a space for a group interrogation. The Terriers versus the forces of law and order needed an appropriate arena. The time was set for six o'clock, which would allow the featured students to finish off their classes and sports sessions. After consultation of the college management, George was allotted the same VIP dining room in which Alena Fosdick and Professor McGraw had first made their plans to devour the Drama School. Liquid refreshment in the form of root beer and Orangina would be offered.

"To soften them up?" asked Mike when he turned up in the trailer shortly after noon.

"I've tried the austere approach," said George. "Maybe this will loosen lips."

"For that," said Mike, "you need TNT. Or better yet, an electric cattle prod. Anyway, want to hear what we found going through those two dorm rooms, Kay's and Derek's?"

"Nothing," said Katie.

Mike looked disappointed. "You spoil everything, Katie. But forensics won't know about bloodstains and organic matter or drugs or gunpowder, anything interesting, until the lab comes through. But from what I've seen, the answer is zero. Kay Biddle left ninety-nine percent of her clothes and books. Apparently took off without much planning. Or maybe she's coming right back. And Derek's been allowed to go in and pick up some odd things in the room he shared with Grover. Under Alex McKenzie's supervision. Of course, forensics has already vacuumed up anything that was Grover Blaine's. Last week. A few stains on a pair of his jeans and a T-shirt. That lab, they just got around to telling me they've got a match with Todd Mancuso's blood. Maybe from Grover's beating of Todd. But who knows? Call later, they say. It's always 'call later' with that bunch."

"But now we've got Derek's deposition on the beating," said Katie. "We won't need the match."

George frowned. "We damn well will. Derek's song and dance may change every hour on the hour. Give me lab tests any day."

"To sum up," said Mike, "Kay Biddle's and Derek's collection of junk in the dorm, it's all pretty much a waste of time, I'd say. But how about I take off—"

"No way," said George. "I've just heard from the hospital that a man in uniform has called on Danton McGraw. Apparently it's Grover Blaine's father. I'd like to see him. Alone. Katie, would you go over and make the request? Mike, go back to the forensics lab and lean on them. Those things from the two dorms. Every shoelace and toothbrush gone over."

Two hours later, George Fitts stood up and shook the hand of Commander Arthur Blaine. And Commander Blaine responded with a serious nod. "I think we do understand each other, Sergeant," he said. "It's damn unfortunate, this whole damn business. As a matter of fact, most of Grover's life could be called unfortunate. But now we've arranged with a mortuary for cremation and shipment of Grover's ashes. As for my wife, for me, I'd say, for better or for worse, it's a kind of closure. For you, the whole assault and murder affair, well, I suppose you'll have to wait a while for an ending. The law's like that; things drag on. But thanks for your time. I have a great admiration for the Maine State Police."

"And I," said George, reaching out to shake Commander Blaine's hand, "have the same admiration for the United States Navy."

Katie Waters had arrived to hear this last statement and stood back to allow the commander to leave the trailer.

"You two make a fine match," she said to George. "Like a lovefest."

"I meant what I said," returned the sergeant. "There are very few organizations these days that reflect an interest in efficiency, order, and courageous action."

"My, my," said Katie, sitting down at her desk. "If you get tired of the state police, you can join the navy."

"Just hand over the personnel folders of our guests to be. And any notes you've made. I want to brush up on exactly who was where. What they've said in their original depositions."

"Six o'clock sharp, right?" said Katie.

"Correct," said George, snapping his teeth down on the last syllable.

The VIP dining room had been rearranged to accommodate a group interrogation. Several tables, tablecloths removed, had been pushed into a rectangle; chairs had been lined up on either side. Recording machinery had been installed, and at the kitchen door and the outside access door stood a uniformed sheriff's deputy equipped with a list of the police attendants and students to be interviewed.

They came, sauntering, hurrying, or moving deliberately, some three or four minutes to six. All dressed rather soberly in clean parkas, jackets, sweats, jeans without visible holes, because this was, after all, a formal occasion. Already in place in chairs facing the student seats were Deputy Katie Waters, Sergeant George Fitts, and Assistant Professor Sarah Douglas Deane. No lawyers were present, as each member of the so-called Terriers, all being of age, had been read his or her rights and waived the right to council. However, Deputy Mike Laaka had been ordered into exile at the local forensic laboratory. Sergeant Fitts felt that the last thing he needed during a difficult group interrogation was the smart mouth and irreverent wit of Mike. Besides, Mike had been in a sour mood since missing the Saturday of Breeders' Cup racing, an event that for him rivaled the Kentucky Derby.

Now Katie leaned over to Sarah. "Have you got all these guys straight in your head? Because you almost need a scorecard for the names."

"I hope so," said Sarah. "After teaching them, helping with their costumes, eating lunch with them, and being abducted by some of them, well, I should remember."

"Quiet, please," said George. As the students, now a subdued lot, sat quietly, he introduced his crew in a formal manner: full names, titles, and departments. "Professor Deane is with us because she knows each of you from class, was present or involved in certain theatre incidents, and, of course, was a passenger during a recent road trip made by some of you. Have any of you any objection to her presence here?"

Silence greeted this question, and as Katie whispered to Sarah, it wouldn't do a bit of good if they did.

Sarah for her part found her mind tried to move away from the emotional aspects of the meeting and so busied her mind by trying to think of the whole affair as a sort of weird reality show. There was the playbill and the list of characters. One by one she went over them. All members of the so-called Terriers. All seniors in the Drama School. First and foremost were the three no-shows now present only in her imagination.

Kay Biddle, absent. The Julio in the Halloween production, confessed assaulter of Danton McGraw and murderer of Grover Blaine. Expert fencer. Possibly in love with Todd Mancuso. Abductor and abandoner of Sarah in a snowstorm. Now driving around somewhere in Mary Donelli's green Subaru Forester.

Next, Todd Mancuso, in jail, owner of sliced ear and knocked head (thanks to Kay Biddle and Terri Colman) and beaten-up body (thanks to Grover Blaine and Derek Mosely). Todd forbidden to play Mercutio—for reasons that may or may not have been valid. A second confessed assaulter and murderer. Expert fencer. Possible lover of Kay Biddle. Crucial question: was he actually too ill to avenge his beating?

Last, Derek Mosely, presently making a short visit along with Alex McKenzie to his mother, Dean Alena. Derek, recent houseguest and animal lover, understudy of Friar Laurence, devoted friend and possible lover of the murdered Grover. Or the lover who had been dumped by Grover and so took his revenge by way of foil. However, Sarah was beginning to have doubts about that. *What* other lover? She couldn't think of a candidate, certainly not a member of the cast. I mean, she asked herself, who—except weak-willed, friendless Derek—could possibly love Grover?

Then on to those present. Weeza Scotini, drama student and nurse's aide, participant in a sting operation of her own devising to capture Grover and Derek. Player of Paris (wooer of Romiette or was it Julio?), star dancer. Athletic, could probably learn a few fencing moves. Active member of the abduction team from the Squeaky Wheel Café.

Next Malcolm Wheelock, captain of the Bowmouth fencing team, player of Tybalt, claiming to having had no time to spear Mercutio because of quick re-entrance to stage in order to be killed and lie in full view onstage.

Griffin Starr, Benvolio, master of stage blood effects, fencing team member, and another quick exit-return actor in the Mercutio death scene.

Who else? Oh yes. That sufferer of hepatitis, expert fencer now sidelined, Seth Nussbaum. Into stage management but had been pressed by Vera to play one of the extras in the crowd scenes. And so quite available for quick violent action.

"Do you agree, Dr. Deane?" said George from the middle of the table.

Sarah came to with a jerk. George was looking at her with an expression that suggested that affirmation was her role. She nodded and told herself sternly to pay attention.

Probably the best description of the meeting that followed would use some of these words: "smoke screen," "ambiguity," "contradiction," "generality," and a continual repetition of the phrase "I don't remember."

George Fitts was more patient than Sarah had ever seen him. Usually during an interrogation, after listening to a certain amount of waffling he would attack with a few sharp remarks that would drill holes in the statements of his "victim." But now he seemed determined to let the students hang themselves. But after a full hour of back and forth, nothing certain had emerged. With two exceptions. As Sarah had expected, the time available for either Benvolio (Griffin Starr) or Tybalt (Malcolm Wheelock) to bash Danton McGraw over the head and haul him backstage was so limited that both students could probably be eliminated from charges of assault. Whether either had pursued Grover to the Green Room for a private duel was another question.

At this point in Sarah's mental deliberations, George suddenly stopped his questions. "I've been listening," he said, "to a lot of babble. Sidestepping. Noting a loss of memory in each of you. Remarkable, since memory is an actor's long suit. But, I think," he said, moving his head to look each student in the eye, "we've come to a place where two of your friends may have done things that you noticed, but don't wish to share. Let's start with Todd Mancuso. Do you remember any one time during the play that suggested that Todd was not too weak to commit an assault? And later a murder? Remember he was dressed to play the parts of both Friar Laurence *and* Mercutio, so he wore the essentials of the Elizabethan costume underneath the monk's habit. We know he was physically able to play the friar. But because of his behavior and sick appearance the director, Vera Pruczak, and Dr. McKenzie prevented him from going onstage as Mercutio. That meant that Todd was free to watch those scenes from the wings. Or, possibly, put on a mask and join in with the crowd scenes. To slip an épée into Mercutio's neck, help Benvolio carry Mercutio offstage, and, since both Tybalt and Romeo—or Romiette—were about to re-enter, he would be free for a few minutes to dispose of Professor McGraw. Hit him, then drag him into hiding."

At which there was a muttered chorus of objections. "Todd wouldn't hurt a flea. No way!" "Todd was really, really sick, Sergeant; you've got it all wrong." "Forget Todd!"

But George shook his head. "Let me finish. The cast party was a moveable feast."

"A what?" exclaimed Griffin Starr.

George peered at Griffin. "You take English?"

Griffin nodded. "Yeah, sure."

"Hemingway. Ernest. Title of one of his books. Look it up. To rephrase, people came and went from the cast party, and this makes it extremely hard to fit departure times in with the probable time of the attack on Grover Blaine. In fact, with very few exceptions almost everyone at the party could have killed him. Including, of course, Todd Mancuso."

"But he didn't," said a loud voice at the door. The sort of voice trained in projecting itself across a room, to the last row of seats in a large theatre.

A sudden turning of necks, moving of chairs. Mouths opened. Eyes widened.

And then George Fitts, rising. "Come in, Kay Biddle. We have an extra chair."

Absolute silence. No movement except for Kay Biddle, née Bungle, walking quietly across the room toward George Fitts. Her face drawn and white, her jacket and slacks looked as if she might have spent the night in a trash bin. But she held her shoulders straight, walked firmly, and stopped directly in front of the sergeant. Then, extending a long newspaper-wrapped object clutched in one hand, she placed it almost tenderly on the table space in front of George.

"I think," said Kay, speaking in a calm, flat voice, "this might help your case? Because maybe you didn't believe Sarah Deane's story." She turned to Sarah. "I see you made it back okay. I thought you had a chance. So did you tell them what I said? About the Mercutio scene and Grover Blaine in the Green Room."

Sarah nodded. "Yes, I did. As nearly as I could remember."

"And no one believed you?"

Sarah looked over at George, who held up his hand. "Ms. Biddle," he said in the weary voice of one who had said this once too often, "you have the right to remain silent. Anything you say can and will be used against you in a court of law. You have—"

But Kay Biddle stopped him cold. "I waive the right to everything," she said. Then turning to Sarah, she repeated her question. Had anyone, anyone at all, listened to Sarah's account of Kay in her murder role?

"I think that Sergeant Fitts thought it might be true," said Sarah. "He got hold of the newspapers, the radio and television people. But he also said that my report might not be useful because it was hearsay evidence. He thought I might be acting under coercion. Under a threat."

"Which," said Kay, "was not true." She turned back to George. "Judging from the latest news I've heard, you've decided to put the screws on Todd Mancuso."

"No," said George. "His was a voluntary confession. He came

to us on his own. He's been arraigned and is right now in the Knox County jail." George paused, studied the rather dirty rolled object in front of him, and then turned to Katie Waters. "Katie, please go back to the trailer and pick up some gloves and an evidence bag. A long one."

The sergeant then turned to his audience of students and told them they were dismissed. That if anything they had seen or heard that evening got loose on campus he would be after them with a lasso. "Don't forget," he added. "All of you may be facing charges for obstruction of justice in the case of a capital crime, plus charges of abduction, perjury, conspiracy, and a number of other things I haven't had time to think of." To Sarah he said, "Please stay seated. And Ms. Biddle, will you also sit down and wait until Deputy Waters returns."

Katie Waters must have traveled on winged shoes. She was back almost before Sarah could collect her thoughts and center her attention properly on the wrapped object.

Katie presented the examining gloves to George and held the evidence bag open. George, moving deliberately, stood up, pulled on the gloves, and slowly unwrapped the object. An object that seemed to have picked up small chunks of dirt from wherever it had rested.

Sarah guessed its identity at almost exactly the same time that George revealed it. A foil. No, wrong, look at the bell guard, Sarah told herself. An épée. An épée with bits of damp, soiled newspaper clinging to its blade.

George looked at Kay. "Where?"

"From the Drama School construction site. That big pile of dirt the workmen haven't finished cleaning up. I wiped the blade after I hit Professor McGraw. But I was in a hurry and I couldn't do a proper job. So you can probably find some bloodstains on the tip."

"The épée used in the Mercutio death scene," said George.

Kay nodded.

"So," continued George, "where is the foil used to kill Grover in the Green Room?"

"I'd gotten rid of the épée, but now I was running out of time for hiding the foil," said Kay. "There were too many people coming and going during the cast party. So I didn't even try and rinse the point off. I just got outside and stuck it into the middle of a bush."

"A bush!" said George, looking as if Kay had said she'd put it on the moon. "What do you mean, 'a bush'?"

"Not exactly a bush. That big clump of evergreens, yew or arborvitae, something like that. Planted by the stairs next to the entrance to the Drama School. They were perfect. You could hide ten foils in the middle of them."

"I'll be damned," said George, who rarely told himself such a thing.

And Sarah, though she didn't speak, thought exactly the same thing. Remembered her fall down the steps when she had rolled close to the same cluster of evergreens.

Sergeant Fitts took a deep breath and turned to Katie. "Stand right next to Ms. Biddle, will you?"

"I'm not going anywhere," said Kay in the same expressionless voice. "I just want to hear that you're going to release Todd. The foil, the épée, I'm sure a lab will find blood on the points. That's what you need, isn't it? Evidence."

"We'll go over to the police trailer," said George. "There, Ms. Biddle, I'll record a complete statement. Sarah Deane, will you go with us? You will be able to compare Ms. Biddle's statement with the one she gave you earlier. Katie, call Mike to meet us in the trailer and get ready to record."

All this was done. But whether Kay Biddle had come back to confess because of her love of Todd or from a sense of justice Sarah could not guess. Certainly Todd himself must have confessed because he loved Kay. The time-honored gesture. Todd, Sarah thought, was something of an old-fashioned romantic. But what an unholy mess. One murderer and six tight-lipped supporting actors. Six students who might soon be spending time behind bars or at the very least find themselves on probation and doing difficult and unpleasing community service—cleaning pigsties for overworked farmers, cat boxes at the shelter, restrooms at the YMCA, for instance. And quite possibly none of these would be cast in any Drama School future play or perhaps marching down the aisle in cap and gown at the Bowmouth graduation. But legal systems grind slowly, and it was doubtful whether any judgments would be given until at least the beginning of December.

Epilogue

IN the waning days of a blustery November, with the Thanksgiving holiday on the horizon for Bowmouth College, the murder of Grover Blaine began slowly fading into the past. No one missed him, and judging from a rumor abroad based on a remark made by Commander Blaine to someone in the college, Grover was one of those sons who were born to inflict worry and pain on their parents and community alike. In fact, only Derek Mosely seemed capable of something like honest grief.

As for Derek himself, a number of things became clear: He was not happy as a student at Bowmouth College; he had few friends. No—not even friends. Not even a few speaking acquaintances. For too long he had been seen as Grover Blaine's shadow and sidekick, and that connection still hung over him like a toxic cloud. Therefore, after much back and forth between psychiatrist Jonas Jefferson, Alex and Sarah, and Derek's mother, Alena Fosdick—she reluctant to express an opinion—it was arranged for Derek to take a leave of absence from the college beginning immediately and to take a position found for him by Sarah with her veterinarian. He would work as a kennel assistant and learn the ins and outs of simple animal care. Also, since Derek was essentially homeless, he could live in an apartment over the veterinary office together with an elderly but kindhearted kennel helper, a Mrs. Consuelo Perez. On days off, by prior arrangement, he would be able to visit his friends Patsy, the Irish wolfhound, and the rapidly growing kitten, Piggy.

More important to Derek's mental health, aided by the advocacy efforts of Drs. Jefferson and McKenzie, and Sarah, one of his teachers, the charges against him were modified to result in a sentence of six months in prison, which was suspended, with probation for two years and mandated community service six hours a week at the local humane society. He must also visit his mother (with her consent) at least once a week. In one group he was positively welcomed. The local town soccer club needed all the help it could get and received him with pleasure. Indoor soccer practice would begin in December. To these positive events was added the ruling of a compassionate judge: if Derek's behavior remained favorable and his veterinarian employer permitted it, he would be allowed in some future time to adopt a cat or kitten from the shelter.

As for Kay Biddle, she was duly arraigned, charged, and jailed. Sentence to be determined when the court had set a date to hear her case. Sarah's last view of Kay showed her with her chin up, a stubborn set to her lips, and her eyes directed straight ahead. Her first visitor after incarceration turned out to be the newly released Todd Mancuso, but what they had to say to each other was anyone's guess. Love between a visitor's grille, Sarah thought, was a tough thing to keep afloat.

As for the action group known as the Terriers, they were ordered to disband and firmly reminded that proper faculty and student channels stood ready to handle complaints of every variety—including of course sexual harassment. But when Dean Alena Fosdick was reminded by Weeza Scotini that the Arts and Sciences committee had not acted promptly enough to suit Kay Biddle, who then resorted to murder, Alena exploded.

"You and your so-called Terrier friends," scolded Alena in a voice she had not used in years, "are not in the clear. You, Louisa Scotini, as I've heard, set that whole business up. It's called entrapment. A sting operation. But you are not part of any law enforcement agency that I've heard of. I'm sure the committee would have decided against Grover Blaine, who was a despicable person, but they shouldn't be railroaded into making a decision because of some murder-minded student can't wait another twenty-four hours to hear the testimony. Of both sides. And I never want to hear the word 'Terriers' again. Half the county probably think the word is 'Terrorists,' which is exactly what Bowmouth College does not need." There, thought Alena, marching away from Weeza, it's high time I began sounding off. Enough of pussyfooting around mere students and people like Danton McGraw.

Curiously, the English Department under the helm of this same Professor Danton McGraw became almost a pool of peace. Arlene rejoiced in the calm and was even able to finish a new Sue Grafton mystery during working hours. As for Linda LaCroix, she began to be worried about the lack of action and wondered what was eating her boss. He was fairly well recovered, though still somewhat pale. Strangely, however, his zeal for a shipshape English Department seemed to have abated. And although he scowled when the name of Vera Pruczak was brought up, no further steps were taken to bring the Drama School to heel. In fact, a great deal of the chairman's time seemed to be spent shut up in his office making long-distance calls—Linda took note of these since she collected the telephone charges before submitting them to the fiscal powers of the college.

"What's he up to?" demanded Linda after a whole morning had gone by without Professor McGraw emerging. After his accident, McGraw's classes had been taken over by Mary Donelli and Amos Larkin. Both had arrived in the office asking when the chairman would resume his teaching duties. But they had been unable to extract an answer from the chairman. It depended, Dr. McGraw had said vaguely, on what the doctors thought.

"I'll bet McGraw's had it here," said Arlene. "Probably trying to hook up with the FBI or the CIA. More his style, I'd say."

"Maybe he had brain damage," said Linda. "That bang on the head. But I don't want him to go. Think who we might have. Professor Morgan!"

"Don't use that tone with me," said Arlene. "I'm crazy about

Professor Morgan. Silas Ulysses Morgan. What a great name. He's an old sweetheart. He brings me a piece of homemade butter crunch every time he comes into the office."

"No wonder we still have mice," complained Linda. "Every day this whole semester I've been very glad we had someone who could manage things. Like Dr. McGraw. Except right now. I do think he should go to a neurologist. He's just not acting normal."

"You lose five units of blood and you won't act normal," said Arlene. But at that exact moment, Professor McGraw opened his office door and handed a sheet of paper to Arlene. "Will you please send this as an a e-mail to Professor Alena Fosdick." Then from his jacket pocket he produced a sealed envelope. "Linda, will you see that this letter is delivered by hand to the Chancellor of the college. Immediately."

"Who do you want to—"

"Are you doing anything this moment that would prevent you from taking it yourself?" said Professor McGraw.

"It's starting to snow," said Linda. Her temper was rising; she had never before been asked to act as an errand person for the English Department. She was the executive secretary. Why was Arlene allowed to type out an e-mail while she was being sent into the storm?

"Snow in the state of Maine in November," observed Dr. McGraw, "is not unusual. Wear your coat and scarf. And please report to my office when you return." He turned to Arlene, his face now showing almost a healthy color, his jacket and tie and trousers neat and crisp. "Arlene, you come to my office, too," he added. "When Linda gets back." And the professor turned and disappeared into his office.

The snow that had returned in force that mid-November morning, some two weeks after senior student Kay Biddle had taken up residence in prison, began to whirl around the campus in what was rapidly turning into an extremely nasty nor'easter. Afternoon classes had been called off, and Sarah Deane and Mary Donelli had picked up Amos Larkin and headed for the hospital cafeteria, where Alex was to meet Sarah. Office hours for most physicians had been canceled and patients in distress were urged to use public transportation or call an ambulance to reach the ER.

After brushing off clumps of snow, the three headed for a quiet corner of the cafeteria, now deserted except for persons keeping guard over bedridden family members.

Alex joined them, his heavy jacket hanging over one arm.

"We should be leaving or we'll have to spend the night here. And believe me, you won't like the sleeping arrangements."

"I'm just getting coffee and a doughnut," said Mary. "I've missed lunch."

"You call that lunch," said Amos. "Me, I'm going to live it up. I have four-wheel drive; I can get home in the middle of three nor'easters. And Mary . . ."

"Mary," said Mary, "now has to retrieve a green Forester which is in the shop. To see what that Kay Biddle did to it."

"At least she didn't wreck it," said Alex. "I'll think I'll have apple pie and coffee. Sarah, you want tea? And something like a Danish?"

But none of these refreshments were destined to be enjoyed. Through the door, her fur-trimmed cape covered with a mantle of snow, came Dean Alena Fosdick. She paused, peering into the room. And then spied the three English professors and Dr. McKenzie. She almost ran across the room, a difficult feat for one who insisted on fashionable spike-heeled winter boots.

"Oh, Dr. Larkin," she said. Then realizing that others of lesser importance were also present, she nodded at Mary, Sarah, and Alex.

"You'll never guess," Alena said almost breathlessly.

"No," said Amos. "I doubt that we will. Please sit down, Alena, and we'll bring you some coffee. Tea. Name your poison."

"I don't have time," said Alena, breathing hard. She rarely tried to run anywhere. "But someone told me you all might be here. Since the college cafeterias are all closed. I've got news. And I'm shocked."

"Another murder?" asked Amos. "Foil or épée?"

"Honestly, Dr. Larkin. I mean Amos. Don't you want to hear?"

"Of course," said Mary, reaching a boot over to press it on Amos's ankle.

"It's Professor McGraw," said Alena, now breathing hard.

"He's dead?" suggested Amos.

"Stop that," commanded Mary.

"He's gone. I mean he's going. After this semester. The first of January."

"January is a good choice," observed Alex, who was becoming irritated by the delay in giving information.

"Dr. Danton McGraw," said Alena, her voice in an upper register, still standing and speaking as from a podium above a crowd, "has handed in his resignation. He has apparently applied to the United States Naval Academy for some sort of job. Teaching, working with the fencing team. He's been in the reserves and now he'll be active. At Annapolis. Oh dear."

"Why, 'oh dear?'" demanded Alex. "Sounds like a perfect fit."

"I mean what *is* going to happen to the English Department?" said Alena.

"I think the English Department can stand the blow," said Amos. "It's been around for a while. We've had lots of chairmen. They come and they go."

"The thing is," said Alena, "we need a chair right now. And I do not mean Linda LaCroix. Professor McGraw is resigning the position as of now and will only teach his own classes. He'll leave the college after exams. Dr. Larkin, Amos, I mean. Would you possibly consider—"

"No," said Amos briskly. "I certainly would not. But I have a suggestion for you. Professor Silas Ulysses Morgan hasn't enough to do. Only two classes. He's very organized. In his own way. He can fill in until January. What you need is some old blood."

"You mean," said Alena, puzzled, "new blood."

"I mean old blood. Old ways. It's called experience. Dr. Morgan was practically born in the English Department. You need someone who can settle things down in a quiet, time-honored way. I vote for Silas Morgan."

"And I second it," said Mary.

"Me, too," said Sarah. "If the vote of an assistant professor is worth anything."

"And now that's settled," said Mary, who avoided Alena Fosdick's troubled face, "I have a small piece of news. Vera Pruczak has announced that the midwinter Drama School play will be—"

"Let me guess," broke in Sarah. *"Hamletta, Princess of Denmark.* Or *Queen Henrietta the Fifth."*

"No way. Vera's been there, done that," said Mary.

"How about turning that Robert Service poem into a play?" said Alex. "You know, 'The Shooting of Dan McGrew.' Just change one letter."

" 'The Shooting of Dan McGraw.' " said Sarah. "Great choice."

"But no cigar," said Mary. "Try again."

Alena tightened her lips. "I certainly hope," she said, "that it's going to be a play that everyone likes."

"Alena," said Amos, reaching for an empty chair. "Please sit down. Remember, none of us bite. Or at least not very hard. Now what play would you suggest?"

Alena sat down and frowned at the circle of expectant faces. "I know you're going to say that I'd choose something like *Little Women.* Which I'm not. And I know I'll never live down writing a dissertation on Raggedy Ann. And that I've been a lousy mother to Derek."

Here Sarah interrupted. "But you're trying to be a good one. Derek told me so."

Alena gave her a small smile. "What I'm saying is I want some play that's not going to attract assault and murder. And stir up the entire county. And wreck the fund-raising campaign. Or bring the Reverend Nicholas Copeland down on our heads."

"I remember someone telling me," said Sarah, "that people accept any production as long as it was a classic or had picked up a Pulitzer."

"You're getting warm," said Mary. "Think Greek. Think ancient comedy with contemporary implications."

Amos and Alex sat up straight and Alena blanched.

And Sarah put it into words. *"Lysistrata,"* she announced. "I should have guessed. I'm going to be teaching Aristophanes. Right down Vera's alley. Women banding together to withhold sexual favors from macho men who insist on waging war."

Mary smiled. "Bingo," she said.